BLACK DOGS

THE IRON KINGDOMS CHRONICLES

THE BLACK RIVER IRREGULARS I
BLACK DOGS

RICHARD LEE BYERS

Published in the United States by Skull Island eXpeditions,
a division of Privateer Press, Inc.

ISBN 978-1-943693-13-9

Printed in the United States of America

www.privateerpress.com
www.skullislandx.com
facebook.com/skullislandexpeditions

First Paperback Edition

Book design by Richard Anderson
Cover illustration by Carlos Cabrera

The text of this book was set in Adobe Garamond Pro

Dedication

For Lawrence, Sid, Seth, and Claudia

— CONTENTS —

— 1 —

COLBIE STERLING PERCHED on a stool in the corner of the work bay while Pog, standing on the uppermost rung of a stepladder, labored over the exposed inner workings of Doorstop's shoulder. Green-skinned and frog-faced with long, pointed ears, the gobber was the size of a human child and utterly dwarfed by the hulking steamjack. Grunting, he heaved at a wrench in an attempt to loosen an uncooperative bolt.

Meanwhile, the glow of the kerosene lamps gleamed on Doorstop's chassis, the detached pieces of it lying at the foot of the ladder, and the tools hanging on the wall. Metal clanked and clattered as Pog's fellow mechaniks toiled in the work bays to either side. The air smelled of oil and burning coal.

This, Colbie supposed, shifting on the stool, was prosperity. She could afford to upgrade Doorstop's capabilities and even pay someone else to do the grunting and straining.

What she couldn't do was leave any mechanik to perform the work without her supervision, not when her life and the lives of her partners sometimes depended on the automaton. Nor would she remove her leather greatcoat, hot and heavy though it was with its attached pieces of armor and tools and weapons. Not here in the Undercity enclave of the Patient Weavers.

Considering that Natak Warbiter and Canice Gormleigh, two of the more notorious members of the gang, had recently been on the verge of killing Colbie and her friends, a more cautious woman might not have returned to the Weavers' stronghold at all. But presumably she and the other Black River Irregulars had laid that quarrel to rest by delivering on their promise to end a problem that bedeviled everyone in the Undercity, and the shop that employed Pog specialized in fitting 'jacks with capacities that the more lawful society aboveground discouraged.

Scurrying up and down the ladder as required, the gobber eventually managed to loosen the recalcitrant bolt and the clamp it secured and replace the short length of hose connecting two pneumatic tubes. Then, poking around inside Doorstop's shoulder, he said, "Huh." His voice was a reedy tenor.

Colbie stood up and approached for a better view. "What?"

The gobber pointed with a long, grimy finger. "If I changed the gearing here, he could carry heavier weights."

Colbie shrugged. "But that's not what he needs to do. He needs to be able to swing a mace or a war hammer as hard, fast, and accurately as possible."

Pog sighed. "Just like every other 'jack that comes through here."

"Well, considering where you work, that's to be expected."

"I know, but I wish every job wasn't turning the 'jack into a better killer. Old Doorstop here, he wasn't built for that, and he could earn you a good wage loading cargo on the docks or stacking goods in a warehouse."

Colbie laughed. "If only I were willing to turn away from my bloodthirsty ways."

The gobber hesitated. "I hope I didn't offend you."

"No. But I can't help wondering—"

Suddenly, somewhere outside the shop, something boomed

and hissed simultaneously. Recognizing the distinctive sound of a steam lobber, Colbie reflexively cast about just as she would have on the battlefield.

Then came a far louder blast—the steam lobber's projectile had exploded somewhere close at hand. A shock jolted her, and she shifted her feet to recover her balance. The same shock knocked the stepladder out from under Pog. He clutched at Doorstop to keep from dropping to the floor. Tools tumbled from their hooks.

• • •

NATAK WARBITER STROLLED AMONG the round tables, gnawing on a broiled chicken and dropping or spitting out bones and gristle. Usually the scraps landed on the floor, but once in a while they fell on the heads or shoulders of the gamblers who tossed rattling dice or hunched over their hands of brag and black argus.

When the latter occurred, no one complained, at least not while Natak was within earshot. Even if the mostly human clientele objected to the boorishness of some other ogrun, they didn't dare take offense with this one, standing a head taller than any of them, with massive steel rings for punching skulls to mush on every finger and a double-edged battle axe hanging from his belt. They knew his reputation for homicidal rampages.

In fact, the patrons seldom accosted Natak for any reason, which made keeping order the least onerous of his many duties amid the tawdry splendor of the Braggart's Smile, with its peeling gold-painted molding and crudely rendered murals of sybaritic indulgence. Accordingly, he was surprised when he spotted a middle-aged woman and a young man making their way in his direction.

Both humans had silver-blond hair, upturned noses, apple cheeks, and an overall fleshiness that suggested a familial connection, and their choice to dress in identical shades of cornflower blue and daisy yellow reinforced the resemblance. Their cloaks and what Natak could make out of the garments underneath were the clean, respectable attire of supposedly decent citizens who'd sneaked down into the Undercity for illicit commerce or fun.

Judging from their smiles, they weren't coming to complain that they'd been cheated or anything like that. Perhaps, like a few brash souls before them, they hoped to boast to their friends that they'd bought an infamous outlaw ale—or at least were on speaking terms with him.

With mingled irritation and amusement, Natak braced himself to suffer their attentions for a moment or two. He supposed it was good for business.

"Natak Warbiter?" asked the young man.

"Who else?" growled Natak through a mouthful of chicken. It made the encounter slightly less obnoxious that such fools expected and even wanted him to be surly.

The young man beamed at the older woman. "You see, Mama? I told you!"

"I know, lovey." She stroked her fingertips down the lad's forearm and gave Natak a smile. "My little boy's so clever."

"What do you want?" Natak asked.

"We were told Canice Gormleigh works here," the young man said.

"And that you and she are the best of friends," the mother added.

"So, we'd be ever so grateful if you'd help us find her," the young man concluded.

"Sit," Natak said. "She'll wander in eventually." He certainly wasn't going to interrupt whatever Canice was doing to accommodate these nitwits.

The son pouted. "I'm afraid we're in a bit of a hurry. If you can't direct us to her, we'll have to prevail upon you to help in a different fashion."

Natak grunted. "How's that?" Then something thundered somewhere outside.

"We'll explain by and by," the mother replied. She raised her arm over her head and her sleeve slid down, exposing black tattooing. With a wink, she snapped her fingers.

Around the gambling hall, half a dozen men leaped up from their seats, ripped the cloaks away from their shoulders, and snatched their swords from their scabbards. Dangling their capes in their off hands, they converged in twos and threes on the other startled Patient Weavers in sight. A customer was slow getting out of the way, and one of the attackers cut him down with a casual slash to the throat.

Mother and son stepped back and away from one another, simultaneously distancing themselves from Natak and maneuvering to flank him. They tore off their cloaks, too—the ogrun wondered fleetingly how the garments were secured to pull loose so easily and reliably—revealing long, straight cut-and-thrust swords hanging beneath.

Natak decided to dispose of one of his adversaries before either could draw. He dropped what little remained of the chicken, cocked his fist for a punch, bellowed, and lunged at the son.

But the young man simultaneously pirouetted out of the way and lashed out with the cloak. The hem clouted Natak's cheek and pointed ear with surprising force. Evidently it had weights sewn in.

The unexpected jolt balked Natak for only an instant, but that was time enough for his foes to finish drawing their blades. He scrambled back from the threat, and they glided after him.

He grabbed an abandoned table by its edge and flung it amid a rain of cards and clinking coins. Mother and son dodged, but the attack held them back long enough for him to ready his axe.

The thundering thing outside roared louder than before, the hall shook, and a piece of the ceiling, painted with a scene of buccaneers playing pirate's dice, crashed down on the patch of floor beneath. Natak wondered what in the name of Holy Mother Dhunia was happening.

Then he thrust speculation from his mind. If he didn't dispose of these two adversaries trying to do the same to him, right here and right now, the broader picture wouldn't matter.

He spotted an overturned chair at the periphery of his vision. He stepped behind it, then booted it at the son. It cracked into the man's knees and knocked him stumbling backward.

Natak pivoted and rushed the blonde woman. He swung his axe at her head, and she whirled her cape at the weapon.

He was accustomed to smashing through the parries and sometimes even the shields with which human opponents tried to deflect his strokes. He sneered at the thought that a piece of cloth, even a weighted one, could do the trick. But the cloak tangled around the axe head, and with a jerk and a twist of her hips, the mother brought it arcing harmlessly down in front of her body. She stabbed her sword at his midsection.

Natak sidestepped. Her blade slid across his ribs, slicing through his leather jerkin and the shirt beneath but only scratching—he hoped—the skin beneath. He jumped forward, let go of the entangled axe with one hand, and swung his fist in an uppercut.

She sprang back and the punch missed, but at least her retreat pulled the cloak off his axe. Gripping the haft anew, Natak started after her, then heard or perhaps merely sensed danger behind him.

He whirled and swung the axe in a horizontal cut. It intercepted the young man's sword in mid-slash, not quite knocking it out of his hand but making him fumble to hold onto the hilt.

Natak stepped in to cleave the bastard's skull. The human snapped his cape at Natak's face, and though it stung, it was not enough to balk him. He feinted low and spun the axe high. Then everything went dark.

The mother had come up behind him and tossed her cloak over his head. He blindly struck at the son anyway but missed.

Then twin shocks, the precursors to pain, flared in the back of his knee and his forearm. He pitched forward, and something—the flat of a blade?—clouted him over the head. He fell to the floor, and a sword slid into his back.

The cape pulled away, revealing carnage. The other Patient Weavers in the hall were dead while, still employing murderously efficient teamwork, their killers were slaughtering the panicked gamblers struggling to shove through the crush at the exit.

Mother and son stood over Natak. "You were perfect," the young man said.

"No," the blonde woman said, "*you* were perfect, and so brave!" She ran her fingers through his disheveled hair, stroking it back into place.

Natak tried to spin himself around and swing the axe at their ankles. But agony ripped through his several wounds, and he just flopped like a newly caught fish.

"That's enough of that," said the plump young man. He pulled the axe from Natak's numb, twitching fingers.

"We promised to tell you how you were going to help us," the mother said, her blue eyes twinkling. "The answer is, as bait."

• • •

A SECOND BLAST rocked the shop. Her ears ringing, Colbie crouched and once again retained her balance. But Pog lost his grip on Doorstop, plummeting down onto the steamjack's foot and the stray parts scattered around it.

Colbie helped him up. "Are you all right?" she asked, realizing as she did that she couldn't hear herself. That probably meant those long green ears couldn't hear her either.

Still, perhaps the gobber sensed her meaning, because he waved his hand in a gesture that seemed to answer in the affirmative. He had a gash on his forearm, likely the result of landing on a sharp metal edge, but apparently he didn't regard it as cause for alarm.

That was good, because he and Colbie had plenty of other causes. Plainly, someone had bombarded the building and might well continue to do so. Swirls of smoke and wavering yellow light revealed a portion of the place was already on fire. Either the shells had been incendiaries or some of the kerosene lanterns had fallen and shattered. Mechaniks from the neighboring work bays scurried for the exits.

It was the only sensible thing to do. But partially disassembled as he was and his boiler cold, Doorstop wouldn't be able to follow, and Colbie couldn't just abandon him. Sentimental attachment aside, she had more crowns in her purse than she'd had for a while but certainly not enough to buy a whole new 'jack, and how could she lead a mercenary company without one? Doorstop was her principal weapon, like Gardek's war hammer, Eilish's spells, and Milo's grenades.

She grabbed the fallen stepladder, hurried behind Doorstop,

and climbed high enough to pour clear liquid from a pewter vial on the coal in the firebox and the contents of a second one into the boiler. Impatient as she was, the viscous fluid seemed to take forever to ooze and dribble out.

The liquids were some of Milo's alchemical concoctions. They'd produce a head of steam more rapidly—if they didn't simply cause the engine to explode.

She struck a match, applied the flame to the firebox, and slammed the hatch shut. The engine shuddered and chugged to life. She circled around to the front of Doorstop just as the focal lenses in his otherwise featureless face began to glow.

To her surprise, Pog was still there laboring to put one of the 'jack's legs back together. Coughing, Colbie set to work on the other.

• • •

CANICE GORMLEIGH KNOTTED THE SILKEN CORD around Harlan Denby's wrist and so finished tying the naked young poet, handsome—in a pallid, skinny, nearly consumptive fashion—to the bed. Such practices weren't necessary for her own pleasure, but she wasn't averse if a partner was so inclined. She liked being in charge, in the bedchamber and elsewhere.

She gave Harlan a lascivious smile and shook out her mane of curly red hair. Men liked it when she did that, perhaps because her tresses were the best feature of a broad-shouldered, muscular, and scarred body that deviated from typical notions of feminine pulchritude.

Then, somewhere outside the Braggart's Smile, something boomed and hissed simultaneously. It had been a while since Canice fought on an actual battlefield as opposed to in the smaller but no less deadly confrontations of Corvis' underworld, but she still thought she recognized the noise of a steam lobber. Then a considerably louder explosion shook the room, and she grabbed a bedpost to keep her balance. A moment after that, screams sounded through the floor.

Canice strode to the dresser and chair where she'd dropped her clothing and gear. Quickly but methodically she dressed, belted her magelock pistols to her hips, hung a conventional pistol in its shoulder rig under each arm, and made sure her little holdout guns were in their hiding places. Then she pulled on her red-and-yellow armored leather greatcoat and headed for the door.

"Wait!" Harlan bleated.

Damn it. She hadn't bound the dainty rhymer all that tightly, but perhaps he truly was incapable of wriggling free on his own. Begrudging the moment it would take to fiddle with a knot, she pulled a dagger from its sheath and sliced one of the hand ties. "Undo the rest yourself."

"Aren't you going to stay with me?" he whimpered.

"Do you pay my wages?" She slipped the knife back into its sheath, drew a magelock pistol, and left him to claw at the cord securing his other wrist.

Peering around the uppermost newel post, she scanned what she could see of the scene at the bottom of the stairs and winced. So many motionless bodies hacked to pieces in just the moments it had taken her to pull on her clothes. No wonder the shrieking had subsided.

Who could have carried out this attack, and why? Of late, the Patient Weavers had been at peace, relatively speaking, with the other criminal syndicates of the Undercity. They'd even been getting along with the Knotted Cord.

She scowled. Questions could wait. Right now, she had to determine if any of her fellow Weavers were still alive. She started down the steps.

Another explosion nearly sent her tumbling, but she grabbed the bannister and anchored herself in place. She spat away a speck of fallen plaster that had ended up on her lip and finished her descent.

Still, all she saw was bodies. The attackers in the gambling hall—swordsmen, by the look of the wounds—had completed their massacre and moved on but not before smashing some of the oil lamps along the walls to set the place on fire. One crackling sheet of flame licked up a mural of a banquet, devouring the rotund gluttons much as they were gorging on rack of lamb and meat pies.

The crackling almost covered the sound of a groan but not quite. Canice turned and spotted Natak. She knew better than most people that luck can run out at any time, but it still shocked her to see the massive ogrun, he of the prodigious might and boundless ferocity, feebly stirring in a pool of his own blood.

She had to haul him out of here before the smoke strangled him or the fire reached him. She hurried in his direction as he, plainly straining, managed to lift his head a little. The wide mouth between his slab of jaw and the nub of his nose worked, but the words were inaudible.

"It's all right," she said. "I'll help you."

His mouth twisted as if in disgust at her failure to comprehend. His dark eyes shifted to one side and then the other, and she realized he was urging her to take another look around.

She spun. A man and a woman, each white-blond, dressed in blue and yellow, and gripping a sword with one hand and a cape with the other, were creeping toward her from two sides. Perhaps playing dead themselves, they must have hidden among the corpses slumped across tables and sprawled on the floor.

Canice pointed her magelock pistol at the young man. Grinning as though a friend had just surprised him with a deft play at some innocent table game, he flipped his cape at her.

She fired and, the force of impact heightened by the magic of its crafting, the rune shot smashed a chair to pieces but failed to find its target. In the instant when the tossed cloak flummoxed her aim, he'd dived for cover.

Pivoting, she holstered one magelock pistol and drew the other. But to her surprise, the blond woman wasn't rushing in to cut her down from behind. Instead she'd hidden somewhere, and despite the bright blue-and-yellow garments, Canice couldn't spot her amid the thickening smoke.

Behind her, a firearm barked. The young man might prefer the sword, but he had a pistol as well. Fortunately, the round missed.

Canice spun back around, and the young man ducked down

behind an overturned gaming table. She fired. Though charged with mystical power like its predecessor, the rune shot failed to punch through the wooden barrier with its covering of stained green felt. But it slammed the table backward into the lad behind it, and he let out a squawk.

Perhaps she'd actually hurt him or, failing that, at least diminished his enthusiasm for the fight. She holstered the second magelock pistol, whipped a non-magical one from under her arm, and scurried to Natak, looking again for the vanished woman; still no sign of her, curse it! Jerking a chair between the young man's last known position and herself—it wasn't much cover, but it was something—she crouched down beside the ogrun.

"How bad?" she asked.

"Bad," he croaked. "Save yourself, korune."

A korune was an ogrun warrior's chosen lord, the master he deemed worthy of his service. Natak had decided Canice was his korune early in their association, after she'd saved his life a time or two, not that she'd ever wanted the devotion. She'd told him repeatedly that she was merely a fellow rogue who just happened to be positioned one tier higher in the hierarchy of the Patient Weavers, but her perspective didn't alter his own.

"I'll save both of us," she said, just as another explosion shook the building, and another chuck of ceiling crashed down in the center of the hall. "Our friends in blue and gold won't linger much longer, not with the place falling apart around them, and when they make a break for the front door, we'll head out the back."

"You don't understand," Natak replied. "They were lying in wait for you in particular. I don't think they'll quit until they've killed you."

What in the name of Markus's holy sword was this all about? "Then we'll just have to make them regret their persistence. Keep watch." She set the pistol in her hand on the floor and started reloading the magelocks. She would likely to need the edge magic could give her.

She readied the first. Then Natak said, "There!" and indicated where he meant with a trembling, bloody hand.

Canice looked in that direction. Leaning around a pillar, the silver-blonde woman was pointing a small, short-barreled pistol but not accurately enough to incline Canice to duck or dodge. Instead, she snatched for the non-magical gun she'd just set aside.

The other woman fired, and as expected, the round missed. Canice was a split-second away from shooting back when she glimpsed a flicker of motion at the edge of her vision. The young man had crawled from behind the overturned table to a different spot where a fat woman's corpse provided cover. Lying on his stomach, he'd drawn a bead on Canice while she was intent on his partner.

She threw herself down as his pistol banged and flashed. The ball slammed into her shoulder. The impact didn't keep her from firing back, but it spoiled her aim, and her round flew wild.

She checked and found to her relief that the armor in her greatcoat had stopped the round. She was going to have an ugly, aching bruise, but she wasn't crippled or bleeding to death.

Still, she didn't like this game. The assassins were far too good at working together, one drawing her attention while the other maneuvered for a killing stroke. She needed to be equally tricky.

She studied the ceiling with its dangling planks and curling, blackening patches of charred paintings. The section above the prone gunman and the body he was employing for cover wasn't in good shape at all.

Grinning, she reloaded the second magelock pistol, took one in each hand, and fired both upward. The double impact of the rune shots brought flaming boards and scraps of plaster banging and clattering down on top of her adversary.

"Fodor!" the blonde woman wailed. She lunged out from behind the pillar.

Canice hadn't expected the frantic, unthinking reaction, so surprise slowed her for a moment. She grabbed for the pistol hanging under her other arm, but by the time she had it ready, her target had thought better of rushing to her comrade's aid and scrambled back behind the column.

Even with the other woman still unscathed, the situation

was considerably better than it had been a moment ago. Canice returned her primary weapons to their holsters and drew one of her holdout guns from a pocket. Then she took hold of Natak's forearm. "Time to go," she said.

To her relief, the ogrun dredged up enough strength to help her stand him up, drape his arm across her shoulders, and walk him toward the door. When they were partway there, the blonde woman stuck her head around the pillar, and Canice fired. Even in the hand of an expert shot, such diminutive weapons were woefully inaccurate beyond close range, and the ball missed. But the threat, and the two shots she fired after it, kept her adversary pinned down.

Eager though she was to convey Natak out of the burning ruin that had been the Braggart's Smile, Canice paused in the vestibule to reload her various pistols. Judging from the booming and screaming coming through the door, she was still going to need them.

• • •

COLBIE HAD TUGGED HER SHIRT up to cover her mouth and nose, but it didn't seem to be helping. The thickening smoke was making her cough harder and more frequently, robbing her hands of the steadiness they needed. It was stinging her eyes too, and she tugged on her goggles to protect them.

Resisting the temptation to look around and check just how close the fire had crept and trying not to think how one direct hit from a steam-lobber shell could obliterate the work bay in an instant, she labored doggedly to reinstall the parts and reconnect the linkages that would restore Doorstop's leg to functionality. Then Pog pushed in beside her.

The gobber inspected her progress and shook his head. He jabbed a finger at one pneumatic pipe. "This, yes!" He pointed to a silvery reflex trigger that ran alongside it. "These, yes!" He indicated another such wire-and-cable pathway. "This, no!"

She realized what Pog was getting at. Without all the reflex triggers connected, Doorstop would move more clumsily than he should. But with luck, he'd still be able to walk out of this deathtrap, and his mechaniks would save precious time.

"You're right," she said. "You finish the leg, and I'll start on the arms." She grabbed the stepladder, noticing as she did so that Pog hadn't bothered to reattach the entire cowling that would normally cover the inner workings of the limb he'd already put back together. That saved time, too.

She put together one shoulder-and-forearm assembly and moved on to the other. Doorstop's head turned in its socket to watch her work, and she imagined he was questioning the hasty, seemingly slapdash work. *Maybe* he was. Over time, steamjacks picked up behaviors some people believed indicated the development of true consciousness and personality, although more prosaic folk argued that these emerged as a simple consequence of divergent learning experiences interacting with minute variations in the construction of the automatons' cortexes.

Once he finished with the second leg, Pog hovered at the foot of the ladder and called up advice. With a flicker of amusement, Colbie wondered if, before the shells had started flying, he'd found her supervision equally annoying.

She tightened a final bolt, jumped back down to the floor, and shoved the ladder out of the steamjack's way. "Doorstop," she said, "walk!"

He regarded her for a moment, then took a step. She could tell he wasn't as surefooted as before or at least that he didn't feel so. Something in the tentative motion reminded her of a human trying to walk when his leg had fallen asleep.

But he didn't fall over. The squat solidity of his frame, hunchbacked like the chassis of every 'jack to accommodate the engine smoking and chugging on his back, helped to steady him.

"Good!" she said. "Now get your mace and shield." The last thing she wanted to do was make him fight in his current condition. But it might be necessary. At the very least, the sight of the huge metal bludgeon with its round studded head might deter potential attackers.

Still moving even more ponderously than was his wont, the steamjack recovered the articles from the corner where he'd set them down. Clockwork turned inside the gaps where Pog and Colbie had left his chassis open.

She opened her greatcoat and took out the heavy slug gun she carried slung around her shoulder. She also removed the 'jack wrench, one of several tools tucked through loops sewn inside the garment, and transferred it to a pocket.

She looked down at Pog. "You need a weapon, too."

The gobber's mouth twisted in seeming distaste. But he picked up a mallet from the clutter of tools that had fallen off the wall.

"All right," Colbie said. "Time to go. The 'jack leads, we follow. Doorstop, go outside."

She was expecting cleaner, cooler air and the darkness of the vaults and tunnels of the Undercity, where few lights shone outside the shacks and burrows in which the residents conducted their business and lived their lives. But she hadn't escaped from smoke and heat entirely, and the scene was brighter than she'd anticipated because every structure in sight was on fire—the Braggart's Smile, the brothel, the thieves' market, all of them.

Screaming shadows fled while other teams of dark figures overtook them, surrounded them, and cut them down. A man, almost as massive in his steam-powered armor as the 'jack he was servicing, was loading projectiles into the steam lobber attached to the automaton's forearm.

Though it was difficult to be sure of anything in the confusion, it looked to Colbie as though some group was eradicating every trace of the Patient Weavers' illicit enterprises while also slaughtering every luckless gambler or brothel customer they could catch. Maybe the point of the wholesale butchery was to ensure that not a single Weaver got away.

If so, the attackers had likely sealed off the obvious exits from the vault. But Pog was a Weaver, or at least a worker in their employ, and might know of a secret way out. Colbie turned to ask him but then heard the thump of running footsteps.

She pivoted. Unfazed by Doorstop's size and enormous mace, two men, each with a sword in one hand and a cloak in the other, were charging in on her flank. The black-bearded one in the lead had gotten his shirt ripped in some previous confrontation. A smear of blood stained the dark, intricate tattooing underneath.

Gripping the slug gun with both hands, Colbie squeezed the trigger. Such weapons were made for punching through warjack armor, and the projectile tore its target's midsection to shreds. The swordsman's top and bottom portions flopped completely apart as they fell to the ground.

Meanwhile, anticipating his mistress' wishes as he had occasionally begun to do, Doorstop pivoted and lumbered to engage the other attacker. Doorstop's mace swept down but too slowly. The attacker dodged, and the weapon merely thudded to the ground. Another horizontal swing, and by dropping into a squat this time, the killer ducked the blow.

Whooping, he straightened up again and snapped his cape at the exposed workings of Doorstop's weapon arm. The turning gears pulled the garment in, and the cloth, or something inside it, made the mechanism grind and falter.

The swordsman whirled, sprang at Colbie, and cut at her head. She just managed to parry with the now-empty slug gun but doubted she could keep doing so until the crippled Doorstop shuffled around to help her. She was a reasonably competent brawler, but it was plain she was outclassed.

Then, scurrying between the automaton's legs, Pog darted out from behind Doorstop and flailed with his mallet. The awkward stroke whacked the swordsman in the back of the thigh, and he stumbled off balance.

Colbie bashed him over the head, and the man fell to the ground. She hit him again and he stopped moving. A third blow made his skull crunch.

It also made Pog flinch. "Did you have to do the last one?"

"You're joking, right?" Colbie transferred another round from her bandolier into the breach of the slug gun. To her regret, she only had one more after this one, but the projectiles were too heavy to lug around very many of them when she wasn't expecting trouble. "I was about to ask you, is there a way out of here these madmen might not know about?"

Pog nodded. "But the closest is almost halfway around the cavern."

"Then we need to move."

They skulked onward, trying to cover ground expeditiously but without drawing further attention to themselves. Doorstop kept experimentally bending his arm until, concerned by more grinding and the jerking action, Colbie told him to stop.

Then Pog said, "I know them!"

When Colbie looked where he was pointing, she discovered that she did, too. Canice Gormleigh and Natak Warbiter were heading the same direction that she and the gobber were, although it might be an exaggeration to say the ogrun was intentionally heading anywhere. Natak was bleeding from several wounds and looked semiconscious at best; holding her companion's arm across her shoulders, the red-haired gun mage was hobbling and panting, close to buckling under his weight.

Colbie frowned. Nothing about her previous encounter with Canice and Natak had endeared them to her. But she was willing to set aside her feelings if that would help save her skin; besides, even if she didn't like them, she did *know* them, and they were fellow practitioners of the profession of arms. Perhaps that was why, despite her better judgment, their plight inspired a twinge of sympathy.

"Gormleigh!" she called.

Nearly fumbling her hold on Natak's wrist in the process, Canice lurched around and pointed a pistol.

Colbie stopped in her tracks and swung the slug gun well to the side, making it clear she wasn't threatening the redhead with it. "Easy! It's Colbie Sterling."

"Yes," Canice replied, "a mercenary captain. Are the Black River Irregulars part of this?"

"No," Colbie said. "From the looks of things, I doubt your ill-wishers felt the need to hire additional muscle."

Pog took a step forward. "Captain Sterling just happened to be here when the trouble started."

Canice gave a brusque nod. "Then go." She started to turn away.

"My thought," Colbie said, "was that we can help one another."

"I don't need your help."

"Don't be stupid. Doorstop's in poor shape for a fight, which means so am I. But he can carry Natak. Whereas you can fight but, lugging your friend along, you're creeping at a snail's pace."

Canice's mouth tightened and then smiled crookedly, as if with grim amusement. "When you put it that way…"

Colbie told Doorstop to drop his mace and pick up Natak. The steamjack stared at her for a moment, then obeyed the order. The group hurried onward.

For fifty paces of so, no one noticed them. Then, just as Canice was slipping past the burnt remains of a little outbuilding, a pile of charred wood fell clinking in on itself, and new flames leaped from the coals. The light glinted in Canice's coppery curls and revealed the distinctive red-and-yellow pattern of her greatcoat.

Toward the center of the vault, someone shouted. Then, silhouetted by the blaze consuming the thieves' market, a 'jack turned in the fugitives' direction. Its arm pointed.

Though Colbie couldn't actually make it out, she was certain the limb had a steam lobber built into it. "Shield!" she cried, whereupon Doorstop poised the armor to protect Natak and himself. She dived to the ground, and Canice and Pog followed her lead.

The enemy 'jack's arm boomed and hissed, and a puff of vapor shrouded it. The projectile flew over Canice, narrowly missed Doorstop, and exploded against the cave wall, producing a burst of flame and a shower of dirt that half-smothered it.

The steamjack advanced. Colbie assumed its controller had ordered it forward, although she had yet to spot him. He was probably moving up behind the automaton as any sensible 'jack marshal would.

"Why are they so interested in us?" Canice asked. "Just because they know you're a Weaver?"

The gun mage shook her head. "For some reason, some of them are after me specifically."

"You didn't think to mention that before?"

"You were so eager to join forces. I didn't want to dampen your enthusiasm."

Colbie bit back an obscenity; there was no time for it. "Doorstop, keep your shield pointed at the other 'jack! Everyone else, stay behind Doorstop!"

The steam lobber thundered. The shot—not an incendiary this time—clanged against Doorstop's shield and sent him lurching backward. Dodging aside, Colbie felt a jolt of fear that he'd topple. If he did, it was unlikely that his half-functional limbs could set him upright again. But though it was close, he didn't quite overbalance.

The enemy steamjack lowered the arm with the steam lobber, perhaps because the weapon was empty. Using its other hand, it hefted an enormous sword and tramped forward.

That meant the fugitives were in about as much trouble as before. In his current condition, Doorstop could neither outfight nor outrun the other automaton.

But if the 'jack with the battle blade was primarily after Canice, it might ignore a target that separated from her. Colbie sprinted away from her companions.

Her objective was to circle around behind the enemy steamjack and blast its boiler or engine to bits. The trick was to get close enough. As she'd learned from failed shots on many a battlefield, slug guns were inaccurate beyond short range.

At her back, Canice's pistols barked again and again, and metal clanged as the rounds found their target. But even rune shots were only slowing the automaton down a little.

Suddenly another firearm banged and flashed, and the breeze of the ball's passage fanned Colbie's cheek. The enemy 'jack's controller had spotted her maneuvering and taken a shot at her. Now he rushed her, a shadow surging out of the darkness with sword in hand.

She pointed the slug gun and squeezed the trigger. Her target threw himself to the side as the weapon roared, and the projectile hurtled past him.

Revealing a mouthful of stained, broken teeth, he grinned and continued his advance, taking his time now that he'd nearly closed the distance. She raised the slug gun like a shield, focusing his attention on it—or so she hoped—and slipped her other hand into the pocket containing the wrench.

He poised the sword for a cut or feint in the low line. Giving ground, Colbie snatched out the wrench and threw it spinning at his head. The tool thudded between his eyes, and he faltered. She charged, hit him with the slug gun, and kept striking until she laid him out on the ground.

She stood, panting, and saw that unfortunately, the controller's fall had done nothing to halt the enemy 'jack. Obeying its last orders, it was still advancing on her companions.

Meanwhile, Canice had stopped firing, presumably because she was out of ammunition. She darted out from behind Doorstop, and for an instant Colbie thought she was making a run for it and abandoning everyone else. But the gun mage stopped several paces away from the automaton and poised herself to dodge. Maybe she'd broken cover in an effort to make sure the enemy 'jack wouldn't notice what Colbie was doing.

Colbie loaded the slug gun with its last projectile and dashed around behind the enemy 'jack. She took aim, exhaled, and fired.

The big gun kicked in her hands, and, with a crash and a screech, the automaton's boiler burst apart. Colbie twisted away and jerked her arm up to shield her head from flying shrapnel and scalding steam. The enemy 'jack took a final decelerating step and froze, its sword arm raised for a stroke it would never make.

Colbie ran back to the others. "That took you long enough," Canice growled.

"At least *my* gun got the job done," Colbie replied. "Let's move! Doorstop, shield us like before!"

There was nothing else of interest in the immediate vicinity to attract notice to the Patient Weavers' bolthole, and a jut of stone concealed the fissure unless an observer was standing right beside the wall of the vault. On his first attempt, Doorstop failed to squeeze through, but Colbie ordered him to discard his crumpled shield. By sidling, he just managed to fit.

The conflagrations at their back provided a trace of illumination for the first few paces. When they rounded a bend, Colbie extracted a jar of bottled light from her pocket and gave it a shake. The black oil and the yellow grease floating on top of it started glowing as they combined.

"We should get aboveground fast," Colbie said, "before the enemy discovers this tunnel."

"Agreed," Canice said. "We should go to the Watch."

Colbie cocked her head. "I was going to recommend that. I wasn't sure a member of the Patient Weavers would go along."

"The Watch can find a physician for Natak quickly, and as far as I can tell, there's no such thing as the Weavers anymore."

— 2 —

JULIAN HELSTROM PROWLED THE PERIMETER of the flagstone courtyard with its wrought-iron fence and glowered. His fingers never strayed far from the hand cannon holstered on his hip, a habit ingrained by decades spent enforcing the law in Corvis. He hadn't started out as watch commander, and even now couldn't find it in himself to dress like a man who spent much of his time behind a desk.

His bad mood was due in part to the city's notoriously foul weather—today, a cold drizzle. But mostly he was disgusted by the slowness and the sloppiness with which the company of men before him was forming up.

Helstrom understood their lack of enthusiasm. It was a rare watchman who liked descending into the Undercity. Given a choice, most behaved as though their responsibilities ended where that criminal warren began. But it wasn't true, particularly when the Watch had received the first confused reports of a massacre that had apparently claimed the lives of not just tunnel dwellers but of respectable burghers fool enough to venture into the depths.

"Lieutenant!" Helstrom shouted. "What's the holdup?"

A squat bulldog of a man whose sandy hair was going grey, Lonan Bartley glanced around. "Almost ready!" he called, and then a steamjack carrying the torn bloody form of an ogrun lumbered through the gate. Two human women and a gobber followed.

The assembled watchmen stared, and after a moment, Helstrom realized he was doing the same. He supposed the universal surprise was understandable. The sudden intrusion was remarkable in several respects.

The steamjack had pieces of cowling missing, exposing the turning gears inside. The round-faced, solidly built redhead in the distinctive yellow-and-crimson greatcoat was Canice Gormleigh, which meant the ogrun was likely Natak Warbiter, two of the last people he would have expected to show up at a Watch station of their own volition. And the willowy, swarthy woman in tinted glasses and clothing as black as her tangled hair was Colbie Sterling. Unlike Gormleigh, Captain Sterling was a respectable mercenary—to the extent that such a thing existed. She and her people didn't hire out to further the ends of outright criminality. Rumor had it that the two women had even tried to kill one another at some point in the past. Thus, it was odd to see them together now.

"The ogrun needs a physician!" Gormleigh shouted.

"You look like you're preparing for a raid," Sterling added, "so I assume you've got someone on call to tend your wounded. Fetch him."

Bartley said, "On call to tend *our* wounded. Not outlaw scum. Especially scum that looks like it's already dead."

"I wasn't talking to the underlings," the gun mage snapped. She fixed her gaze on Helstrom. "Watch Commander! No doubt your men are preparing to head out because word reached you about a battle belowground. Sterling, the gobber, and I just came from there. We can tell you all about it. But only after someone sees to Natak."

Sterling gave the other woman a sour glance that suggested

she'd been included in that ultimatum without prior consultation. "You'll accomplish more by indulging her, Watch Commander. By now the fight's over. The victors are departing the scene, and the losers are dead."

Helstrom scowled. He didn't like the ultimatum either, but he'd employed Sterling and her crew on two occasions, enough times to form an opinion of her reliability, and if she said there was nothing to gain by rushing down into the Undercity, it was probably so. "Lieutenant," he said, "send a runner for the physician, and let's get the ogrun inside." He glared at the two women. "And woe to you if you don't have something to say that's worth my time."

The steamjack was too large to fit through the entrance to the three-story brick bastion that was the station proper. At Sterling's direction, the automaton handed the ogrun off to her, Gormleigh, and the two burly watchmen who Lieutenant Bartley, with manifest disgust, directed to assist them. Together, the four carried Warbiter in out of the rain and laid him on the table in a conference room, where he drew shallow, rasping breaths. The physician completed a hasty examination, said, "Well, he *might* live," then set to work with needles, catgut sutures, and salves.

"There," Helstrom said to the two mercenaries, with the little gobber plainly seeking to remain inconspicuous behind them. "I held up my end."

"It doesn't help to save his life," Gormleigh answered, rainwater dripping from her coat, "if assassins track him down before he regains his strength. Promise to keep him safe while he recuperates."

"That wasn't the bargain," Bartley said.

"Look," Sterling said, "you know what Natak Warbiter is. Who doesn't? But do you have the evidence to charge him with a crime here and now? If not, then the law says you should look after his welfare the same as you would for any other resident of the city."

"Don't tell us what the law says!" Bartley snapped. "We could revoke your company's charter for associating—"

"That will do," Helstrom interrupted. "Gormleigh, something

can be done to keep your friend safe. *If* it's necessary and *if* you actually have something of value to trade for the protection. Lieutenant, go see to your men. No reason to keep them standing in the wet."

"Sir." Bartley stamped out of the room followed by the two watchmen who'd helped carry the ogrun.

Helstrom pulled a chair away from the table, removing it and himself from the physician's way, and, with a wave of his hand, indicated that Sterling, Gormleigh, and the gobber should do the same. When they'd all seated themselves in the corner, he said, "Talk."

Gormleigh said, "Formidable enemies executed a surprise attack on the Patient Weavers' stronghold. The assault was well planned and intended to wipe us out to the last man."

Sterling nodded. "That's my appraisal as well."

"That's why Natak needs protection," the gun mage said. "They aren't done yet."

Helstrom grunted. "I promised we'd get to that. First things first. Who was responsible for the attack? The Knotted Cord? The Anthill?"

Gormleigh shook her head, and her coppery curls swished on the shoulders of her greatcoat. "It wasn't any of the gangs you know. It was a *bratya*, a Khadoran crime syndicate."

Could that be true? Plenty of disreputable characters and smuggled goods entered Corvis surreptitiously via the docks, but could an entire well-armed criminal gang from the empire that was Cygnar's principal foe have crossed the river and established itself in the Undercity without anyone in authority being the wiser? If so, what in Morrow's name were the duchy's tens of thousands of soldiers doing with their time?

"I need light!' the physician shouted. Apparently the gas lamps on the walls were insufficient to his purpose.

"See to it!" Helstrom called, and with a patter of footsteps, one of his subordinates scurried to fetch a handheld source of illumination. Helstrom looked at the women. "How do you know the attackers belonged to one of these bratyas?"

"They operated in pairs and teams to kill their victims," Gormleigh said. "They fought sword-and-cape style. Each of them had the same distinctive type of tattooing. Taken all together, the details say, 'Bratya.'"

"To you, maybe," Helstrom said. "But what makes you the expert?"

Gormleigh's mouth twisted. "Does it matter?"

"If you want me to believe you."

"Fine. I wasn't always a mercenary. Before I came to Corvis, back in Llael, I was a member of the Loyal Order of the Amethyst Rose. We fought to free our country from the Khadoran conquerors."

Sterling cocked her head. "I'd heard that rumor, but I always had trouble picturing you as an idealistic freedom fighter." She smiled. "No offense."

Gormleigh glowered. "I was younger and foolish then."

Helstrom wondered what had happened to change her into the allegedly amoral killer-for-pay he saw before him.

"Anyway," the gun mage continued, "there was—still is, as far as I know—a certain noblewoman in the city of Laedry. I can't divulge her name, but it doesn't matter. She was Umbrean, not Khadoran, but like Viscount Ushka, seemingly reconciled to the Khadoran occupation and flourishing under their rule."

"'Seemingly,'" Helstrom repeated.

"In reality, she was a patriot aiding the Resistance however she could." Gormleigh's tone warmed with a hint of admiration or affection. "Spying, chiefly. Her title, wealth, and charm gave her access to all the great men and women and fashionable houses of the city. Unfortunately, in time, one of our enemies came to suspect her and sent assassins after her."

Helstrom frowned. "Why not simply arrest her?"

"I said *someone* suspected her, not *everyone*. Apparently he couldn't convince his superiors of his suspicions. Perhaps it didn't help that the lady gave lavishly to the needy. It would have outraged the populace if she were taken into custody, especially without proof, and what ruler wants to trigger a riot? At any rate, a bratya had slithered into Laedry with the rest of the Khadorans, and when the chain of command failed him, the spy's ill-wisher turned to them for help."

"A government official—I assume that's whom we're discussing—sought the aid of outlaws?"

"As I was to learn, some bratyas have ties to the kayazy, the wealthy merchants, who in turn cultivate alliances with the Khadoran princes and the Empress herself. As a result, outlaws occasionally end up doing the jobs that no one in a position of legitimate authority would care to admit having ordered."

"It's not like Corvis," Sterling said gravely, "where officials never go behind one another's backs or slip across the line that separates servant of the law from criminal."

Helstrom sighed. "Go on with your story, Gormleigh."

"The first time the killers came after the lady, they failed. She had bodyguards, and she was cool-headed and resourceful in her own right. Still, it was a close call, and when she reported the attempt, the Amethyst Rose sent me to protect her."

Sterling chuckled. "I'm also having trouble picturing you dressed in an elegant gown and jewelry accompanying a fine lady to the ball."

Gormleigh snorted. "You might have been surprised. But I didn't spend all my time shepherding my charge around. I worried that would be a recipe for failure as soon as the enemy gave up on swordsmen and switched to snipers or explosives. When the lady was safe behind the walls of her mansion, I went hunting for the assassins. I had no idea they belonged to a bratya then or even what a bratya was. But I knew from examining the corpses of the first batch of would-be killers that they had distinctive tattooing under their clothes, and I assumed they couldn't avoid displaying those marks in bathhouses and brothels. So that was where I looked."

"And that worked?" Helstrom asked. Behind him came a tearing sound. The physician was preparing a length of bandage.

"Yes," Gormleigh said. "Like everyone else, they had their habits and appetites, and I had money to loosen people's tongues. Eventually a half-grown girl with a black eye and swollen lip gave up one of her new customers. She didn't like the treatment she had to endure to arouse him.

"I waited outside the room listening," the gun mage continued, "and when I judged that he was intent on his pleasure, I threw the door open. With his sword out of easy reach, he locked his hands around the prostitute's neck and swore that if I didn't withdraw, he'd crush her throat. I told him it wouldn't matter except insofar as it annoyed me, and evidently he believed me. He let her go and rolled off her."

"Did you truly not care if he killed her?" Helstrom asked.

Gormleigh flicked her hand as if the question were a buzzing fly and she was shooing it away. "She was my paid confederate. That made me responsible for her. She was also a single life when I was trying to liberate a country. Combine those considerations and perhaps you'll understand what was in my head. What does it matter anyway? You asked how I know about bratyas, and I'm telling you."

"Of course," Helstrom said, meanwhile deciding that in the final analysis, the Llaelese expatriate had dodged his question. "Go on."

"Well, when I started questioning him, he vowed he'd never betray his 'brothers and sisters,' and after two days, I was worried he was right. But then my prostitute friend came up with something ingenious, and he broke down on the third."

Sterling made a spitting sound. "You tortured him?"

Gormleigh sneered. "Perhaps you're too squeamish to do it yourself, but I'll wager you've at least stood by and let others do it a time or two. What mercenary hasn't? So spare me your scorn."

"What," Helstrom asked, "did the prisoner tell you?"

"A fair amount about bratyas in general and how they were moving into Llael along with every other Khadoran opportunist looking to profit from my homeland's humiliation. And more important, the location of the house where he and his friends had holed up, as well as the identity of the official who wanted the noblewoman dead.

"I put together a team to assault the house, four able duelists loyal to the Resistance. We moved on the place in the hours before sunrise when, we hoped, most everyone would be asleep or, failing that, drunk. The bratya kept a sentry peeking out from behind curtains in a gable window, but I crawled over the peak of the rooftop across the street and shot him before he spotted anything amiss.

"When I climbed back down to the ground, a fellow who knew his way around locks picked the one on the front door, and my comrades and I burst in and cleaned the place out room by room. It was easy for the first few moments, less so when the Khadorans started waking up and grabbing their weapons. Still, we kept making progress.

"Toward the end, a gout of fire burned one of us alive, so I knew the other side had an arcanist. But no matter how I tried, I couldn't spot him until, up on the second story, I heard floorboards creak in a bedroom. I rushed in just in time to see a casement open and a shadow—or rather, the enemy wrapped in a spell of concealment—lunge through, jumping down into the alley behind the house.

"I dashed to the window to fire after him, but a blast of magical force shattered the glass and frame, and the shards and splinters flew at me. That's how I got this." Gormleigh touched a little white vertical scar on her forehead.

"But happily, nothing hit me in the eyes, and when I shook off the surprise and peered out the hole, I located the arcanist, shadowy though he was. I put a rune shot in his back as he was trying to run away. Then I rejoined my companions, and we determined we'd killed everybody.

"Except, of course, not quite. The outlaws were gone, but so long as the official who suspected the lady remained, so did the threat. I had to find a way into his apartments and bedchamber and smother him with a pillow to make it appear he'd died of natural causes. Otherwise, someone might have wondered if there hadn't been some truth to his allegations after all.

"Once that was done, and a couple weeks passed without incident, my superiors in the Resistance decided the lady was safe and gave me a new assignment. I never saw her again." Gormleigh barked a truncated laugh. At what, Helstrom couldn't tell. "And that, Watch Commander, is how I know about bratyas."

"Fair enough," Helstrom said. "Why do you think this gang came to Corvis?"

"The same reason they go anywhere. For profit." The gun mage frowned. "Although, given Khador's recent conquests, you'd think there'd be easier places than a Cygnaran city for a bratya to expand its operations."

"Could they be here at the behest of the Khadoran government? To spy, commit sabotage, or foment unrest?"

"It's possible, I suppose. Although when I was a spy operating in hostile territory, I tried to go unnoticed, not make my presence known in spectacular fashion."

"Yes, about that. Why did they strike to eliminate the Patient Weavers?"

"Not because we'd ever had dealings with them or any bratya, at least so far as I know. Maybe they felt they needed to destroy somebody's gang to clear a space for their own and picked the Weavers more or less at random."

"This is all just speculation," Sterling interjected.

"Perhaps," Helstrom replied, "but at least Gormleigh can provide informed speculation, and if there's any chance that the bratya is here to carry out the aims of the Khadoran military, this situation is too important for me to neglect any resource." He shifted his gaze to the gun mage. "So, you'll have protection. I'll provide a safehouse."

Gormleigh inclined her head. "Thank you."

Helstrom looked back at Sterling. "I'm short of manpower as usual, and given what's happened, people will want to see every watchman patrolling and ensuring public safety. Thus, I'd like to hire the Black River Irregulars to guard the house."

Sterling frowned, pondering, and Helstrom surmised the tenor of her thoughts. What with her dislike of Gormleigh and Warbiter, her first impulse was to decline the assignment. But coin was coin, and she also hesitated to forfeit the Watch Commander's goodwill.

"All right," she said at length. "We can be bodyguards. It wouldn't be the first time. But why limit our role to that? Gardek Stonebrow is an accomplished bounty hunter. Eilish Garrity has a gift for solving puzzles. Milo Boggs…" She smiled. "Well, you've met Milo. We can obtain information that will enable you to destroy the bratya before they get themselves so well established in Corvis' underworld that it's impossible to root them out. It will simply cost you a little more."

Helstrom grunted. "The Watch has its own investigators."

"And the Khadorans will be on the lookout for them. They won't know you hired us."

Helstrom considered only for a moment longer before conceding the point. "Very well. It's a deal."

"I don't mind the help," Gormleigh said, "But as the person who's actually hunted a bratya before, I should be in charge."

Sterling snorted. "Forget it. This time, you won't be hunting at all. The Irregulars have worked too hard to build an honorable reputation to work with a murderer-for-hire."

Gormleigh glared. "You're fond of drawing imaginary distinctions, aren't you? Every freelance is a 'murderer-for-hire.'"

"There's no need to argue," Helstrom said. "The fact of the matter, Gormleigh, is that I don't care to risk losing your counsel. So, you'll stay in the safehouse with Warbiter."

"That's stu—wasteful! I'll be more useful in the field!"

"You'd be a liability," Sterling replied. "This whole safehouse plan is predicated on our assumption that the bratya is still searching for any Patient Weavers who escaped. Worse, you told me during the battle that the killers are looking for you in particular."

His armor clinking, Helstrom sat up straighter in his chair. "Is that true? You neglected to mention it before, Gormleigh."

"Because it's not significant. They simply wanted to make sure they neutralized the one Weaver with magic at her command. It was basic strategy, nothing more."

"That reminds me," Sterling said. "You ran out of your magic—rune shots—during our escape. Without them, how much use would you be, really? No more, I imagine, than any common ruffian."

"Maybe I should show you." Gormleigh gripped the arms of her chair and started to stand up.

"That's enough of that!" Helstrom rapped. "I've made my decision. Ms. Gormleigh, you'll stay where I put you. I'll scrape together a few more crowns to compensate you for your time."

"You're making a mistake," the gun mage said.

Sterling gave her a mocking smile.

• • •

TO A SIGNIFICANT DEGREE, the fires had burned down, but the coals and flickering blue-and-yellow flames revealed that little remained of the Patient Weavers' enclave. It was a pity in its way. Had the structures survived, Ivan thought, the Black Dogs could have used them to house their own enterprises.

But combined with the wholesale butchery of the Weavers and any third parties found on the scene, burning the enclave to the ground sent a message. The men and women of the bratya were merciless berserkers, and anyone who resisted them assured his own destruction. Someday, Ivan promised himself, when the Black Dogs were the uncontested masters of Corvis' underworld, he'd rebuild in this vault and make every illicit market and den of vice bigger and gaudier than before.

For now, though, it was time to think about disappearing before the Watch turned up. He might need to butcher a company of them, too, in due course, to convince them to leave him alone, but that was a chore for another day, when he'd mapped out a strategy and his fighters were fresh.

He lifted the bugle hanging at his hip and blew a call. The gobber at the end of the leash in his other hand jumped. He'd beaten the scrawny, half-naked creature often enough that any sudden noise or movement was apt to make the prisoner cringe.

Shadows in the gloom, Ivan's followers left off robbing bodies and sifting through rubble for loot to converge on him. "Coming!" Gridia called.

Ivan's heartbeat accelerated. He'd convinced his superiors in the bratya that Corvis represented an opportunity, and that was true. But he'd also wanted to lead a contingent of Black Dogs here to attend to a personal matter, and he'd entrusted the blonde assassin and her son with the handling of it.

He squinted, trying to make them out by the wavering firelight. Would one be carrying a severed head? Then he'd be content and thank them as they deserved. But he prayed they'd be leading a living prisoner so he could deal with her as she deserved.

But when they and a different team of killers emerged from the darkness, revealed by the burning brands two of the Dogs were carrying, they possessed neither. Limping, Fodor had blood in his hair, and Gridia was cooing over him and helping him along as though he were three years old instead of nineteen.

"Was the target not here?" Ivan asked. Judging from Fodor's condition, he suspected he already knew the truth of the matter, but even with frustration rising inside him, a leader needed to make sure of the facts.

Gridia sighed. "No, she was."

"We almost had her," Fodor said.

"But then she cheated," his mother said, "and hurt my poor little lamb." She kissed her fingertips and touched them to a scrape on Fodor's cheek.

Fodor smiled. "I'm fine, Mama."

Gridia looked back at Ivan. "He's so brave."

Ivan's jaw tightened. "You're telling me she escaped you."

"Yes, taking the ogrun with her. Although he may have succumbed to his wounds before getting very far."

"I don't care about the ogrun!" Ivan snarled. "I gave you one task! One! And you—"

Gridia stepped back, not out of alarm, he was certain, but to give herself sufficient distance to draw her sword and cut. "We what? I understand we've disappointed you, and that saddens me more than I can say, so please feel free to let it all out."

Ivan took a breath. If average underlings had failed him as she and Fodor had, he would have felt free to curse them, slap them, throw them to the ground, and kick them. But the woman and her son were a different matter.

Ivan wasn't afraid of them. An orphan from the gutters of Skirov didn't rise to become an underboss by fearing anyone or anything. But their strangeness notwithstanding, he recognized them as kindred spirits, too dangerous and too useful to provoke without good reason.

"What's done is done," he said. "We have more important matters to concern us." He didn't entirely believe that, not in his heart, but since no one else would agree with him, he needed to behave as if he did.

The lamp affixed to his shoulder glowing with a slightly greenish light, Olekse the ironhead strode up with his laborjacks to join the palaver, each 'jack modified to bear and wield weapons, marching along behind him. In his massive steam-powered armor, smelling of oil and combustion, smokestack fuming on his back, a maul in his gauntleted hands too heavy for mere human strength to wield, he could almost have been mistaken for an automaton himself. Only the square face framed by the domelike open helmet, that face with its pouchy, perpetually bloodshot eyes and a fringe of dark scraggly beard, revealed the truth.

"What have you got to tell me?" Ivan asked him.

"You can see for yourself," Olekse replied. "The 'jacks blasted and burned everything. But we lost one. Unless you want to try to haul it out of here. Then, given time, I might be able to rebuild it. Or at least break it down for parts."

The rage that Ivan had struggled to put aside came surging back. "The gun mage wrecked it, didn't she?"

Olekse shook his head, although the steel shell enclosing it didn't move. "I didn't see. It was the 'jack Padri was commanding. The person or people who disabled it beat him to death as well."

"It was the gun mage," Ivan said. He was sure of it.

"Well, hell take whoever it was. Now we're down to three 'jacks and just one mechanik—me—to maintain them all."

Ivan took another long breath. "What matters is that we won. We'll leave the wrecked 'jack for now. It would slow us down.

Maybe you can return and salvage it after the law has come and gone."

"Do we know," Gridia asked, "how many people we lost altogether?"

Ivan shrugged. "Half a dozen?"

"Oh, no! Their poor mothers! But I suppose it could have been worse. If we all pull together, the next phase of the plan should still work out."

"Olekse and I will make sure of that," Ivan replied. "You and Fodor, finish the chore I gave you."

Gridia's brow furrowed. "Dear heart, no one respects your judgment more than I do. But with so much at stake, is that truly the best use of our time?"

"If you're worried that everything else will fall apart without you, then get the job done quickly."

Gridia spread her hands in a gesture of acquiescence. "If you think it's that important, then of course."

Ivan glanced around at the ring of cutthroats who'd assembled to watch their chieftain and his deputies confer. "It's time to go!" He snapped the rope knotted around the gobber's neck, and the small green creature whimpered. "You! Guide us home!"

Among his fellow tunnel dwellers, the gobber was famous for his knowledge of the labyrinthine passages of the Undercity. Ivan had taken him prisoner shortly after his arrival to help the bratya find a secret refuge and to lead them around until they learned the lay of the land. After that, he supposed, they'd kill him. They couldn't just set him free to carry tales.

Meanwhile, Ivan liked seeing him trudge along with head bowed and scourge-welted shoulders hunched. Perhaps it was a stupid joke, but it always amused him when, even though he was the Black Dog, he had someone else on the end of a leash.

— 3 —

POG HAD BEEN HAPPY TO LET Colbie and Canice do all the talking and was happier still to escape Watch Commander Helstrom's flinty regard. He'd never truly been a Patient Weaver, merely a laborer in their employ, and as far as he knew he'd never done anything absolutely, incontrovertibly illegal. Still, the association was scarcely likely to engender positive feelings in officers of the law, and anyway, he'd always felt nervous around people twice his size if they were arguing.

He wasn't comfortable even now, in part because his two companions were still bickering as they came out the station door.

"You're going to regret this," Canice said.

"Is that a threat?" Colbie asked.

"No, idiot, it's common sense. The bratya's too much for your sad little company of four. You need reinforcements."

"Not just to investigate them. And as I explained inside, if we did need help, it wouldn't be you."

"Please!" Pog said. The strapping red-haired woman and the

lanky dark one pivoted to peer at him, and his face warmed with embarrassment. "I'm sorry. It's just that while you're squabbling, poor Doorstop's standing in this weather with holes in his chassis and the rain getting inside."

Colbie smiled crookedly. "You're right. He deserves better, and there's no point debating what Helstrom already decided. Gormleigh, why don't you ride along with Warbiter in the carriage? I'll join you at the safehouse in a while."

"Where are you going?" the gun mage asked.

"To round up the other members of my 'sad little company of four.' Also, to get a physician who can stay close to your friend over the course of the next few days."

"Then I'll tag along. Helstrom's men will watch over Natak until the rest of us show up, and no bratya hunters will have made their way aboveground just yet."

"Helstrom wants—"

"I don't care what he wants. This is my last chance to stretch my legs before I'm sequestered."

Colbie studied the other woman as though seeking to determine whether some devious intention underlay the suggestion. Then she said, "You wouldn't disappear on me before making sure the ogrun really is safe. So, come along if you must. Good luck, Pog. Doorstop, follow."

The two mercenaries and the steamjack set off for a canal lined with moored houseboats. A soot-stained bridge arched over the murky, rain-pocked flow, and the evening's first stars peeked between the clouds overhead. Her voice hoarse from crying her wares, a woman tried to sell them apples from a wicker basket. The brown-spotted fruit looked as if it might have been wholesome yesterday, or perhaps the day before.

Scurrying to keep up with his companions' longer strides, Pog brought up the rear. At first they didn't pay him any mind—he was used to that from humans unless they needed a 'jack repaired. It was only when his foot splashed down in a puddle in a low spot among the uneven cobblestones, and two women whipped around, that he realized they hadn't known he was still with them.

Colbie's "good luck" had actually been a dismissal; he just hadn't understood because the words weren't used that way in the gobber tongue.

At least the pair didn't appear angry, only surprised. "I figured that once Helstrom finished with us, you'd go your own way," Colbie said.

Pog spread his hands. "To where? I didn't just work in the 'jack shop—I lived there."

"I'm sorry. I didn't realize. Do you have kin or friends elsewhere to take you in?"

"Not in Corvis." He hesitated. "Miss Gormleigh said there are only four Black River Irregulars, so I hoped you might be looking for new recruits."

The women exchanged glances. Then Colbie said, "Forgive me if I note that you don't strike me as the soldierly type."

"Maybe not," Pog replied. "But I can work on Doorstop and tell him what to do."

Colbie's lips twitched upward. "I admit it would be nice if every bit of the repair work didn't fall to me."

"It's nice, too," Canice said, "when there's somebody else to command a 'jack in battle if its marshal is incapacitated." For the moment, the edge was gone from her voice as, thinking like the fighter she was, she pondered the merits of Pog's offer.

Encouraged, he said, "Captain, you've seen I'm a good mechanik, and now you've heard Miss Gormleigh vouch for me, too."

Canice grunted. "'Vouch' is putting it a little strong. I'd seen you around, of course, but until today, I didn't even know your name." She turned to Colbie. "But for what it's worth, during our time with the Weavers, I never heard of him making any trouble."

Colbie chuckled. "That's more than I can say for the people I have already. Pog, if you're sure you want this, I can propose it, but understand it's not up to me alone. I'm the captain, but there are some decisions we vote on."

"Thank you!" said Pog. Cast adrift as he was, he really was grateful, although he also shared the two women's doubts about his inclinations and capacities. Until the notion came to him a minute ago, he'd never imagined himself as a mercenary or any such desperate character.

He decided the best way to cope with his misgivings was to focus on Doorstop instead. As the group tramped onward, he looked for a tarp or oilcloth he could scrounge or prevail on Colbie to purchase. Once they had one, the 'jack could wrap it around himself like a shawl to cover the exposed inner workings of his shoulders and arms.

• • •

LYING FLAT, A CORPSE MADE A POOR TARGET. Eilish Garrity had rectified the problem by strapping the old woman's naked cadaver to a table and then standing the table on end. He focused his will on it and on the words and gestures that, while not truly necessary, would help him channel arcane force to the desired effect, and then a pang of uncertainty assailed him. With a muttered curse, he raised the old book in his hand for another skim of the relevant passage.

Perched on a stool in the corner, Regan Falk said, "Going well, is it?"

Eilish glanced at her in annoyance, but the irritation melted at the sight of her. Her petite form clad in the teal dress that was her favorite, her crystal earrings and necklace glittering in the gaslight, her short brown hair fluffed artfully, she'd made herself look even prettier than usual. And Eilish knew it wasn't so she could sit smelling lye soap, formaldehyde, and putrefaction while watching him putter around with a corpse and a grimoire.

"Just a few minutes more," he said.

"Lied the heartless swain as his sweetheart perished of starvation. You know, you could get in trouble if someone caught you doing this."

"I don't see why. As a proud alumnus of Corvis University, I have the run of the morgue."

"To study forensics, anatomy, and such. Not sorcery."

He waved his hand. "All right, if you insist on being technical.

But of late, the Irregulars have faced some tough opposition. As you should know, since we call on you to patch us up afterward. I need to expand my repertoire of spells to tilt the odds in our favor."

"And studying on your own is a better option than applying to the Fraternal Order of Wizardry for membership?"

"They wouldn't take me. I don't have the right connections."

Actually, though, he thought that might not be true. Back in Ceryl, the so-called City of Wizards, Eilish's mentor in the arcane arts had been a member of the Fraternal Order, which gave Eilish at least an outside chance of gaining admission himself. But for all the senior mages' power and pretensions to wisdom, when his teacher disappeared, Eilish had been the one who'd determined what happened to him. The experience had left the young arcanist disillusioned and averse to accepting any strictures or limits the Fraternal Order might care to impose.

"And I don't need them anyway," Eilish continued. "Behold." He ran his gaze over the page in the spellbook one more time, then recited the incantation that shifted his focus to conjure the appropriate runes. Fingers waggling, he bobbed his hand up and down in a motion that mimicked the rise and fall of leaping flames.

Glyphs of blue light glowed into existence in the air around him. More azure radiance danced on his fingertips and then grew suddenly warmer, although not uncomfortably so. Then, with a crackle, a patch of fire flared into being.

Unfortunately, it didn't do so in the center of the elderly woman's Y-shaped autopsy scar where he wanted it. Rather, it erupted on the sheet shrouding a different cadaver several feet away.

Eilish scrambled to the table, whipped the burning sheet to the floor before it could char the corpse underneath, and then drenched it with the bucket of water he had standing ready at hand. That left a bit of flame still alight, which he stamped on. Meanwhile, Regan laughed.

Her amusement didn't bother him. Much. But he stiffened

when a slow clapping sounded from the doorway to proclaim that someone else had seen him botch the magic. He turned and discovered it was Canice Gormleigh, of all people, with Colbie standing beside her and a little gobber in grimy clothes just visible behind them.

"I take it all back," said Gormleigh in her smoky contralto voice. "With experts like this on the crew, you're plainly ready for anything."

"I'll wager," Eilish said, "that you don't hit the bull's-eye every time you try a new pistol."

"How much would you like to wager?"

Eilish shifted his gaze to Colbie. "Speaking of guns," he said, "I notice that neither of you is holding one on the other. That makes it all the stranger to see you together."

"I'm getting paid for it," Colbie said. "We all are, including you, Doctor, if you're available."

"I can make arrangements," Regan said.

"You'll want your medical bag and a change of clothing or two. Eilish, you'll want your armor."

"What's the job?" He picked up the short, straight sword he'd set aside for comfort's sake and belted it back on.

"I'll explain as we walk."

As they exited the morgue, Regan murmured, "Goodbye, sumptuous supper with dancing to follow. I suspected you were only a dream."

"Courage," Eilish said. "I'll buy you something on the street."

"That poses an interesting question. Would I rather die of hunger or tainted food?"

• • •

IN MOST CIRCUMSTANCES, Gardek Stonebrow rejoiced in being even bigger and stronger than the average trollkin. His might had seen him through countless fights and prevented just as many more when opponents got a good look at his hulking frame crowned with the crest of orange-red quills that added a finger length to his already imposing height.

But his formidable appearance was a detriment if he wanted to lure some quarry like a fish to a fishhook. So were his war hammer and his plate armor and shield with their jutting spikes. In such cases, he had to disguise the former and set aside the latter.

As he did now. Gardek sat slumped in the mouth of a dark alley with his head lolling, wrapped in a filthy ragged cloak. Bits of red molded wax made it look as if open sores dotted his blue-green skin. A crutch, a begging bowl with three copper farthings and a soggy, half-eaten crust of bread in it, and an overturned jug sat around him. Everything about his appearance was meant to suggest he was even more wretched and helpless than the average refugee squatting in the once-fashionable park a block away.

Something rustled in the darkness farther down the alley. Every time Gardek had heard such a noise previously, it had turned out to be rats rooting in garbage. Keeping his eyes narrowed to slits, he rolled them to the side and saw that his patience had finally been rewarded.

Three lean, dark figures with bone-white visages slunk out of the gloom and the rain. He felt a surge of savage anticipation, followed by disgust when they crept closer. The skull faces were only greasepaint, the talons just little steel blades sprouting from the fingers of leather gloves. Still, Gardek supposed that, having come this far, he might as well finish what he'd started.

He slipped his hands into knuckledusters, the motion concealed by his grubby mantle. Thinking it might do some good, he'd paid a priestess of Mother Dhunia to scratch runes on the weapons, but he had determined this was money wasted. Just the same, they'd do fine for breaking heads.

He waited until the newcomers were stepping to encircle him and thus too near to run away easily. Then he simultaneously slapped away the clawed hand that was reaching in stealthy fashion for his face and jumped to his feet.

The imitation undead yelped and recoiled in surprise. Gardek punched one in the jaw. Bone crunched, the human's head snapped back, and his knees buckled.

Gardek pivoted to strike at another one, but both foes skipped back out of range. Neither bolted, though. Evidently they were unwilling to abandon a fallen comrade, at least when they still had their adversary outnumbered two to one. They poised their gloved hands in guards that suggested they had some notion of how to use their talons.

Unfortunately for them, a notion alone wasn't going to be good enough. Gardek made a show of turning toward one to provoke the other into striking at him from behind.

He spun back around when instinct told him to, swinging his arm to block. The defense wasn't as deft as it could have been—his foe's talons raked his forearm.

Happily, he'd only dispensed with the undisguisable bulk of plate armor, not armor altogether. The claws shredded his sleeve but failed to slice all the way through the quilted padding underneath. He drove a punch into the human's solar plexus, and his adversary floundered backward.

Gardek turned and jabbed. The blind punch fell short, because the one imitation undead on whom he had yet to score was backing away. The greasepaint skull mask failed to hide the expression of wide-eyed consternation beneath. In a moment, the human was going to turn tail.

Not inclined for a chase, especially when there were two other malefactors who might rouse and slip away while he was running through the alleys, Gardek lunged. At the same instant, a bolt of blue light flashed past him and hit the false undead in the forehead. The human collapsed.

Gardek looked around and saw what he was expecting: a lanky, yellow-haired human, good-looking by the delicate standards of his kind and dressed in modish blackened steel plate. The glowing sky-blue symbols floating in the air around him were just fading away.

The attacker he'd punched in the solar plexus was still on his feet, albeit unable to do anything but totter and wheeze. Gardek took him by the back of the neck and slammed him face-first into a grimy, crumbling brick wall, saying, "I didn't need help."

"I didn't imagine you did," Eilish said, sauntering closer. "But providing it seemed like the comradely thing to do. What is this? Are you holding out on the rest of us?"

"No," Gardek replied. "There's no bounty posted. I just heard tell undead were clawing up some of the refugees camped in the park, and with nothing better to do, I decided to look into it."

There was no need to explain any further than that. The arcanist knew the living dead had killed Gardek's brother on Corvis' terrible Longest Night several years back, and thus Gardek seized every opportunity to avenge him.

"Sorry you were disappointed," Eilish said. "But we have a real job now. Colbie sent me to fetch you and Milo."

"I trust there's time to turn this scum over to the Watch before we go on our way." Gardek waved his hand to indicate the three humans sprawled amid the trash and filthy puddles.

"I doubt it," Eilish said.

Gardek frowned. "Why's that?"

The other heaved a sigh. "Why is it that people can't see what's right in front of them?" He squatted beside the fellow Gardek had smashed into the wall and pointed to his hair. "Consider this elegantly barbered coif." He took the fallen man's collar between thumb and forefinger. "The quality of this broadcloth." He gestured toward his subject's leg. "The craftsmanship that went to cobble those boots. These aren't common ruffians attacking the unfortunate for farthings and trinkets. They're the sons of prosperous families killing, maiming, and terrorizing for the thrill of it, possibly while telling one another they're performing a service by purging their neighborhood of 'undesirables.'"

Gardek grunted. He wasn't about to let on that he was impressed; the blond mage was conceited enough without further encouragement. But in truth, over the course of their association, Gardek had come to see some value in Eilish's intellectual approach to man hunting, just as he knew the scholar had acquired some grudging respect for Gardek's tracking ability and practical knowledge of the underworld.

"What you're telling me," Gardek said, "is that if we try to convince the law to arrest rich boys for murdering the poor, it's likely to take time we don't have, and we might not even get satisfaction at the end."

"Exactly."

"Damn it." Using his mantle, Gardek rubbed the paint from the faces of the unconscious aristocrats. "Recognize them?"

"No."

"Neither do I, but they don't know that." The trollkin picked up a pebble and scratched a message on the nearest wall: SAW YOUR FACES. KNOW YOUR NAMES. MURDER AGAIN AND I KILL YOU.

Afterward, as he and Eilish were strolling briskly away from the scene, Gardek growled, "That wasn't nearly good enough."

"This might make you feel better," Eilish replied. "If a pauper from the park or just a common scoundrel discovers the 'Risen' still lying helpless, he may well start administering justice where you left off."

Gardek grunted dismissively. "So, what's the new job?"

"A bit of investigation, a bit of playing guard dog." The arcanist grinned. "You'll be delighted when you find out who we're watching over."

• • •

TO ALL APPEARANCES, the gaff-rigged sailboat was just another dilapidated fishing vessel tied up at the rickety pier. Viewed from a distance in the rain and the gloom of night, it showed nothing to attract a customs inspector's attention. Still, Milo Boggs hoped his contacts had taken the sensible business precaution of bribing the official on duty to look the other way.

He tied up the donkey cart he'd rented and walked slowly down the dock, meanwhile making sure the planks creaked under his boots and his empty hands would be visible to anyone watching aboard the boat. The gesture opened his black leather cloak a little, revealing the crossed bandoliers and combat alchemist's armor underneath.

Before long, a low voice called, "Who's there?"

Milo stopped walking. "Me. Who else?"

"Show your face."

Milo had to smile. He was so accustomed to his gas mask that he'd forgotten he was wearing it. Eilish joked it was his true countenance. While that was putting it a little strongly, when a fellow spent much of his time experimenting with alchemical preparations that gave off noxious fumes, contending with the sorts of threats people paid the Black River Irregulars to neutralize, and engaging in transactions the uncharitable might deem illegal, protecting his face could become a habit.

He pulled the gas mask down to dangle around his neck. "Happy?"

"Come on aboard."

As he hopped down into the boat, which truly did stink of fish, Milo said, "All these precautions over such a small cargo. If you boys only knew the amount and value of the contraband that moves through this port every day."

Odger spat. Like the two sons who made up his crew, and even Milo himself for that matter, he was a short, wiry—some would say scrawny—man. His teeth were brown, his right eye milky and sightless, and from the smell of him, he'd been nipping moonshine on the trip downriver.

"Seems like the cargo's big enough to interest you," he said. "Guess you're just small time, too."

Milo sighed. "You've got me there. Can I see them?"

Odger waved at a rectangular shape covered by a tarp.

Milo pulled the cloth away to reveal a crate with a lid on tip. He raised it and peered down at half a dozen black, coppery-banded swamp adders, all somnolent with the coolness of the night. "They look all right."

"Ain't our fault if they're not," Odger said. "The trapper catches them, we bring them, and you buy them. That's the deal. Except maybe it's time to tweak it some. Say, you pay half again as much this time around?"

Milo frowned. "As you were just saying yourself, the deal is what the deal is."

"Come on, city man. After all your big talk, I know you can afford it."

Milo realized he should have chosen his words more carefully. To many people born in Corvis, he'd always be an inbred, pockmarked swampie with mud between his toes. But his attitude had persuaded the half-drunk smuggler before him that he'd put on airs, gotten soft, and thus made himself an appropriate target for real swamp men to take advantage of.

And they were in a good position to do so. Milo placed considerable faith in his grenades and throwing knives, but they worked best when he was over *here* and the foe was over *there*. Odger and his sons were only a stride or two away, and the close confines of the deck made the situation that much more problematic.

Yet Milo couldn't just capitulate. Well, he *could*. And had, when it was the only way to survive. But a fellow couldn't do so in response to every little bit of pressure, or before long, everyone would see him as a mark.

He made a show of scowling. "You're a treacherous smear of dung, Odger. But I really do need them, so I guess I've got no choice. Let me load them on the cart, and then I'll pay you." He picked up the crate.

"Money first!" Odger snapped.

"What?" Milo turned and intentionally caught his toe on the bottom of one of the sheets. He pitched forward and made sure the crate pitched with him—made sure, too, that the lid popped open. Hissing, the adders tumbled out in a tangle that started slithering apart as soon as it smacked down on the deck. The three smugglers recoiled, their belligerent scowls turned to goggling fear.

"Oops," Milo said, likewise backing away. "Sorry. Truly. Once they find hiding places, you'll never locate them all. Well, not in a way you'll like anyway."

Odger pulled a fishing knife with a serrated edge from its sheath, then faltered, apparently deciding that using it in the present circumstance would surely get him bitten. "You let them loose on purpose!" he snarled.

"Never," Milo said. "But now that they've gotten loose, I can round them up for you... provided you offer me a discount. When they're back in the crate, I'll pay you half the price we originally agreed on."

"To hell with you!" Odger snarled.

"If that's the way you feel about it." Milo set down the crate and turned to clamber back up onto the dock. "I notice your younger son is barefoot. You might want to get him some shoes. If he lasts long enough for you to get around to it."

"Stop!" Odger said. "Put them back in the box and get them off my boat."

"And I pay you half?"

"Yes!"

"Do you have a stick with a hook or a crossbar on the end?"

"No!"

"Too bad." Milo had left his back in his laboratory.

He pulled two jars of bottled light from his pockets. "Catch." He tossed one to Odger and one to the son who did have shoes, if just ratty moccasins that left his ankles bare. "Shake them, and whenever they start to go dim, shake them again."

Once the deck was illuminated, Milo advanced on the first adder. The trick was to move slowly so as not to agitate the snake, although swamp adders occasionally reacted aggressively just the same. The creatures had a nasty disposition.

When he was within arm's reach of the snake—which meant he was within its striking distance as well—he eased his left hand to the side. When the adder swiveled its head, tracking the motion, he reached with his right and gripped it at the very top of the body.

At once the adder lashed and squirmed, nearly twisting free before he slipped his left hand under its body and picked it up. Its jaws gaped with hooked fangs extended as he carried it back to the crate and dropped it inside.

"Help!" wailed a voice behind him. He turned. Giving ground before an adder winding in his direction, the barefoot son had retreated into the bow, but now he'd run out of boat. In the youth's place, Milo might have jumped overboard, but perhaps the swampie couldn't swim, or maybe fear prevented him from thinking clearly.

In any case, Milo supposed he needed to keep the fool from being bitten. Otherwise, Odger was unlikely to honor the terms of the renegotiated deal.

He strode toward the viper. He was trying to make haste while being stealthy, but the snake still felt the deck vibrating, twisted around, and struck at him.

Milo snatched his hand back just far enough, and the strike fell short. He grabbed the reptile at the base of the head before it could gather itself to attack again and, panting, carried it writhing to the crate.

He took a moment to control his breathing, slow his hammering heartbeat, and steady his hands before going after the third adder. It didn't give him too much trouble, nor did the fourth or the fifth.

When he tackled the last one, though, he reached for the head too soon, before the motion of his off hand had the snake entirely distracted. It whipped back around and struck, and Milo failed to pull back in time. The long fangs stabbed right through his gloves to penetrate his index and middle fingers.

With a curse, he caught the adder behind the head and squeezed until it let go. Then he nearly threw it overboard. But that would be wasteful, just as it was childish to hate the reptile for simply acting according to its nature. He carried it to the crate to deposit it with its fellows.

By the time he did so, alternating waves of heat and cold were flowing up his poisoned limb, which was also swelling so rapidly that the layers of sleeve around it already felt tourniquet-tight. He fumbled a vial from one of the pockets of his armor, extracted the cork, and gulped the bitter contents down.

As he finished, he noticed the swampies were gawking at him. "Did your glove stop the fangs?" Odger asked.

"No, he nipped me."

"Then why aren't you dying or dead already?"

Milo grinned. "Lucky, I guess."

"Is it the stuff you just drank?"

"No. Nobody's invented an antitoxin that will save a man from swamp adder venom." Yet. Although with luck, his formula would help him shake off the effects more quickly.

"Then how—?"

"How would you rather be paid?" Milo interrupted. "With the secret or coin?"

Odger glowered. "Coin, if you're going to be a bastard about it."

Milo's arm was going numb now, his fingers as big and dexterous as sausages. Still, he managed to take a pigskin purse from his pocket and count out half the crowns inside.

"Now," he said, "how about if one of you boys carries the crate to my donkey cart?" When no one seemed inclined to volunteer, he added, "Or I can try. But you see I'm having trouble with my arm. It would be a shame if I dropped the snakes all over again."

Odger turned to the son with the moccasins. "See to it."

As the youth was stowing the box in the back of the conveyance, Eilish and Gardek came striding up one of the cobbled lanes that terminated at the river's edge. Milo watched their approach with mixed emotions. He'd decided it was a good thing to belong to the Irregulars, good to have people who had become, he supposed, his friends. But there was still a wary, reclusive part of him that was most at ease when he was on his own.

War hammer in hand, armored in the plate and carrying the shield to which he'd affixed spikes to transform himself into the trollkin equivalent of a porcupine—Milo still marveled that he was able to move around without injuring himself—Gardek gave Eilish a grin. "I told you I could track him down."

"Yes," the lanky arcanist drawled, "it was amazing." He gestured to the crate. "What have you got there?"

Milo told him. "I'm trying to make things from the venom."

Eilish snorted. "And I thought playing with fire was chancy."

— 4 —

COLBIE REFLECTED WRYLY that Julian Helstrom had promised a safehouse, not a comfortable one. The dank front room only had two chairs in it, and the fireplace was drawing poorly, tingeing the air with eye-watering smoke. Now that the rain was drumming down harder outside, water dripped in one mildew-spotted corner.

Eilish studied the hearth from several paces away. Then Regan said, "Please don't."

The arcanist grinned. "A little faith would be welcome." He crossed the room and prodded the firewood with a poker in an effort to make the flames burn hotter. After a moment, he glanced at Colbie. "Charming accommodations."

She shrugged. "The important thing is, the house has barred windows and stout doors with sturdy locks."

"Which we aren't supposed to need," Eilish said. "Well, except perhaps to keep her from wandering." He nodded at Canice.

Judging from the gun mage's sneer, she had a sharp retort

to offer. But before she could make it, a groan sounded from elsewhere in the house.

Canice and Regan hurried side by side up the creaking steps, one of which had a dead mouse on it. Everyone else followed.

The watchmen had laid Natak Warbiter on a narrow cot that appeared in danger of collapsing under his bulk. When Colbie had last looked in on him, he'd been unconscious while Regan examined his wounds, muttering grudging approval of the previous surgeon's efforts. He was awake now, though, and the narrow eyes beneath his bushy upward-slanting eyebrows locked on Canice.

"Did you kill them?" he croaked.

"Not yet," the red-haired woman said.

"We'll do it together." He tried to sit up and then cried out.

Regan rushed to his bedside and—her petite frame and his huge one notwithstanding—pressed him back down to lie flat. "You can't do that," she said. "I'm your physician, and I'm telling you."

The ogrun glowered up at her and then surveyed everyone else who'd crowded into the grubby, bare little bedroom or was watching from the doorway. Colbie had the feeling he was just now realizing that he was no longer in the Patient Weavers' enclave, surrounded by other members and servants of the gang.

"Except for you and me," Canice said, "the Weavers are gone. The attackers—outlaws out of Khador—wiped us out. I'm using the Watch to help us take revenge, and they saddled us with this lot." She waved her hand to indicate everybody else.

Eilish looked to Colbie. "How badly do we need this particular job? I thought the moneybox was reasonably full. Unless Milo has been dipping into it on the sly."

"That was only one time," the pock-faced alchemist said, "and it was an emergency."

Regan poured a cup of water from a pitcher and held it to Natak's lips. "Sip, don't guzzle."

Instead of doing so immediately, the ogrun dragged a trembling hand from beneath the blanket and lifted it to hold the cup for himself. When Regan frowned and allowed him to try, he nearly dropped it but not quite.

After he finished drinking and handed back the cup, he transformed Regan's frown into a scowl by brusquely waving her away. "What's the next move?" he asked.

"We were about to discuss that downstairs," Colbie told him.

"The doctor doesn't want me moving around." Natak sneered at Gardek. "I suppose you could carry me. As I recall, you don't fight worth a damn, but you might do as a nursemaid."

Gardek leered back. "Glad to. I'll hold you close." He tapped one of the spikes projecting from his breastplate.

Colbie said, "Warbiter, we don't need you in the conversation, and Doctor Falk says you need to rest."

"But he won't," Canice said, "not while he knows there's a council of war going on that he isn't a part of. We should talk up here."

"If we did," Eilish said, "he could tell us what he experienced during the attack. He may have seen something useful. Besides, it's not as if the downstairs rooms are lavishly appointed. We might as well be cold and chairless up here."

"If that's what everyone prefers," Colbie said. "We have one other piece of business to consider besides the Khadorans. Pog here… Pog, where are you?"

The gobber stepped from the hallway into the bedroom doorway where everybody could see him.

"Pog," Colbie continued, "is applying to join the Irregulars."

For a moment, everyone was silent. Then Gardek rumbled, "And for some reason, you think the idea is worth putting in front of the rest of us."

"He's a good mechanik," she replied, "and able to command a 'jack."

Rubbing his arm through his sleeve, Milo grunted. "Can he do anything else?"

"Like speak for himself?" Eilish asked.

Pog cleared his throat. "Captain Sterling and Miss Gormleigh told me I don't seem soldierly. But Doorstop needs my help, the shape he's in, and I handled myself all right when the bratya attacked." He looked from Colbie to the redhead in her crimson-and-yellow coat and the matching waistcoat beneath. "Didn't I?"

"Yes," Colbie answered. "You kept your head."

"Good for him," Gardek said. "But it's one thing to fend off panic when danger springs up around you. It's something else to go willingly into danger just because someone is prepared to pay you. Pog, are you brave enough for that?"

Pog swallowed. "I hope so."

Eilish smiled a crooked smile. "I don't find that answer entirely reassuring."

"Pog's all right for a gobber," Natak said. "I never had to knock him around for laziness or pilfering."

"Oh, well," Eilish said, "if *you* recommend him, that makes all the difference." He shifted his gaze back to Colbie. "Captain, I vote no for the reason Milo touched on. Pog brings nothing to our enterprise that you aren't contributing already. Why, then, should we give him a fifth part of our profits?"

"I vote the same," Milo said, now repeatedly flexing his fingers.

"And I'm not convinced we can depend on him in a fight," said Gardek, "so it's also no from me."

"I vote yes," Colbie said. "But obviously, the three no votes prevail."

Pog's shoulders slumped.

"But you don't have to go away tonight," Colbie told him. "We'd rather not have you out on the streets knowing where the safehouse is. You can help me repair Doorstop, and I'll pay you for it."

Milo frowned.

"Out of my own pocket, Milo, not company funds."

"Thank you," said Pog. "I'll get started right now." He turned and headed for the stairs.

"That was a mistake," Canice said.

"The company made its decision," Colbie replied. "Now it's time for you and Warbiter to tell us what happened to you during the attack."

The ogrun began. It seemed to Colbie that his gruffness sought to mask a certain amount of embarrassment as he described how the mother-and-son duo had overcome him.

Gardek evidently thought so too, but somewhat to her surprise, the trollkin didn't jeer. Rather, he said, "It was two against one, and plainly the two knew their business."

Natak spat on the floor at what he might have taken as condescension.

Then Canice and Colbie related their experiences during the attack. At the end of the telling, Milo looked at Eilish. "Did you tease anything useful out of that?"

The investigator frowned. He disliked appearing anything less than brilliant, even in circumstances when no sensible person was expecting brilliance from him. "No. If I'd observed the attackers myself, I might have gleaned some information, but our associates' accounts lack the necessary details."

Canice snorted. "Next time, the three of us will be sure to jot down some notes in between fighting and running for our lives."

"As usual," Gardek said, "despite the schoolboy's fancy notions, we'll have to do things the tried-and-true way. A big attacking force complete with steamjacks must have left tracks when they headed back to their hideout."

"You'd think," Canice said. "But I doubt there'll be a trail you can follow all the way to their lair."

"Either you're giving them a lot of credit," the trollkin said, "or me, not much."

"Why not both?" Natak asked, and then he started to cough. Regan poured another cup of water.

"The attack on the Weavers," the gun mage said, "was competent, to say the least. I doubt they got sloppy afterwards or that they ever make many stupid mistakes. That's why you need me—I've fought a bratya before—to help hunt them down."

"Damn it!" Colbie snapped. "How many times must we argue over this?"

"When we talked before," Canice said, "it was just the two of us. Your partners deserve the chance to consider the offer."

"The way I understand it," Gardek said, "the Watch Commander made it clear he wants you kept inside this house."

"True," Eilish said, "but Helstrom's not here, is he? And we have on several occasions disregarded a client's stipulations about ways and means. As long as we achieve the desired ends, the client seldom complains."

Colbie's jaw tightened. Of late, she and Eilish had gotten along better than during the first days of their partnership. But he still possessed a contrary streak that, when he was in a certain mood, inclined him to argue against whatever she espoused. Though she mostly took it in stride, the emergence of that side of him when she was still tired and edgy from the escape hours before annoyed her. And it was worse with a pair of near-enemies looking on.

Eilish gave Canice a smile. "The problem," he continued, "is that you and Natak were once on the verge of murdering the four of us when we were helpless prisoners. A thing like that makes an impression. Gardek was worried he couldn't trust the gobber, but at least Pog wouldn't shoot him in the back."

Canice glared. "Nor would I. When we were going to kill you, that was business, not personal. A professional ought to understand that."

"Besides," Natak said, "you people started it. You were stalking me. Because your guesswork made you think I was the tunnel killer."

Eilish bristled. Colbie was sure the word "guesswork" rankled. But he was seemingly at a loss for an answer, perhaps because the logic in which he took such pride actually had, in that instance, led the team astray.

"You can call me unprofessional, too," Milo said, fumbling a vial of something from a pocket under his crossed bandoliers, uncorking it, and downing the contents, "but we don't need you, and I don't want you."

"Agreed," Gardek said.

Colbie smiled. The others had ignored her wishes where Pog was concerned, but at least all of them—even Eilish, despite initially pretending to think otherwise for the fun of it—were in accord where Canice was concerned. "Then *this* vote is unanimous," she said.

The gun mage shook her curly head in a way that conveyed that the Irregulars were fools. Then, taking care to avoid Natak's feet beneath the blanket, she seated herself on the corner of his cot.

"Now that all that's settled," Gardek said, "what's the plan?"

"We're all sleeping here," Colbie replied. "For the present, I'll pretty much stay on the premises all the time to stand guard and work on Doorstop. You, Eilish, and Milo will look for those tracks you mentioned. There could be some, despite what Gormleigh assumes. If you don't find a trail, you and Eilish will stake out some brothels and gambling halls in the Undercity. Places where the men of the bratya might go to unwind. When you spot one of the bastards, do whatever seems appropriate."

Canice turned to Natak. "She's afraid to have me in the field, but Sterling's happy to steal my tactics."

Gardek chuckled. "Trust me, gun mage, you and your fancy Llaelese spy ring didn't invent the basics of man hunting."

Colbie turned to Milo. "While Gardek and Eilish are doing that, you go talk to your contacts among the gangs. Somebody must know something useful. Questions?"

No one had any.

"Then get some sleep. We're all be busy come tomorrow."

As the group dispersed to discover what else the safehouse had to offer in the way of sleeping arrangements, clanking sounded from the ground floor. Colbie headed downstairs to see what headway Pog was making and to take a look at what, if anything, was going on outside.

• • •

EVERY ANTHILL NEEDED A QUEEN. Sele made a reasonable effort to be a good one, but the way she saw it, that entailed claiming a monarch's share of any bounty that came the community's way. What subject would respect a ruler who did otherwise?

Accordingly, she scooped up the last candied peach from the

tarnished silver tray and stuffed it into her mouth without a trace of guilt, even though Gek, her current paramour, was hard-pressed to hide his disappointment. But if her fellow gobber was so fond of sugared peaches, he could taste them via her kisses. As soon as her belly didn't feel so stuffed.

She chewed, swallowed, and tossed the tray off the low bed to clink on the earthen floor. Then one of her guards called from the other side of the moldy velvet curtain that gave her privacy. "There's a human outside who wants to see you."

"Tell him to come back tomorrow. No, the next day." She could have granted the supplicant an audience right away. But that wouldn't make the point that she was important, and besides, she wasn't in the mood for business. Certainly not at this hour of the night, even though in the Undercity, night and day were matters of convention.

The guard hesitated. "He says he's the boss of the gang that killed the Patient Weavers."

Sele blinked. If that was true, then the visitor could claim to be important as well, not to mention dangerous. "Tell him to wait, and I'll be out in a while. That is, if it doesn't look like he means to kill me, too."

"He asked to call on you inside the 'hill."

"You're joking. No? All right, if that's what he truly wants. Disarm him, blindfold him, and bring him to the throne room."

She pulled on her clothes and made her way to the back entrance of the burrow in question. A guard waiting there gave her a nod to indicate the stranger was already on the other side of the curtain. Deciding the human needed to wait a little while longer—this was, after all, *her* domain—she counted to fifty and then pushed through the hanging crimson silk.

When her diggers had excavated the chamber, she'd told them to make it big. Still, the human was tall enough that his bald or possibly shaved head, gleaming in the light of the two dozen candles, nearly brushed what was for gobbers a high ceiling. His grey eyes were narrow and sharp, his features aquiline, and he had the malformed knuckles of someone who'd dealt out a good many beatings in his time. His leather-and-baft clothing was of fine quality, and his empty scabbard and boots were chased with gold.

The most remarkable thing about him, however, was that he held a scourged, mostly naked, and by the looks of him, thoroughly cowed gobber on a leash. Sele caught her breath—she hoped not audibly—when she recognized Az the tunnel explorer. Az was something of a hero to many denizens of the Undercity, gobbers in particular, and while neither notoriety nor anything else guaranteed one's safety belowground, it was nonetheless startling to see him brought so low.

The human inclined his head as she set her foot on the wooden step she needed to seat herself on her high oaken chair without undignified jumping and clambering. It was the most comfortable throne she'd ever had, although the upholstery had started to smell, assailed by the Undercity's dankness.

"Lady," the stranger said. "My name is Ivan Varnek, and my bratya—my gang—is the Black Dogs. I'm making the rounds of my fellow bosses to ensure we all agree about how things will work from now on."

"'Bratya,'" Sele repeated. "Is that a Khadoran word?"

"Yes, although it saddens me that you guessed. I've tried to shed my accent. But apparently I have more work to do."

"I already figured you must be from someplace out of town. No human who knows the Undercity comes into the Anthill of his own free will."

Ivan chuckled. "I can well believe that those who enter without an invitation have trouble getting out again. Even with my eyes covered, it was plain I was moving through a maze and that many of the passages are so narrow and low that no one bigger than a gobber could walk them easily." He slapped at the dirt smearing his ermine-collared cape. "As the condition of my garments now attests."

"Yet here you are."

"Because I come as a friend, trusting in your goodwill."

"Do you?" Sele gestured to Az. "As a gobber myself, I could take that display as an insult or a threat."

"Truly? I didn't mean it that way," the Khadoran said without appearing even slightly surprised by the suggestion. "I asked the wretch, and he denied being one of your people. If he lied, I'll have to punish him."

Az trembled.

"He's not one of mine," Sele said.

"Then I don't see a problem. Among my people, you're either in the family or you're not. Is it any difference here? The way I heard it, you yourself have hurt plenty of gobbers when it served your interests."

Sele decided to let the matter drop. "You said you wanted to talk about how you think things should be in the days to come."

"Yes. I wish to assure my fellow bosses that my intentions are peaceful. I only want a seat at the table."

"I doubt the Weavers would advise me to take that assurance at face value."

Ivan spread his hands. At some point in his past, he'd lost the last digit of the little finger on the left hand to a blade or a bite. "Occasionally, if you want a seat, you first have to empty a chair. But now that's done, and I merely intend to lay claim to whatever the Weavers possessed and then work with other gangs to our mutual advantage. By all accounts, the gobbers of the Anthill are master tunnelers and experts at moving goods around the city, despite all the military checkpoints and whatnot in the way." He grinned. "I could have used your help when I was preparing my attack. It wasn't easy smuggling armed steamjacks off a freighter and down into the Undercity where I needed them."

Sele was unsurprised that he'd seen fit to remind her that the bratya—ugly word!—had 'jacks with weapons. Likely not as powerful as the warjacks the army used but, as the fate of the Weavers demonstrated, powerful enough to wreak havoc in Corvis' underworld.

The Anthill had none. Still, determined not to appear vulnerable or lacking in confidence, she put on a sneer and asked, "But what if I don't agree that outsiders—outsiders from an enemy country, no less—have the right to just come in and seize a piece of Corvis for themselves?"

"Enemy country? What have flags and wars got to do with the likes of us? It's money we care about, isn't it?"

"You didn't answer my question," Sele said.

"Because I hoped to speak to you in a friendly fashion. But if you prefer bluntness, so be it. The Black Dogs have come to Corvis, and we're here to stay. Those who side with us will profit. Those who oppose us will suffer."

"It might pay you to remember," Sele said, "that you caught the Patient Weavers by surprise. You won't have that advantage a second time."

Ivan nodded. "True. Just as it's true that your burrows are more defensible than the Weavers' freestanding wooden buildings. But that's not the same thing as impregnable. Do you know how hard a projectile from a steam lobber hits? Imagine if my 'jacks bombarded you for days or weeks. Eventually the tunnels in front—the ones that let in air and connect to the vault outside—would collapse."

"Burying us alive? No. We're the Anthill. For every burrow that caves in, we'll have dug three more."

The Khadoran laughed. "Another good answer. I like you, Lady, and I suppose it was foolish to suggest we could hurt you where you're strongest. But what about where you're weak? Your little green rabbits have to come out of this warren to conduct your business, and then, if we were at odds, my men would catch them and skin them."

"We'd strike back," Sele said.

"Some of your followers might try," Ivan said, "the ones too loyal or lacking in sense to forsake you. But then you'd be trying to hurt us where *we're* strong, exhausting your own resources until you couldn't even withstand us when we invaded the Anthill itself. In the end, it would be like this."

With a jerk of the leash, the Khadoran wrenched Az off his feet and started kicking him. Screaming, the captive curled up and covered his head with crossed arms. Bone cracked.

Sele gawked in astonishment at Ivan Varnek's brazenness. He was alone and unarmed in the middle of a hive of criminals who'd come rushing if she called. He didn't even know the way out. Yet he was abusing a fellow gobber right in front of her.

It was, she realized, his way of driving home the truth that she didn't dare balk him in this or much of anything. Because even if she had him killed, his murderers and 'jacks would carry on and avenge him.

Still, it was one thing to accede to his demands. It would be something else to show that he'd managed to unsettle her. The latter might cost her whatever respect he actually felt and lead to unfortunate consequences in the future.

So, with mild regret, she simply sat and watched as the Khadoran kept on kicking Az. Another bone cracked. A rib, judging from where the toe of the gold-bedizened boot slammed in.

Eventually Ivan stopped of his own accord. Breathing heavily, he said, "I trust you take my point."

"Yes," Sele said, "some time ago. After thinking it over, I believe we can do business. Why not? I never liked the Patient Weavers anyway."

Actually, the "why not" might well be that he intended to absorb or eliminate every other outlaw fraternity in the Undercity over time. Certainly, given what he'd already accomplished, it would be foolish to underestimate his ambition. Still, for now at least, Sele could see no prudent course but to accept the proffered alliance.

Ivan grinned. "Wonderful! Sometime soon we'll celebrate, but tonight I have other calls to make. Tell me, now that we're partners, is there any chance of dispensing with the blindfold on the way out?"

"No," Sele said.

"Good. We're going to get along."

— 5 —

YAWNING, EILISH TRUDGED INTO the kitchen to find Gardek and Milo eating eggs and butterless brown bread at a round little table. Someone had hauled in the two chairs from the front room, and thus there were currently four altogether. "It's about time," the trollkin growled.

Eilish's first impulse was to retort that if either of his male partners were capable of attracting a female, he might not spring out of bed at first light either. But it would be boorish to allude to what he and Regan got up to when they were alone—even though, of course, the others already knew.

"The crime scene's not going anywhere," he said. "How are we fixed for food overall?"

"It won't make you want to quit the Irregulars and join the Watch," Gardek said, "but at least they stocked the larder with something."

Eilish moved to the stove, scooped eggs from a wrought-iron frying pan, and took an experimental bite. In the house's attached stable, where a dusty, cobweb-shrouded carriage still sat, metal rang to proclaim that Colbie, Pog, or both were already at work on Doorstop. Then Canice padded into the kitchen.

At some point she must have availed herself of water from the pump to scrub the grime of combat, flight, and the Undercity from her face and hands. She was in her stocking feet and had likewise left her greatcoat, gun belt, and shoulder rigs in her room. Her red-and-yellow waistcoat was unbuttoned.

With her sturdy frame and functional clothes, she still didn't strike Eilish as a particularly attractive woman—his tastes were for the daintier—and he fancied he could discern where a couple of holdout pistols were weighting her pockets. But she looked significantly less thorny, less poised to whip out a gun and shoot someone, than he'd ever seen her before.

"Morning," she mumbled. She filled a plate for herself and then sat down at the table with the rest of them.

After several mouthfuls, she said, "Natak and I wouldn't have made it out of the Undercity without your Captain Sterling, and the way you four run the Black River Irregulars is none of our business. What I'm getting at is, last night I might have spoken out of turn."

Gardek shrugged his massive shoulders. "You'd just lost your friends."

Canice smiled a wry smile. "Honestly, that wasn't it. Except for Natak, perhaps, I wasn't all that close to any of the Patient Weavers. I know they gave me a fair amount of responsibility, but I never pricked my finger and smeared my blood on the cloth in the loom to give my oath. I always made it clear that I was simply a mercenary in their employ, and when it suited me, I'd move on."

Eilish took a sip of tea. It was bitterer than he liked, but the officers of the Watch hadn't provided milk, honey, or sugar. "Then I guess you're just naturally cranky."

The gun mage surprised him by laughing. "You aren't the first to say so. But actually, I was in a vile mood because of what Helstrom demanded of me. All my life, I've met trouble head on. Fought my own battles. I can't get used to the idea that this time,

I'm going to hide away while others face my enemies in my stead. That makes me feel jumpy in a way that blades and bullets never have."

Gardek nodded. "Because you're not in control."

"Before we all wax sympathetic," Eilish said, "let's recall that however restless Gormleigh may be feeling, we already decided we're keeping her shut away for several good reasons."

"I accept that," Canice said.

"But you want something from us, don't you?" Eilish persisted. "That's the reason for this softer demeanor."

Canice ruefully shook her head. "You truly are as perceptive as everybody says."

Eilish grinned. "Perceptive enough to recognize you're still trying to ingratiate yourself. Don't bother. Just ask us, we'll say no, and then we can all get on with our day."

The red-haired woman snorted. "All right. Here's the truth. Last night, I expended all my rune shots escaping, and without them I'm just a shadow of the fighter I ought to be."

Hunched over his plate, Milo swallowed a bite that left a yellow fleck of egg clinging to the corner of his mouth. "Since you're not going to fight, what does it matter?"

"How would you feel," Canice replied, "if you were denied your knives and grenades?" Her gaze shifted to Gardek. "Or you, your hammer and plate?" She regarded Eilish. "Or you, the ability to work magic? Like a piece of you was missing, I suspect."

"Perhaps," Eilish said, "but you're just going to have to put up with being incomplete. They aren't selling rune shots down at the corner market."

"No," Canice said. "Every gun mage makes his or her own with special equipment dedicated to the purpose. And I left my kit in my room."

"Where the fire will have burned it up."

"Maybe," the redhead said, "but maybe not. When a building burns, the flames don't always reduce every stick of it to ash. Sometimes a shell or skeleton remains."

"That's true," Milo said. "I've seen it."

"Wipe your mouth," Eilish told him, and then turned back at Canice. "It's clear where this is going. But in light of our past differences, why would we go to the trouble to retrieve your gear for you?"

She arched an eyebrow. "Making rune shots will quiet my nerves and help me while away the empty hours?"

"I meant, what's in it for us?"

"I know what you meant, arcanist, and as it happens, I have some money stashed alongside the kit. You can keep that."

Milo sat up straighter. "How much?"

"Likely not enough to make it worth annoying Colbie," Gardek said.

Canice said, "She does seem resolved to keep me as toothless as possible. But yours is a fellowship of equals, isn't it? In theory, she's the captain, but you don't feel bound to do every little thing she says."

Eilish grinned. "I don't, that's for certain. Still, that doesn't persuade me it's a sound idea to oblige you."

Canice frowned and twined the callused fingers of one hand with those of the other, pondering or pretending to. After several seconds, she said, "When the Amethyst Rose trained me to be a gun mage, my mentor made me swear never to share our secrets with outsiders. But I've broken the rest of my vows, so why not the last one? Fetch my kit, and I'll show you how I make rune shots. Since the process touches on magic and alchemy, you and Mr. Boggs may both learn something you can use."

If he did, Eilish reflected, running this little side errand could turn out to be worthwhile after all.

"When you put it that way," Milo said, "I'm willing." The genuine intellectual curiosity that existed side by side with his shifty venality was one of the few things he and Eilish had in common.

"But I don't know that I am," Gardek said. "As you may have guessed, woman, I'm never going into a workshop to tinker with spells or acids and such."

"No," Canice said, "but the time will come when you and your war hammer square off against sword-and-cloak fighters. Maybe on this very job, but if not, then surely someday. How much do you know about the system?"

The trollkin scowled. "Not a lot."

"Well, I've seen some of it, and as of last night, Natak has, too. We can teach you what we observed."

"In trade for the kit and nothing more."

"Yes."

Gardek glanced at Milo and Eilish, then extended his enormous blue-green hand for Canice to shake. "In that case, it's a deal."

• • •

GRIDIA BROUGHT THE HAND-SCRAWLED MAP, augmented with notes describing landmarks, close to her kerosene lantern. That way, she could make it out without squinting. Which, alas, didn't necessarily mean she was following it correctly or that Ivan's captive had made it as comprehensive and accurate as it ought to be. The gobber seemed too frightened to attempt deliberate betrayal, but he also appeared to have little experience with cartography. Apparently he'd done all his guiding and exploring based simply on what he observed firsthand and the memories he carried in his head.

In truth, Gridia believed she was on the right path. It was just that these murky depths were unsettling even to a Black Dog assassin. Passages branched and side tunnels snaked away into the darkness, and she could readily imagine that one wrong turn could lose her darling boy and herself so thoroughly that they wouldn't find their way back before the fuel in their lanterns ran out. At certain points the ground crumbled away into sinkholes and fissures, and rumor had it that hideous abominations sometimes crawled up out of them in search of prey.

If so, the legendary terrors were placing themselves in competition with any number of perils whose reality was undeniable. Robbers and kidnappers prowled the fringes of the inhabited areas, while huge, aggressive vermin and even undead lurked in the miles of tunnel that remained unclaimed and unknown.

Occasionally Gridia heard noises too faint to identify. Then, lanterns lifted high, she and Fodor turned and peered into the blackness. But so far, the sources of the various sounds had never been within reach of the light. Perhaps they were nowhere near. As she understood it, noise carried underground. On the other hand, maybe the creatures she was encountering, or near encountering, were adept at hiding.

All Gridia was certain of was that she didn't care for the Undercity. Unlike many members of the Black Dogs, she'd never seen the inside of Skirov Khardstadt, Khador's largest and most infamous prison, but it was hard to imagine these filthy holes were a great deal better, and she couldn't help wishing Ivan had seen fit to build his outlaw empire somewhere else.

But at least she and Fodor wouldn't be stuck down here forever. The established gangs of the Undercity might be content to confine their ambitions to these warrens, but the Black Dogs had grander aspirations. The Undercity was simply a logical place to start.

Up ahead, something made a sound midway between a crack and a thud—the noise of a weapon striking a wooden shield. A guttural voice shouted.

Before heading onward, she took another look at Fodor. Bandages and bruises notwithstanding, he seemed as spry as ever, but after the accursed gun mage had brought the burning ceiling crashing down on him, it paid to be careful. Gridia had spent the night cradling him in her arms, sometimes kissing his hair and neck so gently that it never woke him.

Sensing the tenor of her thoughts, the youth sighed. "I'm fine, Mama. I promise."

"You'd better be. You're my lambkin." She stroked his downy cheek.

As they advanced, the noises ahead made her increasingly confident they'd found their destination. The edginess engendered by creeping through the darkness fell away, and, with reflexive ease, she put on the placid demeanor with which she customarily greeted the world.

She and Fodor came to a bend and peeked around it at the space on the other side. It was a vault, not just a tunnel, illuminated by several torches mounted on poles thrust into the ground. The torchlight sent the shadows of the fighters lunging and striking, retreating and blocking, along the earthen walls.

The combatants were ogrun and trollkin who, Gridia understood, convened here most mornings to practice with other combatants of comparable size and strength. At the moment, three duos were sparring with edged weapons while nine of their fellows looked on.

She stepped out into the open, and Fodor followed. "Good morning!" she called.

The hulking creatures turned to stare at her.

She and Fodor strolled forward. "We're strangers trying to make our way in an unfamiliar place," she said, "and we're hoping you can help us."

"I'll help you," said an ogrun, striding toward the newcomers with a battle-axe in hand. Sweat plastered his shirt to his torso, and the stink of it stung her nose even at a distance. "I'll warn you to turn around. This is our place. No runty humans allowed."

"But we have blueberry scones." She hefted the wicker basket looped over her arm. "Sadly, not fresh baked—I was a little busy yesterday—but still tasty."

"I said, go!"

Gridia pouted. "Please don't be like that. I said we were strangers, but we're also your new neighbors. You want to make us welcome, don't you?"

Some of the big fighters laughed. But the ogrun who'd warned the Khadorans narrowed his eyes, if not in wariness then at least in reassessment. "You're part of the gang that killed the Patient Weavers?"

She beamed. "It's wonderful how quickly news travels in these tunnels. It must help everyone feel like one big family."

The ogrun scowled. "Are you mocking us?"

"Gracious, no. Just trying to see things in the nicest possible light."

He hesitated, and she liked that because she judged that she'd put him off balance, even if he was as disinclined to show it as any swaggering bravo in the back alleys of Skirov or Khardov. Some things remained constant no matter how far a person roamed.

"Well," the ogrun eventually said, "we don't care if your gang got lucky and wiped out the Weavers. Nobody here is afraid of you."

"Of course not, big and strong as you are, nor do I want you to be. I just need a bit of information, and then Fodor and I will let you get back to playing."

"What information?"

"Someone told me Natak Warbiter practiced here. Now he and his friend Canice Gormleigh have gone missing. Fodor and I hoped his other friends might know what's become of them. We can pay for information with coin as well as scones."

The ogrun spat. "You think we'd turn rat for a few crowns?"

"If you're wise," Fodor said.

Gridia shot him a glance. "Lovey! That wasn't polite. Say you're sorry."

"Sorry," he muttered.

Gridia looked back up at the ogrun's face with its slab of jaw, pointed ears, and low, sloping brow. "Boys," she sighed, "forever trying to prove they're rough and tough. Still, he has a point. Kindness is always rewarded in the end."

"I'm sick of this!" a trollkin shouted. "Lorgrul, you gave them a chance to run. Let's make them wish they'd listened." He and his friends raised their weapons and moved forward, spreading out as they came.

"Now, now." Gridia flipped open the lid of the wicker basket and brought out the grenade she'd been carrying tucked among the scones and the little pot of clotted cream. The ogruns and trollkin faltered. "I understand this is all very exciting, but let's not get rambunctious."

"Fine," Lorgrul growled. "It's not worth us trying to beat you down. But nobody here means to help you, either, so just go away."

"That way, *no one* gets what he or she wants. Surely we can come to a better arrangement. At least if, contrary to appearances, you don't really think it would take all fifteen of you just to pummel one weak little human woman and her poor injured son."

"What do you mean?"

"You come here to fight, so let's fight. Fodor and I against you and a partner. If we win, then anybody who has an idea where Warbiter and Gormleigh have gone is honor-bound to share. If you win, then we'll give you all our money."

Lorgrul leered. "If we win, you won't be able to stop us from taking it."

"I suppose that's another way of looking at it. Are you game, then?"

"Let's do it!" shouted a trollkin with slate-colored skin and calcified bumps studding his noseless face like boils. "You and me, Lorgrul! We'll show these pissant foreigners who needs to be afraid of who!"

"Do it!" bellowed another.

"Smash their heads in!"

"Kill them!"

Fodor smiled and reached for the hilt of his sword.

Something in his expression or the movement brought Lorgrul up short. Gridia could see it in him. Frowning, fingering a tuft of his goatish beard, he reassessed yet again.

Then he said, "I couldn't make your boy fight, banged up like he is. It wouldn't be fair. So it'll be just you against just me."

The ogrun's intuition was serving him well. In any situation, Gridia and Fodor preferred to fight as a team. Partly a natural consequence of their intimate bond and partly the result of years of practice, their ability to coordinate enhanced their effectiveness even when they didn't possess a numerical advantage.

Still, she smiled and said. "If that's what you prefer. It's sweet of you to worry about him."

"Something else: I'm happy to knock you around, but I don't want to kill you and maybe start a war. The boss of my gang might not like it. So we'll fight with bated weapons just like everybody else does here." He ran the ball of his thumb down the edge of his battle-axe, then showed her that he hadn't cut himself. "I'm ready. You can choose a practice blade from that crate over there."

Under the guise of minimizing the risk of fatal injury, he was still trying to structure the rules to his own benefit. Wielded with an ogrun's strength, an axe wouldn't need to be sharp to smash Gridia's human body, but she'd find it significantly more difficult to injure him with a dull blade.

She nodded. "That sounds like a fine idea. I said from the start that I want everything to be friendly." She set her lantern and wicker basket at Fodor's feet and unbuckled her sword belt. "Be a love and hold these for me."

"I don't like this," Fodor murmured.

"It's actually better this way," she whispered. "If you're standing ready with the grenade, Lorgrul's friends can't misbehave. I'll be fine. Mama promises, with sugar and spice on top." She brought his hand to her lips and kissed the tips of the longest fingers.

Then she pawed through the box Lorgrul had indicated. Among the contents was a dull-edged sword with a little knob where the point belonged. She hefted it and found that the weight and balance were comparable to those of her usual weapon.

By then, Lorgrul was awaiting her on a relatively flat patch of earth that, as the plentiful footprints attested, was one of the spots where people generally sparred. As she moved to join him, she asked, "Is someone going to say, 'Ready, set, go,' or something like that?"

"I'm going to break your bones," Lorgrul said. "You'll crawl back to your people in a trail of blood like a snail."

"That all sounds quite ferocious," Gridia replied, "but it doesn't answer my question."

"Go!" shouted a female ogrun. At once, Lorgrul advanced.

It wasn't the all-out charge Gridia had hoped for. Despite having set the terms of the combat to suit himself, he was still a little too wary for that. But she retreated quickly, as if alarmed, and that provoked him into coming on faster to close in on striking distance.

The axe whizzed down in a diagonal stroke at the juncture

of her neck and shoulder. She spun to the side, and the blow missed. She whipped the sword in a backhand slash that cracked him across the knuckles.

He grunted in pain but didn't fumble his grip on the axe. Instead, he chopped at her breastbone. She simultaneously jumped back out of range and stretched out her sword arm. It was the basic move many a swordsman would make to impale an opponent who drove in recklessly, and Gridia hoped it would make Lorgrul believe she'd momentarily forgotten her weapon lacked a point.

Sure enough, ignoring a threat that was minimal at best, the ogrun lunged to strike her before she realized her mistake. She spun out of the way, snatched the cape from her shoulders, stooped low, and whipped it around his ankle.

In the hand of a bratya assassin, a weighted cloak could do many things. One was to snag a limb as securely as a hook or lasso, at least for a moment. She yanked, and Lorgrul pitched forward, reeling off balance.

She cut twice to the back of his neck, then, judging that her foe was too stunned to use the axe for at least a second or two, circled in front of him and thrust the dull sword into his solar plexus. Striking there, the tip didn't need to be sharp to stab the wind and the strength out of him.

A final cut to the top of his head dumped him to his hands and knees. When he managed to raise his bloody head, she poised the sword for a jab to the eye. Considering that she had only the blunt little knob to work with, he might well avoid losing the organ, but it was still the sort of threat that gave a person pause.

"Well," she panted, "that was fun and good exercise, too! Thank you! Now, I trust that you, or someone, will pay off our little wager."

"To hell with you!" Lorgrul wheezed.

"Now, dear, nobody likes a bad loser. Especially a blind one."

"We don't know!" said the trollkin who'd hoped to fight alongside Lorgrul.

"It's true," said the ogrun on the trollkin's left. "Warbiter practiced with us, but he wasn't a friendly sort. He wouldn't tell anybody here where he kept a secret hideout."

Gridia ran her gaze over all the assembled ogruns and trollkin. In her judgment, no one was holding anything back.

"Well, then," she said, "the joke's on me. But a bit on Lorgrul as well. We'll all have a good laugh about it the next time we see one another. For now, Fodor and I will give you your privacy. And leave you some scones, of course."

As the two of them tramped back the way they'd come, Fodor said, "Well, that was a waste of time."

"Patience, dumpling, patience. What does Mama say about tracking down a target?"

"You have to work your way through the false leads to get to the true one."

"Clever boy! And while we're about it, we're doing our bit to help the Black Dogs make a good first impression on the Undercity at large."

— 6 —

AS HE OFTEN HAD IN THE PAST, Milo pondered the difficulties of moving stealthily through the darkness of the Undercity. A fellow could step noiselessly and avail himself of every bit of cover. Still, if he needed to carry a light to find his way, someone was apt to spot him coming.

One solution would be to come down here with eyes that saw without light. Some of the creatures that lived underground seemed able to do so. Unfortunately, Menoth hadn't bothered to give humanity the same ability. Milo hypothesized that if one dripped the proper tincture into their optics, human beings could do the same.

But even if he could devise a promising formula, how was he to test it? How could he observe what, say, a dog was doing in pitch darkness if he was of necessity suffering the same condition himself? How could he know it was enhanced vision that led the animal to a morsel and not scent?

He supposed that if he ever got that far, the more practical approach would be to experiment on himself. It wouldn't be the first time, although the thought of working on his eyes specifically made even him a little squeamish.

"I think we're close," Gardek murmured.

Reminded of the business at hand, Milo searched for signs of danger as best he could with the bounty hunter's towering frame, even bulkier armor, and enormous shield mostly blocking the tunnel ahead. It was the same passage through which Colbie, Canice, and Natak had escaped, and it was possible the bratya killers had never found it. On the other hand, they might have, so it only made sense to be careful.

Bringing up the rear, Eilish took a long hissing sniff of the cool, dank Undercity air. "We are close," he said. "You can still smell smoke, and the corpses are starting to ripen."

When the three mercenaries peered out around a jut of stone, the vault before them wasn't wholly dark. Even now, a few embers glowed red to mark the remains of one or another conflagration. But they didn't shed enough light to reveal anything other than the three of them.

It was reasonable to assume that if some of the enemy were still lurking here, they'd need light too, so they must have moved on. Even so, the newcomers listened to the silence for a few moments before Gardek opened his bull's-eye lantern and cast a wary beam into the blackness.

No one called out or fired a shot at the source.

"Well, then." Shield still held where it was likeliest to protect him from a sniper, Gardek stepped on out into the chamber. Milo and Eilish followed.

Milo had been told what to expect, but when he contrasted the scene before him with the thriving outlaw enclave he remembered, the devastation was impressive nonetheless. No structure within reach of the light had escaped the fires, and corpses lay here, there, and everywhere.

Eilish squatted beside the body of a woman that sprawled facedown with a slashed neck in a pool of dried blood. "Cut down from behind," he said. "She was just trying to run away."

"Any money or jewelry on her?" Milo asked.

Gardek made a spitting sound. "Let's check on Canice's kit and get that out of the way. Then the schoolboy and I will see what we can see, and you can play vulture."

"I've watched you rob a corpse or two in your time," Milo said.

The trollkin stalked on without deigning to reply. Milo and Eilish followed. Though it seemed increasingly likely that the three of them were alone, the lanky wizard tested to make sure his short, straight sword would come out of its scabbard smoothly and quickly if need be. The steel guard clicked against the pewter throat when he slid it back down.

Rising at the center of the Patient Weavers' enclave, the gambling hall had been the highest, most imposing structure, and now it was the highest, most imposing burnt-out husk. Perhaps the bombardment had had the paradoxical effect of creating firebreaks that kept the general conflagration from consuming everything or maybe the perpetual dampness played a part.

Whatever the reason, the remains put Milo in mind of jugglers and acrobats he'd watch balance precarious towers of items that seemed as if they'd come crashing down as soon as someone exhaled. There was comparatively little left of the ground floor but charred columns and rubble, but above it, sections of wall, floor, and roof remained. Somewhere wood was groaning, and although it was difficult to be sure with only lantern light to push back the darkness, he had a sense that the whole structure was trembling.

Eilish pointed upward. "According to Gormleigh's diagram, her room was right about there. So something's left, and perhaps her equipment is still intact."

Gardek grunted. "And if anyone climbs up after it, the whole place is likely to cave in on top of him."

Milo turned to the arcanist. "You've been trying to learn new spells."

"Nothing that would let me pull the kit out when I can't even see it," Eilish said. "I doubt there even is a spell like that."

"I was afraid you'd say that." Milo took off his gas mask and set it on the ground.

"What are you doing?" Gardek asked.

"Lightening my load. I'm the smallest among us three."

"Nobody has to go up," the bounty hunter said.

"I know." Milo removed his cloak and bandoliers, then slipped a little vial on a thong from one of the pockets of his alchemist's armor before doffing that as well. Then he put the bandolier with the throwing knives back on again. Extra weight or no, it was a bad idea to go anywhere in the Undercity unarmed.

He hung the vial around his neck, flicked it with a fingertip, and the bottled light inside started glowing. The small quantity of grease and oil shed only about as much illumination as a single candle, but maybe it would suffice.

"Be careful," Eilish said.

If a person could avoid dwelling on the weight of half-burnt wood hanging over his head, the ground floor wasn't too bad. Milo simply had to mind where he set his feet among the debris. It wouldn't do to twist an ankle or tread on something sharp enough to pierce the sole of his boot before he even found a way up.

Once, despite his caution, he stepped on the withered remains of a corpse's hand, and the fingers crunched under his foot. It prompted him to wonder whether any alchemist had ever investigated the properties of human flesh reduced to charcoal.

The best way up appeared to be a blackened set of narrow stairs toward the rear of the building. He stepped on the first riser, and it held his weight. He tested the second, and it was all right, too.

He kept on climbing cautiously, transferring his weight from one step to the next as gently and smoothly as he could. That worked until he was just over halfway up. Then the staircase shuddered. Wood rasped as it toppled away from the mounts that had secured it to the wall.

Milo scurried upward and jumped. He caught his foot on something, giving it a wrench, but then smacked down on a solid surface just as the stairs crashed and clattered amid the debris on the level below.

The section of flooring on which he'd landed creaked and

shivered. He stayed flat and stretched out his limbs to distribute his weight as widely as possible. After a moment, the shaking subsided.

It was only then that he noticed Gardek was bellowing. "Milo! Are you all right?"

Milo drew a long breath, then sought to swallow away the dryness in his mouth. "Yes!" he answered. *So far.*

It seemed safer to crawl from this point forward. Even so, the timbers gave a little under his hands and knees. Ignoring that slight but ominous sagging as best he could, he tried to fit Canice Gormleigh's description of the layout of the building to the wreckage emerging from the darkness.

The door to the left should lead to her quarters. Skirting a ragged hole in the floor, he made his way to it and tried the handle. The door swung open partway, then caught when, with a little snapping sound, the upper hinge pulled loose from the frame.

Milo squeezed through the gap. Revived with a tap of his finger, the bottled light shone on a room that was intact toward the front and an utter shambles at the rear. By the looks of it, a steam-lobber projectile had smashed through the exterior wall and reduced the bed to scraps and splinters before crashing on through the interior wall on the other side.

Though smoke-stained, its veneer charred and cracked in patches, the wardrobe in the corner to the right of the door was one of the pieces of furniture that had more or less survived. Milo crawled to it, pushed aside the pile of Canice's dirty laundry on its floor, and groped for the hidden catch the gun mage had said to look for. With a click, a panel hitched upward just enough for him to grip with his fingertips and lift the rest of the way out. In the space beneath rested a satchel.

As promised, the bag contained lead wrapped in pristine white paper, a brass burner etched with mystic signs for melting it, gold dust to sprinkle into it, bullet molds with raised figures inside to mark a round with a rune, magnifying lenses, and etching styluses. It also held a clinking pigskin purse.

Milo considered transferring some of the coins inside to his own pockets before rejoining his partners. It would serve Gardek right for that "vulture" comment. But then again, if Canice should happen to mention how much money had been in the purse originally, that would be awkward.

With a snort, he repacked the satchel just as he'd found it—and then, with no warning whatsoever, the patch of weakened floor on which he was kneeling broke apart beneath him. Combined, his weight and that of the wardrobe had proved too much for it.

He plummeted, slamming down hard. Some of the objects beneath him were sharp enough to add to the pain, if they hadn't done worse. The world went entirely dark.

Trying to push past the shock of it all, he fumbled at his chest and suffered a stab of fear when he felt the wetness. But no, he wasn't bleeding, or if he was, only superficially. He was wet because the vial slung around his neck had broken, whereupon exposure to the air had killed the glow of the mixture inside.

Gasping, his heart pounding, he told himself things could have been considerably worse. Something could have fallen on top of him. Then, before he finished thinking the thought, something did, clipping him on the shoulder and glancing off to clink and scrape in the debris.

More chunks and scraps of the ceiling banged down around him. Gardek and Eilish were shouting, "Get out! Get out!"

Coughing, Milo staggered to his feet, cast about, and spotted the beams of his friends' lanterns illuminating falling pieces of board, floating ash, and the tangled litter that made walking treacherous. Using the light to guide him, he stumbled two steps toward safety and then remembered the satchel.

He turned back around. The lanterns were less help when he was interposing his body between them and what he was trying to see. "Move the beams around!" he croaked, loud as he could with a throat clogged with grit. At the same instant, a sizable piece of the ceiling crashed down almost within arm's reach on his left.

"What?" Gardek shouted.

As Milo was drawing breath to repeat himself, he caught sight of the wardrobe lying beside a pillar. He hurried to it, peered inside, and found only a shirt and a sock. Apparently, the satchel had tumbled out as it fell.

Pivoting, he looked for the bag. To no avail. Meanwhile, more falling boards smashed down around him. The support column beside the wardrobe cracked with a noise like a gunshot.

Then, although Gardek and Eilish were still shouting for him to run, the light of the lanterns grew brighter. They were coming in after him, perhaps because they imagined he was too addled to make his way out on his own.

The beam from someone's lantern fell on the satchel. He snatched up the bag and, now shielding his eyes against what had become dazzling glare, hurried toward his companions.

He tripped over something. Someone caught hold of him by the forearm and kept him from falling. He turned his head and saw that it was Eilish.

"Gather in!" Gardek said. He was holding his shield over his head in an umbrella fashion. Falling debris clanged and bonged on the steel.

Milo and Eilish did their best to avail themselves of the shield's protection while still staying clear of the spikes jutting from the trollkin's armor. That sufficed to keep anyone from getting brained as they scuttled clear of the building.

Panting and rubbing his shoulder, Milo turned back around. He half-expected to see the entire ruinous shell of the gaming hall collapse. It didn't, but, as evinced by the ongoing bang and crack of falling wood, the chain reaction he'd inadvertently triggered inside continued for half a minute more.

"Are you all right?" Gardek asked.

"Yes," Milo said.

The bounty hunter inspected the face of his shield, found a board stuck on one of the spikes, yanked it loose, and tossed it away. "I warned you it would be dangerous in there."

"But I retrieved Gormleigh's gear anyway, and so you'll get your sword-and-cape lessons. You're welcome."

• • •

THE GREENISH LIGHT OF HIS shoulder lamp illuminating the way, Olekse and his four companions hiked up a sloping tunnel. When they reached the top, another broad space with a high ceiling opened out before them.

Within the vault sat blocks of houses rotting into decrepitude. Still, there was a noticeable difference between them and most buildings that originated down here in the Undercity, structures commonly slapped together out of whatever materials could be scavenged and with inadequate knowledge of carpentry or masonry. A skilled artisan himself, though in a different craft, Olekse had been sneering at such tumbledown shacks ever since the Black Dogs' arrival.

In contrast, someone had constructed these homes properly, which meant they'd originally stood beneath the open sky before the boggy ground of Corvis swallowed them whole and the city grew a new layer of itself on top of them. In Olekse's opinion, only idiots would choose to live in a metropolis where such a thing could happen, but it seemed Cygnarans possessed a different perspective.

Still, the natives of Corvis, or at least the ones living like voles in this particular cave, had enough sense to scurry for cover upon sighting the Black Dogs. Maybe news of the extermination of the Patient Weavers had already reached them. Or maybe it was simply the spectacle of the swordsmen, as fierce- and hungry-looking as the two-headed black argus from which the bratya took its name, and especially of Olekse himself, tramping like a giant in his smoking ironhead armor with maul in hand, that alarmed them.

Were it up to him, he'd make sure they stay scared, and that would be that. But Ivan had a more nuanced strategy for dominating the Undercity. Intimidation was the cornerstone, but he also meant to persuade the tunnel dwellers that the Black Dogs could be kindly masters so long as everyone obeyed them.

And so, Olekse thought, here he was when, given the option, he'd rather be performing maintenance on the surviving 'jacks.

Still, he had to admit that, as errands went, this one would likely prove pleasanter than most.

"Get to it," he said to his companions, "before they're all quaking and pissing themselves indoors."

A gaunt fellow whose wavy tattooing crept all the way up the sides of his neck to the undersides of his cheeks, Iakshen laughed phlegmily. Six years of forced labor in freezing temperatures had afflicted him with a catarrh that never cleared up completely. "I joined the Dogs to take money, not to throw it away."

Still, he started tossing the silver denesckas the gang had brought from Khador, and his fellow swordsmen joined in. Olekse did not. The steel gauntlets encasing his hands weren't made for taking hold of something as small as a coin.

Instead, he called, "Grab it, friends! It's yours! Then follow along! The party's just beginning!"

The residents of the vault were probably still wary. But money was money, greed was greed, and, Olekse supposed, curiosity was curiosity. Snatching and scrabbling for coins, they started following the Black Dogs. Before long, he'd gathered quite a parade.

He led it to one of the largest houses. Someone had painted the four-story building bright pink overlaid with the red silhouettes of naked men and women. The workers, however, had neglected to do an adequate job of scraping off the old, peeling coat of paint beneath. The results were either enticingly carnal or leprous, depending on how closely one looked.

Olekse climbed up on the porch, which creaked under the weight of his armor but, to his relief, didn't break. He pushed open the door and sidled through, the steam engine on his back scraping the frame in the process.

In the parlor beyond, with its plush cushions and drapes of crimson and purple, scantily clad women and men gaped at him. Few were as svelte and generally comely as the painted silhouettes promised, but they all looked capable of satisfying a customer. Never picky, especially since prison, Olekse felt his interest quickening. It had been a while.

Clad in a gauzy vermilion gown with a neckline that plunged between her breasts, the madam—a plump, buxom woman well into her middle years—sauntered out from behind the bar. Though she was trying to appear confident, he could see the tension underneath the rouge and the green mascara.

"I was wondering if you'd be dropping by," she said.

He grinned. "And hoping we wouldn't?"

"I..." She took a breath and squared her shoulders. "Before you do anything rash, I think you should know the Pink Palace has never been required to pay tribute to any of the gangs. Everyone likes it that way. They like having someplace nice to meet that's neutral territory."

"Don't worry," Olekse said. "My bratya—my organization—isn't laying claim to your place."

Not today. In a month, perhaps, within a year, certainly, but not today.

She heaved a sigh. "You don't know how good it is to hear you say that. People told me you were from somewhere foreign, and—no offense—I can hear it in your speech. I was afraid you might not understand the way things work."

"Oh, we understand." *How to use your hopes and expectations to eat you up a bite at a time.*

"Then I imagine," the madam said, "you and your friends came to celebrate your victory. We're honored! And today, whatever you want is on the house."

"You're almost right," he told her. "We're inviting everybody to celebrate. Show her, Iakshen."

The swordsman set a bag on the bar and scooped out a handful of Khadoran koltinas. The gold coins glittered in the gaslight as he strewed them clinking along the polished oak. A harlot, her hair dyed almost the same metallic yellow as the money, caught her breath.

"Free girls, boys, and drink for whoever wants them," Olekse said. "Look outside. You'll see we've already got some takers."

He and the other Black Dogs stepped to one side or the other to give her an unobstructed look out the door. She snorted when she saw the crowd waiting beyond the porch.

"Half those... *people* of modest means have never been inside here before," she said. "I hope they aren't so eager that they tear the place apart."

"My friends and I can handle troublemakers," Olekse told her, "in between our own fun. Speaking of which, point me to a room. It'll be mine and mine alone while I'm here."

It needed to be, since he'd be storing his armor in it. There was no point in wasting fuel, and while he was as accustomed to his suit as any ironhead could be, it was still cumbersome, hot, and even less convenient for fornication than for handling coins.

• • •

GARDEK WATCHED AS EILISH circled the fallen steamjack. Whenever he saw something of interest, he dropped into a squat and held his lantern to more closely illuminate the bit that had captured his attention. There was something about his bobbing up and down that might have been comical if he weren't proceeding in such an unhurried, methodical manner.

As it was, Gardek was growing impatient. "Anything?" he asked.

The wizard pointed to a string of characters engraved in one of the curved pieces that made up the chassis of the automaton's forearm. "This is Khadoran. I can't read the language, but I recognize it."

"So what? Assuming we believe Gormleigh—and little as I trust her overall, I see no reason not to—we already know the new gang hails from Khador."

"I suspect it's a maker's mark, or the equivalent thereof. If we find someone who can read it, it might tell us exactly where the 'jack was assembled." Eilish removed a small notebook and a crayon from one of the pockets of his cloak and jotted the characters down.

"What will it matter if we do?" Gardek asked. Exercising the caution that had kept him alive through a decade of man hunting, he turned and looked for movement in the darkness. He didn't see any. "The 'jack and its masters are here now."

"The information might still tell us something useful," Eilish said. "A properly trained investigator attends to every datum."

"It's a steamjack," Milo said, his voice slightly muffled and tinny coming through the gas mask. His brush with death inside the gaming hall had apparently stifled his desire to wander around looting bodies. Instead, he was sticking close to his partners. "Too bad Colbie's not here to look at it. Or Pog."

"Having seconds thoughts about letting him join?" Gardek asked.

"Not really." Then, after another moment, he added, "Maybe. I remember when the rest of you weren't sure I was fit to join."

Gardek grinned. "I'm not sure *now*."

Milo answered with a gesture that, had it not come from a friend, might have had Gardek clenching his fists.

Meanwhile, Eilish had finally worked his way down to the disabled 'jack's feet. "You want something of immediate practical use? This could be it."

Using a magnifying lens, he peered closely at the mud clinging to the 'jack's extremities. Then he sniffed it, scooped up a dab of it on his fingertip, touched it to his tongue, and spat. His mouth twisted.

Gardek sensed that the arcanist's sour expression had more to do with disappointment than a foul taste. "No luck?"

Eilish shook his head. "The soil from certain portions of the Undercity has identifying characteristics," he said in his pedantic way. "Contaminants seeping down from manufactories on the surface and things like that. But this dirt is merely that. It could have come from any of a thousand vaults or tunnels."

"Then if you're done wasting time," Gardek said, "I'll do the thing that's really of 'immediate practical use.'"

The arcanist sighed. "Have at it."

Now it was Gardek's turn to repeatedly stoop as he led his companions around the cave from one exit to the next. After a time, he pointed to a footprint. "This must be the mark of a Khadoran boot. Clearly, they're different than the ones the cobblers make hereabouts. Look at the shapes of the heel and toe."

"I see it now that you point it out," Eilish said, the faintest hint of admiration in his tone.

"I don't," Milo said. "I barely even see a print. You're sure?"

"Yes," Gardek said. "The people wearing this type of boot were marching along with the steamjacks. You see *their* tracks, right?" Milo spread his hands. "Then take my word for it. They came out of that tunnel there and fanned out to make their attack. When they finished, they left the same way."

"Then let's find out where they went," Eilish said.

At first the trail led toward the smallish vault where Gardek knew a community of dwarves had established itself, supposedly because the majority had fled the mountains of Rhul after committing one crime or another. Their territory was one of the better-guarded and fortified portions of the Undercity, and it seemed unlikely that the Khadorans had even passed through it, let alone established a hideout within its boundaries.

And sure enough, the tracks soon ran off into a twisty, downward-sloping side passage. When Gardek headed into it, Milo grunted. "No one knows what's in this section," the alchemist said, "but everybody says it's nasty."

Eilish chuckled. "The two halves of that statement are mutually contradictory."

"To hell with your quibbling, wizard. You know what I mean."

"The Khadorans plainly found a safe path through," Gardek said, "and since we're following them, we should be all right, too. Just keep your guards up."

They skulked on down the passage. The shadowy mouths of side tunnels yawned to the right and the left, and, somewhere, water dripped. Convoluted like brain tissue, a patch of grey fungus caught Milo's eye, and he paused long enough to slice off a portion and cram it into an empty vial.

Meanwhile, the prints led onward. Until Gardek felt a sudden stab of alarm. His instincts were warning that something was wrong, but what?

He stopped and played the beam of his lantern across the space ahead. There was nothing there but earth and stone, nothing he hadn't been seeing all along.

"What is it?" Milo whispered.

"Quiet," Gardek replied. He listened, straining at it, and heard nothing.

Next he tasted the cool, moist air. All he smelled was earth and the chemical tang that clung to Milo's garments.

"I don't see anything," Eilish said.

"I don't either," Gardek answered. Still, he didn't advance. Instead, he stood and pondered until it occurred to him that if there was nothing perceptible stirring or lurking in the gloom ahead, then he must be reacting to something about the trail itself, some difference he'd spotted without consciously realizing he was seeing it.

Bending down, he studied the ground. "Damn it," he growled.

"What is it?" Eilish asked.

"There are fewer tracks than there were starting out, and no steamjack tracks at all anymore. I should have noticed sooner."

Milo shrugged, and his black leather cloak rustled. "Still, if any of them went this way, the trail could still lead us where we want to go."

"No." Gardek pointed to a footprint. "See how it's scuffed and blurred and the weight is on the heel? The man who made it was walking backward setting his feet in the tracks he made before. This is a false trail likely meant to send us into danger."

"When you put it that way," Milo said, "I think we should turn around."

They did, trying to retreat quickly but silently as well. Every couple of steps, Gardek glanced over his shoulder, and on the fourth glance, he glimpsed a shifting in the darkness. He turned and shone the beam of his lantern at it.

Pale eyes gleamed in the head of a hunched creature the size of a dog. Its slavering mouth was full of fangs, the three toes of each foot ended in long, curved claws, and a row of spines rose from the coarse, bristling fur on its back. Gardek saw it for only a moment before it squealed and scuttled clear of the light, but that was time enough for him or anyone who'd spent much time in the Undercity to recognize it for the dangerous beast it was.

"Devil rat," he said.

Milo shifted his free hand, the one that wasn't carrying the satchel with a lantern handle looped over the wrist, close to his bandoliers. "Thanks be to Corben we didn't go any nearer the nest. I've seen men die of devil rat fever, and it isn't pretty."

"We're too near as it is," Gardek said. "Be ready."

He pulled his war hammer from the sling that secured it to his back. He had a crossbow hanging from his belt, but a single quarrel would at best kill a single rat, and then, he feared, several more would be on top of him before he could either reload or change weapons.

Meanwhile, Eilish drew his sword, and a vertical furrow appeared in the center of his brow. The latter meant he was focusing his will to cast spells.

In the gloom at the very fringe of the lantern light, low shapes brushed past one another, their aggregate motion a seething in the dark. Together the spurs on their backs were like blades of grass waving in the breeze, although, making himself breathe slowly and deeply, Gardek wasn't sure if he could actually make out the spines or was just imagining it.

Suddenly, as though some master had given a command, the devil rats exploded forward. Reminiscent of piss and rotten meat, their eye-stinging stink engulfed the mercenaries, and their claws clicked when they landed on stone instead of earth. Their foaming jaws were half-open in anticipation of the initial bite.

Eilish rattled off one of the short rhyming phrases that helped him channel power to the proper purpose and held out his sword. Symbols made of blue light danced in the air around him, and an azure bolt shot from the point of his blade. The magic struck one of the devil rats in the snout and jolted it off its feet. Gardek couldn't tell if the arcanist had killed the thing, because the creatures behind it instantly scrambled over its body in their haste to reach their intended prey.

Milo lifted his gas mask, brought a grenade to his mouth, pulled the pin with his teeth, and threw the studded metal cylinder. It landed short, but in an instant the foremost devil rats raced over it, and then, with a flash and a bang, it exploded. The blast threw chunks of vermin tumbling through the air.

The surviving creatures hissed, squealed, and cringed away from the explosion. Still, the tide kept rushing forward.

A silvery light flowered around the mercenaries. This time not bothering with an incantation, Eilish had conjured the glow. In another moment, they'd be fighting with blade and hammer, and illumination didn't require them to manage the lanterns and their weapons at the same time.

Gardek set his lantern down. Then Milo threw a second grenade.

This one burst into hissing vitriolic fire. Dazzlingly bright, the cloud of flame threw off a heat that Gardek could feel even at a distance and set devil rats ablaze to collapse screeching, thrashing, and rolling against their fellows. Those adjacent to their afflicted pack mates recoiled and jostled, clambered over, and lashed out at one another in panicky attempts to avoid being set ablaze themselves. Meanwhile, the original splash of fire hung in the air for a few seconds before dwindling away.

The surviving rats stopped charging. They hadn't liked the concussion grenade, and they'd liked the cinder bomb even less.

Milo snatched a third grenade from its bandolier and held it over his head. "You see, you filthy beasts? I have more!"

"Nice work," Gardek said. "Now let's get out of here."

They backed up the tunnel to keep their eyes on the devil rats. Once more a vague churning mass at the fringe of the light, the creatures skulked after them. The distance they maintained reflected an uncannily accurate sense of just how far Milo could pitch a grenade.

Still, so long as the beasts kept their distance, things would all right. But as the seconds crawled by, as Eilish's silvery light faded and the mage rekindled it, even as Milo caught his heel on a bump on the floor and lurched off balance for an instant, Gardek couldn't believe it was going to be that easy. The cunning vermin weren't just seeing the trespassers out of their territory. They were waiting for something that would alter the tactical situation to their advantage.

He glanced over his shoulder, then snarled a curse. There were devil rats farther up the tunnel too, beasts that had used the side passages to maneuver around behind their prey. There they waited silently for the intruders to witlessly back within reach of their fangs and claws. As soon as they saw Gardek looking at them, they squealed and hurtled forward.

He bellowed, "Watch out!" as he spun and assumed a fighting stance. Rats sprang, and he thrust his shield at them, using its mass to smash and its spikes to stab. But big as it was, it could hold back only a couple of the creatures. Others circled his feet like a whirlpool, snapping, clawing, rearing, scrambling as they sought to climb his body. The spikes on his boots and greaves jabbed some of those, too, but not enough to stem the onslaught.

From behind him came a bang and a flash. Milo had thrown the third grenade, no doubt because the original horde of vermin had commenced another charge. Gardek doubted the blast would balk them this time, not when their comrades had already closed to striking distance.

Nimble even in his fitted black plate, Eilish lunged and pivoted across Gardek's field of vision. The arcanist drove his short sword into one devil rat and then another. Then, the tips of the spines along its back burning like candles, one of the huge vermin snatched with its claws, snagged Eilish's billowing cloak, and jerked it. Eilish reeled backward, and while he was off balance, yet another rat snapped its fangs shut on his ankle. He fell on his back, and his attackers drove in from all sides and cut off Gardek's view of him.

Swinging his war hammer up and down, Gardek struggled to break free of his own ring of attackers and go to the caster's aid. He pulped flesh and smashed bone with every blow, but another rat always pounced forward to take each dead one's place. Meanwhile, some still writhing and raking, rat bodies hung on the spikes of his armor like fruit on a tree. Strong as he was, their weight and bulk hindered him, but if he took the time to get them off, the rest of the vermin would overwhelm him.

At his back, Milo cried out. It was all too likely that, his grenades useless against foes that had already closed to striking distance, the masked alchemist was in serious trouble too, but Gardek couldn't fight his way in two directions at once. In truth, he wasn't even making any headway toward Eilish.

Suddenly flame erupted just beside the spot where the arcanist lay buried beneath his assailants. Devil rats squealed and flinched away. Eilish rolled to his knees with a claw scratch on his cheek, more scratches and dents marring the ebony finish of his armor, and a savage cast to his expression. Glyphs of blue light flickered around him as he jabbed with his gory blade.

More flame leaped up where he pointed, first to burn and repel the rats nearest him, then at various points throughout the pack. The creatures screeched in pain and consternation.

The general confusion included Milo's attackers. He had a bloody leaf-shaped knife in each hand, and when the creatures faltered, he dropped the blade in his right, snatched another grenade from its bandolier, and flung it over their heads at rats farther away. Vitriolic fire exploded in their midst.

Finally demoralized, those devil rats that were still able fled, streaming into side tunnels. In moments, they'd all disappeared, although their squeals still echoed.

Taking care that the ones clinging to life didn't bite or claw him, gripping and crushing their throats as necessary, Gardek divested himself of the rats impaled on his armor and shield. Then he strode to Eilish, who was still on his knees with one hand planted on the ground. "Are you all right?" he asked.

"Just give me a minute," the arcanist panted.

Spellcasting, Gardek understood, taxed a wizard's stamina. Eilish was more resistant to the resulting fatigue than some arcanists, yet even so, it was no wonder that creating several fires in quick succession had taken a toll.

Gardek turned. "Milo?"

"Scratched a little," the alchemist said. His dark leather cloak was in tatters, and the matching armor beneath was scarred. "Looks like we all are. But it's bites that carry the fever, and I have a salve that'll stanch the bleeding and keep the wounds from getting infected."

Gardek looked himself over and discovered that Milo was right. One of his spiky pauldrons was dangling partly loose. A devil rat's claws had jammed under the shoulder armor to tear one of the straps securing it, the layer of padding beneath, and the blue skin under that. Fired up with fury and desperation, he'd never felt it.

Milo gave Eilish a nod. "That was a good trick."

The lanky arcanist grinned. "I told Regan I'd master the spell. I merely needed the proper motivation."

"Let's move out," Gardek said, "before the rats get motivated for a third try."

He offered his hand. Eilish allowed the trollkin to heave him to his feet but declined assistance thereafter, preferring to totter along on his own. At first he looked like he might well fall down again, or drop his sword or lantern, but then his gait steadied and he stood up straighter.

After a while, when there was no indication the devil rats were still stalking them, Gardek decided he could afford to divide his attention between watching for the animals and scrutinizing the ground. At a spot where the passage branched, he said, "Here."

"Here what?" Milo asked.

"Here's where our quarry turned aside. If you know how to look, you can see how they tried to set their feet on stones and firm, dry earth instead of damp and how they tried to sweep away any tracks."

"Then onward," Eilish said.

"Or not," Milo said. "We're tired and bloodied, and I'm down four grenades."

"We're only scouting," the yellow-haired arcanist said, "and you can bet Helstrom isn't counting on us and us alone. He has watchmen out looking for the bratya, too. You don't want them to beat us to the prize, do you?"

Gardek snorted. "Not much chance of that. But I agree we should press on."

Milo sighed. "Of course you do. Let's at least tend to our cuts and catch our breath first."

The alchemist's ointment burned and had a smell that reminded Gardek of onions. He wasn't surprised. Milo rarely gave any thought to making his preparations pleasant to use. To the little swampie's credit, though, they worked more often than not.

When they finished smearing their scratches, the three of them tried to brush and slap the filth from their persons. Their efforts were only minimally effective. Their foray into the remains of the gambling hall had dusted them with ash, and now they'd spattered devil-rat blood over that.

Gardek didn't much care, and he doubted Milo did, either. He grinned when they gave up but Eilish kept on fussily swiping and picking at himself.

"We're not paying a call on the High Prelate," the trollkin said.

The corners of Eilish's mouth twitched upward. "No, I suppose not. Lead on, then."

Before long, the trail took them to a place where the floor went from being mostly earth to primarily exposed stone. Gardek bent low to inspect the surface. Then, to bring his eyes even closer, he crawled on hands and knees, and Eilish conjured magical light to augment the glow of the lanterns.

Finally, Gardek growled, "May their balls fall off and their pizzles rot."

"People don't leave tracks walking on rock," Eilish said, "but perhaps the steel feet of a steamjack leave scratches?"

Gardek suppressed the urge to snap at the human for presuming to think he could teach him how to track. Annoying though he often was, Eilish was only trying to help, while he himself was just frustrated.

The bounty hunter took a breath and said, "Not if you wrap the feet in cloth. Which they must have done. And up ahead, you can see how the way divides." He stood up. "We've lost them."

"If no one could track them," Milo said, "then why bother

leaving the false trail to the devil rats?"

"For the same reason they slaughtered every living soul back in the vault," Eilish said, "whether the victims belonged to the Patient Weavers or not. To impress Corvis with just how vicious, cunning, and generally dangerous they are."

"Well," the swampie said, "*I'm* convinced."

— 7 —

FODOR PICKED UP THE CLEAVER from amid the raw pork ribs on the chopping board. Weighing it in his hand, he said, "I've never thrown one of these before."

A tall man with receding sandy hair and a natural pallor that had turned positively ashen, the trembling cook let out a moan. But he knew better than to attempt to bolt from the spot against the kitchen wall where his captors had ordered him to stand. Knives now jutted to either side of him, as Fodor tried to outline the man's form with the available utensils. He wasn't the best knife thrower among the Black Dogs, but he didn't especially care if he stuck the prisoner instead of landing a blade an inch to the right or left.

"Oh, go ahead," Mama said, stroking his forearm. "You're a natural marksman, and besides, practice is the only way to learn."

Fodor grinned. "You're right." He hurled the cleaver.

Even as it left his hand, he could feel that his aim was off, and sure enough, the cleaver thumped into the center of the cook's high, sweaty forehead. But everything about the throw was clumsy, so it was the flat and not the edge of the blade that struck him. The man screamed, and the cleaver fell to his feet with a clank.

Fodor cursed. "That was terrible."

"Don't be so hard on yourself," Mama said. "It was fine for a first effort. Try again."

His skin split where the cleaver hit him, blood flowing down over the bridge of his nose, the cook said, "Please! I'm telling the truth! I've heard of Canice Gormleigh, but I don't know her! She never ate here! Never!"

"Now, dear," Mama said, "how likely is that, really? Your many loyal customers say you prepare the most authentic Llaelese cuisine in the Undercity, perhaps in all of Corvis. And wanderers crave food that reminds them of home."

"I'm telling the truth!" the cook repeated.

"No," said Fodor, picking up the cleaver while watching to see if the cook would try to kick him or yank a knife out of the wall and stab him. It was unlikely—the wretch was paralyzed with terror, and Mama was standing ready with sword drawn—but it paid to be careful. "You're not."

"Do you know," Mama said, "he might be. We don't know why Miss Gormleigh left Llael, but if there was some painful tragedy involved, if she doesn't want to be reminded of the old days..." She smiled at the captive. "Give me your word, one cook to another—not that I'd ever for a moment suggest I'm in your class—that you have no idea where the gun mage might have gone to ground."

"I swear by every Ascendant!"

Mama turned to Fodor. "I believe him, lambkin."

"All right, then. If he's of no use to us." Fodor threw the cleaver.

This time he'd actually aimed for the center of the cook's forehead but hit him in the neck. Still, in one respect, the throw was an improvement. It was the cleaver's edge that struck the target.

The cook collapsed, and when he flopped down thrashing,

the cleaver popped out of the wound. Blood spurted, and Mama stepped back to avoid getting soiled.

As the rhythmic gushing and the prisoner's death throes subsided, she said, "Dearie, I never want to keep you from your fun. But I did promise that if he cooperated, we'd let him live."

Fodor felt a familiar mix of sheepishness and resentment, the latter because he was a grown man and a fighter of the bratya who shouldn't be meekly taking orders or enduring scoldings from his mother. But he knew deep down that he'd never show that resentment any more than he'd ever hire a whore or take a mistress.

"I'm sorry, Mama," he said. "I didn't think."

"Oh, it's not important," she said, fluffing his hair with her fingertips. "Perhaps it's even for the best. Even if not everyone realizes yet, this is all our territory now, and Ivan doesn't like being reminded of Llael either."

• • •

AS THE THREE MEN with the barrows pushed them clattering up the cobbled street, Colbie glanced right and left without, she hoped, being obvious about it. She was trying to spot anyone following her or eyeing the oilcloth-covered contents of the barrows with larcenous intent.

She would have felt more confident of spotting trouble in open country or even in a forest or swamp. Before landing in Corvis, she'd spent several years as what she still occasionally thought of as a real mercenary, chasing brigands and river pirates and fighting to put down petty insurrections and repel probing Khadoran raids into northern Cygnar. Since then, her comrades had taught her a little something about recognizing cutpurses and ruffians in the City of Ghosts, but she still wasn't the thief taker that Gardek or Eilish was.

Be that as it may, as best she could judge, no one was checking out the procession with more than casual curiosity, and when a rumble of thunder and a flicker of lightning behind the towers to the north announced the imminent return of the rain, even that stopped. People were more interested in hurrying on to their destinations and getting indoors.

Though they too picked up the pace, Colbie and her hirelings didn't quite beat the rain. As they rounded a corner and the safehouse came into view, the first cold drops spattered them and the nearest buildings—dark, grimy, square-built structures originally adorned with statuary and carving. Vandals had defaced most of the decoration, although if she looked carefully, she might still notice a staring eye, fragmentary symbol, or serpentine curve that gave her a shiver without her even understanding why except that it was Orgoth.

The Orgoth were the hated conquerors who'd founded Corvis, and much of their ugly architecture survived to this day. Colbie had occasionally thought it a pity that such monstrosities endured while more recent structures crumbled or sank into the ground, but perhaps it was just as well. The Undercity could be unsettling enough already without tossing Orgoth strongholds, torture chambers, and wizards' workrooms into the mix.

She rapped on the double doors to the safehouse's attached stable, and Pog opened them a crack. She peered over his green, long-eared head, then pulled the doors all the way open and told the men to unload the tools, 'jack parts, and groceries onto the floor by the derelict carriage. When they finished, she tipped them a handful of copper farthings and sent them and their barrows on their way.

Just as she barred the doors behind them, the rain started drumming audibly on the roof. Then Canice came through the door connecting the stable with the rest of the house. She still wasn't wearing her greatcoat, but she'd put her hip and shoulder holsters back on. Probably, Colbie thought, a hired murderer felt naked without them.

"I saw you peeking in," Canice said. "Did you think that if I was in the stable—which I was, bothering Pog, because with Natak asleep and Dr. Falk off looking in on a couple of her other patients, it was the only thing to do—I wouldn't have sense enough to get out of sight?"

Colbie shrugged. "Would you have checked if you were me?"

Canice snorted. "Maybe. But all this caution is excessive. Even if the Khadorans are interested in chasing Natak and me all the way aboveground—"

"'Even if?' Talking to Helstrom, you seemed pretty certain."

"The massacre made an impression on me, and if worst came to worst, Natak needed a safe haven. As he still needs a place to recover and a physician's care. But as I was saying, even if our enemies are willing to look for us aboveground, they have no way of tracking us to this house."

"Unless one of the Khadorans," said Pog, "one you didn't kill, I mean, got a good look at Captain Sterling." He carried a bundle of reflex-trigger wire from one of the piles to the carriage, which he and Colbie were using as a work platform in their efforts to restore Doorstop to full functionality. Dull-eyed and inert with a cold boiler, the 'jack himself stood beside it. "In which case, she shouldn't be wandering around outside either."

Colbie frowned. "Pog, you're not helping."

"But he has a point," Canice said.

"No, he doesn't," Colbie said, peeling off her armored greatcoat. She'd be cooler and more comfortable working on Doorstop without it. "We did kill everyone who got a good look at me, and even if we hadn't, I wasn't one of the bratya's primary targets, and with Eilish, Gardek, and Milo investigating belowground, *somebody* has to run errands."

"I volunteer to handle that from now on," Milo said.

Colbie turned. The alchemist was coming through the door into the house proper. Eilish followed, and, stooping and twisting to slip his hulking frame and bulky, spiky armor through the opening, Gardek brought up the rear.

She caught her breath at their filthy, battered, and blood-smeared condition. "Is everyone all right?" she asked.

"More or less," Gardek said. "We just thought we might as well clean up properly."

"What happened?" Colbie said. "You were only supposed to do reconnaissance."

"The bratya happened," Canice said. "I warned you—"

"Quiet!" Colbie snapped. "You weren't there. I need to hear from the people who were."

The other Irregulars told the story in turns. Although perhaps her reaction was childish, it annoyed Colbie that their first move had been to attempt to retrieve Canice's gear and irritated her still more that they'd managed to do so.

"So," said Milo, "we succeeded at something, anyway." He held out the satchel to Canice.

The gun mage gave him a smile that for once seemed devoid of swaggering superiority or sneering challenge. Instead, it bespoke pure gratitude. "Thank you. You found the money?"

"We did," Eilish said, leaning against the wall, "and a tidy sum it was. But I'm still primarily interested in learning how rune shots are made."

"You will. I keep my promises."

Colbie scowled. "Let's get back to what actually matters here."

"As you wish," Eilish said. He described finding an inscription on the steamjack Colbie had disabled and then tossed her his notebook with the characters copied in crayon. "Does this mean anything to you?"

"No," she said. She couldn't speak or read Khadoran either.

"Can I see?" Pog asked. She handed the little book to him. "Hmm." He hesitated in a way that almost seemed apologetic. "Captain, you probably never ran into these because they aren't real warjacks. But I've seen a couple. They manufacture them in Skirov."

Eilish smiled at Gardek. "I told you."

"And I ask again," the trollkin rumbled, "what good does it do to know that?"

"Well," Pog said, "I didn't recognize the make before, not at a distance in the dark when I was running for my life. But now that I do, I can tell you a couple weak points to hit at if you have to fight another one."

Gardek snorted. "All right," he said to Eilish, "that's one for you, and I do mean *one*." He turned back to Colbie. "Anyway, after the schoolboy looked over the 'jack, it was time for me to search for footprints." He proceeded to tell of the trap involving devil rats and the trail that even he had been unable to follow to its end.

When he finished, Colbie said, "Thank Markus you all made it out in one piece. It's unfortunate that you couldn't track the killers, but we already planned for that contingency. So, whenever you feel ready."

"Meanwhile," Canice said, "your leader will stay safely locked away here to tinker."

Eilish chuckled. "Apparently so."

"It's important," Colbie gritted, "that Doorstop be put back in order. He's a vital weapon for this company."

"Vital to you, anyway," Canice said. "You're useless without him."

Colbie took a breath. "I believe you've seen that isn't so."

The gun mage blinked. "Well, perhaps that wasn't entirely fair. But the fact remains, your partners nearly died today, and if you aren't presently able to back them up, somebody should. Even without my magic I'm a crack shot, and I can cut and dye my hair and leave the red-and-yellow outfit behind."

"And likely be recognized anyway," Colbie said, "notorious character that you are, when others are trying to go unnoticed. So, *no*. For the hundredth time, you'll stay here as Helstrom ordered."

Canice glowered.

Eilish drawled, "We hear and obey, O Captain. But if I end up meeting Morrow for want of a pistoleer, I'm going to be upset."

• • •

POG WAS EXCITED TO HAVE new tools and parts for restoring Doorstop to perfect working order and was accordingly surprised when he found himself unable to concentrate fully. He gave a bolt a final twist, then set down the wrench and said, "I'm going to take a break."

As he hadn't taken one hitherto, he was a little worried that Colbie would find the declaration suspect. But, intent on her own labors, she simply waved a greasy hand in dismissal.

Pog clambered from the top of the carriage into the coachman's seat and then down a set of three folding steps to the floor. Once inside the house, he paused to drink from the kitchen pump and splash more water on his hot, sweaty face. Then he went in search of Canice.

The one closed interior door on the ground floor gave her location away. He hesitated and then rapped on the panel.

"What?" the gun mage snapped.

"It's Pog," he answered. "Can I come in?"

"If you'd interrupted me in the middle of a prepping a rune shot," she replied, "I'd have come out and blasted you with it. But I'm not that far along yet. So yes, if you must."

He opened the door. The room on the other side was small and gloomy, with spider webs in the corners of the ceiling and nose-tickling dust on nearly every surface and no doubt suffusing the drapes as well. But it contained a chair and a writing desk, and Canice had wiped the latter clean to serve as her worktable.

She'd set a brass burner with engraved mystical symbols in the center of the space and adjusted it to produce a blue teardrop of steady flame. A short hose connected the apparatus to a tank no larger than a fist. Ordinarily, such a vessel wouldn't hold enough fuel to feed the burner for long, so Pog surmised that magic, alchemy, or mechanika was involved. Collapsible when not in use, a little steel tripod held a pot full of miniature lead ingots suspended above the fire.

"Well," Canice asked, "what is it?"

"I thought you were going to wait until Mr. Garrity and Mr. Boggs could watch."

"They'll get their chance. It's a slow process, and I can only make one rune shot at a time." She sneered. At herself, apparently. "I should never have let my supply dwindle. That's one of the first things my mentor taught me." For a moment, she seemed lost in memory, perhaps even wistful, and then her expression hardened. "You didn't answer my question. What do you want?"

Pog hesitated. Now that the moment had arrived, he suspected he would have done better to keep to his own affairs. Still, he said,

"It doesn't do any good to keep poking at Captain Sterling in the same old way. It only puts her back up."

"It's the only way I know to poke, and if all it does is irritate the bitch, at least that's a moment's entertainment. What do you care, anyway?"

"I just like it when people get along."

She laughed. "Then I suspect you're fated to be unhappy, the world being what it is."

"Is it truly so important for you to go face the bratya yourself?"

"How could it not be? Aside from the reasons you've already heard, right now I'm the mercenary who was responsible for the Patient Weavers' gambling den, couldn't keep enemies from killing everybody inside and burning it down, and ended up running away."

"No one could think less of you for the way things turned out."

"The hell they couldn't. I'm also the person from whom the Watch Commander is expecting additional information about the Khadorans. Just between you and me, I haven't got it. I pretty much told him everything I knew to get this far. Somehow, I have to turn all that around, or with my reputation in rags and Helstrom bearing a grudge, my future prospects will be pretty bleak."

"You could start over somewhere else. When Mr. Warbiter is able to travel, I mean."

Canice shook her head. The motion tossed the coppery curls on her head, and some of them caught a gleam of the blue firelight. "No. I forsook one home. I won't give up another."

Pog reflected that, frustrated though the gun mage was, in one respect she was luckier than she realized. It must be nice when simply being in a city you found congenial made you feel at home.

He liked Corvis too, mostly, but its towering spires, fuming smokestacks, barge-choked canals, and tangled streets with their teeming multitudes were simply too big to afford him a sense of belonging. He required a circle of friends, and now that his coworkers were dead and the Black River Irregulars had rejected his application, he had no idea where or when he'd find another.

His shoulders slumped. "I'd better get back to Doorstop."

• • •

EILISH HEARD THE ECHOING CLAMOR before the entrance to the vault came into view. It was a mix of boisterous conversation, other voices roaring out a ribald drinking song, and woodwinds, mandolins, and drums playing a galliard unrelated to the vocal music. The instruments stumbled periodically, their harmony breaking into dissonance, as the singers' tempo seemed to addle the players' sense of rhythm.

Eilish and Gardek exchanged glances. One of the bounty hunter's contacts, a foxy-faced beggar with an allegedly withered leg—Eilish had discerned the contorted positioning and pigment used to create the illusion—had given them some idea of what to expect, but the sound of such widespread, unbridled merriment still seemed incongruous in the Undercity. It reminded Eilish of the festival held every spring on the grounds of Corvis University, where during his student days he'd flirted, drunk the tart new white wine up from the Southern Midlunds, and contended in the comical lecture competition satirizing the learned discourse of the professors.

He grinned at his companion. "Suddenly, it seems ludicrous that we're being paid to track down the bratya. I'll feel guilty pocketing my share of the fee. Well, almost."

The trollkin grunted. "Don't underestimate the Khadorans. Remember the rats."

"I'm not underestimating them. I think they're clever to exterminate the Weavers, then turn right around and host an orgy. If you want to exert influence, terror and treats make a potent combination. Still, unless they simply paid for the party and vanished into the darkness—which I doubt—we've got them."

"Just be wary and not only of the Khadorans. Chances are, there'll be other people in the crowd who dislike thief takers."

They tramped onward, descended a slope, rounded a final bend, and entered the vault. Shortly after that, the celebration came into view. If it had ever all fit into the Pink Palace to begin with, it had since spilled outside as it attracted revelers from across the Undercity. The resident harlots must be exhausted, although in the dark aisles between the dilapidated houses, competitors were taking up the slack.

It was somewhat reassuring that the party had drawn some gobbers, dwarves, ogrun, and trollkin. Unless they were deviants—of which the Undercity had its share—they weren't interested in human prostitutes, but everyone liked free drink. At any rate, maybe Gardek wouldn't be horribly conspicuous, even though one rogue flinched and scurried into the crowd at the sight of him.

The bounty hunter chuckled. "Not today, Mago. Probably not ever, unless you fall into my lap. The last time I checked, you were only worth five crowns. I can make that in one hand over yonder."

Eilish discerned that his partner was looking at a table someone had hauled out of one of the houses lining the street. Around it sat three men, an ogrun, and a gobber playing brag. The ogrun loomed over his fellow gamblers, while if the gobber had been sitting any lower, he could easily have rested his receding chin on the tabletop.

"You're not here to play cards," Eilish said.

"I should do something to make it look like I belong, and this is as good a place to sit and watch the crowd as any."

"Fair enough. Just don't get so caught up in the game that you forget why we're here. I'm going to circulate."

"Try to look like you're hunting for a streetwalker. One of the really cheap ones. People will believe that."

Eilish snorted, and, taking care not to impale his hand on a spike, clapped the trollkin on the shoulder. Then he sauntered onward.

Pale of face and doughy as a slug, a man was dispensing red wine from a cask. There were no cups left, so Eilish poured the water from his canteen and allowed the other fellow to refill it. A wary sip of the sugary vintage pulled the corners of his mouth back in distaste, but at least now he was drinking alcohol like everybody else.

After that, he watched a woman juggle daggers. Dull ones, evidently, since she fumbled and caught one by the blade instead of the hilt and didn't cut herself. Still, amused, he tossed a farthing into the scatter at her feet.

Then, drifting on toward the gaudily painted brothel itself, pondering the advisability of joining the queue waiting for admittance, he spotted a swordsman, skinny to the point of gauntness, stalking in his general direction. The fellow had wavy black tattooing slithering up the sides of his neck to the bottoms of his hollow cheeks and, incongruously, given his generally knavish appearance, the alert air of a watchman charged with maintaining at least a vague semblance of order.

By themselves, the thin man's tattoos and demeanor were enough to snag Eilish's attention, but once they did, he also noticed the cut of the fellow's cape, made to leave the sword arm uncovered and only hanging to the hip. He knew nothing about cloak fighting specifically but inferred from his general understanding of combat that a person needed a relatively short garment to whip it around with finesse. This particular cape, moreover, draped and swung as though it had weights sewn into the hem.

Clearly, Eilish had identified a member of the bratya. The real trick would be doing something about it in the midst of the mob of revelers.

For want of a better idea, he decided to shadow the Khadoran. Maybe he'd observe something helpful. Or perhaps the scoundrel would even be obliging enough to stray into a patch of darkness removed from the heart of the celebration.

• • •

THE CONGESTION MOVED AROUND from day to day. Sometimes it was in Iakshen's head and sometimes in his chest. Unfortunately, though, it never wandered all the way out of his body to afflict some new unfortunate.

This evening—he'd been told it was evening, although how, and come to think of it, why did anyone keep track inside these caves?—his malady had nested in his lungs. A coughing fit seized him, and he welcomed it even though it would burn and, while it lasted, give him the scary feeling of being unable to draw in air.

If he brought up enough phlegm to ease him for a while, a few moments of discomfort would be worth it.

He bent over hacking and in due course spat a meager and thus disappointing quantity of greenish sludge into the dirt in front of his boots. Then he straightened up too quickly, before the lightheadedness of anoxia had passed, and staggered a half-step before catching his balance.

That lurching motion turned him partway around, and, blinking moisture from his eyes, he glimpsed a lanky man with blond hair at the periphery of his vision.

The stranger's appearance was less than immaculate. His cloak was torn, and the armor beneath was dinged and scratched. But it had started life as expensive plate with a foppish ebony finish when, as Iakshen could see by surveying the crowd, any sort of metal armor was comparatively rare among the rogues and paupers of the Undercity. His general demeanor seemed unusual, too. He carried himself confidently but not with the sneer and swagger of a ruffian.

Could he be an officer of the Watch in disguise? Iakshen doubted it, and he trusted his ability to sniff out a lawman, whether Khadoran or Cygnaran, in uniform or otherwise. But the same instincts told him the man would bear watching.

He walked on, looking this way and that as he had been all along, and managed to keep track of the yellow-haired man ambling behind him. It was interesting that the Cygnaran was trailing along in his footsteps, but at this point, conceivably just coincidence.

Ahead was a trestle table where one of the flunkies who normally worked inside the brothel was dispensing brandy. Iakshen had already discovered that he disliked the taste, and he was unimpressed by the potency. If Ivan truly intended the bratya to make Corvis its permanent home, they needed to import *vyatka*, and sooner rather than later.

Still, the brandy provided an excuse to pause. He shoved through those who were waiting for the flunky to serve them and grabbed a bottle from the dwindling supply. Meanwhile, the man in the black armor passed him by without a glance.

So maybe the stranger wasn't stalking him, but his intuition remained unconvinced. He prowled onward, and after he passed a cockfight, the blond man emerged from the circle of spectators, who shouted in unison every time one bird scored on the other, and fell in behind him once again.

Taking a meandering path, Iakshen drifted on through the crowd and its various amusements. Whenever he changed course, his shadow did as well. After three turns, he was certain.

He stifled an urge to confront the blond man straightaway. Not that he was afraid of him. But only idiots fought "fairly" when they could bring superior numbers to bear. Instead, he headed for the Pink Palace, where he shoved aside the patron at the front of the line to unblock the doorway.

There were so many pasty tunnel dwellers jammed into the parlor that, even though he had no compunction about pushing, and all but the boldest were eager to make way, it took a few moments to get to the madam, who was laughing with each arm looped around a different man. Her makeup was smeared, perhaps from giving and receiving kisses, or possibly she was just sweating it off. Despite the dank coolness that generally prevailed in the Undercity, the overcrowded room was stuffy and warm.

"Olekse!" Iakshen said, raising his voice to make himself heard. That evoked a fresh little rasp of pain in his chest but fortunately not another coughing spasm. "Where is he?"

"In his room," the madam answered. "I think."

Iakshen worked his way to a hallway that ran off from the parlor and onward toward a space that had been a dining room before Olekse ordered the prostitutes to bring down a bed from upstairs. He could do many useful things in his steam-powered armor, but he couldn't easily negotiate the average flight of interior stairs. He'd left scrapes and gouges on the corridor walls just getting as far as he had.

Iakshen rapped on the door. "Olekse!"

"Come in," the ironhead said.

Olekse was lying in bed with a slender black-haired harlot. Both were naked.

This exposed the tattooing that covered Olekse's barrel-chested, hairy body, some of the signs and images skillfully executed, others the cruder marks that men jabbed into one another in prison. In addition to the tattoos that any Black Dog might carry—skulls, daggers, and, of course, snaky lines and the stylized two-headed hound above the heart—he bore inked clockwork and pneumatic tubes, as if it pleased him to imagine he was half-machine.

The prostitute had a split lip and bruises coming up on her throat.

Olekse's armor stood in the corner partly disassembled, as it needed to be for him to squirm out of it. His enormous maul leaned beside it.

"Good," Olekse said. "You brought a fresh bottle. Give it here."

Iakshen tossed it.

The ironhead uncorked it and took a long drink. "Now, is something wrong?"

"Maybe," Iakshen said.

Olekse growled at the black-haired woman to get out, whereupon she jumped out of bed, snatched her clothes off a chair, and scurried from the room as though grateful to make her escape. Then Iakshen told him about the man in the scarred black plate.

When he finished, Olekse said, "I don't suppose you saw anything that links your yellow-haired bastard to the gun mage."

"No."

"Too bad. Ivan set our mad mother and her mad son on the bitch's trail, but if we found them first, we'd be the ones to win his gratitude."

"Why does he hate her so?" Iakshen suspected that whatever its source, the malice had even influenced Ivan's decision to attack the Patient Weavers. Fortunately, that had worked out, but the fact remained that there had been easier targets.

"I don't know." Olekse grinned. "You could ask him."

Iakshen snorted. "Or I could hold my tongue and spare myself a fist in the face. What do you want to do about the man who was shadowing me?"

"Catch him and question him." Olekse picked his trousers up off the floor. "Go collect the other Dogs."

— 8 —

EILISH FOUND GARDEK STILL SEEMINGLY INTENT on the card game. Yet the trollkin sensed that someone was approaching him from behind and looked around when his partner was still a stride away.

Eilish beckoned. Gardek threw away his five-card hand, scooped up the coins in front of him, picked up his hammer and shield, and departed the table, ignoring the taunts and jeers intended to make him stay. He was clearly leaving with some of the other players' money.

"I take it you spotted someone," the bounty hunter rumbled. "I admit, I haven't yet."

"Probably because the Khadorans are mostly staying inside the Pink Palace," Eilish said. "It makes sense. That's where the most appealing prostitutes and the best wine and liquor are. But a member of the gang comes out periodically to keep an eye on things. I saw one of them wandering around."

"Where is he now?"

"Back inside. Where we would be ill advised to follow. But if we wait and watch, he or one of his fellow scoundrels will come out, and then perhaps we can grab him."

The trollkin grunted. "Worth a try."

They separated as they sauntered in the direction of the brothel. Eilish sat down on the moldy remains of what had once been a horse trough and nipped at his supply of cloyingly sweet wine. Gardek joined the ring of spectators watching a pair of human boxers with wrapped fists pummeling one another bloody. The mercenaries' positions allowed them to keep an eye on the entrance to the Pink Palace and on each other as well.

The spectators watching the fighters cheered or groaned as one pugilist gained the upper hand and meted out punishment to the other. Then the same Khadoran Eilish had seen before emerged from the brothel. Apparently it was his particular duty to patrol the vault.

Eilish glanced in Gardek's direction to make sure he'd spotted the gang member. The trollkin responded with a twist of his wide mouth that seemed to reply, *Do you really think I could have missed him?*

Still moving separately, hanging back as far as they could while keeping their quarry in sight, the two mercenaries ambled after the Khadoran. The outlaw led them past a sinkhole with a high, narrow, tower-like house all but tottering on its brink, and an entrepreneur hawking cheap, likely stolen good-luck charms hanging from the lining of his cloak. Then the Khadoran paused to peer at a pimp loitering between two homes or, more likely, at the streetwalker plying her trade in the murky space beyond.

The Khadoran spoke to the pimp. No coin changed hands, but given who the gang member was, the fancy man probably had better sense than to ask for any. The pair continued chatting until, still buttoning his trousers, the harlot's previous customer sidled past them. Then, coughing twice and spitting once, the thin, tattooed swordsman walked into the shadows to take his place.

Eilish smiled. It was by no means a perfect situation, but it was as good an opportunity as he and Gardek were likely to get. He counted to fifty and then, judging that had given the trollkin enough time to maneuver into position and for the Khadoran to become fully occupied with his pleasure, he advanced on the pimp.

The procurer gave him a leer. His incisors were yellow, the rest of his teeth absent. "One shield. She's pretty, and she's clean."

"I'm skeptical," Eilish replied, "but I'll pay you two shields to take a stroll."

The pimp frowned. "Whatever you've got in mind, forget it. That's my livelihood back there, and I watch over her."

"That's sensible. But I mean her no harm. With you, however, I could go either way. I'm a skilled arcanist and just as able a swordsman, and if you don't accept the coins and remove yourself from my path, I'll do it for you." He smiled and put his hand on the grip of his blade, bone carved with grooves to help a combatant hold it that much more securely.

He tried not to let his smile and the air of menacing confidence he hoped it conveyed waver as, his eyes shifting back and forth, the fancy man considered his options. Eilish suspected he could pretty much guess the other man's thoughts.

Could he snatch out the holdout pistol weighting his hip pocket, cock it, and shoot before Eilish drew and cut with his sword? If he cried for help, would the Khadoran come to his aid and do so expeditiously enough for it to matter? Ultimately, who was more to be feared, the gang member or the arcanist?

Finally, a drop of sweat seeping forth on his brow, the pimp whispered, "I'm going to get a drink. We never talked, and for certain, you never bribed me."

"Of course not." Eilish slipped the other man the coins, and the latter scurried away.

As far as Eilish could tell, the Khadoran had no idea what had just transpired. He had the streetwalker's face pressed against the left-hand wall and her skirt pulled up.

The vaguest of shadows in the gloom, Gardek appeared at the far end of the aisle between the houses. He crept forward, and Eilish did too.

After just a step or two, some trick of acoustics made the

noise of the celebration appreciably fainter, even as the darkness deepened. Eilish grinned. Now that he was inside it, this space felt more secluded, and the odds of spiriting the Khadoran away consequently better. No doubt silver would buy the streetwalker's silence just as it had purchased the pimp's cooperation.

Then the thin man stepped away from the woman and pivoted in Eilish's direction. The arcanist just had time to notice that the Khadoran had never really even opened his breeches yet. Then the outlaw snatched out his sword with one hand and ripped off his cape with the other.

Apparently the fellow had realized someone was following him and had decided to lure the stalker in close. It might have been a bold but reasonable idea—had Eilish been operating alone. But as things stood, the Khadoran was still the trapped and not the trapper. The thief takers just needed to subdue him before the confrontation could attract unwanted attention.

Eilish drew his own sword. "Run," he told the prostitute, a dark-haired woman dressed in the bedraggled remains of what had once been a gaudy spangled dress.

To his annoyance, she stayed right where she was, inconveniently near the criminal. For a moment, he imagined she was simply paralyzed with surprise or fear. Then, despite the dimness, he saw that she was staring at something behind him.

Despite the foe before him, he risked a glance over his shoulder. Swords in one hand, capes in the other, three newcomers were creeping into the aisle between the houses. When they saw that he'd spotted them, they advanced more quickly, uttering threats and taunts in Khadoran. He didn't know the words, but the poisonous tone was unmistakable.

Quashing a pang of fear, Eilish told himself that despite the enemies' superior numbers, everything was still under control. Gardek would swiftly take down the coughing man from behind and then move up to aid his partner. And while Eilish was good at close combat, the trollkin was extraordinary.

Eilish just had to keep himself alive for the next few moments. To that end, he focused his thoughts. In a fight, magic was often no more lethal than a sword cut or a gunshot, but people who couldn't work it themselves sometimes found it intimidating and balked in the face of it.

Concentrating, he shaped power to the desired end, willed the spell to manifest, and suffered a momentary twinge as it took the unavoidable toll on his vitality. A bolt of blue light shot through the air and splashed against the chest of the man in the lead. The impact jolted him backward as if a sledgehammer had hit him.

But to Eilish's disappointment, the other two Khadorans didn't falter. They kept coming, whirling and snapping their cloaks in a display made that much more deceptive and confusing by the inadequate light.

Eilish rattled off a quick incantation. Yellow flames leaped up on one of the capes, and the man holding it gave a startled yelp.

Hoping to neutralize him before he recovered from his surprise, Eilish lunged and cut to the head. But, perhaps prompted by pure trained reflex, the outlaw stepped backward and parried. Steel clashed on steel.

At the same instant, Eilish glimpsed movement from the corner of his eye. While he was busy with the one Khadoran, the other had maneuvered onto his flank. The mercenary wrenched himself around to confront the new threat, and the weighted hem of his adversary's cloak clouted him in the jaw.

The blow didn't quite stun him, and that was good, because instinct screamed that it was supposed to render him helpless to defend against a follow-up attack. With the cape dragging across his face, he was momentarily blind, but he jumped back and swept his blade in a panic parry. With a clang, it stopped a cut to the midsection.

He retreated two more steps, and his foes glided after him. Even the man he'd struck with his mystic bolt was returning to the fray. Evidently the Khadoran was tough enough to bear the pain of bloodied flesh and cracked ribs in exchange for a chance to hurt Eilish in his turn. Which meant that so far, all the arcanist had really accomplished was to deprive one opponent of the cape he'd dropped burning on the ground.

"Gardek," Eilish gritted, shifting his sword back and forth to threaten one Khadoran and then another, "whenever you finish disposing of one sickly foe, feel free to join the real fight."

Just as he finished speaking, he heard movement at his back. Grinning, he waited for the Khadorans' alarmed reaction to the hulking trollkin's approach. Then something bashed him in the back of the head.

• • •

GARDEK WATCHED THE THIN MAN whirl around, ready for combat, and then the arrival of the Khadoran's comrades, just visible as shadows at the far end of the murky corridor between the two houses. He wasn't unduly concerned because he judged that, intent on Eilish, none of the bratya killers had noticed him. In fact, the realization that everybody had been scheming to trap everybody else made him grin.

He just hoped no one would think to threaten the woman's life. That would complicate matters. But with luck, Gardek would lay the nearest wretch out before he even realized someone was sneaking up on him, and that would clear a path for the woman to flee. A shove would set her in motion if that was what was required.

Preparing to deliver a blow that would knock the average human unconscious without smashing his skull, a thump he'd mastered relatively early in his bounty-hunting career, Gardek raised his war hammer. Then he smelled coal smoke and oil and heard the *tick-tick-tick* of turning gears.

He turned around. Vague in the gloom, gripping a maul even bigger than Gardek's hammer, a metal figure was advancing on him, and the amusement he'd been feeling at the notion of one trap surrounding another withered away. Plainly, it was the Khadorans who'd out-tricked their opponents and their box containing the enemies they wanted to snare.

For another moment, as he shifted his spiked rectangular shield into what he expected would be the best position to protect against the maul, he took the approaching figure for a light steamjack. Then he noticed the human face with its fringe of dark beard inside a helmet like an overturned bowl with a square window in the front.

Not a 'jack, then, but a so-called ironhead, a Khadoran clad in steam-powered armor. Gardek had never fought one before, but he suspected they were easier to contend with than a true warjack. No doubt the pneumatic tubes and whatnot augmented the strength of the wearer, but perhaps to the detriment of speed and agility, and in any case, he was good at driving his hammer through plate to pulverize the flesh and bone inside.

He just had to get into striking distance. The maul, a two-handed weapon with a long haft, gave the ironhead a longer reach, but Gardek didn't expect that to pose a problem, even though it wasn't a situation he encountered all that often.

He stepped in, inviting an attack, and it swept in on the arc that the Khadoran's guard had led him to anticipate. He angled his shield to make the maul glance off instead of hitting squarely.

As he'd expected, metal crashed against metal. What he hadn't anticipated was the flash of pale light leaping from the point of impact. And the piercing cold that seemed to originate in his shield, surge up his arm, and stab into his torso.

The shock of it staggered him and made it impossible to deliver the riposte he'd intended. The outlaw heaved the maul back in preparation for another blow.

Snarling, Gardek strained to shake off surprise and shivering clumsiness and to shift his shield. He blocked but less deftly than before. With another clang and burst of silvery light, the weapon met the barrier dead-on.

To Gardek's dismay, the shield cracked, and the chill that leapt from it to his body was even colder. It might have stopped the heart of a creature less hardy than a trollkin.

But this time he was braced for it, and, bellowing away the shock, he simultaneously pushed the shield forward and twisted it.

He was striving to catch the head of the maul in the projecting spikes. He'd worried that as he banged and ground the armor against the weapon, he himself might trigger more surges of cold, but apparently the mechanikal device had to swing through the air or strike with considerable force for that to happen.

When the Khadoran attempted to swing back the maul, the spikes caged it. He then tried to pull it straight back like a cork popping out of a bottle.

Gardek drove forward. That both kept the maul contained and brought him close enough to use his hammer. He struck at the criminal's exposed face.

The Khadoran bent at the knees and twisted, and the stroke smashed down on top of the dome of the helmet instead of through the opening. Well, that could still work if Gardek bashed the bowl and the head inside it flat.

He struck twice more, denting the helmet but nothing more. He wondered if he should shift behind the ironhead and attack the engine. That had worked in Colbie's recent battle when she'd disabled the 'jack.

Then the ironhead let go of the maul with his right hand. Whirring, a panel in the armor protecting his forearm slid back, and a rod-like device popped up from the shallow compartment inside. With its little hole at the end, it resembled the nozzles Milo used for spraying liquids.

Gardek couldn't disentangle his shield from the maul in time to defend against the new threat but was sure he mustn't let the spray hit him in the face. He flung himself back and to the side, and fluid jetted past him to the splash against the wall of the house behind him. Foaming and hissing, the acid ate into the wood even as it trickled down to the ground. The fumes stung Gardek's eyes and filled them with tears.

As he frantically blinked to clear his sight, the maul smashed into his leg with another ring of steel and silvery flash. When he'd recoiled, the ironhead had managed to free his primary weapon. Combined with the stab of bitter chill, the impact knocked Gardek off his feet. Sidestepping, the Khadoran raised his weapon high for a blow to the head.

• • •

HIS SKULL RINGING from the blow he'd just endured, Eilish pitched forward. One of the men in front of him tossed a cape over his head and blinded him.

Eilish's body was a numb, flopping thing like an ineptly manipulated marionette. But despite the punishment he'd just endured, his brain was still working, and so he realized two things.

The first was that it was the thin Khadoran with the cough who'd just struck him from behind. Which meant something had kept Gardek from neutralizing the man.

The second was that the thin man had struck with the flat of his blade, not the edge. Otherwise, Eilish would be in worse shape than he was. His foes must want him alive for questioning even though, in the face of his own straightforward efforts to kill them, some of the other swordsmen had reflexively made potentially lethal attacks of their own.

Sure enough, it was fists and perhaps pommels that now started pounding his body. The leather cloak that was hooding him seemed to cushion the blows a little, but he was sure he had at best a few seconds remaining before they beat him insensible.

He strained to focus his mind despite the repeated jarring impacts and somehow reached the clear, calm place where magic waited. He silently told it to ward him and for an instant felt a coolness flowing over his body. A protective layer of force was covering him—Gardek too, if the trollkin was close enough.

Only a fool would expect such a spell to stop every sword cut and gunshot. It wasn't powerful enough for that. But combined with the cape and Eilish's suit of plate, it diminished the beating his foes were trying to administer to a harmless pattering.

He fell to his knees. That should persuade the Khadorans they were making progress and so give him another moment or two to recover his strength.

When he was ready, he gripped his sword and stabbed. He was reasonably confident of hitting someone's leg when his foes were clustered all around him, and as he'd hoped, the blade bit. A man squawked.

At once, Eilish thrust in the opposite direction, only higher, and felt his point slide into flesh. He yanked it back, wrenched himself around, and cut at what he hoped was the coughing man's location.

This time he didn't connect, but he sensed his foes recoiling from the unexpected onslaught. He simultaneously scrambled to his feet and clawed the cape off his head.

Two of the Khadorans were still unscathed. One was on the ground, doubled up on his side and clutching his perforated belly. The one with the newly gashed leg turned out to be the same fellow Eilish had previously struck with a flare of magic. He was hobbling now and leaving a trail of blood in his wake but was still game for the fight.

What did it take to discourage these maniacs? Eilish drew a deep breath and placed his back to the wall. At least that way, he wouldn't have to worry about another attack from behind.

• • •

SHAKING, TEETH CHATTERING, Gardek rolled onto his side and tried to raise his shield to intercept the maul. He was afraid the defense would prove inadequate. The ironhead might well batter through it before Gardek shook off the effects of the last blow he'd taken.

But as the maul hurtled down, a tingling flowed over Gardek's body. He recognized the sensation. Eilish must have worked the magic that gave them an extra layer of paper-thin but resilient armor—and about time, too.

The maul crashed down on the shield in a burst of white and then glanced away, snapping off a spike at the base as it skipped. New cracks erupted in a spider web pattern from the point of impact.

But the chill that pierced Gardek's body wasn't quite the debilitating jolt it had been before. Evidently Eilish's enchantment protected against even that.

As the maul cocked back over the Khadoran's head, Gardek bellowed, hooked his war hammer behind the ironhead's ankle, and pulled. The Khadoran's steel-booted foot jerked forward and, his balance possibly further compromised by the weight and position of his own weapon, he toppled, banging down on the fuming smokestack rising from his back and the engine and boiler beneath it.

As Gardek knew from past experience, if a fellow knocked down a 'jack or, presumably, an ironhead, many of them could stand back up again. But few could do so quickly.

Gardek wasn't feeling all that spry himself, but he clambered up to take advantage of his adversary's vulnerability, At the same time, faster than he expected, the Khadoran floundered to one knee and pointed his left arm. A hatch in the bulky cowling whirred open, and a miniature cannon sprang up. It fired with a bang and a puff of steam.

Gardek covered himself with his shield. The resulting impact knocked him stumbling backward just the same, and his shield shattered, leaving him with only the straps and a jagged piece no bigger than a buckler.

Considering how the strokes of the maul had hindered him even when he was catching them on the shield, its loss boded ill. Still, if he just could strike before the ironhead finished using the weapon like a staff to heave himself to his feet. Gardek advanced once more, and then Eilish cried out.

The trollkin looked around. On the other side of the cowering prostitute, who'd apparently either never found an opportunity to get clear of the fight or lacked the courage to seize it, Eilish stood at bay with his back against the right-hand wall. His face was bloody and the back of his head more so, the yellow hair there now dark and matted with gore. He was defending himself with all his considerable ability, but three against one was long odds for any swordsman. As Gardek watched, he parried two cuts by the narrowest of margins and failed to riposte either time.

Gardek roared and charged in his friend's direction. Startled, the Khadoran swordsmen jerked around, stared, and gave ground. The two unwounded ones were quick enough to keep away from him. The one limping on the bleeding leg was not.

Instead, the outlaw whipped his cape around the hammer, entangling it, and made a sword thrust with his other hand. Luckily, his point failed to penetrate Gardek's breastplate. Gardek kicked, and the spikes jutting from the toe of his boot plunged into the swordsman's guts. Without setting his foot back down, he kicked again, and the action shook the Khadoran loose to drop backward onto the ground.

It felt good to finally hurt somebody. But Gardek's momentary satisfaction dissolved when he saw that the two surviving sword-and-cape fighters—the skinny, coughing dastard and one with jug-handle ears and a wide simpleton's grin—had stopped running and that the ironhead was just finishing the process of standing up.

Gardek took another appraising look at Eilish's battered face and considered his own condition as well. He no longer felt like he was on the verge of freezing to death, but a certain unsteadiness remained, periodically aggravated by trembling fits and a kind of raw ache.

"Unless you can work some really powerful magic," he whispered, "we aren't going to win this."

"Whatever happens," Eilish panted, "we aren't likely to take a prisoner alive for questioning, and that was the errand. So, if you see a way, I propose we withdraw."

"Agreed." Gardek let go of his war hammer, and the weapon dropped to the end of the leather thong that looped around his wrist. He grabbed Eilish, startling a yelp out of him, picked him up, and thrust him at the window of the derelict house beside them. The arcanist crashed through into the darkness on the other side.

Gardek then jumped and struggled to squirm through himself, while the spikes on his armor caught on the frame and then tore free in little bursts of rotting wood chips. Impacts clanked on the back of him, but as far as he could tell, the sword strokes weren't penetrating his plate. He hoped not, anyway.

Hands gripped his ankles and tried to pull him backward. He kicked them loose and then managed to drag himself inside.

The interior of the house was even darker than the alleyway running between it and its neighbor. Eilish was just a shadow picking himself up off the floor amid broken glass and oiled paper. "A little warning next time," he gasped.

Then he pointed his sword, and glowing blue symbols flickered in the air around him. A bolt of azure light streaked past Gardek and out the window. A man squawked.

Gardek cast about and found a rectangular shape that he took to be a cabinet standing against the wall. He heaved it to the window and pushed, and it toppled out amid a rattling and crashing of dislodged crockery. It smashed into the ironhead, who had his maul poised to smash his way inside, and knocked him stumbling backward.

For an instant, Gardek considered making a stand in this place. But two fighters couldn't defend every door and window, and besides, given the chance, the ironhead and his comrades might summon reinforcements. Now that the bounty hunter and Eilish had disengaged from their foes, they'd do better to keep running.

Gardek grabbed a chair and flung it after the cabinet. Then he ran toward the front of the house, where he was sure of finding a door. Eilish pounded after him.

Gardek tripped over an unseen something lying on the floor. Behind him, something thudded as Eilish bumped into it, and the arcanist snarled an obscenity. Then they stumbled into the front room, where the light of the fires and lanterns illuminating the impromptu festival shone through the windows bracketing the door.

The bounty hunter opened the door. To his relief, the Khadorans weren't waiting right outside. He suspected they were still beside the house, maybe regrouping or discussing tactics for breaking in. In any case, it appeared the mercenaries had a moment or two—likely no more—to lose themselves in the crowd.

Eilish sheathed his sword and pulled up the hood of his cloak, no doubt to conceal his yellow hair and the blood soaking it. Then walking fast but not so fast, Gardek hoped, as to draw attention, the two thief takers strode out to join the revelers.

Slurring, a drunken human tried to divert Eilish for some indecipherable purpose, and the arcanist shook him off. Gardek's leg started to ache where the maul had struck it. The smells of roasting meat and too many unwashed Undercity dwellers rubbing shoulders hung in the air.

"I trust," Eilish said, "that you're leading me to the nearest exit."

"Yes. There's a tunnel up ahead."

"Good. I confess I'm not feeling my best. I'm seeing double, and—"

At their backs, a rough voice shouted a word in what Gardek took to be Khadoran.

He glanced around. The ironhead and the two swordsmen who were still on their feet had found their way back into the center of the vault. Worse, they'd spotted their retreating foes.

"It's not enough that you're enormous," Eilish said. "You have to affix spikes to your armor to make yourself even more conspicuous. Are you beginning to see the problem with that?"

"Shut up and keep moving," Gardek growled. Maybe they could stay ahead of the ironhead. He and his bulky armor might have difficulty making his way through the throng. And if the swordsmen were reckless enough to race ahead of their ally, well, Gardek would deal with them. He shifted his grip on his hammer.

Then the ironhead bellowed, "One hundred crowns for the men who help us take down the trollkin with the spikes and the wizard in black plate!"

Gardek sensed a kind of ripple run through the crowd. A wolfish hunger lit up their eyes.

He brandished his hammer. "Come and try."

Meanwhile, brow knit in concentration, Eilish rattled off an incantation that produced a burst of flame at the feet of a pair of the nearest ruffians. They yelped and jumped backward.

In fact, for a moment, it appeared to Gardek that he and his partner had succeeded in daunting all the scoundrels in their immediate vicinity. Then the ironhead shouted, "*Five* hundred crowns!"

A man in patched, filthy leather eased his hand toward the

short sword half concealed beneath his coat. Gardek lunged and smashed his skull.

That was one down, but other humans, ogrun, and gobbers were likewise readying weapons. A pistol flashed and barked. The shot missed Eilish and hit a man behind him. Better aimed, a throwing knife caught Gardek in the shoulder but glanced off his pauldron. Other people who opted to attack at range made do with flung bottles, rocks, and clods of mud. Something hard thumped the back of Gardek's head.

The Khadoran swordsmen were loping forward, and the man with the maul was tramping along behind him. The crowd wasn't slowing him down after all—not anymore, anyway. They were scurrying out of the way.

Gardek had been in a plenty of tight spots in his time. Yet even so, for an instant, fear flickered through his mind because this one seemed truly inescapable. Then, casting about, he realized that as they made their way toward the now unreachable tunnel, he and Eilish had wandered close to a high, narrow house.

Swinging his hammer back and forth, he pushed in that direction while, sword in hand, Eilish slashed and stabbed. Their combined efforts sufficed to clear a path, in part perhaps because the mob believed they were about to fetch up at a spot from which there was nowhere else to go.

Three men dodged aside, two to the left and one to the right, like curtains parting, and then the sinkhole yawned before the mercenaries. Eilish gave a crooked smile. "This is the new plan?"

"If you have a better idea, now's the time to trot it out." Gardek nodded to indicate the mob, the Khadoran swordsmen who'd nearly closed to striking distance, and the ironhead with his belching smokestack only a pace behind them.

"Sadly, no." The arcanist sheathed his blade and stepped over the edge of the drop, and Gardek followed.

— 9 —

AS MILO UNDERSTOOD IT, the Undercity existed because of its proximity to the Black River and the Dragon's Tongue, the great watercourses that diverged in Corvis. Over the ages, subterranean side channels and tributaries had carved out the tunnels, sinking the buildings on the surface into the mire below.

Despite that aqueous origin, there were vaults and passages where water was hard to come by. Since his arrival in the City of Ghosts, Milo had watched clans and tribes fight vicious battles for control of a well or a stream.

He did not, however, recall any such contention over Poison Pond, the small dark lake currently reflecting the glow of his bottled light. Many people believed it unwholesome because of runoff from manufactories on the surface. Others maintained there were tombs on the bottom, and the occupants resented their submergence. A few held that a drowned Orgoth relic tainted the water or that the city's unpleasant founders had practiced unholy rites hereabouts.

But everyone agreed it was dangerous to drink from the pond, eat the malformed fish that swam and spawned in it, or breathe the dank mist that sometimes formed above it. In fact, Milo knew of only one group that would willingly live on its shore, and that, of course, was the gang that had built the ramshackle little palisaded fortress yonder.

As he circled the lake, Milo walked slowly and held his bottled light high so no one could imagine he was trying to sneak up on the stronghold. Meanwhile, the snake in the box he carried tucked under his arm stirred and hissed as though even it disliked the polluted atmosphere.

"Hush," Milo told it. "You're venomous yourself. You should feel right at home."

"Who goes there?" called a voice from the top of the palisade.

Milo tensed. The Undercity being what it was, he was sure he now had an arrow or a rifle trained on him, and unlike his fellow Black River Irregulars, he'd never quite mastered the knack of facing such threats with unruffled aplomb. Still, the crisp military style of the challenge bemused him. Perhaps the sentry had once been a soldier. After all, Corvis was crawling with them, which meant its shadow self served as a refuge for a fair number of deserters.

Juggling the snake and the bottled light, he tugged his gas mask down around his neck so it wouldn't muffle his voice. "Milo Boggs! I want to talk to Druce Keller! He knows me, and I brought a gift for him!"

"Approach the gate!"

Milo did as he'd been told. Something that sounded bigger than anything in such a small lake ought to be broke the surface, swam a sinusoidal course, and dived back down without him ever getting a good look at it. He suspected hearing it was better than seeing it up close.

He had to stand outside the gate, plainly constructed of whatever scavenged or pilfered lumber had come to hand but sturdy-looking nonetheless, before it creaked open on unoiled hinges. The two pale men on the other side gave the impression of deformity without him being able to pinpoint why. Did this one have a right ear larger than the left? Was that one walking on legs that didn't have their knees at quite the same height, or did his mouth extend a little wider on one side than the other? A person might need calipers like those Eilish employed in his forensic examinations to tell for sure, but there was no doubt that in the aggregate, all the miniscule, indefinable asymmetries scraped at an observer's nerves like a picture hanging crooked on a wall.

"Box," said the one with the possibly mismatched knees.

Milo handed it over. "Be careful peeking in. He's just eaten a mouse, so he should be sleepy. But then again, you never know."

Funny Knees unlatched the hinged lid with its air holes, lifted it just enough to peer at the contents, then hastily lowered and fastened it again.

"Weapons," said Mismatched Ears.

Milo surrendered his bandoliers and then allowed Mismatched Ears to frisk him. "I'll take the box back if you don't mind. That's my present for your boss."

Funny Knees returned it. Mismatched Ears waved him on across what amounted to a castle courtyard, if a person was willing to dignify the rotting, rickety structure with that term. To its credit, at least it had gaslights burning again. When Milo had last visited, the gas company had discovered and shut off the illegal tap, but evidently the Jagged Knives had turned it on again.

The illumination aided Milo as he peered about, counting gang members and noting their locations. He had no reason to think he'd need the information, but having and not requiring was vastly preferable to the other way around.

When his taciturn escorts ushered him into the large building at the back of the palisaded enclosure, the look of the place improved. The basic construction was no less shoddy, but the furnishings—a ticking clock with brass weights here, a porcelain vase of fashionable blown-glass roses there—might have been stolen from the home of some well-to-do burgher in the city above.

The two Jagged Knives ultimately conducted Milo to a spacious laboratory, brightly lit and well appointed with racks of vials and jars, mortars and pestles, burners, alembics, and athanors. It too might have looked out of place in the Undercity except for the brain, eyeballs, and heart currently floating in sealed glass containers with low flame burning underneath each.

Druce Keller was a stout, ruddy-faced man with a luxuriant white moustache and side-whiskers. In seeming contradiction to Poison Pond's ominous reputation, his appearance bespoke robust vitality. Upon seeing Milo, he left off dripping blue-green oil from a pipette into a beaker of cloudy liquid and bustled over to wring the other's hand.

"My dear fellow!" Keller said in his plummy voice. Then he turned his smile on his subordinates. "You can leave us. Mr. Boggs and I are colleagues."

"Yes, sir," said Funny Knees. "We'll be close if you need us." He and Mismatched Ears went back through the door and shut it behind them.

"Remarkable," Keller said. "Many of those poor fellows die well before their times serving me, and at the end, the cold requirements of commerce deny them even a decent burial. The substances that collect in their tissues are simply too valuable to leave unextracted. Yet their devotion never wavers. Would you say that reflects the basic nobility of the human spirit or our fundamental shortsightedness?"

Milo shrugged. "People who live down here can't depend on a long life or a funeral in any case. Gang members run out their time in pleasanter circumstances than most, especially when they work for the alchemist who concocts some of the more interesting—and addictive—narcotics in town."

"I can always depend on you to focus on the practical aspects of a question. I suppose that's why you concern yourself with natural philosophy to the exclusion of the more ethereal sort."

Milo disliked the condescension implicit in the other man's remark but saw no advantage in saying so. Instead, he proffered the box. "I brought you something."

Keller set the box on a clear corner of a worktable. When he opened it, his blue eyes widened beneath their bushy white brows. "Is that a swamp adder?"

"Yes. I suspect the venom is useful. For more than the obvious, I mean."

"It's the first one I've ever seen, which makes it a handsome present indeed. So handsome, in fact, that I infer you're hoping for something in return."

"Now that you mention it."

Keller closed and latched the box. "Well, rest assured I'll oblige you if I possibly can. Let's talk about it in my study." He gestured to a second door.

The room on the other side was also the preserve of a scholar but full of bookshelves instead of alchemical equipment. One crimson-bound set of two dozen volumes comprised Keller's own experimental journals, penned over the course of several decades. To all appearances, the skull on the mantelpiece was nothing more than the standard academic affectation, but Milo had heard it once belonged to a rival criminal who'd made himself particularly obnoxious.

Keller moved to the sideboard, poured two generous drinks, and conveyed the snifters and crystal decanter to his desk. "I trust you still like brandy. This is the good stuff, up from Caspia."

"I like it all right." Seated on opposite sides of the desk, the two alchemists saluted one another. As far as Milo was concerned, any rotgut that had a kick and didn't make you blind qualified as "the good stuff," but he privately conceded that the brandy burned pleasantly going down.

"Now, then," Keller said, "how can I help you?"

"You know about the Patient Weavers getting wiped out?"

Keller's eyes narrowed. "Certainly. I daresay most everyone dwelling in the Undercity has heard by now."

"I'm trying to find out about the new gang that did it."

"And why, my fellow seeker of truth, are you interested?"

"In case they want to hire someone like me."

The stout man chuckled. It made his pink jowls wobble. "Or me."

"You already have a thriving business to finance your research.

I don't. If there's work to be had, let me take it, and I'll cut you in for a finder's fee."

"I am busy, and that does sound reasonable." Keller topped off the two snifters. "But may I speak frankly?"

"You should." Milo took another sip of his drink.

"Some rumormongers whisper that you're not the same Milo Boggs we knew of old. That these days, you've partnered with Gardek Stonebrow and Eilish Garrity, thief takers both in their respective fashions."

Milo's mouth abruptly felt dry. He swallowed. "There are always crazy rumors flying around."

"But how crazy are these, really? Before you answer, remember, I myself collect information as assiduously as I can. It's the best way to survive down here, and it's the very reason you came to consult me, is it not?"

Milo felt a drop of sweat ooze from his hairline down onto his brow. "All right, I am a partner in the Black River Irregulars. But we're mercenaries, soldiers for hire, and mostly not thief takers."

"'*Mostly* not.'"

"When we caught the tunnel killer, that came as a relief to everybody in the Undercity, and anyway, if you really know that story, you know I didn't have a choice."

"And afterward?"

"Since then…" Milo swallowed again. "I admit there have been a couple times we've worked for the Watch. But never to do anything worse than the clans and syndicates do to one another."

"What about now?"

Milo's pulse beat in the side of his neck. He took a long breath in the hope of quieting it. "Look. You got me. The Watch needs information to root out the new gang before they get themselves established, and the Irregulars are going to provide it. But why is that bad? These new killers are strangers, outsiders, and you see how ruthlessly they dealt with some of our own."

"Yes, it would be hard to miss that."

Milo opened his mouth to say, *Then help me*. But suddenly Keller's form rippled before him as if he were viewing it at the bottom of a stream. A tingling pricked his fingertips and toes, and a dazed confusion overtook him.

Though the twinges in his digits persisted, after a second his sight and thoughts returned to normal, and then he knew. The dry mouth, sweating, and throbbing pulse hadn't been just because he was edgy. In addition to trading in narcotics, Druce Keller had at one time been the Undercity's foremost poisoner for hire, and now the genial old murderer had poisoned *him*.

• • •

UPON REACHING THE CRUMBLING RIM of the sinkhole, Eilish had discerned that Gardek's escape plan wasn't quite as suicidal as it could have been. The wall below him wasn't perpendicular. Rather, there was a slope, albeit a steep one.

When he'd jumped, he'd tried to land and slide on his rump, and for a second or two, he managed it. Then his foot jammed into some sort of protrusion, and that spun him. Suddenly he was bouncing and tumbling like a log rolling down a mountainside in a choking shower of earth. Meanwhile, the firelight shining down from the vault overhead dimmed to blackness. Somewhere off to his left, Gardek's armor clanked and rattled.

Eilish was certain he and the trollkin had no chance of surviving this plunge if they couldn't see. He dug a vial of Milo's bottled light from an inner pocket of his cloak, but another bounce jolted the container from his hand even as it clacked his teeth together. The mixture inside the tumbling bottle flared to life for an instant. Then the vial smashed against a lump of rock, and darkness swallowed everything once more.

Eilish realized it didn't matter that his bumping descent was stabbing fresh pain through his battered head or that he'd already cast several spells in quick succession. He needed to find the wherewithal for another. He gasped and grunted out an incantation.

Silvery light flowered around him. The glow illuminated what might be some semblance of a narrow ledge farther down. Despite the glimmering magic now pushing back the dark, it was hard to be sure. But even if it was what he hoped, it wasn't directly underneath him.

"There!" he shouted and ended up with a mouthful of dust and grit. With a shove and a wrench of his shoulders, he sought to alter the path of his descent.

For a long moment, there was no solidity beneath him, and a pang of fear told him that his frantic effort had flipped him far enough away from the slope that now he would simply fall and fall and fall. Then he slammed back down and rolled some more.

He crashed down on the rounded little ledge and started to bounce and slide onward. He clutched madly for something to arrest his plunge. His right hand found a hollow in the dirt, and his left, a piece of rock sticking out of it. With a jerk he felt from his fingers up into his shoulders, the double grip arrested his descent.

Realizing his feet were sticking out into space, he drew them onto the ledge and then lay there shuddering, panting, and coughing. Only for a second, though. Only until he remembered Gardek. Then, his eyes stinging, full of grit and the tears it brought, he raised his head and cast about him for his companion.

When he did, he discovered that, perhaps because of irregularities in the slope, he'd descended faster than his partner. Sliding feet first on his stomach, Gardek was a moment away from hurtling past the end of the ledge. Grimly aware that the trollkin's momentum might well snatch him from his perch, Eilish nonetheless extended his hand. Then he perceived that Gardek was too far away to reach it in any case.

With a noise that was half roar and half grunt, the trollkin jammed his war hammer into the surface beneath him. Steel grated on stone, and he too jerked to a halt.

Panting, he clung to the hammer for a moment. Then he spat dirt from his mouth, studied the several feet of wall that separated him from the ledge, freed his weapon from the crack where it had lodged, and started to clamber across. Prepared to extend his hand again if required, Eilish watched his partner's progress.

Grasping handholds that the wizard would have hesitated to trust even if he recognized them as such, Gardek made it halfway. Then objects rained down from overhead. The mob back up in the vault was throwing them. A bottle shattered on the bounty hunter's shoulder armor but fortunately without shaking his grip or flinging glass in his eye.

"You had to light us up," Gardek growled.

"Would you have seen where to stick your hammer if I hadn't?" Eilish replied. "I recommend you hurry up."

"Shift back and give me room." Eilish did, and the trollkin hauled himself onto the ledge. "Now we find out if there's anywhere to go from here. Stand up and hug the wall."

When Eilish rose, dizziness assailed him, and for an instant he felt like he was toppling backward. And perhaps he actually did, for Gardek grabbed him by the forearm.

Once the trollkin released him, he sidled while the harassment from above continued. A fist-sized stone bounced past him. A firearm banged.

"Before long," Gardek said, "someone with a gun or crossbow will decide to circle around to the other side of the top of the sinkhole. It's a longer shot, but the angle's better."

"You always know what to say to cheer a person up," Eilish replied. Then his magical light revealed a vertical fold in the wall. When he moved directly in front of it, the narrow gap writhed away into the earth past the point where the glow gave way to shadow. "This might be something. If you can squirm through."

"Go. I'm right behind you."

Eilish clambered into the gap. Meanwhile, Gardek tore at the buckles securing his spiky cuirass and shoulder armor, then dropped the metal to slide, roll, and clatter down the slope. He managed to edge in after his companion, although he still filled the space around him like a cork in the neck of a bottle and couldn't advance an inch without the spikes on his remaining pieces of armor snagging and scraping on the walls.

But to Eilish's relief, Gardek never got so stuck that he couldn't strain his way forward, and eventually the space widened out into something approximating a proper tunnel. At that point, the arcanist sat down on the floor.

"How bad is your head?" Gardek asked.

"Not so bad," Eilish said. He hoped he was correct. "I just want to catch my breath. Unless you think someone climbed down the sinkhole and is about to overtake us."

"I doubt that even the Khadorans are that crazy." The trollkin sat down with his back against the opposite wall.

"Perhaps they aren't crazy at all. After all, they out-played the two of us. I hate that."

"And I hate being outfought, even by a living warjack with an ice-cold war club."

"The Khadorans call them ice mauls."

"Whatever they call them, how the hell does it freeze and shatter steel?'

"It's a mechanikal weapon. There's magic in the mix."

Gardek spat. "Well, that won't stop me next time."

"Let's hope there is one. First, we have to find our way out of here. How lost are we?"

The bounty hunter snorted. "Not too. I hope. An unfamiliar tunnel can always surprise you, but I have a hunch where this one comes out. Someone back at the celebration may have an idea, too, so if you're ready, we should get moving before he sells the information to the bratya."

"Right." Trying unsuccessfully to squint away his double vision, Eilish struggled to his feet.

• • •

KELLER EYED MILO CURIOUSLY. Specifically, Milo now realized, with the interest of a poisoner watching to see if his victim was going to succumb to the dose forthwith or if a brief period of consciousness remained.

Milo prayed it was the latter. His mentor, the apothecary who'd taken a grubby swampie boy in off the street and made him his apprentice, had also been a poisoner, and early on in his studies the novice alchemist had hit upon the idea of ingesting nonlethal quantities of a variety of toxins on a regular basis.

The process was supposed to increase his resistance, and over the years, it had demonstrated its value, protecting him against potentially fatal laboratory mishaps and even adder venom just the other night. But by itself it was unlikely to save him from whatever Keller had slipped into his drink while topping it off.

Milo was willing to wager his life on his ability to mix an antidote from the other alchemist's extensive supply of minerals, herbs, and compounds—but only if he could identify what he'd been given. And only if he could reach the laboratory next door and do the work, even though he was already impaired.

"Are you all right?" Keller asked.

"Fine," Milo mumbled, trying to sound as if he were still addled. "I just… I'm fine." He reached for his snifter.

Raising it back to his lips required as much willpower as anything he'd ever done. He sniffed, and then, when that told him nothing, took a far more modest sip than the hearty slug he'd gulped before and swished it around in his mouth like Eilish at his most pretentious.

The contaminant in the liquor smacked of bitter cinnamon. It annoyed him that he hadn't recognized the subtle taint before, although how would a man like him know how fine brandy was supposed to taste?

The important thing was that he recognized somnolence elixir now and so knew he wasn't on the brink of death. The compound only rendered a man insensible. That seemed preferable, even though he knew that if he passed out and Keller handed him off to the Khadorans, his long-range prospects were bleak at best.

Trying to be surreptitious about it, he spat his mouthful of brandy back into his glass and set it down. Then he swayed, flopped his head forward, and let out a little moan.

"My dear fellow!" Keller said. "Are you unwell?"

Milo glared at him. "You drugged me!"

"Well… yes."

Milo swallowed twice, the first time because his mouth truly was going dry again, the second for show. "Why?"

"Because the Khadorans will want to question the man who came snooping around trying to pick up their trail. You see, unfortunately, you're late to the game. The boss of the new gang already paid me a call. We've come to an understanding." He smiled. "No hard feelings, eh? It's just business."

The rippling came back. Milo blinked it away and kept blinking after it departed. "Why would you make that deal?"

"Because a syndicate that destroyed the Patient Weavers could easily do the same to my modest operation."

"And will, when they're ready. Or else take it away from you."

Keller sighed. "Those possibilities have occurred to me, but at least this way I have the chance to prepare for eventualities. You know how it is, my friend. In the Undercity, even the best of us must address the task of survival one day at a time."

The tingling in Milo's fingertips and toes stung its way onward into his hands and feet. "The best way to guarantee your survival is to help me."

"And in so doing, help Helstrom and the Watch? Forgive me if I doubt that they would make my welfare a priority. Too many fools from prosperous families have come to grief from overindulgence in my product. No, I prefer to cast my lot with my fellow outlaws. At least I understand how they think."

The prickling was advancing on Milo's elbows and knees. His thoughts slipped away, and at first he didn't even want to snatch after them. He just wanted to let his eyes close and rest. Then a stab of panic jolted him alert. For a few more seconds, anyway.

He swallowed and found that it scarcely helped the parched feeling anymore. "Where are you taking me?" he croaked. "Where's the Khadorans' hideout?"

"I have no idea," Keller said. "It's a secret. But I'm sure that one of them will pay me another call in due course. Or that one of my fellows will run into one of theirs when they're both out and about. Meanwhile, you'll enjoy my hospitality."

Damn it. Milo had hoped that Keller might reveal information to someone he imagined he'd rendered helpless, but apparently the stout man actually didn't know anything of importance.

Time then to set about the task of saving himself, not that he could afford to delay any longer in any case. He'd been exaggerating his reactions to the somnolence elixir, but the pretense was swiftly becoming reality.

"To hell with your hospitality," he croaked. "I've… I've got something to… to counter your drug."

He fumbled with one of the pockets built into his leather armor. His hand was so numb that it truly was difficult to take hold of the vial inside.

Everything depended on what Keller did next. If he shouted for Mismatched Ears and Funny Knees, then Milo's playacting had been for nothing. But if he believed that the drug had so weakened his prisoner that assistance was unnecessary…

Keller rose, circled the desk, and took hold of Milo's wrist. "I'm sorry, but I can't allow you to take that."

Using his free hand, Milo punched at the older man's solar plexus.

The numbing drug in his system was making him clumsy. In addition, he disliked close combat. His preferred style of fighting was to throw grenades and knives at a foe who had no way of attacking at range and then, if said foe kept advancing, run away.

But no one survived in the swamp or the gutters of Corvis without learning to scuffle, and his fist landed hard and on target. Keller's mouth fell open and the air *whuffed* out of his lungs.

Milo lurched up from his chair, and the floor tilted underneath. He avoided falling down by grabbing Keller's shoulder. He wrestled the stout man facedown on top of the desk and gripped the fleshy sides of his neck in a blood choke.

After several seconds, Keller slumped into unconsciousness. Just in time. The rippling came back, only now there was a greyness to it, as though the gaslight were dimming. It reminded him that he had more pressing concerns than revenge.

Milo finished extracting the vial from his leather vest, uncorked it, and gulped the metallic-tasting contents. Then he threw back his head and groaned through gritted teeth as his muscles clenched.

When they unlocked, he was sweating even more copiously,

and his heart was pounding even harder than before. But the numbness and somnolence had abated. Unfortunately, the stimulant he'd just imbibed would only hold them at bay for a little while. He still needed the specific antidote for somnolence elixir.

Hoping that no one had heard him struggling with Keller or was in the habit of looking in on the laboratory just on general principles, he stumbled toward the door and threw it open. The space beyond the threshold was empty.

Seeking the ingredients he needed, he hurried from shelf to shelf. Praise be to Corben that Keller was a methodical sort with a penchant for alphabetical order. For a moment, the rippling came back and smudged the labels on the bottles and jars into illegibility, but Milo closed his eyes tightly and willed the distortion away. When he opened them, he could make out his fellow alchemist's crabbed handwriting, if only barely.

Certain he didn't have time for measuring, he scooped and poured his ingredients into a beaker, estimating as best he could then stirred while they bubbled and steamed. When he'd combined them thoroughly, he guzzled the compound down.

Nausea racked him. Clutching the edge of a worktable, he strained to keep the antidote from coming right back up. Then the sickness subsided, and he took stock of himself.

The effects of the knockout drug were gone. The stimulant was still in his blood, making his heart slam and ratcheting his nerves tight, but he could tolerate that as he had on many previous occasions. It was time to make his escape.

He pulled his gas mask back up onto his face. Then, again availing himself of Keller's supplies, he prepared two beakers of clear liquid.

Holding one in each black-gloved hand, he stood beside the door though which he'd initially entered the laboratory. Then, doing his best to imitate Keller's rich, jolly voice, he called, "Lads! Come here! I need you!"

The door opened immediately and in so doing hid Milo from whoever was entering. Peeking around the edge of it, he spied

Mismatched Ears and Funny Knees. They'd been hovering near as promised.

He splashed the contents of one beaker on the back of Mismatched Ears' head. The acid sizzled, dissolving hair and skin. Mismatched Ears gasped and staggered.

Funny Knees lurched around, and Milo tossed the remaining acid. In the process, a bit of it slopped out onto his fingers, but that was all right. It couldn't eat through his glove.

The acid spattered Funny Knee's left arm, and his mouth contorted as it burned through his sleeve. "Listen to me!" Milo said. "I can neutralize that. Save your arm and maybe even your friend's life. Tell me where my bandoliers are." Meanwhile, still stumbling about, trying to claw away the stuff eating into his head and merely succeeding in burning his fingers as well, Mismatched Ears started shrieking.

Funny Knees probably had screams welling up inside him, too, but he forced out words instead. "Right outside. On the table."

"Good." Keeping his eye on the two Jagged Knives, Milo sidled backed toward the exit.

"Please," Funny Knees gritted, "you promised."

So what? Milo thought. But then, on impulse, he said, "Big green bottle in the far left corner."

The bandoliers were where Funny Knees had said they'd be. Milo hastily donned them, pulled his long coat back on top of them, and considered going back into the lab and putting a knife in Mismatched Ears. The man was still howling, and someone was likely to hear. But then, passing out or dying, he fell silent.

Milo prowled onward, listening all the while. He didn't hear anyone else moving around in this building or any commotion outside.

He cracked open the door to the courtyard. Previously, he'd noted three Jagged Knives besides Mismatched Ears and Funny Knees: the sentry on the wall and two men in the vicinity of the long shed where the gang manufactured and packaged its more easily compounded narcotics. At the moment, he could see none of them.

He decided he'd rather keep moving than hold his position

until he pinpointed their locations. Crouching low and keeping to the shadows, he crept toward the gate.

"Halt!" shouted a voice from overhead. It was barking the command in the same sharp, soldierly manner he'd noted before.

Raising his hands, Milo turned and looked up. As expected, the man on the wall had a rifle trained on him.

"Take it easy," Milo said. "Keller and I finished our business, and now I'm just making my way out."

"Where are your escorts?" the guard replied.

"Right," Milo said. "About that..."

He lunged for the cover of a small cart. As he dived down behind it, the rifle banged, but the round missed.

Milo considered striking back at his attacker while the man was reloading, but it was a long throw at an elevated target, and he doubted he could make it. Instead he yanked a grenade from its loop on the bandolier, pulled the pin, and hurled it at the long shed.

The missile exploded in a flash of vitriolic fire, which then hung in the air. For a second, Milo feared that despite the fierce heat and the blazing cloud's persistence, the damp, rotting structure wouldn't catch, but then blue and yellow flames rippled up the wall.

The sentry cried out in dismay. Milo wasn't surprised. The building was likely full of necessary supplies and equipment, perhaps even narcotics awaiting distribution.

The other two men he'd seen before scurried out of the shed. They were on the same side of the cart that he was, so it couldn't shield or hide him from them. But they were too intent on the blaze to notice him.

He tossed a smoke grenade a few feet ahead of the cart. After a moment, it blew apart, and thick grey vapor billowed forth and engulfed him.

Inside it, he could see almost nothing. Even the cart was just a ghost of itself, while the burning shed and the gaslights were only smudges of glow.

Good. That meant no one should be able to see him either. He ran toward the spot where he reckoned the gate ought to be.

It was. As he slid the bar in its brackets, the rifle banged, and the shot cracked into the wood mere inches from his head. He realized the gate was at the fringe of the cloud he'd created where it didn't really conceal him anymore and that the sentry had been waiting for him to appear there.

Milo yanked the gate partway open, flung himself through the gap, and kept on running through the darkness, relying on memory to keep him on course. That was preferable to kindling a light for the sentry to shoot at. Periodically he tripped, and after a while his boots splashed in water when he blundered into the edge of Poison Pond.

But nobody fired at him again. Perhaps the sentry had decided his time would be better spent fighting the fire before it consumed the shed or, worse, found its way to whatever the Jagged Knives had improvised in the way of an illegal gas line.

Panting, glancing over his shoulder periodically, Milo decided he might enjoy seeing the gang's lair disintegrate in a spectacular explosion. But in that regard too, he was disappointed.

— 10 —

DESPITE HIS RECENT SUCCESSES, Ivan was in a foul mood because Gridia and Fodor had failed to pick up Canice Gormleigh's trail. It had only been with difficulty that he'd refrained from heaping abuse on their heads, contenting himself with knocking around his leashed gobber instead.

Still, as the four of them entered the vault, he forced a smile. He wanted to arrive at the celebration he'd provided like a beneficent lord.

Unfortunately, it soon became apparent that something was wrong here, too. Some people were still drinking and partaking of other amusements. No doubt others were still enjoying the carnal entertainment in the red-and-pink brothel up ahead. But he hadn't found quite the atmosphere of riotous, all-encompassing abandon he'd expected. A number of the wretches of the Undercity were standing in small groups talking among themselves, and when they spied Ivan and his companions, they fell silent and watched them pass. With some measure of fear and respect, certainly, but also with speculation.

What the hell had happened?

Ivan strode into the brothel. "Everybody out!" he bellowed.

People gaped at him but didn't move. Perhaps drunkenness made them slow to understand the implied threat.

Gridia gave them all a sunny smile. "Please run along, dears. I know you wouldn't want to make us cross."

That got everyone moving. In a few moments the parlor emptied out, leaving a red-and-purple chaos of strewn cushions, emptied and spilled cups and bottles, and discarded clothing. Ivan didn't know whether to be pleased or annoyed that Gridia had succeeded where he'd failed. Apparently even his roar was less intimidating than the happy light of madness shining in the plump woman's eyes.

"Olekse!" he shouted.

The ironhead came out of a door partway down the hall that ran off the parlor. His forehead was bruised, and he held his dented helmet in his hands. Evidently there'd been a fight.

"Where are the others?" Ivan asked, switching to their native tongue.

"I've got Iakshen and Ladimir walking around patrolling. Jachemir and Rajko both got stabbed in the stomach. Jachemir bled out already, on the inside mostly, and Rajko isn't going to make it either."

Now it was plain why, their annihilation of the Patient Weavers notwithstanding, the vermin outside were questioning whether the Black Dogs truly were the invincible conquerors they made themselves out to be. Ivan's jaw clenched. He shivered with anger, and the tethered gobber cowered.

As well he might, but before venting his feelings, Ivan needed to sort out exactly what had happened. He glowered at Olekse. "Tell me about it."

The ironhead then explained that Iakshen had noticed a man in black plate shadowing him, whereupon Olekse had decided to lure the stalker into a snare and question him. Things went awry when the Cygnaran turned out to be a spellcaster and to possess a trollkin ally. Ultimately the two fought their way clear of the trap and then, even though the mob outside tried to hinder them, jumped down a pit, landed on a ledge, and from there disappeared into what appeared to be the entrance to a tunnel.

"And nobody jumped after them?" Ivan asked.

"My armor's not made for climbing walls," Olekse replied, "and I wasn't going to order Iakshen and Ladimir to do it. It would have been suicide. It took amazing luck for the arcanist and the trollkin to end up on that ledge."

"Or maybe just courage and skill." Olekse started to reply, but Ivan raised his hand to forestall him. "Never mind. At least you made them run, and the mob saw it. That's something, I suppose. Who the hell were they?"

"According to people in the crowd," the ironhead said, "Gardek Stonebrow and Eilish Garrity. The trollkin's a bounty hunter. The spellcaster has a reputation for solving puzzles. People hire him when something mysterious has happened and they need to figure out how, why, and who's to blame."

Ivan grunted. "So, a pair of thief takers. How can they come down into these tunnels without people killing them?"

"Well," Olekse said, "I gather that sometimes someone tries. Once I offered coin, it was easy enough to persuade the crowd to turn on them. But it seems to me that as a general rule, people down here don't go out of their way to borrow trouble." He smiled. "And that's the way we want them, isn't it? Congratulating themselves that it's the Patient Weavers who are dead instead of them, as opposed to uniting to drive out the Khadoran intruders."

"It's how we want them for now," Ivan said. "Once we control the entire Undercity, we'll get them organized. Then nobody will come down here and live to tell the tale. Not unless we give permission."

Gridia ran her fingertips down Fodor's arm. "I hope you're paying attention, lovey. I want you to display this kind of leadership when you're an underboss."

As if, Ivan thought, she'd ever let him beyond the reach of that caressing hand to command a chapter of the bratya or do anything else. "Why were they after Iakshen? Not because of anything he's done off on his own. When has he even had the chance? It can only be because they were out to snatch whichever of us they could lay hands on, probably to sweat information out of him."

Olekse nodded. "I think so, too." He picked up a half-empty green glass bottle from the bar and raised it to his lips.

"And they wouldn't do it for free," Ivan said, "so who hired them? Is one of the other Undercity gangs going to try to push us out after all? Or is it the Watch? Don't they have snoops of their own?"

The ironhead wiped his mouth with the back of his hand. "Maybe their snoops aren't as good."

The front door opened. Ivan looked around and was surprised to see Druce Keller standing there. The stout, snowy-whiskered alchemist had bruises—the marks of a strangler's hands, almost certainly—on his florid, flabby neck.

"This is good luck," Keller said. "I came because I'd heard that you Black Dogs were presiding over a celebration hereabouts, but I didn't know I'd find the boss himself."

"What's happened?" Ivan growled, switching back to Cygnaran.

"A man named Milo Boggs, a fellow alchemist, came to see me. Not realizing that you and I had sealed a pact, he wanted to know anything I might be able to tell him about the… bratya, is that the word? I gather he was inquiring on behalf of the Watch."

Ivan frowned. "Why would the Watch employ an alchemist for that?"

"Well, somewhat like myself, Mr. Boggs is a criminal alchemist and a familiar face in the Undercity. He's conducted business with a good many of us. So, people will talk to him. Yet he's also a member of a small band of mercenaries called the Black River Irregulars, and Watch Commander Helstrom seems to trust them. He's employed them on more than one occasion."

"These Irregulars," Olekse said, "do they include a trollkin in spiked armor called Stonebrow and an arcanist named Garrity?"

Keller cocked his head. "I take it those two came poking around here."

"Did you capture this man Boggs?" Ivan asked.

The stout man spread his hands. "I tried, but luck wasn't with me. He did a lamentable amount of damage in the process of escaping as well. Did you catch Stonebrow and Garrity?"

Gridia chortled. "Apparently luck wasn't with anyone on our side today. But I'm sure we'll all do better next time."

Ivan stared Keller in the eye. "Did you tell Boggs anything?"

"My dear fellow, you wound me! Besides, what do I really even know except for what everyone in the Undercity already understands?"

"If they haven't found out anything," Olekse said, "that's good. Still, two attempts in one day? And they get away both times? We can't let that go. It'll make us look… well, not weak, probably, but less strong than we need to look."

"I agree," Gridia said. "Fodor and I will hunt them down and put an end to this. In a way that will make an impression on everyone who hears the story."

"No," Ivan said. "Or at least not yet. You need to finish the task I already gave you."

Olekse frowned. "Boss, we understand that there's something between you and the Gormleigh woman. But she'll keep."

"Not if she slips out of the city."

"Well, if she does, she does, and maybe you'll catch up with her down the road. Meanwhile, we have work to do, the work our chiefs sent us here to accomplish."

Ivan took a long breath. There was a thing he never talked about. Nor was he willing to share the whole truth now. But maybe he needed to tell some of it, mixed with some lies, to avert a mutiny.

"You remember four years ago," he said, "when the bratya sent men to Laedry to help the Empress's government eliminate resisters. If they were effective, we'd be given free rein to set up our usual sort of businesses."

Olekse nodded. "I heard that at first things went well, and then our fellow Dogs stopped reporting back. You went to find out what had become of them, and it turned out they were all dead." He hesitated. "Killed by this Gormleigh?"

"And her confederates," Ivan said. "One of the men they murdered was my little brother Yaro."

"I'm so sorry!" Gridia said. "That's very unfortunate. But are you certain Gormleigh was responsible?"

"Yes," Ivan said, "because unlike the other Dogs, Yaro wasn't killed in the fighting. He was only wounded. Gormleigh took him prisoner, tortured him just for fun, and then left him to die. He didn't die quickly, though. I found him in his last hours—what was left of him, anyway.

"He told me what had happened, every cut and every burn, and I vowed I'd track down the woman responsible and kill her." He looked at Gridia. "Imagine if it had been someone you loved. Your son, for instance."

The plump, silver-blond woman shuddered. "I can't imagine that. Not really. Just the thought is too awful to bear. But of course, I'd have to avenge him."

"As you must have tried," said Olekse to Ivan. "Right then and there."

"Yes," Ivan said, "but by then, Gormleigh had already departed Laedry, and I couldn't hang around endlessly in a strange country in a forlorn effort to pick up her trail. I had a duty to return to Skirov and report, and then our bosses had other tasks for me. All I could do was wait and pray that someday, word of the bitch's whereabouts would reach me."

His mix of truth and lies completed, he studied the other Dogs' faces. He found a trace of sympathy there, though compromised by calculation and suspicion. He realized he shouldn't be surprised.

"So, that's why you really convinced the higher-ups that this was a good idea," Olekse said. "Why we're all buried alive in a hole under a hostile foreign city when there was plenty of money to be made back in Khador."

"No," Ivan said. The others eyed him skeptically. "We have a grand opportunity here. We're tough and smart, but back in Khador, there was a limit to how high we could rise. There were too many people above us. But in Cygnar, there's no limit. First, we control the Undercity. Next, all the crime in Corvis. In time, all the outlaws in the kingdom. Each of you will have your own duchy to run."

Keller cleared his throat. The diffident little noise surprised Ivan, who'd all but forgotten the apothecary was still present.

He gave Keller a smile. "And of course, my new friend, you'll fare well under the new system. You're one of us now." And if the old man was fool enough to believe that, he deserved whatever he got.

Gridia gave Ivan a smile. "We know you'd never use us as dupes and pawns purely for your own selfish purposes, dear. I mean, if we for one second imagined *that*… well, things would become unpleasant. So, with that reflection in all of our minds, I once again recommend forgetting Canice Gormleigh—only for the time being, naturally—and dealing with these Black River Whatever-They-Are."

"We can do both," Ivan said.

"It saddens me," Gridia said, "that I have to disagree. Our little family is filled with talented people. You know I think the world of each and every one of them. But when it comes to tracking down enemies, Fodor and I are far and away the best. Yet even we can't follow two trails at the same time."

Ivan abruptly decided he'd had enough of coaxing and explaining. Any more in the same vein, and his subordinates might well take it as a sign of weakness.

"Then follow the trail I ordered you to follow," he snapped. "Prove you're as good as you say you are. Bring me Gormleigh and not more excuses."

Gridia and Fodor shifted ever so slightly apart, the possibly unconscious move so subtle that most people would have missed it. But Ivan, who had in his time worked as a member of a team of assassins, recognized that they were preparing to flank him.

Had it really come to this? Were mother and son so dissatisfied with his leadership or so affronted by his harsh words that they were about to draw on him? And if so, which side would Olekse take? Ivan glanced in the ironhead's direction, but Olekse's blocky, beard-fringed face betrayed no hint of his intentions.

Ivan flipped the weighted hem of his cape outward. That too would have struck most people as a small, inconsequential gesture if they noticed it at all, but in reality he was making sure the garment wouldn't be in the way if he needed to grab for his sword hilt. Gridia and Fodor unquestionably recognized the preparatory action for what it was and understood the underlying message: He was ready for them, and he was not afraid.

Then Keller, who, despite his lengthy criminal career, seemed not to understand what was happening or to sense the gathering tension in the air, said, "I vote with the lady. The mercenaries are the actual problem, and that has to take priority over any one individual's desire for retribution, natural and even commendable though it is."

Swift and sudden as a striking serpent, Gridia snatched for her blade. Ivan was about to do likewise when he discerned that as her weapon emerged from its scabbard, she was pivoting. Then he held himself still and tried to look as if he'd never for even an instant believed he was in danger.

As she spun, she cut. Keller squawked and reeled backward, clutching his cheek. Blood welled out between his pudgy fingers.

Gridia dropped her sword to clank on the floor. "Oh, my poor sweet dove! I'm so sorry! Let me see that."

She stepped forward. The alchemist cringed back against the door.

"I promise, I never meant to hurt you," the round-faced woman said. "I'm so clumsy sometimes! I simply needed to make the point that there are limits. You're our trusted friend now, just as Ivan said. But when the brothers and sisters of the bratya are working out a problem among themselves, then outsiders, even those we cherish, should hold their peace. Do you understand, and can you find it in your heart to forgive me?"

Keller took a ragged breath. "Of course."

"Thank you. I'm very grateful. Fodor, love, most any sort of liquor will do for cleaning the wound. And if you can find clean towels or napkins, that would be lovely."

The young assassin sheathed his sword and scurried to fetch his mother the items she'd requested. Meanwhile, Olekse glowered.

"So, are we all in agreement now?" he asked.

"Oh, yes," Gridia said. "It was just a momentary tiff. Of course Fodor and I will find Ms. Gormleigh first, if that's what Ivan wants. Surely we'll locate her soon, and then we can pay a call on the Black River people." She raised a whiskey-soaked towel to Keller's face. "All right, dearie, away, take your hand away. And be brave. This may sting a little."

Keller sucked in a hissing breath. "Speaking of the mercenaries, there's a fourth one, their captain, a woman named Colbie Sterling. I take it that no one's spotted her sneaking around."

"Describe her," Ivan said.

"Tall, thin, dark. Greatcoat, tinted goggles. Usually travels around with a steamjack to do her fighting for her. When the 'jack's not enough, she pulls out a slug gun. Nasty, almost ridiculous weapon, that. It'll blow a man to pieces."

Olekse muttered an obscenity. "When we attacked the Patient Weavers, it was a slug gun that took down our 'jack."

"Are you suggesting," Ivan replied, "that it was this Captain Sterling who fired the shot?"

The ironhead shrugged. "I can't know. But a slug gun's a specialized military weapon made for wrecking warjacks, not something the average tough carries around, and for certain, these mercenaries are meddling in our business now. If it wasn't Sterling, it's quite a coincidence."

"And if it was," Ivan said, "maybe she and Gormleigh fled together. Maybe they're holed up together now." No one could know that for certain either, not yet, but his intuition told him it was so.

Still dabbing at Keller's cheek, Gridia laughed. "My goodness! What a joke! Our little spat really was all for nothing, wasn't it?"

Ivan's mouth tightened. "Yes. As it turns out, I do want you and Fodor to go after these Irregulars. You know what to do when you find them. Meanwhile, the bratya needs to look strong even though we're down two men and, for the moment, the wretches who killed them are still alive. Olekse?"

The ironhead nodded. "I'll take care of it."

• • •

AS WAS SO OFTEN THE CASE in Corvis, the rain clouds were blocking the sun. Still, the enfeebled grey light that made its way to the ground was the best available for reading, and with Natak in no immediate need of tending, Regan had shifted her chair in front of a window to take advantage of it.

The manuscript in her hands was Eilish's current work in progress, a monograph on the distinctive calluses and stains various trades left on the hands of their practitioners. He'd brought it along to the safehouse on the optimistic assumption that the current job would leave him time to work on it.

Regan read another paragraph of her sweetheart's handwriting—precise yet replete with flourishes—and smiled. Eilish's intelligence pervaded the work but so, too, did his smugness.

The door creaked open and bumped against the wall. She turned and caught her breath.

Gardek was helping Eilish inside. The bounty hunter was missing half his armor, and both of them were filthy. What concerned her most, though, was that Eilish's head was bruised and matted with drying blood. She could tell even though he had his cowl up, perhaps to make himself less conspicuous as he traversed the streets.

Regan dropped the parchment pages and stood up. "The kitchen table," she said.

"Right," Gardek replied. He half-carried Eilish in that direction. As he did, she noticed he was limping and made a mental note to look into that in due course.

"What do you think of my treatise?" Eilish croaked.

That was encouraging. If he'd observed what she was reading, he was more alert than he'd first appeared.

"You misspelled 'cartilaginous.' Lie down on the table."

"Best offer I've had all day. And mind you, that's from a man who's newly come from a brothel. Well, give or take."

"Are you hurt anywhere besides your head?"

"I might have a bruise or two somewhere under my armor."

"Gardek, take it off him." The trollkin started to do so, making a clinking pile of the pieces on the floor, and she set about examining Eilish's head. A knot of tension in her stomach dissolved when she decided that, the plenitude of sticky blood notwithstanding, his injuries weren't life-threatening.

"Tell me your symptoms," she said.

"I had some double vision, but that's going away. Now I mostly just hurt."

Colbie and Pog appeared in the kitchen doorway. They must have heard everyone's voices from the stable. "Is he all right?" the human mechanik asked.

"He will be," Regan said, "but he needs the gash in his scalp sutured. Someone go up to Mr. Warbiter's room and get my bag."

"I'll do it," said Pog. He scurried off.

Colbie turned to Gardek. "Come into the next room and tell me what happened." The two of them went out the door.

"I could have answered that," Eilish said. "Dismal failure followed by humiliating flight." He started to laugh, then winced when it evidently made his head throb. "The Khadoran bastards out-thought me. Can you believe it?"

"It is almost inconceivable," Regan said drily. Pog trotted through the door, and she took her medical kit from his grimy hands.

"These are the moments," said Eilish, "when I could almost wish my investigations consisted solely of unmasking embezzling bookkeepers and profligate sons who feared Father was about to amend the will. They were that way for a little while."

Regan threaded a needle and sewed a first stitch. Pog abruptly looked queasy, swallowed, and retreated into the parlor.

"If that's what you really want," Regan said, "you could go back to it."

"No," Eilish replied. "We Irregulars already had our little crisis of confidence back when Gormleigh and Warbiter got the better of us. There's no need for another. Ultimately, we caught the tunnel killer, and we'll deal with the Khadorans, too. But we need to alter our approach."

"If that means what I think it does, Colbie won't be happy to hear you say so."

Eilish grinned. "Good."

• • •

NOT PANICKED BUT AGITATED VOICES sounded through the door. Canice quashed the urge to go find out what was going on. She could tell it wasn't a battle, and if she stopped now, the rune bullet would be ruined.

Instead, she kept whispering the ritual incantation and, squinting, etching the proper symbol on the round. Meanwhile, a bit of vitality flowed out of her. It wasn't the sudden pang that an arcanist felt when casting a spell but rather something gradual. A sensation she would never even have recognized for what it was if her mentor hadn't taught her to do so, so she'd know if her magic was working as intended.

With the ease of long practice, she finished her murmuring and engraving at the same instant. As far as she knew, no one had ever proved that absolute simultaneity infused the enchantment with extra potency. But many gun mages believed it.

She tucked the finished shot in a loop on her gun belt and stood up from her makeshift worktable, reflexively registering the weights under her arms and riding her hips. There might not be a battle raging right this second, but she always wanted her pistols ready to hand.

When she stepped into the parlor, Gardek was reporting to Colbie while Pog hovered, listening. The kitchen doorway afforded a glimpse of slim little Dr. Falk with her cap of chestnut hair, tending to an injured and recumbent Eilish.

Canice's first inclination was to stay where she was and listen to what the trollkin had to say. But then something—simple curiosity, perhaps—prompted her to cross the room and take a closer look. In the process of wrapping bandages around Eilish's head, Regan gave her a nod to signal that the blond man was going to be all right.

Her curiosity satisfied, Canice returned to the conversation in the parlor, where Colbie gave her a scowl. "Good of you to show an interest," the mechanik said. "Even if it took a while."

Canice sneered. "Was I supposed to be full of concern that one of your incompetents had gotten hurt? Why would I be? And as for hearing every word of Mr. Stonebrow's report, why would I need to? It's obvious that your plan went off just about as well as I predicted it would."

Colbie glowered back. Pog peered at the two of them and looked as unhappy as he generally did when they were bickering. But Gardek's wide mouth twitched upward in grudging appreciation of the gibe.

At that moment, the door to the street opened and Milo shuffled in. When, his gloved hand shaking, he pulled down his gas mask, his pockmarked face was ashen, even his lips.

"Are you sick?" Pog started toward the alchemist, likely to help him to a seat.

Milo raised a black-gloved hand to signal that he could manage on his own. "I'm all right. I've just had too many drugs in too brief a time." He grinned. "I don't think I've ever said those words before."

"Regan is tending to Eilish," Colbie said, "but as soon as she's done—"

Milo collapsed into a chair. "No need. If I needed a gash stitched or a bone set, then yes. But when it comes to stimulants and sedatives, I do better taking care of myself." His pupils contracted to pinpoints, and he blinked. "What happened to Eilish? Is he going to be all right?"

"Fortunately, yes," Colbie said. "But he and Gardek ran into trouble. I take it that you did, too."

Milo sighed. "Yes. The Khadorans have done a good job of terrorizing people. Or persuading them that they're going to make life better. Or both. Anyway, I couldn't find anyone willing and able to tell me anything useful, and when I called on the Jagged Knives, Druce Keller tried to take me prisoner so he could hand me over to his new friends."

"So, he knows where they're hiding," Gardek rumbled.

"He said not," Milo replied. "But he was expecting them to pay a return visit to Poison Pond."

"Damn it," Colbie said. "All right, Milo, rest." She looked to Gardek. "All three of you need to rest. We'll figure out our next move when you're all feeling up to it. Pog, you and I should get back to Doorstop."

After the two mechaniks tramped back into the attached stable, Canice said, "She has no idea what to do next."

"You underestimate her," Gardek said.

"We hope," Milo added.

The trollkin shifted his weight. He appeared to be favoring one leg. "You said that if we fetched your rune bullet-making gear, you and Warbiter would teach us about Khadoran-style fighting. Well, it's time for the first lesson. Mine, anyway."

Canice said, "I take it that the men you went up against impressed you. But are you sure you wouldn't rather rest first, as your captain ordered?"

Gardek made a spitting sound. "I'm fine. Is Warbiter well enough to give me pointers?"

"Yes, and bored to the point of madness. He'll be glad to have something to occupy his mind." Canice grinned. "And for an excuse to insult and disparage you, I expect."

• • •

AS FODOR AND HIS MOTHER CLIMBED the ramp that linked the Undercity to one of the streets above, the night sky opened overhead. Black clouds hid the moon and stars, and spat cold rain down on their heads. The buildings that rose to either side of the exit seemed ponderous and as ugly as the guardhouses and cellblocks of a prison, perhaps because, in this rundown section of Corvis, there was a paucity of light to pick out architectural flourishes and make the shapes less stark.

Still, taking a deep breath, Fodor felt as if he were escaping a prison. To a degree, he'd grown accustomed to the tunnels. He supposed a person had to or else you'd go crazy. But now that he was out, he realized the claustrophobic depths were as oppressive as… as… He glanced at the woman by his side, and his mind shied away from whatever comparison it had been about to make.

Mama gave him a smile. "It's nice to breathe fresh air again, isn't it?"

"Yes." Although even with rain trying to wash away the smoke and myriad stinks of a big city, he wasn't sure the atmosphere of Corvis qualified.

"But we mustn't let the pleasure make us careless. Down below, the law comes reluctantly when it comes at all. Up here, it's different. The Watch regards these streets as its proper concern, and there are thousands of soldiers and plenty of checkpoints as well."

Fodor sighed. "I know, Mama." And she knew he knew. Sometimes he wished she didn't feel the need to repeat the same cautions over and over again. But it was because she loved him, so he always felt guilty when it rankled.

They'd come up in the northern bourg of the city, a district of countless manufactories and the tenements housing the workers who labored therein. Keller believed Milo Boggs lived somewhere nearby, apparently because the immediate area was a prime location for the shadier sort of alchemist to filch materials from the warehouses where they were stored or to persuade the caretakers of those warehouses to sell the alchemists a little something on the sly.

It seemed a slim lead to Fodor. But he and Mama had to start somewhere, and at least, according to Keller, their quarry had a distinctive appearance: long black coat and alchemist's armor to match, bandoliers loaded with knives and grenades, gas mask hanging below a pockmarked face or sometimes covering it, even when there was no apparent need.

Keeping an eye out for the authorities, stepping aside and standing respectfully as any patriotic Cygnaran would when a company of army riflemen came marching down the cobbled street, Fodor and Mama started asking people if they knew Boggs. A bit of the bridge that spanned the Black River, just prior to the point where it forked, alternately appeared and disappeared in the gaps between buildings as the two assassins worked their way along.

Mostly, Mama did the talking. She was the one with the knack for putting people at ease when she didn't intend to frighten them instead. Occasionally, though, she urged Fodor to take the lead, and then, vaguely resentful yet wanting to please, he smiled or glowered—depending on which seemed appropriate—through the interaction as best he could.

At first it didn't matter who was speaking. No one admitted to knowing Boggs or to seeing a person fitting his description. But eventually they encountered a thin man with a spade-shaped beard loitering in a recessed doorway where he could watch passersby while staying out of the rain. His coat was made of vertical black and white stripes as if to mimic the pelt of some exotic animal, and rings set with gems so large they could only be paste adorned several of his fingers.

The bearded man peered back, sizing Fodor and Mama up in their turn, and then relaxed back against the grey twin-paneled door. Whatever he was selling, he didn't expect that a young man and a middle-aged woman, the two of them bearing a familial resemblance, would be interested.

Mama surprised him by giving him a wide smile. "Excuse me," she said. "I wonder if you can help us. We're looking for a man named Milo Boggs."

The man in the doorway took another look at them. Fodor was keeping his tattoos covered, and he and Mama had made some effort to dress like honest citizens of Corvis as opposed to outlaws from the tunnels below or the empire north of the river. But there was no hiding their swords or, he suspected, some trace of a Khadoran accent, no matter how accomplished his mother's Cygnaran sounded to him.

Unconsciously, it seemed, the bearded man gave the tiniest of nods. It indicated his appraisal was complete. "Who's asking?" he replied.

"People who need an apothecary's help," Mama replied. "My husband—this poor boy's father—well, I'm ashamed to say it, but when he drinks, he can be very cruel. We need a cure. One that will last." She paused a beat. "If you follow me."

"Yes," said the man in the doorway. "And I know Boggs. But he won't help you just out of the goodness of his heart." He leered. "Come to think of it, neither will I."

"I completely understand." Like a housewife preparing to pay the greengrocer and making sure she didn't drop a coin while she was about it, Mama carefully opened the pigskin purse buckled to her belt. "And I wouldn't dream of drawing you out into the cold and the wet without giving you something for your trouble." She extracted a silver piece from the bag. "Will this do?"

"It will, and I'll get you where you want to go." As the man in the striped coat spoke, his face turned ever so slightly to the side. That was what card players called a tell. Mama had trained Fodor to recognize these even if she'd never managed to teach him to charm people and, when expedient, deceive them in the effortless way that she did.

Mama proffered the coin.

The Cygnaran shook his head. "After we find the alchemist." He turned up the collar of his coat, stepped out of the doorway, winced when a first raindrop plopped down on his bald spot, and then led the Khadorans back the way they'd come. Eventually he turned down a dark, narrow, unpaved alleyway puddled with muddy water on the brink of overflowing the low spots.

Mama hesitated. "Are you sure this is the way?"

"A man who peddles the sort of goods that Boggs does," the Cygnaran replied, "doesn't set up shop in the main street."

"Well," Mama said, "all right, then." She looked at Fodor. "Please, lamb, try not to get your feet damp. We don't want you catching cold."

They headed down the passage. Relying on his peripheral vision, Fodor looked ahead. Crouching in their hiding places, the bearded man's confederates were so easy to spot that he had to hold in a sneer. The outlaws of Corvis *needed* Black Dog bosses to teach them how to rob and murder competently.

He wondered where the treacherous guide usually promised to lead his victims astray. A bawdy house? A drug den? Maybe he was skilled at reading whoever was slinking by and offering whatever vice that person desired.

Fodor pivoted as an ambusher on the left leaped out from behind an abandoned cart with a broken wheel. The Khadoran swept his sword from his scabbard and put his point in line. Lunging with an upraised club, his foe would either stop short or impale himself.

Just a shadow in the murk, the ambusher did stop in time, then backed up and circled, putting the disabled cart between Fodor and himself. Fodor turned, following the motion, then realized that was exactly what his adversary intended. A burst of movement at the periphery of his vision revealed another robber was rushing to take him from behind.

Fodor spun, cut to the head, and the thief fell, his body splashing in a puddle. He pivoted yet again and was easily in time to threaten the first ambusher with his sword before the man finished scurrying around the cart. Meanwhile, a different man cried out as, no doubt, Mama either disabled him or killed him outright.

Fodor's remaining adversary now had his club in one hand and a long knife in the other. Still, he balked at the Black Dog's longer weapon and took a step backward.

Fodor suspected that if he let the Cygnaran retreat any farther, he was going to end up chasing the man either down the alley or around and around the cart. He lacked the patience for either. He whipped off his cape and snapped it in the robber's face to startle him, then stepped and thrust. His sword drove into the thief's belly.

Framed by a shaggy mustache drooping down the sides, the robber's mouth made an O. He took a tottering little half step backward and feebly waved his weapons as if he couldn't decide whether to use them or drop them to clutch at his wound.

Fodor cut to the knife hand. The blade fell to the ground—and a finger or two along with it. A slash to the side of the neck brought blood spraying to mix with the puddles, and the Cygnaran collapsed.

"Oh, lovey," Mama sighed. Her tone was one of exasperation tempered with affection, as if he were still a toddler and had gotten his newly laundered clothing dirty. "We can't question them if they're dead."

Fodor's face grew warm. Before the fight began, he'd had some sense that he ought to strike simply to incapacitate, not kill. But such restraint didn't come naturally to him, and once the second man rushed him, his instincts had taken over. "I'm sorry, Mama," he said.

She smiled and stroked his cheek. Her fingertips tugged at bristles and told him he needed a shave. He sometimes wondered what he'd look like if he let his beard grow out like many of the other Black Dogs, but though they'd never talked about it, he was sure the idea would displease her.

"It's all right," Mama said. "The important thing is, the bad men didn't hurt my sugar dumpling. And we still have a couple left who may be able to help us." She pointed with her sword.

Fodor followed the gesture. While he'd been disposing of his pair of robbers, she'd accounted for the other three.

One lay dead with a split skull and his brains leaking out.

The second was wheezing his way through what were likely his final breaths with bloody froth bubbling on his lips.

The third was their faithless guide. Leaning against a grimy brick wall, eyes rolling, he clutched at the long gash in his forearm that had evidently shocked the fight right out of him. The wound was deep but not, in Fodor's judgment, immediately life threatening, which made him the best prospect for interrogation.

Still, Mama started with the man with the punctured lung, likely because with him it was now or never. She squatted down beside him and stroked his forehead. "You poor dear. I'm terribly sorry. But you can still be saved. Just answer a question or two, and we'll take you to a physician straightaway. Do you know an alchemist named Milo Boggs?"

The gasp that came in reply was nearly inaudible. "No."

"Thank you anyway." Mama stood up.

"I… answered…"

"If it makes you feel any better, a surgeon couldn't have helped you anyway. Maybe you should pray in the time remaining." She turned toward the man in the striped coat. "But you, dearie, truly needn't die. Not if you actually know where Milo Boggs makes his home, and since you're both criminals, it seems conceivable you might. Do you?"

"I think so," said the guide. "I mean, yes! Yes, I do! He lives in the cellar of a boardinghouse on Needle Street."

Mama shook her head. "If that's true, you could have taken us there as requested and earned your silver. But you and your friends just had to try for *all* our money, didn't you?" She looked at Fodor. "This is a valuable lesson for you, lambkin. Greed can be an awful thing."

"We should get moving," Fodor replied. "We don't want the Watch to find us standing over all these bodies."

"That's very wise," Mama said. She smiled at the man in the striped coat. "If you'll please lead the way."

He hesitated. "I don't know if I can walk that far, bleeding like I am."

Mama raised her sword, and the prisoner flinched. She wiped the blood and rain from the blade with a cloth and returned it to its scabbard. "I have faith in you, dear. I know you'll manage somehow."

The captive led them back the way they'd come, and the death rattle of the man with the bubbling mouth sounded behind them. Once they were back on the street, Fodor divided his attention between watching for the prisoner to try to escape and keeping an eye out for anyone who took too much interest in their little procession. Panting and swaying, the Cygnaran seemed too enfeebled and cowed to make trouble, and at this hour in this precinct, few people were abroad in the rain. Still, it paid to be careful.

For a time, they walked along a canal that smelled of sewage and was lined with low little houseboats. The night obscured the vessels, and Fodor was no mariner in any case, but even so, something, a whiff of wood rot perhaps, gave him the impression that many of the boats had floated neglected and deteriorating at their moorings for years and would likely fall apart if the people living aboard had tried to sail them anywhere.

Eventually their course diverged from the water and led them past a little Morrowan chapel with a tarnished bronze statue out front. Fodor assumed it was an image of one of the Ascendants, although, raised in the Old Faith to the meager extent that Mama had bothered with religion at all, he had no idea which one.

By now, the guide was white as snow and tottering with every step. Increasingly certain that the Cygnaran would faint before taking his captors to their destination—if, in fact, he even knew where Boggs resided and wasn't just pretending—Fodor wished he'd shoved him into the canal to drown when he'd had the chance. It would have been easy, and it would have saved time.

But then the man in the striped coat staggered around the corner of a tenement into an alleyway not unlike the one where he and his partners had laid their trap. Unwilling to stop clasping his wound, he indicated with a bob of his head a rectangular hole in the ground and several wooden steps leading down to a door below street level.

"Very good," Mama said. "Now go down and knock. Don't worry. We'll be right behind you."

Two risers down, the captive nearly pitched forward but then regained his balance. At the bottom of the steps, he knocked by kicking.

No one answered.

"Give me some room, dear." Mama descended the steps, tried the door handle, and then, kneeling and employing a set of picks, went to work on the lock. "There we are!" She moved back up onto the steps. "After you."

With a grim expression that conveyed that, based on what he knew of Milo Boggs's character, a booby trap or summarily thrown knife was by no means out of the question, the captive eased open the creaking door. Nothing happened in response. The space on the other side was dark.

Mama struck a match on the wall, used her other hand to shield it from the rain and the breeze, and stepped over the threshold. Following, hauling the man in the striped coat along, Fodor discovered a one-room abode that was mostly given over to trestle tables, shelves, sand baths, athanors, aludels, and other tools of alchemy. Boggs's living area was at the very back and was jammed full with a narrow cot, a chamber pot, a chair, and a trunk that, judging from its placement, doubled as a footstool.

Mama's match went out. She struck another and used it to light a gas lamp, and as she did, the contents of the crowded space came into clearer view. Fodor relaxed because now he could see with absolute certainty that no one was hiding here.

Which had its good and bad sides, when he thought about it. "Do we lie in wait until Boggs comes back?" he asked.

"Perhaps not." Mama indicated what at first glance appeared to be a box of grenades, some armed simply by pulling a pin, others by thumbing the protruding rim of a toothed cog to start the clockwork timer inside. "Do you see these?"

"Yes," Fodor said.

"They're all empty casings. Unfinished." She moved to the back of the room and opened the trunk. "Hmm. If Mr. Boggs owns a spare pair of socks and set of smallclothes, they're not here now either."

"You're saying he cleared out and took what he needed with him. But how would he know anyone was going to pursue him back here? From what I understand, the scum of the Undercity don't generally make trouble aboveground."

Mama shrugged. "If Ivan's right, if these Black River Irregulars truly have associated themselves with Canice Gormleigh and she understands that the Black Dogs are out to catch her no matter what it takes… but that's all speculation. I think we do have to assume, though, that Mr. Boggs won't return anytime soon. We'll need to search elsewhere."

Through a huge, unfamiliar city, while beneath their feet, other Dogs were likely claiming choice bits of what had been the Patient Weavers' dominion for their own particular preserves. Fodor scowled, and then his gaze fell on a burner atop one of the trestle tables. Moved by a sudden impulse, he turned on the gas and struck a match.

"Lovey," Mama said, "what are you thinking?"

"I wonder what a fire would do," Fodor said, "what colors it would turn, if it reached all these acids and such."

She sighed. "Mama knows you're frustrated, but we *will* find Mr. Boggs and his friends. Meanwhile, you can't burn down a boardinghouse full of people just to vent your feelings. We're trying to be inconspicuous."

Pouting, Fodor shook out the match and turned off the flow of gas. "I never get to enjoy myself."

"Now that's just silly. In fact, we can play a game right now. Help our guide to the back of the room."

Fodor shoved the man in the striped coat to the desired location. "Now what?"

"Look over here." She indicated a stack of cages. "I imagine those snakes are poisonous. But they don't seem very lively at the moment. I think we can set them free without getting bitten."

"Why would we bother?" Fodor asked.

"To give our friend here a choice. He can stay where he is and continue to bleed with little hope of medical assistance. Or he can try to make his way back to the door even though the snakes are in the way."

The captive stared at her. "Please," he said. "I'm weak. I'm dizzy. I could fall right on top of them."

Mama beamed. "That's what makes it a challenge."

— 11 —

COLBIE TOLD POG SHE NEEDED SOME AIR and then slipped out the stable door. With luck, none of the other Irregulars would come looking for her within the next few minutes, and if someone did, once the gobber relayed her excuse, he wouldn't think anything of her absence.

As she tugged her armored greatcoat with its added weight of slug gun and tools to hang more comfortably, she reflected with a pang of bitterness that nobody was likely to come looking anyway. His whirling hammer a hazard to all who happened by, Gardek was busy lunging and pivoting around the front room while, sprawled on a pallet in the corner, Natak Warbiter growled criticism. Colbie questioned whether a person could actually learn to contend with sword-and-cape fighters without an actual flesh-and-blood sparring partner, but apparently the trollkin's understanding of close combat and powers of visualization were such that he believed the lesson would be effective.

Meanwhile, Milo and Eilish, the latter wearing a crown of

white gauze bandage, were receiving instruction in the art of making rune bullets. When Colbie had peeked into the little room that Canice had usurped for her workspace, the three were having an animated and cordial conversation. For the moment at least, their common enthusiasm softened old grudges on the one side and habitual arrogance on the other.

Colbie knew that, happily occupied though they were, none of her comrades would have consented to let her descend into the Undercity alone without even Doorstop to accompany her and keep her safe. But with their opening moves thwarted, the Irregulars still needed information, the sooner the better, and after the ordeals the others had undergone, she couldn't send them right back into danger without so much as a single day of rest.

Except, she admitted, weaving her way through countless workers hurrying to report for their morning shifts, that wasn't really true, was it? Gardek was still favoring his bruised leg, but if he could exert himself under Natak's tutelage, then he was fit enough to come along with her and watch her back.

The truth was that with her chief weapon out of commission and her initial plan a failure, she felt the need to prove herself. She'd told herself the impulse was foolish but in the end succumbed to it nonetheless.

She came to a ramp-like path that descended from the edge of the cobbled street down into gloom. She sensed speculative eyes on her as she started down. Allegedly moral, law-abiding citizens visited the Undercity fairly often for all sorts of reasons, but even so, first thing in the morning, a lone woman of somewhat striking appearance inspired curiosity.

That was no catastrophe, but she hoped to be less conspicuous once she reached the passages below. To that end, she removed her tinted safety goggles and stuck them in a pocket, and tucked her curls up under a soft, shapeless cap. It would have been an exaggeration even to call the alteration a disguise, but perhaps she was a bit less obviously Colbie Sterling than she'd been before.

At the bottom of the ramp, she shook a jar of Milo's bottled light aglow and then made her way to the point where, spottily illuminated by the occasional kerosene lamp or open flame, a vault opened out before her. Shanties and larger but equally rickety structures lined the rutted pathway down the middle. In contrast to the teeming thoroughfares overhead, only a couple of figures were slinking about here. That, Colbie supposed, was an advantage of the outlaw life. A person might end up hanged for his crimes but meanwhile needn't rise at the crack of dawn.

Despite the seeming lack of activity, she watched for any sign of the bratya as she prowled ahead. That, after all, was the reason she'd opted to visit this particular section of the caverns. Seemingly to establish themselves as terrifying madmen, the Khadorans had utterly destroyed the Patient Weavers' stronghold. But Canice's former associates had controlled other patches of territory scattered across the Undercity, and it seemed likely the newcomers were now in the process of informing the residents that they still owed tribute, just to a different set of protectors than before. If so, Colbie might get a chance to spy on them.

She swung wide to avoid a relatively fresh corpse, and several rats stopped gnawing to watch her pass. Just beyond was the shabby office of a "surgeon" likely barred or hounded from practice in the metropolis above, and she reflected that a body sprawled near his doorstep was unlikely to encourage trade.

Next came a door marked with a swampie fortuneteller's staring-eye symbol, then a shop supplying canaries to those intending to venture into portions of the tunnels where the air was likely to be bad. Somehow sensing the coming of day even though caged in the dark, the yellow birds in the window had started twittering.

On the other side of that shop was a tavern, if that wasn't too grand a term for a place so squalid. Behind it, crammed in between the building and the cavern wall, were a pair of moonshine stills and a mastiff on a chain that evidently guarded them and their output. Unlike the canaries, the dog was asleep with its big, short-muzzled head on its forepaws.

Colbie tested the tavern door and found it was open. When she stepped inside, though, four ruffians turned to glower at her.

"We're closed," said a stocky man with a wine-colored birthmark covering the greater part of his left profile. Based on his filthy apron, she assumed he was the proprietor.

"No, you're not." Colbie took a gold crown from her pocket and spun it on a tabletop. "I'm supposed to meet someone today, but my boat docked earlier than expected. I just need a place to sit and wait. I won't bother anybody." Clattering, the coin wobbled and fell.

The tavern keeper eyed the money. "Drink's extra," he said at length.

Colbie produced a silver shield and set it beside the crown. "Tea if you have it. Cider if you don't."

It turned out that even cider was too optimistic. She had to settle for ale. She sat down at a table in the corner, the proprietor brought her a tankard, and then he returned to palavering with his fellows.

They tried to keep their voices low and their conversation private, but she possessed hearing that, despite a career that frequently brought her into proximity to clanging metal, pounding engines, and thundering artillery, remained as keen as when she was a child. She also did her best to look uninterested and lost in her own thoughts, and perhaps that undermined the conspirators' caution. As a result, she caught most of what they had to say, and context enabled her to guess the rest.

"It's a chance to get out from under," said the tavern keeper.

"Or a chance to get dead," said a short man whose faded shirt with its rank and insignia patches had once been part of an Army corporal's uniform. The blade hanging from his belt was military too, a trench knife with a studded brass "skull crusher" hilt.

The man with the birthmark scowled. "When did you turn into a coward?"

"You know he's not," mumbled a third man. Sandy-haired, he had a diffident way of bowing his head when he talked, and, watching from the corner of her eye, Colbie thought she knew why. He had wooden false teeth and was apparently embarrassed about the way they looked. "He's just being sensible. Why take a chance when things won't be any worse than before?"

"You can't count on that," the tavern keeper said. "These Black Dogs could raise our taxes tomorrow. Even if they don't, they aren't a part of the . . ." He waved his hand as if seeking to pluck the right word from the air. "The *system* down here, and that makes it not all right."

The former trencher chuckled. "You make it sound like we were all just one big loving family before."

"You know what I mean. They're outsiders."

"Outsiders who wiped out the Patient Weavers," said the man with the wooden teeth.

"Because they took them by surprise," said the tavern keeper, "and even so, I'll bet the Weavers killed some of them in their turn. And did you hear? Yesterday, Gardek Stonebrow, that bounty hunter, killed a couple more and got away clean."

It would have annoyed Eilish to know he'd been omitted from the story. Colbie suppressed a smile.

"So now we're on a bounty hunter's side?" asked the man with the dentures.

The tavern keeper spat. "Of course not. But don't you see, it proves the strangers aren't as tough as they want people to think. They might be stretched thin trying to take control of everything that once belonged to the Weavers."

"Or maybe there are hundreds of them," the man with the false teeth said.

The trencher turned to the fourth man. "What do *you* think, Vidor?"

Vidor frowned, fingered his chin, and pondered before answering. His wrinkles and shock of white hair made it plain he was older than his friends, but he looked spry enough that Colbie suspected his crook-handled cane was for self-defense, not hobbling around. A small bronze button pinned to the collar of his black coat proclaimed his devotion to the Ascendant Rowan, patron of the needy and oppressed.

"My instincts tell me," he said at length, "that our friend Dunley has a point. The Patient Weavers were a gall. These Black

Dogs could turn out to be gangrene, and the longer we wait to cut, the more difficult and dangerous the surgery will be."

Scowling, the other men worked their way through the metaphor. Then the tavern keeper—Dunley—said, "So you agree with me. We should kill them when they come back around."

"Perhaps," Vidor said.

"'Perhaps?'"

"I never recommend violence lightly. The outcome is never certain, even when a person has taken proper measure of the foe, and in this case we definitely have not. But it may still be the wiser course."

The trencher chuckled. "That's about as straight an answer as anybody ever gets out of you, isn't it?"

Vidor's smiled. "You know me so well."

"Yes, and if *you* say to do this . . . well, I guess we could try."

"Then I'm in, too," sighed the man with the wooden dentures. "Even though it'll probably get us killed. What we need to do now is carry word up and down the street. Persuade others to help if they're willing and to stay out of the way if not."

He and the trencher headed for the door.

"The dog could be useful," Dunley said. "I'm going to bring her in." He strode toward a door in the back wall.

When he went out, Vidor turned and gave Colbie a smile. She realized that if he wasn't certain she'd been eavesdropping, he at least suspected it. "If there's anywhere else to wait until time for your rendezvous," he said, "you might prefer it."

Colbie shook her head. "I don't know these tunnels. I wouldn't want to risk getting lost."

Vidor studied her for another second. Then, he said, "I understand. If you get hungry, Dunley fries up a decent scramble when someone can badger or bribe him into lighting the stove."

As Vidor finished speaking, Dunley and the mastiff came inside, and Colbie was left wondering exactly how much the man with the cane really did understand. More, she suspected, than she would have preferred, but her instincts told her he wouldn't use that comprehension to her detriment.

She also wondered how best to react to the situation in which she found herself. It appeared that the bratya—these Black Dogs—hadn't yet scared the entire Undercity into abject surrender. Assuming the former soldier and the man with the wooden teeth could rally support, the inhabitants of this buried street would attack the Khadorans the next time the intruders showed their faces.

The question was, what should Colbie do about it? Reveal her identity and offer to join in? That seemed chancy in light of their animosity toward Gardek. It might also commit her to a battle her side had no hope of winning. She had no doubt some of her potential allies knew how to roll a drunkard or slide a dagger into an unsuspecting victim's back. That didn't mean they could hold their own against the Khadorans.

Though it scarcely made her feel like a dauntless hero in a ballad, she'd come here to gather intelligence, and that was still what she was resolved to do. If a battle broke out while she was hanging around, and if it progressed in a way that made it seem like she ought to take a hand, well, perhaps at that point she'd reconsider. Otherwise, she'd watch, learn, and slip away before harm befell her. That rear exit would do nicely.

She finished her ale, bought another, and nursed it while the dog watched her suspiciously. The corporal and False Teeth returned, conferred with Dunley and Vidor, and went back out again, and she idly conjectured about the shared history that bound them all together.

Time dragged after that. Eventually her stomach growled, and she consulted her pocket watch. It was past noon. She wondered if she could convince Dunley to light the stove, and then Vidor abruptly closed the little green leather book he'd been reading and sat up straight.

"They're here," he said.

Even as he spoke, Colbie sensed it, too: a vibrant tension she'd occasionally felt in the field that signified the enemy was nigh. Or perhaps the sensation was just her nerves reacting to the sudden quiet that had in reality alerted her. In a wood or some farmer's barley field, the birds and beasts would have fallen silent. Here, it was the muffled sounds of the vault.

The mastiff stared at the front door and growled. Dunley reached under the bar and produced a repeating crossbow. As he cocked it, he shot Colbie a glare. "You wanted to be here," he said. "Now keep your head down."

Meanwhile, Vidor rose, hung his cane on his forearm, closed his eyes, and pressed the opposing fingertips of his two hands together. He whispered, and Colbie caught her breath as she felt a tingling flow over her limbs and leave a cool, thin, flexible layer of an invisible something behind. She supposed she ought to be grateful that the old man had seen fit to include her in his aura of protection.

She waited to hear a rattle of gunfire, battle cries, or perhaps the crash of heavy objects being hurled from rooftops onto the targets below. But everything remained quiet, and then the oiled paper in the front windows glowed green.

Colbie looked at Dunley. "Hide the crossbow! Fast!"

He scowled. "This is none of your concern."

"Are you deaf? For some reason, your neighbors didn't attack! You don't want to be the only one caught holding a weapon!"

"She's right!" said Vidor, sitting back down. "Put it away!"

The window glowed brighter. The source of the light was visible now as a discrete circle on the other side. Dunley thrust the repeating crossbow back in its hiding place, and then a swordsman with a tattooed neck and hands opened the door. He wore a hip-length cape that left his fighting arm exposed.

The mastiff bristled and growled. Putting his hand on his sword hilt, the Khadoran grinned as if he hoped the animal would attack. But Dunley snapped, "Queenie! Lie down! Stay!" The dog reluctantly settled where she was.

Meanwhile, outside the open door, a steamjack with dark coal smoke fuming from the stack on its back tramped into view, and Colbie scowled. The automaton was the same make as the one she'd wrecked during the assault on the Patient Weavers' enclave, and no doubt it was the reason why, when the moment arrived, the residents of the vault had balked at following through on their plan.

Colbie had fought on proper battlefields and was conversant with true warjacks. Yet even she respected the lethal capabilities of the modified laborjacks the Black Dogs had smuggled into Corvis. To the inhabitants of the Undercity, the machines must seem truly daunting.

And so the Khadorans were parading them around. It was a show of force to stifle thoughts of resistance.

The source of the green light appeared in the doorway. For a moment, with the beam shining right into her eyes, Colbie took the figure for a squat 'jack of a different design that included a lamp mounted on its shoulder. Then she made out the bearded human face inside the helmet and the enormous maul in the steel gauntlets. She was actually looking at a man in steam-powered armor, surely the same one Gardek and Eilish had encountered.

The ironhead had to turn sideways to come through the door and still scraped gouges in the frame. The floorboards groaned under his weight. He took little shuffling steps as he pivoted to take in all the occupants of the room. Apparently he couldn't twist his head, or rather, the helmet wouldn't twist with it. Colbie filed that nugget of information away.

"I have your money," Dunley said.

"Good," said the ironhead. "But we need to talk."

"About what?" the tavern keeper asked.

"No one was on the street when we came in. But people were crouching behind the windows. People with guns."

"Yet no one opened fire," Vidor said.

The ironhead made another shuffling, thumping turn to glower at him. "I wasn't talking to you, old man."

Vidor shrugged. "I'm just pointing out that you must have known what sort of place the Undercity is when you decided to come here. You must have understood if you demanded tribute and then showed weakness, people would lash out. But instead, you showed strength, and so they'll bow to the new order. It's just the way these things work, isn't it? No need to take it personally."

The ironhead sneered. "So I should just collect the tax and go?"

"That's not what I said. Although, in this enclosed space, it won't be too long before the smoke from your stack starts to choke us all, including you."

He had a point. The black fumes were already stinging Colbie's eyes and nose. But, turning back to Dunley, the Khadoran said, "You're a leader in this dung pile. People told us. I suspect the ambush was your idea. Maybe I should make an example of you."

"Then who would pay his tax next week?" Vidor asked.

The armored Black Dog pivoted, the motion still ponderous but faster than Colbie would have expected from watching him hitherto. Nearly brushing the ceiling, the maul swung up and over to crash down on the old man's table. Ice covered the wooden round even as it shattered into pieces.

Colbie winced at the possibility that the maul, still hurtling downward, would freeze and break Vidor's leg as well. But it smashed into the floor instead, though the man with the cane still gasped in reaction to the frost that splashed him. Meanwhile, Queenie the mastiff sprang up, and Dunley bellowed another command to hold her where she was.

"I told you," said the ironhead to Vidor, "nobody's talking to you." He turned back to Dunley. "Double tax, this week and next."

"I'll get it." The tavern keeper went behind the bar, reached underneath it, and counted out coins from wherever they were kept. Smirking, the ironhead's swordsman comrade took them and tucked them away in the sabretache clipped to his belt.

With that accomplished, the ironhead turned to Colbie. "And who are you?" he asked.

Inwardly, Colbie cursed. She'd hoped no one was paying attention to her sitting passively with head bowed over her ale in her dark corner, but evidently that wasn't the case. "I'm just waiting for someone," she said.

The ironhead leered. "Maybe it's me."

Colbie decided to make her own little show of strength. She stared the ironhead in his pouchy, bloodshot eyes. "I guarantee you, in the end, you'd be sorry you went to the trouble to take off all that armor."

The Khadoran glared. "You'd do better to make friends with me."

"It seems to me," Vidor said, "that you already assessed a penalty, Dunley paid it, and that should be the end of the matter. If you now harass his patrons, that's gratuitous. And if you want the Undercity to regard the Black Dogs as both fearsome and honorable, it's counterproductive."

The ironhead swung back around with one armored forearm poised to clout Vidor in the head. The white-haired man avoided the blow by jumping out of his seat and backing out of range. Seeming to take this purely defensive action as tantamount to a threat, the other Khadoran drew his sword. Dunley's eyes flicked from his crouching dog to the spot where his crossbow was concealed.

Colbie poised herself to thrust back her chair, spring up, and open her greatcoat. She'd decided that if there was a fight, she was going to sit it out, but how could she if it erupted because the old man, the tavern keeper, and even the dog were trying to protect her? And maybe the slug gun could neutralize the ironhead if she readied it in time. Though she was less than sanguine about what would happen after.

Then Vidor pointed to the little bronze button on his collar. "Perhaps you've heard," he said, "it's bad luck to hurt a priest. I was only trying to look out for you."

Just as he finished speaking, a voice called from outside. Colbie recognized the first word, *Olekse*, as a Khadoran name. Since she didn't speak the language, she couldn't understand the rest, but the impatient tone suggested it might be something on the order of "Is there a problem in there?" Or possibly "What's the holdup?"

Whatever it was, it broke the gathering tension. The ironhead—Olekse, presumably—spat and said, "Not bad luck, but not worth the trouble either. This time." Scraping loose more chips and splinters, he squeezed back out the doorway. Bidding a mocking farewell with a flick of his blade, the swordsman followed.

Dunley shut the door after them and then rounded on Colbie. "Damn it, woman! I knew I shouldn't let you stay, and your gold should have warned me I was right. Who spends crowns in a pigsty like this?"

"Easy," Vidor said. "It wasn't her fault."

The tavern keeper stooped to pet Queenie. "Trouble's trouble," he said. "Speaking of which, if our white-livered neighbors refuse to fight, maybe we really are stuck with these bastards."

"I don't know about that," said the man with the cane, "but my intuition tells me that perhaps it isn't our job to root them out after all."

"Whose job is it, then?"

"Possibly Captain Sterling's." Vidor gave Colbie another smile.

• • •

THE RAIN HAD FINALLY STOPPED, although many of the people in the street still had their umbrellas, broad-brimmed hats, and slickers, mute testimony that they didn't expect the break in the foul weather to last for long.

Lacy Murrough took a deep breath and resolved to enjoy it while it did. It would be wasteful to do anything else when there were even discernible golden sunbeams shining through gaps in the overcast.

Strolling on, the mail shirt under her tabard clinking faintly, she sought to twirl her truncheon and fumbled it instead. Someone nearby laughed, and, blushing, she took a firm grip on the weapon and let it hang at her side. She didn't want to look like any more of a green recruit to the Watch than in fact she was.

Soon, she thought, she'd learn to spin a truncheon as well as any grizzled veteran. More important, she'd prove herself capable of more challenging tasks than walking a beat in a comparatively quiet neighborhood. She'd bring the most despicable lawbreakers to justice and rise through the ranks.

With a snort, she reminded herself that she needed to earn such opportunities not by daydreaming of triumphs to come but by acquitting herself well in the assignment she currently had.

Otherwise, she suspected, her apple cheeks and eager smile would hold her back, inspiring her superiors with a paternal urge to keep her out of harm's way. She'd been that sort of "cute" since she was a toddler, and she was sick of it.

Keeping her eyes moving as she'd been taught, she looked for signs of trouble. Even in broad daylight in this placid district, she shouldn't have to search too hard, Corvis being what it was. Surely she could spot a pickpocket plying his trade, a thief snatching an item from a vendor's pushcart and running, or an altercation requiring intervention before one angry participant struck the other.

But alas, all the adults in view appeared to be honest citizens calmly going about their business while a boy on the corner waved a broadsheet over his head and yelled about "slaughter" in the Undercity. The editors of such publications knew their readers had an appetite for reports of outrages in the tunnels beneath their feet, and for better or worse, the stories didn't need to be accurate, merely lurid.

Lacy didn't see how this particular story could possibly be accurate considering that even the Watch had little idea of what was currently happening down below. She'd heard more than one officer say he didn't want to know, an attitude that irritated her. Perhaps someday, when she was a lieutenant, she'd organize an elite squad to clean up the Undercity once and for all. She could see herself shouting orders and pointing with her truncheon to send her men in pursuit of fleeing felons.

"Excuse me," someone said.

Startled, Lacy jumped, and then, annoyed that she'd once again gotten lost in her own thoughts despite resolving not to, turned toward the person who'd spoken. That produced another twinge of surprise.

Lacy was young, and the woman who'd approached her was older. But they were of about the same middling height, and both were plump—"pleasingly plump," Lacy's mother had called it when her adolescent daughter groused about her looks. They both had round, dimpled faces framed by short blond hair, although hers was like straw, and the older woman's was silvery. In short, they so resembled one another that, if she hadn't known better, she might have imagined she was meeting a long-lost aunt.

From the way the older woman's eyes widened, she saw the resemblance, too. But that flicker of surprise came and went in an instant, giving way to an expression that combined worry and hesitation in equal measure.

"I hate to bother you," the older woman said. She had a trace of an accent that Lacy couldn't place, but there was nothing extraordinary about that. People came to Corvis from all over.

"It's no bother, ma'am," Lacy replied. "I'm here to help when I can. Is there a problem?"

"Yes. I was supposed to meet my son on his houseboat. But he didn't come out on the deck to meet me, even when I called."

"Did you go aboard?"

The white-blonde woman shook her head. "I should have, but it all just felt funny to me. Like something was wrong. I didn't want to step on by myself." She grimaced. "I know I'm being silly. He just forgot me or was called away or something. But still, would you take a look along with me? It's just over that bridge and down the side canal."

"Of course."

As they walked, Lacy asked if the son's health was good and if he was having any problems in his life. So far as his mother knew, the answers were yes and no, respectively. So in all probability, whatever had happened, the young man was all right. Lacy told herself she should be glad of that, not disappointed that the current errand likely wouldn't offer a chance to prove her mettle.

The "side canal" was the White Canal, presumably named not for its murky water but for the whitewashed facades of the buildings looming on either side, although in fact those were soot-stained to a dingy brownness, too. The sunbeams shining elsewhere hadn't found their way past overhanging eaves and balconies to the waterway and sidewalks beneath. Rather, the walls channeled a chilly breeze that made Lacy shiver.

The son's houseboat bore a figurehead in the form of a golden seahawk, a pretentious if not ridiculous ornament that looked recently repainted while more fundamental repairs remained unattended to. Lacy tried to sense the ominous atmosphere the mother had described, and perhaps she did, a little. More likely, it was just the cold breeze or merely her imagination.

"What's your son's name?" she asked.

"Ryleigh," the older woman replied. "Ryleigh Bray."

"Mr. Bray!" Lacy called. "I'm Officer Murrough of the Watch! I'm with your mother! She's worried about you! Are you there?"

No one answered.

"We're coming aboard!" Lacy stepped down onto the deck and then, when her companion hesitated to follow, offered her hand. Mrs. Bray took it with a nervous little smile.

"I know the boat's right up next to the land," Ryleigh's mother said, "but I'm always afraid my foot will go through the crack."

"It's all right," Lacy said. She looked around the deck, making sure there was nothing of interest there. "If Ryleigh's here at all, he's inside. Let's take a look."

The houseboat's cabin was partly above deck and partly below. Lacy descended a steep little three-step companionway and tried the handle of the hatch. It was unlocked, and she pushed it open.

On the other side was a space that appeared to serve as living area, sleeping quarters, and galley all in one. A somewhat pudgy young man with silver-blond hair lay sprawled on his back at the far end. Spying him over Lacy's shoulder, Mrs. Bray gasped.

Lacey rushed to Ryleigh and dropped to one knee beside him. Trying to remember what little she knew about resuscitation, he put her hand in front of the stricken man's mouth and nose in hopes of feeling him breathing in and out.

Ryleigh's hand shot up and grabbed her by the throat.

Stunned, she froze for an instant while his fingers squeezed and cut off her breath. Then, suddenly frantic, she lifted her truncheon to beat him until he let go.

Something snatched hold of the cudgel and twisted it out of her grasp. "Now, now, dearie," said Mrs. Bray, "you wouldn't want to mark that handsome face."

Lacy's vision was already dimming. She raised both hands and clawed at the fingers cutting off her air. Ryleigh snatched his arm back.

Lacy jammed her own arm backward, and her elbow rammed into some portion of Mrs. Bray's anatomy and made her grunt. Lacy floundered to her feet and knew exactly what should happen next: she'd bolt back out the hatch to safety. But her foot caught on something or one of her attackers tripped her, and she stumbled, banging her shin against the built-in bench that ran along the side of the compartment.

By the time she recovered her balance, both her assailants were on their feet, too, with cut-and-thrust swords in their hands. The weapons must have been sitting where mother and son could snatch them easily, but, intent on aiding someone who might be dying, Lacy hadn't noticed them until now.

She abruptly remembered she had a short sword of her own, for situations when a truncheon wouldn't suffice. She snatched the blade from its scabbard.

Meanwhile, Mrs. Bray circled in a way that both precluded any chance of an unopposed scramble to the hatch and made it even more difficult for Lacy to keep track of both her opponents at the same time. "Please, love," the older woman said, "put down the sword before anyone gets hurt. I promise, we only want to talk."

Lacy yelled and rushed Mrs. Bray. She feinted high and then thrust to the belly as the drillmaster had taught her.

The silver-blonde woman parried Lacy's blade with her own. The block spun into a bind that twisted the short sword out of her fingers.

Mrs. Bray swung her sword to the side and charged. Lacy tried to stop her by thrusting out her arm, but the strike missed the other woman's face. Mrs. Bray bulled her backward into the waiting arms of her son, who whipped them around her.

Lacy strained to wrestle a hand free, but it was impossible. What had the drillmaster said to do when she was grappled from behind? Snap her head back into the outlaw's face. Kick back into his leg, rake down, and stamp on his toes.

She tried and made glancing contact a couple times. But Ryleigh's grip didn't slacken, and his mother had her hands raised to strangle.

At that moment, Lacy spied a figure beyond the porthole. Dressed in a long forest-green skirt, carrying a wicker basket on her arm, a woman was walking briskly along the sidewalk beside the houseboat. And if Lacy could see her, then the passerby would see her too if only she turned her head.

Lacy screamed, "Help!" But the woman just walked obliviously on, and then Mrs. Bray's hands clamped around her victim's throat.

Lacy tried to kick her away. That didn't work either. Within just a moment she needed air, *needed* it, and a tightness in her chest intensified until it was as agonizing as the compression of her neck. Then blackness swallowed her.

She woke up gasping, able to breathe but with her throat still hurting and the tang of blood in her mouth. When her eyes fluttered open, she saw that mother and son had laid her on the bench she'd blundered into before.

Mrs. Bray was on the bench, too, sitting with Lacy's head in her lap. The silver-blonde woman had the fingers of one hand curled in the captive's hair, not tightly but no doubt ready to tighten if need be. She held a dagger in the other.

Ryleigh was kneeling on the floorboards beside Lacy, penning her in, making her even more helpless, if that was possible. He was studying her with wide eyes and a strange little smile on his face.

"Well," said Mrs. Bray, "now that we've all had our exercise for the day, it's time for some conversation. You don't mind some questions, do you, dear?"

"What questions?" Lacy rasped. Her throat hurt worse when she spoke, and the taste of blood grew stronger. The strangulation had truly injured her, perhaps seriously. She trembled.

"There, there," said Mrs. Bray, "everything's all right. As long as you cooperate, we wouldn't dream of hurting you. Isn't that right, lambkin?"

Her son nodded. "I'd never hurt anyone so pretty."

Mrs. Bray's eyes narrowed. "She *is* pretty, isn't she?" she said with frost in her tone.

Ryleigh flinched. "A little. Not like . . . I mean, I was just trying to put her at ease. Like you do."

His mother smiled, but there was still a trace of coldness hiding underneath. "You don't have to be embarrassed. You're a young man. It's natural for you to notice such things. As long as you remember your manners, it's fine."

Ryleigh inclined his head. "Yes, Mama," he said.

Mrs. Bray returned her attention to Lacy. "Now where were we?" the older woman said. "Oh yes, you were going to give us some information, or at least I hope you can. Fodor and I are at our wits' end. We've been to their homes. We've even been to this magnificent university of yours. And the Black River Irregulars have vanished without a trace."

"Who?"

"Mercenaries, dear. Ordinarily, I wouldn't expect a fine, upstanding young officer like you to know anything about such ne'er-do-wells. But I'm told the Watch hires them for special jobs on occasion, and that that's the case at present. If you can point Fodor and me in their direction, that will be lovely."

And if not, Lacy thought, her captors would torture and ultimately kill her. She struggled to think, and after a terrible moment of blankness, a memory presented itself. "I heard something. On the night of the big battle in the tunnels, a Watch company was going to go down. But then they didn't. Two mercenaries, both of them women, showed up and told Watch Commander Helstrom something that made him call it off."

"What?" Ryleigh—or Fodor—asked.

"I don't know! I wasn't on duty, and I'm new! The higher-ups don't tell me what they're thinking!"

"It's all right," said Mrs. Bray—that was surely a false name, too, but it was all that Lacy knew to call her. "You're doing fine. Was one woman swarthy and lean, and the other one a redhead in a red-and-yellow coat?"

"That sounds right. From what I heard."

Fodor grunted. "There it is. Sterling and Gormleigh, absolutely, positively linked together. Ivan will be happy."

"Only if we find them." His mother beamed down at Lacy. "Dear, this is the really important part. Imagine your Watch Commander hiring mercenaries to act against the new gang in the Undercity. For whatever reason, he doesn't want them to sleep in their own beds while they're doing it. Where does he put them up instead?"

"I don't know!" Lacy croaked. "You'd have to ask him!"

Mrs. Bray sighed. "I'm flattered that you have such a high opinion of our abilities. Honestly, we think rather well of ourselves, too. But extracting information from such an important official is a little more than we care to take on. Perhaps you can think of something else we could try." She raised the dagger a little, no doubt to remind Lacy of its proximity.

At first, Lacy's head was empty yet again, as if fear were a strangler choking off the breath of thought. Then, just as she was about to break down and simply beg for mercy, an answer came to her. "Lieutenant Bartley was there! It was his men who were going below! He'd know!"

Mrs. Bray and her son exchanged glances. "Still a somebody," Fodor said.

"But not as important as the official in charge of all the law enforcement in Corvis," the silver-blonde woman replied. "I think he might be reachable. If he is, and we can befriend him, that could benefit the bratya forever after."

"Did I give you what you need?" Lacy asked. She was ashamed of the eagerness in her pained whisper of a voice, but that feeling was a small thing compared to the hope of survival.

"You certainly did." Mrs. Bray gently lifted Lacy's head from her lap, shifted out from underneath it, set it down, and stood up. "And once you give your solemn promise not to tell anyone about our meeting, we can go our separate ways."

"I swear," Lacy said. She was still afraid—deathly afraid, if she was honest—but even so, she already knew she had no intention to keeping that pledge. Reporting all this would assuage the feeling that she'd been craven and inept. Her superiors might even commend her for bringing them word of a problem they'd known nothing about.

Still imagining it, she started to stand up, and then Mrs. Bray slashed the arteries in the side of her neck. Fodor gave a soft little cry that might have reflected dismay.

His mother shot him a glance, then pivoted back around with a scowl on her face and raised the bloody knife high. Legs shaking and twitching but no longer able to move of her own volition, Lacy flopped back on the bench. She realized it was no longer sufficient simply to kill her. Mrs. Bray felt the need to stab away her face.

• • •

WHEN COLBIE OPENED THE FRONT DOOR of the safehouse, she found herself face-to-face with Gardek and Eilish, who were on the verge of coming out. The latter had the hood of his cloak up, perhaps to make the bandages wrapping his head less conspicuous.

The trollkin's black eyes glowered down at her. "There you are!"

"We were just about to come looking for you," Eilish said. "What possessed you to sneak off without telling anyone where you were going?"

Colbie bristled. "I'm the captain of this company. I don't need your permission to act as I see fit."

"But you do need to behave like you have a brain in your head," the arcanist replied.

"If you want to continue with this assignment," said Julian Helstrom, speaking from somewhere beyond the door.

Colbie winced and strode forward. Gardek and Eilish made way for her. Milo, Natak, Regan, Pog, and, unfortunately, Canice were in the front room as well. Colbie was glad to see that at least the others had had the sense to give the Watch Commander one of the chairs, but that courtesy hadn't prevented a frown from settling on his face.

Colbie gave him a respectful nod. "Watch Commander. I take it you've come for a progress report. I'm sorry I made you wait."

"You didn't," Helstrom said. "I arrived to find your wizard with a head wound, your alchemist in the midst of a shivering fit, and your bounty hunter shouting at the gobber for 'allowing' you to wander off by yourself. Naturally, I asked questions. So I've already heard about all the narrow escapes and dead ends."

"Investigators have to take chances and venture down blind alleys on the way to uncovering the truth," Colbie said. "I'm sure you understand that better than anyone, Watch Commander."

"He understands that nothing's getting accomplished," said Canice, leaning against the frame of the door that led to her improvised workroom.

"I'd like to believe that something is," Helstrom said, "but I haven't heard much cause for hope. Captain Sterling, I hired your company because you suggested your partners could investigate without being noticed as my own men could not. Plainly, at this point, you've lost that advantage. Perhaps, then, it's time to limit your responsibilities to guarding Miss Gormleigh and Mr. Warbiter as I originally intended."

"And reduce our payment," Milo said, brow shiny with perspiration.

Helstrom gave him a sour look. "I have a budget, Mr. Boggs. I have to justify expenses."

"What have the Watch's own investigators discovered?" Colbie asked.

"To date, very little," the lawman said. He stretched out one leg, and the poleyn made a tiny clink. "The difference being, I'm obliged to pay them no matter what."

"Then we're ahead of them," Colbie said. "I've just been down in the Undercity, and I *did* pick up some information." She started to tell the story. When she got to Vidor and how his three friends had deferred to his opinion, Gardek nodded.

"You know him?" Colbie asked.

"Vidor Rusling," the trollkin answered.

"Is he really a priest?" Eilish asked.

Gardek shrugged. "Some say yes, others that the Church tossed him out for some unforgivable transgression. All I know is, he's helped quite a few people in the Undercity. He was in the thick of it on the Longest Night." The bounty hunter's wide mouth tightened, and Colbie surmised he was recalling his brother's death at the hands of the risen dead.

"He worked a bit of magic," she said, "although I don't know if it was really a prayer or a spell like one of Eilish's." She continued her tale and, after another minute, said something that made Canice catch her breath.

"'Black Dogs,'" the gun mage repeated. "You're sure that's what he said?"

"Yes," Colbie replied.

"Then they're not just a bratya. They're *the* bratya. The same one I fought back in Laedry."

"Then they really were after you in particular," Helstrom said.

Natak Warbiter nodded. "It's why, out of all the gangs in the Undercity, the Khadorans chose the Patient Weavers to attack."

"We can even conjecture," Eilish said, "that it's why they're in Corvis in the first place." He smiled crookedly. "Clearly, it's working out for them so far. Still, it's a risky endeavor to try to establish a beachhead in a hostile foreign country."

"But this doesn't make sense," Canice said. "Obviously, they'd take revenge if they figured out who I am and then got their hands on me. But to go to this much trouble? When people like them kill and get killed all the time?"

"It does seem . . . extravagant," Helstrom said. "Still, you were right to trust the instinct that told you to flee the Undercity and then go to ground."

Colbie was certain the Watch Commander meant to commend the red-haired woman's prudence, not to imply any measure of cowardice, but to her amusement, the remark made Canice's jaw clench even so.

"It's interesting," Milo said, "that these Black Dogs have a special grudge against Canice, but unless we're going to dangle her like bait—not that I'm ruling that out—is it helpful? What else did you find out, Colbie?"

"Not a great deal," she said. "I had a close-up view of this

Olekse, his armor, and the ice maul. I noticed a couple of details that may help when we fight him again. I also discovered that even after a day in the Pink Palace, he's still lickerish." She related what had happened at the very end of the encounter, when the Khadoran had turned his attention to her.

"And that proves my point," Eilish said. "Only a dunce would have gone on this madcap excursion by herself."

He might even be right, but Colbie still resented him scolding her in front of Helstrom, Natak, and particularly Canice. "You've already made your opinion known," she said in her steeliest tone. "Now let the matter drop."

He didn't. "You're a distinctive-looking woman, and as the Watch Commander observed, the Khadorans now know that the Black River Irregulars are stalking them. What if the ironhead or his friend had recognized you?"

"I would have handled it."

"Without your steamjack?" Canice said. "Not likely."

Colbie drew breath to snap back, then sensed that losing her composure would only undermine her authority. "As I already said, we need to stop blathering about what might have happened and decide what's going to happen next. Old vendettas and such notwithstanding, I'd say the most useful thing I learned is that the Black Dogs are patrolling parts of the Undercity the Patient Weavers once controlled. What can we do with that?"

Natak shifted on his pallet of pillows and blankets, none too clean to begin with and now stained with a little blood that had leaked through his bandages. "Follow a patrol back to their hideout."

Gardek grunted. "Possible. But Milo, the schoolboy, and I walked into a trap the last time we tried to track them. It might be better to ambush one of the patrols, take a prisoner, and sweat him for the location of the hideout."

"These people are tough and loyal," Canice said. "Still, it might work if you've got the stomach for it. Or you could turn the prisoner over to Natak and me."

"You'd have to take the right man alive," Milo said.

Eilish cocked his head. "How so?"

"You've been down below often enough that you forget how confusing it is to strangers. Even the settled parts. In every patrol, there'll likely be one man who's started to figure out his way around and can lead the rest. The others won't be any use to us."

"He's right," Gardek said. "It also occurs to me that if we capture a man but it takes a while to wring information out of him, that gives the bratya time to move to a different lair."

"Maybe," said Pog, sitting on the floor in the corner with his knobby knees drawn up to his chest, "it isn't the *men* you should be thinking about."

Colbie blinked. The more she'd seen of the gobber's mechanikal ability, the more she'd come to respect him. Yet even so, he was so shy and retiring in a group that it was easy to forget he was there.

"What do you mean?" she asked.

Now that he was the focus of everyone's attention, Pog hesitated, and for a moment his cheeks flushed a darker shade of green. "Well, you said it's not just people patrolling. The Black Dogs are marching their steamjacks around."

"So we should knock down another one of those?" Eilish asked. "Worth doing for its own sake, conceivably, but I've already been over the first one and didn't find any clues to point to the location of the hideout."

"And I doubt that even you and I working together," said Colbie to Pog, "could prevail on a captured 'jack to lead us there. Not in a reasonable period of time. We'd have to repair it, then establish control over it—and who knows what those Khadorans used as its cortex lock codes—then make it understand what we wanted it to do."

"I know," Pog said, "but what I'm thinking is, the bratya can't have all that many of them. Right?"

Helstrom grunted. "Not unless the customs officials are totally incompetent."

Canice grinned. "Incompetent or susceptible to bribery. But let's not get into that. The truth of the matter is, I didn't try to count steamjacks when the bratya attacked the Weavers. I was a little busy. But from what I saw and heard, I don't think there were more than half a dozen."

Colbie nodded. "Probably fewer."

"And you wrecked one," said Pog. "I don't think they'd care to lose any more. I also don't think they have a whole big team of mechaniks to work on them. They can't have just hundreds and hundreds of people, can they?"

"We'd better hope not," Eilish said, "or we were beaten before we even started. Pog, I see where you're going with this. In broad outline, anyway. But please, carry on for the benefit of those who are less astute." He flashed a taunting smile in Colbie's direction.

Pog frowned as though he disliked being drawn, even minimally, into his companions' efforts to needle one another. But he didn't protest out loud. Rather, he said, "The repair shop in the stronghold was the only one the Weavers owned outright, but there's another they collected taxes from. Suppose somebody ambushes a patrol right near there and knocks down a 'jack. Not beyond all hope of repair, but damaging it pretty badly. Then a mechanik comes out of the shop and helps get the machine running again, not perfectly, but well enough to limp back to the hideout."

Milo grinned. "You're thinking the Khadorans would take the mechanik along to keep working on the 'jack. Then you could sneak away and lead us back there."

Colbie frowned. "It would be tricky to leave the 'jack wrecked yet not *too* wrecked. But, Pog, you and I could figure that out. I'm more concerned about you serving yourself up to the Khadorans. What if they recognize you and want to kill you along with the rest of the Patient Weavers?"

Pog smiled wryly. "Really, Captain, what are the odds of that? This is the first time such a thing has even occurred to you, Miss Gormleigh, or Mr. Warbiter. It certainly didn't when we were all running from the Black Dogs. Nobody suggested to Watch Commander Helstrom that *I* might need a safe place to stay."

Colbie felt chagrined. "I apologize for that."

Pog held up a long-fingered hand. "Please don't. My kind only come up to your belt buckles." He glanced at Gardek. "Or sometimes not even that high. It's natural for you to overlook us until you want something. And me, well, I'm quiet, and that makes it worse. Anyway, the point is, the Black Dogs aren't hunting me. I'm beneath their notice."

"Even if you're right," Gardek said, "you'd be running a big risk."

"I know," Pog said, "and if I get you what you need . . . well, I don't mean to be pushy, but I'd like something for it. A second vote on whether I'm fit to join your company."

Colbie looked at her three partners, and read the same thought in each of their faces. That made it unanimous, then. After the friction that had plagued them of late, it felt good that they were all in accord.

"We won't need to vote," she said. "If you make this work, you're in."

Pog grinned. "Really? Thank you! Thank you all!"

Milo snorted. "Don't get too excited. It's basically just risking your life for not enough money over and over again."

"How many of my men do you need for this ambush?" Helstrom asked.

"None," Colbie said.

"Nothing against your men," Gardek rumbled, "but we'll have better luck sneaking to a good spot and hiding if it's just us. The Undercity takes special notice when the Watch is moving through the tunnels."

"And then someone sells the information to the gangs." Milo hesitated. "Not that *I've* ever done that."

Eilish grinned. "Perish the thought."

"There's another reason it should just be us," Colbie said. "We want the Black Dogs to underestimate the Watch's commitment to getting rid of them. When we determine where their stronghold is, that will be the time to strike with overwhelming force."

Helstrom nodded. "I see the logic. When do you foresee all this happening?"

"Pog needs to establish himself at the 'jack shop. Milo, Eilish, and Gardek could use a little more time to recover."

"I need to get hold of a new shield and pieces of armor, too," the trollkin said. "Maybe even stick some spikes on."

"A couple days, then," the Watch Commander said. "I wish it could be sooner, but I suppose it's not an emergency. Whatever these Black Dogs do next, it won't happen aboveground."

— 12 —

AS LONAN BARTLEY TRUDGED up the avenue, he lifted his eyes to look at the illuminated spires of the Cathedral of Morrow rising above the gabled rooftops of the houses. He liked living close to it, as though its sanctity protected his home and family from the ugliness he dealt with every day. And perhaps it really did, in that contemplating its holy beauty lifted his spirits. It washed the accumulated grime off his soul and allowed him to be the husband and father his loved ones deserved.

His step quickened as the brick facade of his own house came into view. Like the other residences on the street, this one was flush with the cobbled pavement, but Islene, his wife, was a devoted gardener and insisted on having some greenery out front. A dwarf crape myrtle in a terra-cotta pot stood to either side of the front door. The rain had only recently abated, and water dripped from the leaves.

Lonan wondered if the children were still awake. They were both young—he'd come to marriage and parenthood relatively late in life—and it was more likely Islene had already put them to bed. But he hoped not. The long hours he put in as a lieutenant of the Watch kept him from spending as much time with them as he would have liked.

He unlocked the door with one of the several keys on his ring and stepped into the foyer. The house was quiet. That almost certainly meant the boys were asleep. With a sigh, he turned in the direction of the dining room. At least there should be a welcome-home kiss and a hot supper waiting for him.

But Islene was nowhere to be seen nor was there food on the table. Confused, he looked through the doorway that led to the kitchen. Carrots from the garden out back lay on the cutting board, some chopped into pieces but others not. As though she'd been interrupted.

Above his head, a high voice shrieked, and then the wail blurred into sobbing. Wyatt, his two-year old, was in distress.

Lonan assumed that since his wife wasn't on the ground floor, she must be upstairs with the children attending to whatever was the matter. He strode to the foot of the stairs and called, "Islene?"

It took her a moment to answer. "I… Wyatt's sick! Can you come up?"

She sounded almost as upset as the crying child. What if the boy was seriously ill? His armor clinking, Lonan pounded up the steps, then faltered in shock.

Islene, Wyatt, and Brunner, the four year old, were in the master bedroom—and they weren't alone. A middle-aged woman and a younger man, both with pale blond hair, both round-faced and a little plump, were there with them.

The strangers were sitting on the bed with the children held in front of them. Her heart-shaped face blotchy and red from crying, snot on her upper lip, Islene was tied up in the corner chair she and Lonan mostly used as somewhere to drop dirty clothes.

The white-blonde woman held Brunnor close. The young

man—her son, perhaps?—had a grip on Wyatt.

Lonan snatched for the hand cannon hanging on his hip.

Islene cried, "Don't!"

The blond woman tightened her grip on Brunnor. His eyes wide, rolling, the four-year old strained against his captor's bosom. It was like a hideous parody of the way he squirmed when making himself comfortable in his mother's lap.

Lonan froze with his hand on the ivory grip of the hand cannon, the heavy pistol not yet clear of the holster. He had to assume they had weapons he just couldn't see. Slowly, he let the pistol settle back into the leather holder.

"Let them go!" he said. The command sounded weak, half-lost in Wyatt's wailing. Raising his voice, he repeated himself.

The blonde woman started to answer, then made an exasperated face that indicated she too recognized the difficulty of making herself heard over the sobbing. She looked to the other captor. "Sweetness, could you quiet him, please?"

The plump young man shifted his right hand. Islene gasped, and for an instant Lonan believed the intruder was reaching to strangle Wyatt or break his neck, believed he'd have to draw and shoot after all despite the threat to his other son. But the intruder simply clamped his hand over the toddler's mouth.

The woman beamed. "There! That's better, isn't it?"

"My pistol's loaded," Lonan said. His voice was shrill, and he struggled to make it deeper. "After that, I have my sword. It's up to me if either of you leaves this room alive."

"I understand," the woman said, "that you're a fearsome lawman and have surely killed many over the course of your career. Though you might not think it to look at us, my lambkin and I have also survived difficult situations in our time. Are you sure you want to resort to violence? When Fodor and I have these darling shields?" She stroked Brunnor's cheek. "When a stray blade swinging wild could slice your wife's pretty face?"

"What do you want?" Lonan asked.

"Your friendship," the woman said. "My name is Gridia, by the way."

"My friendship? Are you insane?"

Gridia sighed. "I understand how it might seem so. But we need a friend. We travelers have been having a trying time of it here in this city of yours."

"You're from the new gang. The one that wiped out the Patient Weavers." Which was to say, they were mad-dog killers.

"Very good!" The woman smiled at Fodor. "I told you he'd be clever. A man has to be to rise to such a responsible position."

Fodor made a spitting sound. "He doesn't look so clever now."

The woman shook her head, as though she regretted the other captor's insolence but not enough to put a stop to it. "As I said, the poor boy's frustrated. And grumpy. The way to put him in a better mood is for us to reach an understanding."

Her reasonable, pleasant demeanor was making the situation that much more ghastly. To Lonan, it somehow felt dreamlike and overwhelmingly, terrifyingly real at the same time. "Tell me what you want," he said.

"To begin with," Gridia replied, "three things. Canice Gormleigh. Natak Warbiter. And the Black River Irregulars." She cocked her head. "Or does that count as six things?"

"What do you want with them?" Lonan asked.

"By and large," Gridia said, "I think we should ask the questions, and you should answer them. That's pretty much the way it works in a conversation like this. But really, I don't mind satisfying your curiosity. We have a few reasons, some personal, some professional. Years ago, the gun mage killed our leader's brother. On top of that, we need to eliminate her and the ogrun so we can honestly boast that we've dealt with every single Patient Weaver. And the mercenaries are interfering with our efforts to get our business running." She smiled. "So, if you can see your way clear to send them into a trap, that will be splendid."

Lonan didn't want to acquiesce and make himself an accessory to murder. But Gormleigh and Warbiter were murderers themselves, and mercenaries were little better even if their violence technically fell within the law. He couldn't jeopardize his family to protect scum. At least in the short term, he had to play along.

Unfortunately, he wasn't sure how. "Captain Sterling and the others take their orders straight from Watch Commander Helstrom," he said. "I can't send them anywhere."

Gridia frowned. "What if you claimed you were relaying Helstrom's wishes?"

"He wouldn't use a lieutenant just to carry a message and especially not me. He knows I don't approve of the Watch employing mercenaries. Colbie Sterling knows that, too."

"And so they might be suspicious," sighed the woman. "Bother! Can you at least tell us where they're staying?"

Lonan felt like he was about to step off a cliff. He swallowed. "Yes. They asked for protection, and the old man put them in a safehouse. On Cooper Street."

A broad smile spread across Gridia's face. "Thank goodness you knew! Fodor and I have looked up and down, thither and yon, day and night for that one simple piece of information." She reached behind her, produced a leather bag, and upended it. Clinking against one another, pattering on the bedspread, gold coins poured out.

"What's this?" Lonan asked.

"Your first payment," Gridia said. "I'm afraid that many of the coins are Khadoran. You'll want to be careful where you spend them. Once we Black Dogs get ourselves established, we'll make sure to pay you in Cygnaran money."

"I don't want a bribe. I just want you to go away and leave my family alone."

"I'm terribly sorry, dear, but it won't be quite that easy. I told you, tonight marks the start of a friendship. You work for the Black Dogs from now on and will be well rewarded for it. While you grow accustomed to the idea, little Wyatt will be staying with us. Once you've collaborated enough that Corvis would surely hang you if your misbehavior came to light, we'll bring him back."

"Please!" Islene sobbed. "Don't do this!"

"As one mother to another," Gridia said, "I promise to take the very best care of him. Does he have a little cap? We don't want him catching cold in the evening chill."

• • •

BRUSHING HIS HAIR OUT OF THE WAY, Regan inspected the stitches she'd put in Eilish's scalp. "Am I going to live?" he asked.

"It appears so," she said. "But if you had any sense, you'd keep the bandage on for added protection."

"I can't go into battle looking like I'm already wounded," he said, rising from the bed. "It would encourage the enemy. How about playing squire and helping me don my armor?"

"If you're fit to fight, you can put it on yourself."

"Lady Una did it for Sir Alvy in the ballad."

"She also drowned herself when Alvy failed to return. If you get killed, that won't be happening, either."

Eilish laughed and picked up his scarred black backplate and breastplate from the chair he was using as an improvised armor stand. "Well, let's hope it won't come to that." He set the backplate on the bed.

Next, she knew, he'd lie down in it and snap and buckle the breastplate onto it, joining the two, and she decided that, after all, she lacked the patience to watch the awkward process. "Wait," she told him.

She then picked the backplate back up and held it against his spine while he fastened the chest armor in place. He was wise enough not to jape at her change of heart.

"It's not likely to 'come to that,' is it?" she asked. "The Watch Commander offered additional men and Colbie turned them down, so you must feel confident that you can do what you need to do and get away safely."

"Of course." Eilish picked up a vambrace and secured it around his forearm. "I'm more concerned that the excursion will turn out to be pointless. We haven't heard from Pog since he returned to the Undercity. We're taking it on faith that he managed to secure employment in the proper shop and that the Black Dogs are still parading their armed steamjacks through their new dominion. This could be one of those ideas that sounds promising but turns out to be too clever for its own good."

She looked at his leg armor, the greaves and cuisses, and

decided she absolutely wasn't going down on her knees to help with those. Talk about sending the wrong message. Instead, she fastened on the assorted pieces of his other metal sleeve.

"'Too clever for its own good,'" she repeated. "Like you."

He grinned, sat down on the bed, and picked up a cuisse. "Is that your diagnosis, Doctor?"

"I think," Regan said, "that it still galls you that even though you're the brightest member of the Irregulars, you're not the leader. That you believe you've made your peace with it. And that you can be nastier to Colbie than you realize."

He cocked his head. "You're serious."

"Yes."

"I'm not nasty. I respect Colbie. Hell, I even like her. That's why I was upset knowing she could have come to grief without any of the rest of us there to help her."

"And the way you expressed your concern was to call her reckless and stupid. In front of Helstrom and Canice."

"I'm reasonably certain I didn't use those words, and even if I did, weren't they justified? It *was* foolish to slip off by herself after Milo, Gardek, and I had already had near-fatal run-ins with the Black Dogs. I don't know what she was thinking."

"It bothers her that Canice is around."

His leg armor in place, Eilish rose and belted on his sword. "Well, that's understandable, considering that it wasn't so very long ago that Canice wanted to kill us."

"It isn't that, or not that chiefly. Canice is a famous fighter. Colbie's an able soldier, too, but a mechanik's role in battle is more… specialized, sometimes verging on useless if her steamjack stops working. Canice is a seasoned leader who's commanded dozens of subordinates. Colbie's a novice captain still getting the hang of leading just the three of you. And with the Patient Weavers gone, Canice is in need of a new berth."

Eilish whirled his long cloak around his shoulders. "You think Colbie fears the rest of us will desert her to follow Canice?"

"It wasn't that long ago that you, Milo, and Gardek were averse to joining forces in the first place. So yes, on some level, she does.

Even if she won't admit it to herself. And it doesn't help when you snipe at her."

"She's been a mercenary years longer than I have, and from what I gather, good-natured chaffing is just the way we ruffians behave."

Regan heaved a sigh. "I don't know why I thought I could persuade you to hold back anything you're in the mood to say."

"Honestly, neither do I. Shall we head downstairs? I imagine the others are ready, or nearly so."

They were.

Gardek had replaced his lost shield and pieces of plate with others just as massive and had even managed to convince the armorer to weld a few spikes on. Enough to make an enemy wary, even if the bounty hunter wasn't quite the hulking steel hedgehog of yore.

Milo already had his gas mask on. That made evaluating his condition more difficult, but, studying the way he carried himself and noting the absence of sweat on the visible strip of his forehead, Regan decided that the last of Druce Keller's poison and the rough-and-ready remedies he'd taken to counter it were likely out of his system.

In her long black greatcoat, Colbie looked cool and businesslike enough to make the physician wonder if Eilish wasn't right after all. Maybe she hadn't ever truly questioned her ability to hold onto the loyalty of her team, or if she had, perhaps she'd gotten over it.

Sprawled on his pallet, Natak gave Regan a grunt and a nod. He had yet to thank her for tending him, but he seemed to have decided she was useful and of late had sometimes borne her ministrations with greater patience than before.

Then Canice emerged from her makeshift workroom with a rune bullet in her hand. She held it up to her light, turned it, and then slipped it into a bullet loop.

Regan observed that all the bullet loops on the hip belt and shoulder rigs were full now. The gun mage had been working hard to rearm herself, and the little show she'd just put on had drawn everyone's attention to the fact.

Colbie plainly understood the point of it. Her mouth tightened, and her brown eyes narrowed behind her tinted goggles.

"Are you taking the steamjack?" Canice asked. Regan suspected the gun mage already knew the answer.

"No," Colbie replied. "Doorstop's fully functional again, but he's never been all that good at sneaking. We'll hold him in reserve until the assault on the Black Dogs' hideout. And before you resume your wheedling, you're not coming either."

"Are you sure?" Milo asked. "Maybe another fighter would come in handy."

"Even if it's *her*?" Colbie replied.

"Miss Gormleigh no longer has a reason to wish us ill," Eilish drawled. "You'd recognize that if you could see past your own prejudices." He gave Regan a wink.

It was his way of signaling that he'd decided she was right. His gibes and naysaying were vexing Colbie at a vulnerable time. But the knowledge had merely encouraged him, and at that moment, Regan could cheerfully have kicked him.

Yet at the same time she recognized that, however insolently expressed, his perspective had merit. He and the other Irregulars were headed into danger. Taking Canice along would be prudent, and as Regan wanted Eilish and his partners to come back safely, she hoped Colbie would agree to it, even if it scraped at her insecurities.

"I'm not saying we *need* reinforcements," Gardek rumbled. "The four of us have always managed to come out on top so far. But the schoolboy's right that there's no need to cling to old grudges. Natak's taught me a useful trick or two. From what I understand, Canice has shared secrets of her craft that Eilish and Milo can turn to their advantage. That's not enough to make me trust them anyplace and anytime, but in a fight with the Black Dogs, I expect Canice would occupy herself killing them and not shoot me in the back."

The redhead grinned. "Thank you for that heartfelt endorsement."

"We've been through this," Colbie said. "My decision stands. Especially now that we know for a fact that the bratya is absolutely determined to hunt her down. That resolve would make it more difficult to accomplish our purpose and slip away."

"Nonsense," the red-haired woman said.

"I'm not going to argue," Colbie replied. "I'll simply point out that if every one of us mercenaries goes to the Undercity, we leave Natak unprotected. And Eilish, Gardek, Milo, and I *are* going. So what does that suggest to you?"

"Actually," Milo said, "if the problem is that someone ought to stay, I—"

Colbie shot the alchemist a glare. He shrugged his shoulders and fell silent.

"All right," Canice growled. "When you put it like that. But damn you."

Her greatcoat swinging around her long legs, Colbie pivoted toward her three partners. "Let's move out." Eilish came to Regan for a kiss, which she gave him despite her exasperation, and then he followed the other Irregulars out into the grey, drizzling morning. Canice retreated into her workroom and slammed the door behind her.

Regan moved to check on Natak, but he scowled and waved her off. Plainly he wasn't in the mood to be fussed over. He rolled over to face the wall, perhaps for a nap, and, for want of any better occupation, she returned to Eilish's monograph.

She found it difficult to focus because she couldn't help worrying about him. Over the course of the past several months, he and the other Irregulars had proved themselves capable of dealing with Corvis' native crop of the felonious and depraved, but the Khadorans had come close to killing him once already.

A door banged and made her jump. She turned to see Canice stalking back out into the front room. Apparently the gun mage couldn't concentrate either.

"She could have sent to the Watch for men to stand guard," she said.

Though Regan privately disagreed with Colbie's decision, she nonetheless felt the need to stick up for her. "If Helstrom guessed why she was asking, he would have refused. Remember, he also thinks you should stay put. Anyway, the way I hear it, some officers of the Watch are more dependable than others. Would you have entrusted Natak's life to the luck of the draw?"

Canice scowled. "I don't know. But maybe. I hoped that Eilish, Milo, and even Gardek would argue harder on my behalf."

"Considering that you tried your best to ingratiate yourself with them."

"If that's how you want to put it."

"It worked about as well it could have. But as much as they all bicker, you were never going to shake their loyalty to Colbie. You might have done better to offer her a measure of respect yourself."

Canice sneered. "Humble myself before a leader who doesn't have a tenth of my experience?"

"The point is that she *is* the leader."

Canice made a spitting sound. "I just don't understand why she's so set against me."

Just as Regan had been unwilling to express disagreement with Colbie's decision, she was also disinclined to suggest the mechanik felt threatened. "The past aside, she's determined to establish the Black River Irregulars as a reputable, law-abiding company." She smiled. "Despite Milo's natural inclinations. That scheme doesn't mesh with people's impression of you."

"Be that as it may, it's a ridiculous posture. People hire mercenaries on the assumption that we'll terrorize and slaughter whomever we must to get the job done." The gun mage twisted a strand of her coppery hair between thumb and forefinger. "I wondered if the tension was because she had a yen for me but was too stiff-backed to admit it."

That surprised a laugh out of Regan. "I'm fairly certain the captain's not inclined that way." She hesitated. "Are you?"

Canice grinned. "Now and again, it makes for a change." Her expression soured again. "I already explained why I need to go back in the Undercity and take the fight to the bratya. It's truer than ever now that I know who they really are."

"Because they're even more of a threat to you than you first supposed?"

"That's only part of it. Eilish was right. They chose the Weavers to exterminate because of me. It was my job to keep things safe, and instead, my being there got everybody killed."

"You lost friends," Regan said.

Canice sighed. "You people are so sentimental. The only real friend I had there was Natak, and I got him out. Still, it's my responsibility to avenge the rest."

"Then go get started," Natak said, startling Regan, who'd thought he was asleep. Grunting, the ogrun lifted himself up on one elbow.

"You heard Sterling," Canice replied. "It would mean leaving you and the doctor unprotected. Now, if one of you could command the steamjack—"

"To hell with the steamjack! I'm Natak Warbiter, and thanks to the doctor here, I'm a lot stronger than the night you hauled me in here. If worst comes to worst, I'll protect myself."

Canice turned to Regan, who hesitated, torn between her concern for Eilish and the ethics of her profession. After a second, the latter won out. "I think Mr. Warbiter is being optimistic," she said.

The ogrun glared. "What do you know?" He shifted his gaze back to Canice. "Two things. First, it would disgrace me if a trivial matter like my safety prevented my korune from acting as her honor requires. Second, nothing's going to happen here. That was the whole point of finding a secret refuge aboveground, wasn't it?"

Canice nodded. "Yes, by all the Ascendants, it was." She strode into her workroom and reemerged, pulling on her red-and-yellow greatcoat.

"Be careful," Regan said. "If the bratya has put a price on your head and someone recognizes you—"

"I'll shoot him," the gun mage said. With a wave, she bustled out the door, leaving Regan to marvel at how happy the other woman suddenly seemed now that she was finally going forth to risk death and mete it out.

"Find me a weapon," croaked Natak, slumping back down again. "I need one ready to hand."

Regan frowned. "You just said we're safe."

"We are," the ogrun said. "Probably."

• • •

IF PRESSED, Canice would have had to acknowledge that Colbie had chosen a good spot for the ambush. The stretch of broad, high-ceilinged tunnel connected to the gas-lit vault of homes and illicit businesses in which Pog had presumably established himself, near enough that a curious mechanik might credibly hear a commotion and come to investigate, yet removed enough from the noncombatants who might otherwise have complicated the situation.

It was also dark, with burrow-like side passages opening a short but steep climb above the level of the tunnel floor. The openings would provide cover and concealment, and, when the 'jack was disabled, allow retreat into a mazelike area that ought to leave the Khadorans stymied and bewildered, even any who'd started to learn their way around.

At the moment, everything was quiet, and if not for the friction between Colbie and herself, Canice would have revealed herself to the Irregulars. That would have facilitated her coordinating with them. But she wasn't in the mood for yet another argument with the 'jack marshal. She could already hear it in her mind, the captain berating her and ordering her back to the safehouse, she refusing, the bickering dragging uselessly on and every jabbing word infused with venom.

It would be better, or at least more tolerable, to conceal her presence for now. With her skills, she could still attack to good effect when the fighting started, and afterward, when she'd demonstrated her usefulness to all four Irregulars, surely even Colbie wouldn't try to exclude her from subsequent operations.

Canice had helped herself to a couple of Milo's finger-sized vials of bottled light when the alchemist wasn't looking. She shook one to life, and the glow illuminated the nearer reaches of the tunnel before her. Only for a moment, though. Then she thrust the alchemical lamp inside her greatcoat and crept from her secondary passage into the larger one, guided by memory alone.

When she needed to see more, she turned her back on what lay ahead, the section of tunnel where the Irregulars were supposedly lurking, and, using her coat to shield the light, shone the candle-like glow back the way she'd come. The third time she did so, she found herself in proximity to one of the openings several feet above the tunnel floor. She put away the vial and scrambled blindly up the steep slope that led to the mouth of the burrow, wincing when, despite her desire for stealth, pebbles pattered away beneath her boots.

But none of the Irregulars sent a slug-gun shell, a grenade, a flare of magic, a crossbow bolt, or even a shouted inquiry in her direction, and in truth, that wasn't surprising. Even if one of them had heard the noise or noticed the light despite her attempts to conceal it, she plainly wasn't a bratya patrol complete with steamjack, and so they would see no reason to accost her. They would assume she was simply some random Undercity dweller embarked on business that had nothing to do with their own.

Groping, she found a bulge in the burrow wall. In the hours that followed, she couldn't make up her mind whether that narrow, downward-sloping makeshift bench was more or less uncomfortable than sitting on the ground. Occasionally she sipped water from her canteen or, touching her fingertip to each rune bullet in turn, whispered the name of the enchantment that resided therein. The exercise ensured that she'd always load the desired one without needing to pause and look.

Meanwhile, she peered out into the main tunnel. Once in a while someone passed obliviously below her, but so far, not the prey that she and the Irregulars awaited.

She never heard or glimpsed any sign of Colbie and her partners. Either they were accomplished, patient hiders or, she thought with a fleeting grin, she'd taken up a position in the wrong section of tunnel and the Irregulars were nowhere near. But that was unlikely. Canice had paid attention when the other mercenaries were planning the ambush, and she'd spent enough time in the Undercity to navigate her way around the better-traveled parts.

At one point, she felt a presence at her back. Leaping up and pivoting, she drew a magelock pistol with one hand and shook the vial of bottled light aglow with the other.

The light revealed only emptiness. Yet the sense that something was staring at her intensified. Her mouth went dry, and her lungs wanted to pant.

People called Corvis the City of Ghosts, and it had earned the reputation on the Longest Night and other occasions as well. Canice herself had once run afoul of one of the malevolent phantoms called pistol wraiths, and the thing had nearly been the death of her. And rumor held that people were particularly likely to encounter restless spirits in the black depths below the city streets.

She wondered if she should speak to whatever stood before her now. Then the sensation of being observed faded away, leaving her to wonder if the lengthy vigil in the dark had simply been playing tricks on her mind.

She was still wondering when a beam of greenish light shone down the tunnel below her perch. Although Canice herself had yet to see Olekse, the ironhead Black Dog Colbie had encountered, she assumed from the captain's description that it was his shoulder-mounted lamp piercing the darkness.

He and his companions were marching toward what Canice hoped was Pog's new place of employment and the other enterprises and habitations in the same vault. The Irregulars hadn't been able to predict whether they'd catch their foes coming or going. In truth, they'd had no way to be certain the patrol would traverse this stretch of tunnel at all. But they'd deemed it likely, and now the Khadorans were proving them right.

The mercenaries had also thought it probable that Olekse would once again lead the patrol, but on that point they'd hoped to be proven wrong. Unfortunately, they were just going to have to cope with him, steam-powered armor, ice maul, and all. With luck, they'd accomplish their purpose and vanish into the darkness quickly before he could bring his formidable weaponry to bear.

Canice peered up the primary tunnel. Behind the greenish light were dots of yellow glow. Some of the Black Dogs were carrying lanterns. Despite that illumination, though, she still couldn't tell how many there were. On her scouting expedition, Colbie had counted a dozen, but the Khadorans might well have strengthened the patrols in the wake of Vidor Rusling's aborted attack.

At least Canice could make out the towering form of the steamjack tramping along in their midst, its steel contours glinting in the lantern light. Since the 'jack was here, the Irregulars' plan was on track.

As the patrol passed beneath her, she slipped one of her conventional pistols from its holster on her hip. Ordinary firearms would do at the start, and she could switch to the magelocks and their enchanted ammunition when she needed them.

She aimed at the back of one of the outlaws, then waited. She shouldn't be the first to attack. Fire from an unexpected source might well confuse the Irregulars and make them hesitate. It would be better to let one of them make the first move and then join in.

After that, time seemed to drag, and she wondered what her allies were waiting on. Finally, flame exploded into being in the midst of the procession. Canice had keen eyes, but even so, the gloom had prevented her from seeing Milo throw the grenade, and from the looks of things, the Khadorans hadn't spotted the danger either. The blast caught them entirely unaware.

The sudden light dazzled Canice, but her eyes adjusted quickly, and then the floating cloud of flame silhouetted potential targets nicely. She shot the one she'd selected. He jerked, and his knees buckled underneath him.

Meanwhile, a blue bolt of Eilish's magic flashed down at one of the outlaws. Probably Gardek had loosed a crossbow bolt, and Milo was readying a second grenade.

Although the attackers were happy to kill any Black Dogs who fell to their assault, the real point was to provide a distraction. Of all the weapons at their disposal, it was Colbie's slug gun, coupled with her understanding of steamjack design, that had the best chance of crippling the Khadorans' automaton in precisely the manner intended. But because slug guns were at best accurate only at short range, the mechanik's allies had to create an opportunity for her to get close, fire, and retreat unscathed.

Canice thrust the pistol she'd just discharged back into its holster and drew its twin. It only took an instant, but it was time enough for the Black Dogs to shake off their surprise and surge into purposeful action. They scrambled, seeking cover, readying weapons, and peering upward to find the foes who'd attacked them. The ones who'd been carrying lanterns set them down, and when Milo's floating fire burned itself out, the space below Canice was mostly just a swirl of shadow.

Still, she picked out a scuttling target. She aimed at the Khadoran, and then greenish light washed over her. Olekse's lamp had found her, and an instant later, a steam lobber boomed and hissed. The bratya's 'jack had fired at her.

It was instinct that made Canice leap, but as she landed on the tunnel floor, reason caught up and assured her she didn't want to be inside the burrow when the projectile arrived. Even if it didn't hit her, an explosion in that tight space could have pulped her or collapsed the roof on top of her. And sure enough, just as she was thinking it, a blast hammered her ears and splashed dirt and pebbles down on her head.

She shook off the shock of it. Ears ringing, the sounds of battle suddenly muted, she cast about. A Khadoran was rushing in on her flank with a sword in one hand and a cape in the other. As her finger tightened on the trigger, he whirled the cloak before him.

The darkness made the action even more deceptive than it would have been ordinarily, and the instant she fired, she sensed that she'd missed. He lunged and cut at her head.

She stepped back and blocked with the empty pistol, but the impact jolted her arm. At the same time, she drew one of her magelocks with her off hand and shot him in the chest.

Charged with additional force as it was, the rune shot punched all the way through him, leather armor and all, and dropped him on his back. Of course, at point-blank range, a properly placed round from one of her little holdout pistols might have killed him just as well, and as she looked about for the next danger or opportunity, she wondered if expending the rune shot had been a tactical error. She decided not. The mistake would have been to allow a skilled swordsman any chance to keep slashing at her.

Nobody else was threatening her, not right this moment, but the greenish light had picked out Milo in the mouth of his burrow. Instead of jumping out as Canice had, he scurried back out of sight, and then a steam lobber roared. When the projectile exploded, it raised a cloud of dust that made it impossible to tell how much of the roof had come down. Perhaps the opening was sealed and the alchemist's body, alive or dead, was buried. Perhaps not.

Canice was sure that someone needed to extinguish Olekse's lamp before it lit up anyone else for the steamjack to shoot at. She drew her remaining magelock pistol and waited until the shifting figures before her parted to give her a clear shot at the lantern.

Infused with extra force like its predecessor, the rune shot smashed the shoulder-mounted device to pieces. The alchemical fluid inside ran down Olekse's armor, its glow fading away on contact with the air. Now only the discarded kerosene lanterns, the flames dancing on a pair of corpses, and the occasional azure flash of Eilish's sorcery remained to light the scene, which became even murkier and more confusing than before.

Canice put her back to the tunnel wall and reloaded the four pistols she'd fired. Then, hoping that in the gloom and the confusion the Khadorans might mistake her for one of their own, she started toward them. A pistoleer ordinarily sought to maintain distance from the enemy, but surely Colbie would make her move soon, and Canice didn't want to be far removed from her allies when that happened. And perhaps, if she advanced, she'd be able to tell if there was anything to be done for Milo.

As she skulked along the wall, she coughed on smoke and dust. The blue light of Eilish's magic stopped flickering, and she hoped he was simply catching his breath and not incapacitated or slain. The mouth of Milo's burrow was only half-full of newly fallen dirt, so maybe he wasn't entirely covered over. Yet nothing moved inside.

The only thing Canice was certain of was that the onslaught

was flagging and so depriving Colbie of the distraction she needed. Plainly, Gardek thought so as well, for with a roar of a battle cry that sounded loud even to the gun mage's half-deafened ears, he sprang from his perch and into the primary tunnel. His towering frame and swinging war hammer were more intimidating, more likely to rivet every foe's attention, than a series of crossbow bolts, but by breaking cover and placing himself within reach of the Black Dogs' slashing, stabbing blades and whipping cloaks, he'd put himself in more danger than before.

Hooting, the Khadorans moved to surround him. Olekse snapped an order to the steamjack, and it readied the huge sword it carried. The ironhead hefted his ice maul, and then the two metallic warriors advanced on Gardek.

Canice shot one Black Dog in the back, but apparently without piercing his armor. He and others whirled to face her. Meanwhile, a blue shaft of light stabbed into Olekse's torso. Eilish was alive and back to casting spells, but his effort didn't even make his armored opponent break stride. The ironhead raised the ice maul high and swung it down.

Their previous encounter had taught Gardek to dodge instead of block. He sidestepped, and the maul missed. Before Olekse could heave it up again, the bounty hunter struck at some vulnerable bit of the ice-generating mechanism just behind the head; Colbie had told him where to aim.

One massive weapon smashed into the other, and white light flashed at the point of impact. Judging from Gardek's leer, he was confident that the maul couldn't freeze its targets anymore.

Maybe he was right. But in Olekse's gauntleted hands, the maul could still pulverize an opponent, and just a step behind its master, the steamjack was tramping up to assail Gardek as well. It seemed impossible that the trollkin could stand against both of them, and Canice couldn't help him more than she already was. She was busy contending with the Black Dogs spreading out to flank her behind a bewildering display of snapping, whirling capes.

Having emptied all the others, she was down to her holdout pistols, one gripped in either hand. Retreating, she waited for a moment when she felt assured of hitting the target. Meanwhile, Eilish tried spattering Olekse with blue-and-yellow fire, but none of it landed inside the open helmet or in any other vulnerable spot, and the ironhead simply ignored the flame while it briefly burned before flickering out.

Then at last, Colbie lunged out of the darkness behind Olekse and the steamjack. Her slug gun roared. The 'jack lurched forward, banged into its master to stagger him, rebounded, and fell on its back. If the projectile had flown true, it had hit the automaton in a vulnerable spot, in what would be a human being's pelvis. The damage should have deprived it of the ability to walk but, by leaving the cortex and steam engine intact, allowed a reasonable possibility of repair.

Startled by the noise and the collision, Olekse looked around, a somewhat ponderous operation given that he had to turn his whole body to do it. Gardek hit him between the shoulder blades and knocked him off balance again. The other Black Dogs hesitated, momentarily uncertain of what they should be doing or whom they should be doing it to.

For a second, Canice thought she and the Irregulars had accomplished their purpose and could now run away. Then the steamjack rolled over, using its giant sword as a crutch, and started to raise itself. Apparently it believed that despite the damage, it could still stand and walk, and if it thought so, it might well be right.

It was also likely on the lookout for the foe who had attacked it from behind. Colbie wouldn't be able to get in close again. But if Canice acted quickly, she might.

She darted around one of the startled Black Dogs who'd been trying to flank her and, for the next few steps, kept covering them with her holdout pistols. Then, praying that darkness, chaos, and a little distance would protect her, she jammed the guns back in her greatcoat pockets, drew a magelock, and started reloading it.

In the midst of the operation, a swordsman rushed her, and she poised herself for what was apt to prove a futile attempt at defense. Then an azure bolt of power stabbed the Khadoran in the face, and he reeled back, screaming and clutching at his eyes.

Canice finished reloading just as the steamjack clambered upright. It tottered and hobbled a step but was still mobile.

She fired. Even had she augmented the raw force this particular rune shot delivered, it wouldn't have hit as hard as a projectile from a slug gun. But she was shooting into the ragged breach that Colbie had already made in the 'jack's armor, and she'd infused this particular round with a different enchantment, one that corroded metal in an instant.

The 'jack stumbled and swayed again, flailed its arms, and collapsed.

Perhaps its fall startled Olekse anew, because he didn't lurch back around to face Gardek. The trollkin pounded him over the head, and although it didn't look like the blow breached his helmet or dented it sufficiently to crush the flesh and bone inside, Olekse fell to one knee beside the automaton.

Gardek raised his hammer again. Fury had helped to keep him alive with the Black Dogs swarming all around him, but now it was making him lose sight of the plan. He and his comrades had achieved their objective, and it was time to go.

"Run!" Canice shouted. But if Gardek heard her call, he didn't heed it.

Then, filthy from head to toe, Milo scurried out of the darkness up to the trollkin's side. He tugged at Gardek's shield arm by gripping one of the spikes projecting from it and jabbered something Canice couldn't make out.

Whatever it was, it got Gardek moving in the proper direction, sweeping his war hammer back and forth to hold the Black Dogs at bay. Milo followed in the bounty hunter's wake. For the most part he allowed his partner to clear their path, but at one point, he hurled a throwing knife and caught a swordsman in the cheek.

Colbie and Canice dashed to join their allies. Colbie swung the slug gun to and fro, and the threat of it balked the foes who might otherwise have closed to striking distance. Canice emptied her holdout pistols and then had to trust her companions to protect her. She didn't dare stop running to reload.

Blue flares of magic shot over their heads to assail the Black Dogs. One such spell blasted a lantern to pieces and splashed burning oil across the floor.

When Canice and the others reached the patch of floor immediately beneath Eilish's burrow, she climbed up first. Once she was up there, she could reload in relative safety and help everyone else. The arcanist gave her a grin as she reached his level.

Colbie arrived next, stood, turned, and discharged the slug gun.

Milo clambered up a moment later and threw a grenade over Gardek's head. The metal orb exploded into blinding, choking smoke.

The barrage flung back or balked the Black Dogs. Nearly braining Milo in the process, Gardek threw his shield up into the burrow to free up his left hand, then hauled himself up after it.

Eilish conjured a haze of silver-blue glow, and the five of them ran onward. The arcanist stumbled, but when Canice and Colbie both moved to support him if need be, he waved them off. Meanwhile, Milo threw smoke and knockout grenades behind them to hinder pursuit.

Now that Canice and Colbie had drawn close together, the gun mage gave the thin woman a leer that said, *You see? You needed me.* Colbie glowered back at her.

— 13 —

FIRELIGHT TINGED THE DARKNESS AHEAD. Pog could make it out but nothing more; this ought to mean that if the surviving Black Dogs were looking in his direction, all they could see was his own lantern. Which was to say, they hadn't seen enough to make them take any serious interest in him, not with everything else Miss Gormleigh and the Black River Irregulars had given them to think about. He could still turn around and go back the other way, and no one would chase him.

Maybe he should. Anxiety had pulled his nerves tight, and he'd already found a new job. He'd sought it out as a necessary step in the plan to fool the Khadorans, but why not just keep it? Why was he, who'd never raised his hand to anyone since he was a child, about to risk his life to join a company of mercenaries?

Well, he liked the Irregulars, despite their quirks or perhaps even because of them. He respected Captain Sterling's ambitions to make Doorstop more than he currently was and would enjoy assisting her. He was also grateful to her, the steamjack, and Miss

Gormleigh for helping him escape the massacre in the Weavers' stronghold.

Conversely, he didn't like the Khadorans and hated to think what they'd do if nobody stopped them. The Undercity was a brutal, lawless place already, but he had little doubt the bratya would make it worse.

Still, was his scheme going to prevent that? It had seemed workable when he proposed it, but back then he hadn't understood how he'd shiver and how his bowels turn watery when it was time to put it into action. Wouldn't the Black Dogs know something was wrong as soon as they looked at him? And then wouldn't they kill him on the spot, or worse, torture him to find out what he'd been playing at?

He took a deep breath and ran his trembling fingers from his temples back over his head, pressing down the pointed tips of his ears in the process. It didn't matter if he belonged in a fellowship of soldiers or if his scheme was sound. He'd made a promise, and he had to follow through. Perhaps his nervousness wouldn't betray him. Surely the bratya expected people to fear them.

The wheelbarrow with its load of tools and parts rattled as he pushed it forward, and he was glad that, like his lantern, the noise announced his coming. The Black Dogs couldn't possibly imagine he was trying to sneak up on them.

Unfortunately, that didn't mean they were happy to see him. By the light of the kerosene lanterns that hadn't gotten broken in the fight, some of the survivors were tending to the wounds of others or nursing their own less severe punctures, gashes, bruises, and burns. Olekse, who'd discarded his armor in the interest of dexterity and stripped to the waist, was laboring over the fallen 'jack. Everyone who was able turned and gave Pog a glare.

"Go back," said a Khadoran holding a bloodstained cloth to his cheek. He drew a half-inch of blade, then clicked his sword's guard back down against the throat of the scabbard.

Pog tried to speak and found his throat was clogged. He swallowed and attempted it again. "I, uh, I heard a steam lobber and came to find out what was going on. Then I watched the fight. Then I ran back to get tools so I could help with the 'jack. Because I'm a mechanik. From the shop down the tunnel."

The Khadorans just kept staring at him. He had to strain against the impulse to keep babbling just to fill the silence, even though he didn't know what else to say.

Finally, Olekse said, "Bring the barrow over here."

Pog obeyed.

Though temporarily abandoned, the ironhead's empty armor was still standing upright, the torso and leg sections open like doors, and Olekse had already hung a lantern from its gauntlet to illuminate the 'jack lying prone at its metal feet. The Khadoran took Pog's lantern from the wheelbarrow and set it on the automaton's back, where it would provide additional light to guide him, then dumped out the remaining contents to clatter to the ground.

After that, he tossed Pog a silver coin. "Go. I'll leave the tools here for you to pick up later."

Pog felt a fresh jolt of anxiety that had a trace of guilty relief mixed in. It had never occurred to him that Olekse might want the tools and parts but not his labor.

He nearly took Olekse's dismissal as a reprieve from Holy Mother Dhunia and fled. Instead, he steeled himself anew and just backed a few steps away. To his relief, Olekse already appeared too intent on his task to notice him lingering, while the other Black Dogs were evidently too tired, sore, and dispirited from the recent skirmish to care.

Olekse sweated, grunted, got his hands and forearms increasingly filthy with grease, and scraped his knuckles bloody as he rooted in the breach Colbie's slug gun had punched. He growled what were presumably Khadoran curses. Eventually he shouted an obscenity that echoed down the tunnel, and he straightened up from his task.

"I could try," said Pog, his own voice a sort of quavering peep.

Olekse looked around and scowled. "I told you to go."

Pog spread his hands. "You have my lantern, and there are

things in the tunnels. I didn't want to grope my way in the dark."

Olekse spat. "And you think you're a better mechanik than me?"

Pog hoped he was, at least when it came to working on 'jacks as opposed to ironhead armor, but it seemed like a bad idea to say it outright. "We all have our own tricks, sir. And small gobber hands are better than human ones for digging around in tight places." He raised his own for the Khadoran's inspection.

"All right. Come try," Olekse said, standing up. "If you can get the 'jack walking again, I'll give you gold to go with the silver. But if you're wasting my time, there just might be a payment for that, too."

Pog shuddered. He hoped the Khadoran couldn't tell. Reminding himself that he and Colbie had discussed exactly what the slug gun would likely do and how to make an emergency repair in the field, he walked over, knelt down where Olekse had been, and lifted his lantern to better illuminate the interior of the breach. Then he sucked in his breath in dismay.

He'd seen Miss Gormleigh fire into the jagged hole the slug gun had made, but he'd assumed her shot had simply done the extra bit of ordinary damage required to cripple the 'jack. But now he discerned the pitted, eroded inner mechanisms and connections. Without comprehending how it would complicate the repair job, the gun mage had used a rune bullet that spread rust like cancer. No wonder Olekse hadn't made any headway.

He had, however, just picked up on Pog's consternation. "I knew it," he said. "You can't fix it either. Damn it! I had Colbie Sterling right in front of me for the killing in that stinking little privy of a tavern, and I didn't realize who she was!"

And you're about to take it out on me, Pog thought. "Please, sir. The damage isn't what I expected, but I can fix it! Just give me a chance!"

The man with the bleeding cheek grumbled something in Khadoran.

"He says we can't just linger here forever," Olekse said.

"It shouldn't take too long to get the 'jack walking," said Pog.

"Not like it should but well enough to take it someplace safe."

Olekse regarded him with manifest skepticism. "I'll give you thirty minutes."

Thirty minutes? Pog's pulse started throbbing in the sides of his neck. He closed his eyes for a moment and ordered himself to calm down. Then he inspected the damage anew.

Whether ruined by brute force or rust, most of the parts that he'd expected to be damaged actually did need replacing. The problem was that the corrosion produced by the rune shot had spread to eat at portions of the mechanism he hadn't anticipated touching. He wasn't sure he could even see the full extent of the damage just by peering into the breach. He might need to remove sections of cowling, but there was no time for that.

He spied a reflex trigger that might not be too corroded to carry impulses. Using all the delicacy at his command, he slipped his fingers under it and tried to lift it for a closer look. It came away from its connections, not breaking so much as disintegrating into grit and tiny fragments that dinged and clattered down inside the chassis. He winced.

"What happened?" Olekse asked.

"Nothing!" Pog yelped. Then, fearing he might have sounded impertinent, he had to stifle the urge to cringe. "I'm sorry! Truly! Sorry! But I can think better, work better, if nothing distracts me."

"I'll leave you alone," Olekse said. "For another twenty-nine minutes."

I can do this, Pog insisted to himself. Essentially it was the same job he'd done already, when he'd gotten Doorstop moving during the attack on the Patient Weavers. Never mind that then he'd known exactly what condition the 'jack was in and was working in concert with another mechanik in a proper service bay. The trick was to remember that the 'jack only had to stand and keep its balance while putting one steel foot in front of the other. A relatively crude arrangement of reflex triggers, pneumatic tubes, hoses, and valves, and braces should suffice for that.

Grabbing a wrench, he started removing cables. Big or small, if damaged, they had to come out, lest garbled feedback reach the cortex. But he replaced just the big ones because he cared only about restoring gross movement and some crude semblance of a kinesthetic sense.

Sweat stung his eyes, and he wiped and blinked it away. He caught himself rushing, and he struggled to slow down. The repair would surely fail if he got sloppy.

After the reflex triggers, he tackled the pneumatics. Then he bolted in crossbars meant to keep the steamjack's own weight from crumpling its damaged portion and crushing his work.

Somehow he finished in less than thirty minutes—or if he hadn't, Olekse hadn't seen fit to call time. A part of him wanted to keep checking, rechecking, and tinkering until the human stopped him; after all, his very life might be at risk. But really, he believed he'd done all he could, and if he wanted to appear competent, perhaps the way was to show confidence in his work.

He looked around at Olekse. "We're ready to light the firebox," he said. While the 'jack lay crippled, the ironhead had shut the vents that fed air to the steam engine to conserve coal and water.

"Then let's see what you've accomplished." The Khadoran opened a hatch, splashed an accelerant on the chunks of anthracite, and struck a long-handled match. Flames leaped up at its touch.

As the boiler heated, the 'jack stirred. It raised its head and shifted the hand still clutching the sword.

Olekse said something in Khadoran. Pog assumed the Black Dog was ordering the automaton to stand. He held his breath.

The steamjack clambered to its feet, and something clanked and groaned within the breached section. Pog squeezed his eyes shut. But there was no follow-up clangor or thud to indicate that his work had come apart and the 'jack had fallen back down, and when he dared to peek again, it was walking. Well, limping, really, the left foot dragging, but mobile nonetheless.

Some of the Black Dogs exclaimed in surprise and approval. Olekse clapped Pog on the back and knocked him lurching forward.

"Good work," the ironhead said. He reached into his pocket and tossed several gold coins to the ground.

As before, the craven—or was it the sensible?—side of Pog wanted to scoop up the coins and scurry away. And he did crouch to pick them up. But he also said, "Thank you, sir! I'm grateful! But I… well, can I ask for something else, too?"

Olekse's pouchy, bloodshot eyes narrowed. "What?"

"People say your gang is strong and only going to get stronger. That in a few years, you might be running the whole Undercity. It that's true, you're the people a wise fellow would want to work for. And it seems like you can use me." He waved at the steamjack.

A Black Dog with blisters covering much of the exposed portions of his body rattled off something in his own language.

"He says," Olekse observed, "that our new home is supposed to stay secret for the time being. But I'm tired of doing all the mechanik work myself. Besides, we're trying to look unstoppable. Deadly. If we leave you running around loose to tell people that the mercenaries ambushed us and got away *again*, that won't help. So really, it's either take you along or cut your throat."

"Sir, I swear—"

The ironhead laughed. "Relax, gobber. I said I can use a helper, and I know how to make sure nothing bad can come of it."

With that, he turned to the task of donning his armor while the other Black Dogs made their own preparations to depart. Pog returned the scattered tools to the wheelbarrow. He doubted he'd have the chance to get them back to the shop, but it felt wrong to leave them lying in the dirt.

Besides, the chore gave him something to do besides wondering whether he'd just done a cunning thing or a stupid one.

When everyone was ready, Olekse spoke to the Black Dog with the blisters. That man produced a black sack, walked over to Pog, and pulled it over his head.

Pog had to choke back a kind of terrified giggle because the hood answered his question. Stupid, beyond a doubt.

He was going to the bratya's lair just as he'd wanted. But since he wouldn't be able to see the path, how was he going to find his way back?

• • •

IVAN HAD LEFT HIS GOLD-BEDIZENED SCABBARD and boots in the Undercity and exchanged his fur-trimmed leather-and-baft garments for nondescript Cygnaran clothing. His companions had made similar adjustments to their appearances, and as he led them up Cooper Street in the dark, he trusted that no one would see a difference between them and Corvis natives. This was, after all, a city where many people went well armed, even aboveground.

Still, Gridia quickened her stride, caught up with him, and murmured, "Are you sure you wouldn't rather wait until later, when more people are asleep? This looks like a respectable neighborhood. Well, somewhat. And if the gun mage and the others are asleep themselves—"

"We're going now," Ivan said.

In reality he knew that, crazy though she was, on this occasion his lieutenant was talking sense. But he just couldn't bear to wait any longer, not when Canice Gormleigh was finally within reach. The Black Dogs would hit hard, get in and out fast, and everything would work out.

Set back farther from the street than its neighbors, three gabled stories high with a stable for horses and a carriage built onto the side, the safehouse had lights burning behind a couple of the shuttered windows on the ground floor. Ivan, who'd strolled past the building several times already over the course of the past few hours, looked it over once again, searching for signs that the people inside expected trouble.

As far as he could tell, they didn't. He glanced up and down the street to make sure no one was watching and then skulked toward the house. Some of his companions followed. Others broke off so the attackers could breach at multiple points.

Creeping along the side of the building, Ivan came to a window with no light shining behind it. He pointed to it, and Gridia worked a knife into the crack between the shutters and started prying. After several seconds, the latch yielded with only a soft crunch of breaking wood.

The plump woman looked back and beamed at her son. "Here's

a useful lesson," she said, her voice low. "I'll bet you a bowl of my walnut cookies that the doors are solid, but any fortress is only as strong—"

"Shut up," Ivan snapped.

She pouted but obeyed, then swung the shutters open and set to work on the leaded panes behind them. That latch yielded even more quickly and quietly, and she pulled the casement open.

Ivan scrambled up and through. The bratya expected a leader to lead, but he would have gone first in any case, so he could come face-to-face without a single extra moment of delay the woman who'd tortured his brother. The prospect of vengeance made him feel lightheaded.

The little room he was negotiating heightened the feeling. Just enough light leaked in through the window at his back to reveal the tools set out atop a little desk. He knew nothing of the arcane secrets of the Llaelese, but he'd watched ordinary gunsmiths at their labors, and enough of the devices and supplies were familiar to him to suggest that Canice Gormleigh had claimed this space for her workshop.

Light shone under the door. He pressed his ear to it. Although he couldn't make out the words, a deep voice was grumbling on the other side.

Drawing his sword, he glanced back to make sure his companions were readying their weapons as well. Then he jerked open the door and lunged through.

That brought him into a corridor just a few paces long. At the near end was a shabby, sparsely furnished parlor where, stripped to the waist, Natak Warbiter sat on a straight-backed chair made for a human, not for an ogrun's burly form. A petite woman with short brown hair was standing over him. Judging from the length of gauze in her hands, she was changing his bandages.

Ivan crept toward them. He wanted to close to within striking distance before they realized he was there, but perhaps eagerness made him stride when he should have tiptoed. The floor creaked, and Warbiter and the physician, if that was what she was, turned in his direction and then gaped in surprise.

The ogrun grabbed the implement lying at his feet—a pitchfork, likely procured from the stable—and sprang up out of the chair, bellowing, "Run!" The doctor started for the door but, dashing out from behind Ivan, Gridia and Fodor cut her off. From elsewhere on the ground floor came smashing and banging sounds as other Black Dogs entered with less finesse than their boss.

"Up!" Warbiter shouted. The physician bolted for the stairs, and this time no one was in a position to intercept her. The pitchfork leveled, the Patient Weaver backed after her but halted partway to the second story, high enough that the Black Dogs couldn't flank or surround him as were their tactics of choice.

Gridia beamed up at him. "That would be sound thinking, love, if we always relied only on our swords." She shifted her blade to her off hand and pulled a short-barreled little holdout gun from her pocket.

"No!" Ivan snapped. "I've got him!" He pulled the cape from his shoulders—not made for fighting like the ones Black Dogs normally wore, but it would have to do—and started up the stairs.

Had things been proceeding as expected, he would have been happy to let Gridia shoot the ogrun dead. But Canice Gormleigh and the Black River Irregulars should be rushing forth from wherever in the house they were to fight the intruders, and that wasn't happening. It was possible he needed Warbiter alive to explain what was amiss.

"You're still wounded," Ivan said. "Weak. Drop the pitchfork and you won't have to die."

"You do," Warbiter said. He thrust the fork at Ivan's eyes.

Ivan simultaneously swept the cloak to entangle the tines and pivoted aside. For an instant, he'd forgotten that the stairs allowed scant room for footwork, and the latter action landed his foot half-on, half-off the edge of a riser, nearly costing him his balance. Still, when the initial thrust proved to be a feint, when the pitchfork dropped beneath the sweeping cape and stabbed through the space his belly had occupied just an instant before, he was glad he'd dodged.

He expected Warbiter to pull the fork back in preparation for another thrust. It was what the average human combatant would have done. Instead, twisting at the hips, the ogrun spun the improvised weapon sideways and caught his opponent in the ribs. Even though the improvised weapon traveled only a few inches, it clouted Ivan with sufficient force to slam him into the banister.

Wood cracked, and for an instant he thought the barrier would break and send him plunging back to the floor of the room below, but it held after all. Pretending the impact had stunned him, he swung his sword arm to the side. The movement opened his guard and invited attack.

When Warbiter obliged, Ivan sidestepped and beat the shaft of the fork with his sword. That didn't knock it out of the ogrun's hands, but it made him fumble to maintain his grip. For a few moments, wounded though he was, the hulking outlaw exerted an ogrun's prodigious strength but wasn't able to keep it up for long. Ivan lunged higher and cut at the ogrun's leg that already had a bloodstained bandage wrapped around the knee.

His blade sliced deep into Warbiter's thigh. The ogrun pitched forward, his massive body nearly knocking Ivan down the stairs along with him.

The Patient Weaver didn't slide all the way down on his belly, nor did falling jolt all the fight out of him. He started to flounder over onto his back and raise the pitchfork anew. But Gridia and Fodor were faster. They darted up the steps and, having gleaned that their boss wanted the ogrun alive, battered his bandaged head with the flats of their blades. Fresh blood welled forth, and Warbiter collapsed.

A second later, Ivan heard a female voice calling for help. Most likely the doctor had been yelling for a while, but he'd been too intent on Warbiter for the shouts to register.

He ran up to the second floor, where he paused and listened to make certain the cries were coming from this story and not higher up in the house. Then he followed the sounds to the right.

He discovered the doctor sitting in an open window. Her legs were hanging outside, and she was calling in the direction of the street. As he appeared in the doorway, she sucked in a ragged breath, perhaps to bolster her resolve, and jumped.

Ivan dashed to the window and looked down. He hoped to see the doctor lying just below him with a broken leg or worse, but she wasn't there. Instead, calling for help once more, a shadow was hurrying toward the street.

Ivan cursed. He should have left someone in the yard, although really, how could he have anticipated this? He waited a second for a Black Dog on the ground floor to hear the yelling and run outside to catch the physician. When no one did, he spat another obscenity, sheathed his sword, and jumped after her.

The drop jolted him and threw him forward onto his hands and knees. When he got to his feet, he found he hadn't broken any bones either, and that was all that mattered.

He charged after the doctor and, as he closed the distance, noticed she was hobbling. She must at least have twisted her ankle or done something similar when she fell. Lucky for him. Otherwise, she might have reached the street and help already.

He pounded up behind her, and then, catching him by surprise, she lurched around. She had some sort of sharp little tool in her hand, something she'd likely been using to minister to Warbiter, and she slashed it at Ivan's face. He jerked back, and the stroke fell just short of his eye.

"Dammit!" He broke her nose, brought the wind *whuffing* out of her with a follow-up punch to the belly, and while she was stunned, twisted her fighting arm up behind her back until she dropped her weapon. Then he drew a dirk and pressed the edge to her throat.

"Back inside," he whispered in her ear. "Any more trouble, and I'll kill you."

Smiling, Gridia opened the door for him. Someone had dragged the unconscious Warbiter to the foot of the stairs, and Fodor was in the process of binding the ogrun's hands. There was still no sign of Canice Gormleigh or the other mercenaries, surely proof positive, had Ivan needed more, that they were nowhere in the house.

"Where are your friends?" he asked.

Blood running from her now-misshapen nose to stain her mouth and chin, the physician didn't answer.

He pressed a little harder with the knife, just hard enough to break the skin. She trembled but still kept silent.

Ivan looked to Fodor. "Take him apart. He doesn't need eyes or fingers to answer questions." Fodor leered and drew his own dagger.

"No!" the physician cried.

"You'll answer in Warbiter's place?" Ivan asked.

"Promise not to hurt him any worse."

"You have my word. Now, I already asked you what I want to know."

The brown-haired woman hesitated. Then she said, "They went down into the Undercity. They found out you have patrols marching around your new territory. They were going to ambush one of them."

"When?"

"Whenever it happened by. They didn't know how long they'd have to wait."

"Where, exactly?"

"I don't know. I've never even been down to the Undercity, and they weren't looking at a map or anything."

"Hmm." Ivan considered what she'd said and the manner in which she'd said it and decided it was likely the truth. He shoved her toward one of his underlings. "Tie and gag her, too. Then we'll wait to welcome the mercenaries home."

His comrades stared at him. After a moment, Gridia said, "I realize how much catching the gun mage means to you, dear. But are you sure that's the best idea?"

He gave her a stare. "Are you questioning my orders?"

Gridia looked back at him as if he'd suggested something astonishing. "Me? Never! It's just that if the ambush hasn't happened yet, shouldn't we try to warn our friends?"

"I'll send someone."

"I assume you don't mean yourself. That leaves Fodor and

me—no one else has learned his way around the Undercity well enough. Do you want to try to fight the mercenaries without us?"

Ivan sneered. "Every man here knows how to kill."

"Well, of course. And now that you come to mention it, Olekse and his men are fierce fighters, too. That means that when these Black River Irregulars spring their trap, things could go against them. They could all end up dead, and that would leave us lurking here for nothing."

"But if they survive, we can catch them with their guards down."

Gridia sighed. "Lovey, the time will come when we can do whatever we want wherever we want in Corvis, aboveground or underneath, but that happy day isn't here yet. We took a big risk raiding a Watch safehouse, and we'll be taking a bigger one if we linger. Especially since we couldn't keep the pretty young lady there from screaming for help. Someone may have heard. Someone may be hurrying to the authorities even—"

"All right," Ivan snarled.

His hatred was telling him to stay. But Gridia, damn her, was right. There were too many unknowns and too many dangers. And he could still set a trap, now that he had bait.

He looked to the man he'd told to bind and gag the doctor. "Forget that. Untie her." He glared at the captive. "Get Warbiter awake, cleaned up, and ready to walk. Yourself, too."

The physician pulled the gag down from her mouth. "I don't know how badly your people beat him, how deeply—"

"You have smelling salts, don't you? Other medicines? Don't play for time, Doctor, or you'll see me angrier than you have so far. Just get it done."

• • •

GARDEK AND HIS FELLOW MERCENARIES had taken a circuitous route through mostly deep, uninhabited tunnels to minimize the chances of a second encounter with the Khadorans or any outlaws looking to curry favor with the newcomers. As a result, it was well into the night when they finally reached a ramp that ran up the surface. They could see a square of black sky dotted with stars at the top.

Gardek smiled at the sight. Although he was hiding it as any trollkin warrior would, he was feeling the weight of his hammer, shield, armor, and the dull ache of the bruises underneath. It would be good to reach the safehouse and relax.

Still, he didn't feel entirely satisfied. "We had the advantage," he said, starting the ascent, which had cobbles planted in the mud like stepping stones but which wasn't entirely paved. "We could have killed them all."

"Which would have ruined the plan," Eilish said, sounding a little out of breath. He was hardy for a human, but his style of pride didn't require him to hide all signs of fatigue. "It would have left no one to recruit Pog and escort him back to the bratya hideout."

"I know," Gardek said. "But it's still a shame."

"I don't share your bloodlust," the arcanist replied. "I'll be quite content to locate the enemy, report to Helstrom, and let the Watch handle the bulk of the slaughtering."

Still smelling of gun smoke, her red-and-yellow greatcoat flapping around her legs, Canice gave Gardek a grin. "*I* share it. When the time comes, I want to be in the fore shooting as many as I can."

"Well, you've earned the right," Eilish said. "We might not all have survived our skirmish with the patrol if not for you. Isn't that right, Colbie?"

"It might be," Colbie said, her tone as cold and flat as a sheet of ice.

Gardek fancied he understood humans pretty well, well enough, certainly, to take care of his requirements as a bounty hunter and gambler. He could often tell when they were afraid or lying and when someone was bluffing or slow playing a big hand at the card table.

Yet even so, their kind and his were different, and occasionally certain twisty nuances of their behavior eluded him. Thus, it had taken him a while to perceive that Colbie wanted to keep Canice shut away in the safehouse, not just because she distrusted the pistoleer who had once proposed to murder them all but for other, less obvious reasons.

He wasn't entirely sure what those reasons were. Colbie couldn't view the gun mage as a threat to her leadership, could she? Her partners had given her their loyalty, and they were steadfast people. Even Milo, in his shady fashion.

Gardek slowed down for a moment, and Colbie's long stride brought her up even with him. "Your plan worked," he said.

She scowled up at him as though she thought he was patronizing her and she resented it. Then, however, her expression softened into a crooked smile. "It was Pog's idea, really, and then we all worked to flesh it out. But thank you."

Gardek was glad that the rain had stopped for a while and that the fog had decided not to roll in from the river. Maybe others were glad of it as well, for there were a fair number of people in the streets despite the lateness of the hour. He scrutinized them as he and his companions hiked over the arching bridges that spanned canals, past grimy brick factories that shook with the rumble of the machinery within and dirtied the stars with smoke as the crews inside labored on the nighttime shifts.

By the time he and the other mercenaries reached Cooper Street, he was confident no one was tailing them. He nodded in private satisfaction, then stopped short when the safehouse came into view.

Eilish sucked in his breath. "There's a ground-floor window open."

"Your doctor friend's not one of us," Milo said. "Maybe she's just been careless?"

"Not her," Eilish replied, "and besides, that's the window of the room where Canice has been making rune bullets. Regan had no reason to go in there while the rest of us were away."

"I agree," Colbie said, "This isn't right." She opened her black leather coat and pulled her slug gun from the loops that held it in place.

"Do we sneak?" Milo asked.

Colbie shook her head, and her wavy dark hair swished across her shoulders. "If we have enemies waiting in the house, they're watching for us. We go hard and fast."

Canice grinned. "Nothing like a frontal assault to fill up the casualty roll."

The captain rounded on the gun mage as if she meant to snap at her and order her to be still. Then, however, she took a breath and, in a tone milder than Gardek had expected, said, "If you have a better tactic, tell us."

The red-haired woman hesitated. "Actually, no. The way you said is the way I'd do it, too. I was just making a joke. Not a funny one, perhaps."

"All right, then," Colbie said. "Everyone, get ready."

Milo shifted his gas mask up onto his face and pulled a grenade from its bandolier. Eilish drew his sword and Canice, both of her magelock pistols. Gardek pulled his crossbow off his belt, cocked it with the goat's foot, and set a quarrel in the groove. It would be less accurate shooting one-handed, but he was used to it, and he wasn't going to leave his war hammer and shield behind.

"Everyone, stay behind me," he said. The shield, his plate, and his size couldn't provide total cover for everybody else, but they were better than nothing.

The others fell in behind him. Then Colbie said, "Go!"

Gardek dashed toward the house while trying to cover up with the shield and peer past it at the same time. He was especially concerned with the gabled windows on the upper stories. Had he been planning to repel an assault, he would have stationed gunmen or archers up there for certain.

One of the casements was even open. But no one appeared to shoot from there, or anywhere else either. By the time he reached the stoop, Gardek suspected that whoever had invaded the house had come and gone, and when he tried the front door and found it unlocked, he was all but sure. Still, he kept the shield in the proper defensive attitude as he threw open the door and sprang inside.

No one was in the front room or anywhere else in view. But there was blood smeared down the staircase and pooled at the bottom, and a pitchfork lying against the bannister. Discarded strips of stained bandage lay scattered on the floor by one of the chairs.

A scalpel pinned a piece of paper to the wall. Entering behind Gardek, Eilish strode up and read the words that were scrawled on it: "We took them." He pulled the blade out of the paneling and turned the page over to reveal lines of smaller script. "This is from my manuscript," he added, not, Gardek thought, because he believed that to be of any significance but because for once shock and dismay had rattled his quick, resourceful mind.

"Search the house," Colbie said. "Make sure the Khadorans—and our friends—are really gone."

They were, and when the five mercenaries finished checking, they returned to the front room. Gardek removed the bolt from his crossbow and eased the string back down. "How did the Khadorans find the safehouse?"

Colbie shook her head. "I have no idea. I didn't think they'd dare to look for us aboveground. We underestimated them."

"My fault," Canice said, uncocking a magelock pistol and sliding it back into its shoulder holster. "I was supposed to be the expert."

"Be one now," Eilish said. "What's the point of abducting Regan and Natak? Are they hostages seized to compel us to leave the Black Dogs alone?"

"In the short term, that's part of it. But remember, the bratya's been after me from the start, and at this point they have reason to hate you, too. So, they won't rest until they take revenge. That's their way."

"Revenge that includes torturing and killing their prisoners?"

"Very likely."

"Then we have to keep hunting them."

"Maybe we can figure out a way," Milo said. "But if they find out we're still poking around, they might start sending us body parts. It's what I'd do." Everyone turned to stare at him. "If I was evil and ruthless, I mean."

"If we can't search for their hideout," Colbie said, "then it all comes down to Pog."

• • •

THE STEAMJACK LAY PRONE ONCE MORE, this time in the middle of a lantern-lit room with brick walls and a filthy plank floor. Pog had taken much of its midsection apart to get at the corroded parts he hadn't been able to reach in the tunnel and to facilitate the rest of the permanent repairs. Olekse was a few feet away, thumping a dent out of his suit of armor with a mallet that had leather pads on the faces.

For the moment, Pog was trying hard to focus only on his work. It was better than fretting over the alarming truths that he was in a den of murderers and had no idea where that den was located, or what to do when the moment came that Olekse left him alone and gave him the chance to play spy.

He was bolting a whisker-thin reflex trigger to its terminus when footsteps and voices sounded in the corridor beyond the workroom doorway. In a moment, two men tramped into view. They were dressed like Cygnarans, not in the short, sword arm-baring capes and fur-trimmed garments he'd come to associate with the Black Dogs, but obviously they could be nothing else.

Then Dr. Falk and Mr. Warbiter trudged into view. They both had their hands tied behind them. The physician had a bruised, squashed nose, and the ogrun was in worse shape than that. He was tottering, maybe only half-conscious, and by the looks of him, someone had beaten him about the head, reopening the old gash and making new ones.

It belatedly occurred to Pog that he might well have gasped when he saw the prisoners and that for certain he was staring at them now. He hastily looked back down at his work lest someone discern that he knew them.

But perhaps it was already too late. Footsteps clumped toward him, and a pair of boots stopped beside him. He swallowed and forced himself to look up at the man to whom they belonged.

The Black Dog's crown was either bald or shaved, and his beak of a nose reminded Pog of a hawk. So, too, did the narrow grey eyes peering down at him.

"For a moment," the human said, "I thought my pet gobber had gotten loose."

“No,” Olekse said, stepping closer, “this one has the sense to help us willingly. In fact, he asked to come here.”

The man with the grey eyes grunted. “That doesn’t mean you should have brought him.”

“We hooded him, he’s a good mechanik, and I need a helper. Today more than ever. While you were up in the real city, your friend the gun mage and the Black River Irregulars ambushed the patrol and nearly took a second ’jack out of commission.” He gestured to the damaged automaton.

“Yes, we found out that was coming, but too late to warn you. Did you get Gormleigh? Or any of them?”

The ironhead grimaced. “No. They all got away.”

“Damn it! You worthless—”

“Now, lovey,” said a plumpish woman with white-blond hair, “there’s no need to be rude. I’m sure it was just bad luck.”

The grey-eyed man rounded on her. “Stay out of it.”

“Of course. You know I hate to interfere. But first, please, just let me remind you that our little group *was* lucky. We procured our guests.”

The Black Dog with the hairless crown—who, Pog had decided, must be the boss of the rest of them—scratched his chin. “Actually, Gridia, that’s a good point. And they’ll be no less useful if we have some fun with them.”

“No less useful as hostages,” Regan said, her voice breathy on the first syllables but stronger thereafter. “But if I know my friends, they hurt some of your men pretty badly. I’ll take care of the wounded if you swear not to mistreat Natak and me.”

The boss sneered. “You tried to defy me back in the safehouse. I threatened to maim Warbiter, and you gave in.”

“And I see where that got me,” Regan replied.

“Our brothers and sisters,” Olekse said, “deserve better care than we can give one another. *Need* it if we’re to continue shaking tithes out of the locals and looking strong.”

“And it isn’t the good doctor or even the ogrun you’re truly upset with,” the blonde woman said. “They’re simply a means to an end.”

The boss raked her, Olekse, and Regan with a glower. "Have it your way. But, Doctor, my warning stands. If you try anything funny, you'll wish you hadn't."

Regan stared back at him. "I'm a physician… Ivan, was it? *We* have ethics."

"Show me," Ivan said. He waved his hand, and he and his underlings marched the captives on down the corridor and out of sight.

Leaving Pog alive and free—well, freer than he might otherwise have been—and his friends seemingly headed for a more promising fate than immediate torture. He closed his eyes, and his shoulders slumped.

It only took him an instant to realize he shouldn't make a show of his relief. But that was time enough for Olekse to notice and say, "Hey."

Pog jerked. "I'm all right!" he babbled, meanwhile wondering what that statement even meant in this context.

Olekse gave him another jarring clap on the shoulder. "Yes, you are. I'll make sure everyone understands you're my helper and treats you right. And don't worry. You won't always be shut away here. When we have the rest of the Undercity allied with us, afraid of us, or both, you can go wherever you like. Only this time, you'll do it with coin in your pocket and the bratya's protection."

Pog managed a smile. "Thank you."

He and Olekse went back to work for perhaps an hour more. Then, when the ironhead finished bolting a new alchemical lantern onto his armor, he asked, "Are you hungry?"

Pog hesitated. "I'd like to finish what I'm doing."

"Suit yourself. I'm done for the night." The human pointed in the direction that Regan, Natak, and their captors had gone. "Food and drink's that way. You should be able to find some blankets, too." He ambled out the door.

Pog felt strange being left alone. Was it truly this easy? Did he really have the run of the stronghold now?

Maybe. Olekse seemed to trust him and had vouched for him to the others.

Or maybe not. Maybe this was a trap, and the Black Dogs were watching to see what he'd do.

But no. He couldn't let that possibility balk him or he'd never make a move in time to do anybody any good. He had to believe that the Khadorans were incapable of imagining that a lone little gobber mechanik would dare insinuate himself into their midst to work against them.

All right, then. Exactly how was he going to do that?

He wished he could rescue Mr. Warbiter and Dr. Falk. But the former was too badly hurt to run, and the latter might be busy and thus under scrutiny for hours. The best way for Pog to help them was to get away himself and then send the Black River Irregulars and the Watch back to save them.

He looked up and down the corridor. A few torches burning in sconces illuminated more crumbling brickwork with additional doorways yawning on one wall and a few narrow windows, the kind that made it possible for a defender to shoot out of but difficult for an attacker to shoot in, on the other. They were at human height, but he could grip the sills and hoist himself up to view what was on the other side. Heading in the opposite direction from the one Olekse had taken, trying to look as if he were just taking a stroll and not attempting anything the Black Dogs would find objectionable, he proceeded to do that.

There was a little light outside, presumably because the Khadorans had provided it to illuminate the hideout's immediate surroundings. Unfortunately, it didn't illuminate anything Pog recognized as a landmark. As he worked his way along, he spotted a couple of openings in the walls of the cave containing the stronghold, but he had no idea where those passages might lead. If he simply tried one at random, his chances of blundering his way to a spot he recognized would be slim at best. He was far more likely to lose himself forever or stumble into one of the Undercity's countless other dangers.

As he turned one corner and then another, his heart thumped and he panted as if he'd been running. He struggled to push fear to the back of his mind and clear some space for thinking.

If no outsider knew where this place was, it was likely somewhere deep and surely well removed from every other Undercity habitation. But how had the bratya found it when, newly come to Corvis, they couldn't have known the parts belowground even as well as Pog did?

Maybe they'd procured an old map. Usuallly alleged to show the way to lost caverns full of treasure, forged maps were one of the Undercity's signature confidence tricks, but supposedly the genuine article turned up from time to time.

If the bratya did possess such a map, it surely wasn't lying around in an otherwise disused portion of the building. It was in the area where the Khadorans spent most of their time and where Pog was even more afraid to venture. But he had to look for it where it might conceivably be found. He retraced his steps toward the part of the stronghold where Olekse had told him to come for supper.

Up ahead, voices echoed. Then a pair of Black Dogs sauntered out of the gloom. They were passing a bottle back and forth.

Pog held in a flinch. He made himself smile, raise his hand, and say, "Hello."

One of the Khadorans charged. Pog froze in shock for a moment, then turned and ran.

But the long-legged human caught up with him, grabbed him by the shoulder, and spun him back around. Jabbering in his own language, the Black Dog slapped him, backhanded him a second stinging blow, and then marched him toward the top of a staircase. It was only as they started down that they realized the other Khadoran, the one who'd been left in charge of the bottle, was laughing.

The outlaws talked back in forth in their native tongue. Then, with a slightly embarrassed frown, the Black Dog who'd been dragging Pog to an unknown but surely hideous fate let go of him.

When the human with the bottle resumed speaking, it was in heavily accented Cygnaran. "Fedko can't tell one gobber from another. He thought you were Az. But I told him you are Olekse's new helper."

Az the tunnel explorer? Had the bratya taken him prisoner and forced him to serve as their guide? That would be better than a map.

Pog tried to smile as if he too thought that being mistaken for an escaping prisoner and treated accordingly was funny. "I'm lucky you were here."

The Black Dog proffered the bottle, and Pog took a cautious swig. He wasn't used to anything stronger than ale or cider, and the brandy made him cough and brought tears to his eyes. The Khadoran laughed again, and this time Fedko joined him.

When the humans proceeded on their way, Pog gave them a couple of minutes to get well ahead of him. Then he returned to Olekse's workroom, selected a few of the smallest tools, instruments used for the most delicate manipulations, and slipped them into his pockets. After that, he tiptoed down the same stone stairs that Fedko had sought to drag him down before.

At the bottom was a dungeon, a cellblock lit by a single lantern. The cell doors were mold-spotted wood reinforced with rusty iron. Like the windows upstairs, the sliding panels intended for peeping in were too high for a gobber to look through easily, and Pog was reluctant to shout out Az's name. Fortunately, the doors also had hinged flaps at the bottom, presumably so dishes could be slid in and out, and, kneeling repeatedly, he made his way from one to the next.

The lantern light barely seeped through the flaps to illuminate the cells. Still, Pog could tell the first two were empty. Then he came to one with a big form sprawled by the back wall. It wasn't moving, and it smelled of blood.

Mr. Warbiter, surely. Keeping his voice low, Pog called the ogrun's name, but the Patient Weaver didn't stir.

Pog hurried onward. When he lifted the next flap, a much smaller form shuffled forward and crouched down. It was a fellow gobber, mostly naked, bruised from beatings, shoulders striped by a whip or bastinado, and a raw circle around his neck. Even the dim light made him squint.

"Az?" Pog asked.

"Yes," the explorer croaked. "Who are you?"

"My name is Pog. I'm going to get you out of this cell, and then you're going to get the both of us out of this whole terrible place."

Pog stood up, selected tools from his pockets to serve as a torsion wrench and pick, and set to work unlocking the door. The instruments weren't perfectly suited to the purpose, nor was he an experienced locksmith. But it would have been a poor mechanik indeed who couldn't manipulate a simple arrangement of levers, and after a minute, the lock clicked open.

Az stumbled through the door into the room beyond, where Pog could take a better look at him. If anything, the explorer appeared more battered and shaky than before. Previously Pog had worried that Mr. Warbiter was incapable of making the trek out of the Undercity, and now he wondered if Az would manage any better.

Possibly sensing his doubts, Az took a deep breath, stood up straighter, and smiled a startlingly malicious smile. "Don't worry. I *am* going to get out of here, and then we're going to bring the wrath of our people down on these Khadoran bastards."

Pog smiled back. "That's just what my friends and I had in mind. Well, the wrath part, anyway. Are you ready to move?"

Az nodded, and they hurried to the foot of the stairs. Then they heard leather creaking higher up. His boots or other garments making the noise, one of the Black Dogs was starting down.

Pog looked to Az. "Give me a tool," the explorer whispered, "something that will stab or cut. Pick one for yourself, too. Then you stand on that side of the door, I'll stand on this one, and we'll jump him when he comes in."

"Right," Pog replied. He did as he'd been told, and then shivering, waited as footsteps bumped lower. Closer.

He didn't know if he could stick a sharp object into another person. He'd never done anything like it before.

But he had to! Though Az was the brave one, he was also the one weakened by days of abuse. Even with surprise on his side, he didn't have a hope of disposing of a human outlaw unless Pog also brought his strength to bear.

The Black Dog came through the doorway. To Pog, he was just a pair of legs because some instinct warned him not to look up. If he saw the whole person, he'd falter. He swung the point of his screwdriver at the back of the human's knee, involuntarily closing his eyes as the makeshift weapon began its arc.

The screwdriver lurched in his grip as it hit the target. His eyes popped open, and he saw it was sticking in the outlaw's leg a couple of inches higher than the spot he'd been aiming at.

Az was slashing at the other leg. Off balance, the Black Dog staggered forward. Two bowls, one of food and one of water, fell from his hands and smashed on the floor.

Pog stabbed again and then a third time. Despite his and Az's frenzied efforts, however, the Khadoran stayed on his feet. His leather breeches and boots didn't protect him altogether, but they softened the attacks that might otherwise have bitten deeply enough to bring him down.

The Black Dog darted forward in an attempt to put some distance between his assailants and himself. Pog and Az scrambled after him but couldn't quite keep up. The human whirled and grabbed the hilt of the sword hanging at his side.

A stride ahead of Az, Pog snatched the dangling hem of the Black Dog's cape and yanked. For an instant, it looked like the gobber might actually drag the human off balance and onto the floor, but then the clasp of the cape came open. The loose garment flopped down over Az's head, and he floundered blindly.

The Black Dog stepped back, and his sword cleared the scabbard. It appeared as if he meant to cut down Az while the guide was helpless. Then his eyes shifted toward the onrushing Pog, and the blade swept at the mechanik's head instead.

Pog's momentum wouldn't let him stop short. He dived to the floor, and the sword whizzed over him. Gasping, he jumped up and stabbed the screwdriver at the Khadoran's stomach.

At last the improvised weapon punched in deep, almost up to the handle. The human froze and made a little whimpering sound. Then Az, who'd rid himself of the cape, bulled into his leg and knocked him down, an action that had the side effect of jerking the screwdriver from Pog's grasp before he could pull it out of the outlaw's body.

With the Black Dog on the floor, Az resumed cutting. Shaking off his momentary paralysis, the Khadoran tried to fend off his assailant. After several failed snatches to retrieve the screwdriver, Pog settled for kicking the writhing, flailing human repeatedly in the back.

The outlaw struggled to one knee. That was bad. It meant he could use the sword to better effect. But as he raised it, blood arced from the side of his neck. Though Pog had missed seeing it, Az must have slashed the artery there. The human pitched forward onto his face, shuddered, and then, as the rhythmic spurts of blood subsided, lay still. Pog felt a kind of dazed relief and also sick to his stomach.

Panting, Az said, "Help me hide the body."

Pog shook his head. "There's so much blood…"

"It's dark in here, and we can mop up some of the blood with his clothing. Hiding him's worth a try."

They dragged the corpse into the cell Az had occupied. It occurred to Pog that he might still need a weapon, but now that the fight was over, he found he didn't want to touch the screwdriver. He took the sword instead. In theory, it was the superior weapon anyway, although in his hands it felt too big, heavy, and generally awkward for an untrained gobber to use it to any effect.

Once Pog and Az had hidden evidence of the killing as best they could, the explorer crouched over the broken bowl of food. The meal appeared to consist of scraps from the Black Dogs' table, but Az gobbled it anyway.

"Garbage," he said through a mouthful, "but I need my strength."

"Why do they treat you so cruelly?" asked Pog.

"It's how they treat anyone who tells them no. Especially Ivan. He likes having a slave to bully."

After Az finished eating, the gobbers crept up the stairs and onward. Every time they approached a corner, Pog worried they were about to run into Black Dogs coming the other way.

They didn't. During his captivity, Az had discerned the layout of the stronghold and noted the passages that people seldom used. But at one point, wailing—eerie and heart-rending in equal measure—echoed through the building. It sounded like hopeless misery beyond measure.

"Is that a child?" Pog whispered.

"I think so," Az replied.

"Why is it here?"

"I don't know. Keep going."

Along the way, they stole two lanterns, then exited through what was plainly a secondary way in and out. After that, they hurried onward toward one of the tunnels. Their best hope was that no one was looking, the next best was that anybody who was looking would mistake them in the dark for Black Dogs.

As they clambered over the soft uneven ground, Pog glanced back at the building. Despite the lights burning here and there, its blocky shape was vague in the darkness and provided no clue as to its original occupants or purpose.

Pog drew breath to ask Az if he knew. Then a voice shouted from somewhere in or atop the hideout.

Unfortunately, it was calling in Khadoran. Pog waved and hoped that wordless response would satisfy the sentry.

It didn't. The Black Dog shouted louder and with more of an edge in his voice.

Az said, "Run!"

— 14 —

CANICE FINISHED THE INCANTATION and felt a bit of her vitality flow into the newly enchanted rune bullet. It actually hurt a little, as if a ghostly finger had given her insides a poke. That was because she was tired.

Despite her fatigue, she suspected she wouldn't be able to sleep. So, she might as well replace the magically augmented ammunition she'd expended during the ambush. That way, she'd be fully prepared…

She scowled as the rationalization abruptly lost its power to convince. She knew what she was postponing by shutting herself away in her little workroom, and she felt an unaccustomed self-disgust for avoiding it. She rose from the little desk and strode into the front room.

From there, she could smell coal smoke and hear Doorstop clanking around in the stable. It seemed Colbie couldn't sleep either and had resorted to a similar strategy to occupy her mind and pass the time.

Specifically, she was putting Doorstop through his paces. At some point, she and Pog had either made or found the steamjack a new mace, and now, in response to her commands, he was assuming various guards and executing various strikes at half-speed.

As the door creaked open and Colbie glanced around, it occurred to Canice that the captain might greet her with the hostility that had become habitual between them. But she simply said, "Doorstop's ready. Now I have to pray to Markus and Corben I get the chance to use him."

"You will," Canice said.

Colbie shook her head. "I could have left him awake when we went below. But to save a little coal..."

"Could he have fought off the Black Dogs without you here to command him?" Canice asked.

"If the orders I left him with were simple, yet well-conceived enough to cover the situation, it's not impossible." The mechanik's mouth twisted. "We'll never know now, will we?"

"What happened is my fault," Canice said. "I promised Helstrom I'd stay in the safehouse. You told me to. Yet I couldn't bring myself to do it."

"We don't know if you being here would have improved the outcome. Maybe you would have ended up in the bratya's hands as well. Whereas I am fairly certain Eilish was right. We Black River Irregulars would have come to grief during the ambush if you hadn't been there to back us up."

Canice snorted. "It feels strange trying to make one another feel better."

For an instant, Colbie smiled. "Yes. It doesn't come as naturally as sneering and sniping."

Then the door opened once more. Eilish had taken off his armor but was still wearing his sword. He blinked and said, "Sorry, Colbie. I didn't realize you were busy."

"Come on in," Canice said. "Everyone else is apologizing. You might as well get it out of the way, too."

"If it helps any," Colbie said, "I was just admitting to Gormleigh that you were right."

Eilish cocked his head, and the gaslight glinted on his tousled yellow hair and the day-old stubble on his chin. "About what?"

"About her usefulness."

"You likely would have come around on that if not for me provoking you. Regan told me to stop, but I wouldn't heed her. I don't know what ailed me."

Colbie squeezed his forearm. "It's growing pains. Yours. Mine. The company's. Despite our victories, we're still learning how we fit together."

"Perhaps, but that's unacceptable when it gets in the way. Even after the first skirmishes, we failed to recognize how much of a threat the Black Dogs really are. We were too busy squabbling. And as a result…"

"We'll get Dr. Falk back," Canice said. "Natak, too. Pog will bring us what we need."

• • •

THE BLACK DOGS' VOICES CARRIED in the tunnel, and every time one of them spoke, Pog flinched. He kept glancing over his shoulder expecting to see that the pursuers had come into view. They hadn't yet, but it was only a matter of time.

Hobbling along a pace ahead of him, determined yet manifestly slowed by the effects of the ill treatment he'd received, Az pointed to a narrow opening in the left wall. "Thank the Mother," he wheezed. "We made it."

With the Black Dogs gaining on them, Pog was prepared to follow the explorer wherever he led. Still, he hesitated at the stink, a rank smell seemingly compounded of bodily waste and rot, wafting out of the gap. "Do you think we can shake them off our trail by going in here?"

"Not exactly," Az said. "We want them to know where we went. Find soft dirt and make some nice clear footprints."

Pressing his feet down hard, Pog did as he'd been told. Then he followed the guide into the passage.

They came around a bend, and the glow of their lanterns reflected in beady white eyes, half revealing the hunched, shadowy dog-sized shape behind them. The creature turned, displaying the row of quills on its back and its long, hairless tail, and scuttled deeper into the darkness.

"Devil rat!" Pog halted and raised the sword even though the beast was running away. Because if life in the Undercity had taught him anything, it was that the rat might well be going to fetch its pack mates.

"Keep moving," said Az. "And don't use that blade. Not unless you're certain we're dead no matter what."

They crept onward, and the tunnel gradually widened out, allowing the two of them to walk abreast. Unfortunately, it also enabled several devil rats to mass, barring the way.

Then a sound that was half-screech and half-squeal sounded right beside Pog. He jerked around and accidentally swatted Az with the flat of the sword. The guide was the only living thing within reach of the weapon.

"Don't do that!" Az whispered. "Don't do anything sudden." He took a deep breath and then squealed a second time.

Pog was so astonished that for a moment he nearly forgot to be afraid. He'd never heard of a person perfectly imitating the cry of a devil rat and, if he hadn't experienced it himself, wouldn't have believed it possible.

One of the vermin shrilled in response. Then they turned and disappeared into the murk.

"Come on," said Az. He started forward.

"Are they really going to let us through?" Pog whispered.

"I can sound like a devil rat, and that's how they communicate. But we don't look or smell like them, and even if we did, they've been known to eat one another when they're hungry. So, it's a gamble. But if we lose, we'll die faster and easier than if the Khadorans caught us. Now shut up and stay close."

At first Pog didn't see how he could do anything else. But the tunnel continued to widen until it terminated at a ledge. At the bottom of the slope running down from the ledge was the floor of a vault where dozens of devil rats were crawling around. The reek stung his eyes and made them water.

Az let out another squeal and then headed down the incline. Trembling, Pog balked. He couldn't descend into the midst of so many of the vile, scurrying creatures. It just wasn't in him.

But unless he was prepared to surrender to the Black Dogs, to suffer whatever punishment they meted out, and to fail Dr. Falk, Mr. Warbiter, and his other friends, he had no choice. And so, swallowing repeatedly, he set his foot on the slope.

Partway down, loose earth slid under his boots and cost him his balance. Terrified that if he fell, his obvious vulnerability would provoke the devil rats into attacking, he struggled to stay upright and finished the descent at a staggering trot.

At the bottom one of the beasts spun around, and he was certain it was going to lunge at him anyway. But Az gave another screech, and the rat responded in kind and backed away.

The gobbers crept onward. Rats brushed around Pog's legs, and he had to stifle the urge to scream, recoil, or flail with the sword when he hadn't seen them coming. Other vermin screeched, bristled, and seemingly poised themselves to attack. Presumably they were warning the newcomers away from the carrion they were gnawing or simply declaring certain patches of floor their private territory.

After what felt like years, Pog and Az drew near to a gobber skeleton with just a few scraps of rotten flesh still clinging to it. Teeth had marked the bones and sometimes broken them in pieces.

"Too bad it's not fresher," said Az. Laying his lantern on its side, he set it near the remains. "But then again, if it was, it might still be covered in rats and we'd never get close. Put your sword by its hand."

Pog hated the idea of disarming himself even though he knew the weapon wouldn't save him if the swarm decided to attack. But he did it anyway.

"Now take off your tunic," the explorer said, "tear it a few times, and leave it on top of the body."

Pog did that too, and as they skulked onward, he wondered if the seemingly inadequate tableau they'd created—*one* body, *one* lantern—would really convince the Black Dogs that both fugitive gobbers had perished in the vault. Maybe it would, in the dark. The Khadorans surely wouldn't approach any closer than the ledge if they even came that far. Nor would they believe their quarries could pass through the devil rats unharmed. He still wasn't sure he believed it either, and he became abruptly less confident when Az faltered.

"What's wrong?" Pog asked.

"There's the way out." Az pointed to a hole in the wall. "But to get there, we'll have to pass close to the matron." He pointed again.

Though Pog had never before seen one, nor ever wanted to, people had told him the matron of a devil rat swarm occupied essentially the same position as the queen of a beehive. This one was a pale, bloated, enormous thing, hairless and three times the size of the attendants scurrying around and in some cases climbing over her to groom her, mate with her, and carry meat to her jaws. Some of the servants turned to glare at the gobbers.

Pog cast a yearning glance back in the direction of the sword. Then, squealing repeatedly, Az started to maneuver around the matron and her guardians, and the mechanik followed.

They could keep their distance for a while. But because the matron had chosen to lie close to the wall and the exit, they had no choice but to draw near to her in due course.

Jaws wide and slavering, claws clicking on stone, a devil rat charged. Pog started to scramble backward, and Az caught him by the forearm and held him in place. The rat stopped just short of them and backed away.

One or two at a time, other rats did the same thing. Pog realized it was a more aggressive and intimidating version of the warning displays he'd seen previously. But it didn't have to be. There was no way to tell the beginning of such a scuttling feint from the start of a real attack, and each one stabbed a jolt of terror through him.

Attracted by the commotion, other rats advanced on the gobbers. Some swung wide to encircle them to enable the swarm to rush them from all sides and bury them under gnashing fangs, raking talons, and sheer blinding, suffocating bulk.

Feeling feverish, lightheaded, as if his spirit were already vacating his body, Pog was certain he and Az would never make it to the far side of the cave. Yet soon they reached the double row of devil rats that had slipped around in front of them. The wall and the exit were just on the other side.

Az screeched, and the rats parted to let him through. But, crowding one another, shifting back and forth, the vermin closed the hole back up before Pog could follow.

He kept moving anyway, taking tiny steps and so giving the rats the gentlest of nudges with his legs. One bared its fangs, and he heard himself whimper. But he continued nudging, shuffling in place to do it, and a different creature sidled to open a narrow aisle, scarcely more than a crack, between it and the coarse-furred flank of its neighbor.

Still treading slowly, fighting the urge to scramble, Pog started through. Despite his caution, his trembling hand brushed one of the long spurs curving up from the spine of the beast on the right. The rat twitched and snarled but did no more. Two more steps, and he was through.

"Now on up the tunnel," said Az, hoarse from the squealing. "Keep quiet and keep walking slowly. We'll be in their territory for a while yet."

If the explorer said so, Pog believed it. But as the vault with its dozens of devil rats receded into the darkness, when he and Az didn't come to face-to-face with any new ones, his legs went rubbery, and he could almost have sat down and wept with relief.

"How did you know you could do that?" he asked.

"I told you," Az replied, "I wasn't sure I could. But I've been watching devil rats ever since I started roaming the Undercity. I spent years practicing their calls, and it's gotten me out of trouble a time or two before." He snorted. "Didn't pull me out of the Khadorans' dungeon, though, did it? I needed you for that. Now let's get topside and make them sorry it did."

• • •

VIDOR RUSLING GENERALLY LIKED WALKING the streets of Corvis, even when a cold rain was falling, as it was at the moment. Clear or grey, the vast openness of the sky made for an exhilarating change from the confined spaces and eternal darkness of the Undercity.

But today he couldn't enjoy it. He was too angry and disgusted at having been impressed into the service of evil men. But someone had to carry out the task he'd been given lest innocent people suffer, never mind that in all probability, some were going to suffer anyway.

The three-story brick Watch station had a courtyard with a wrought-iron fence around that. The pewter ferrule of his sword cane clicked on the flagstones as he walked to the entrance.

The sturdy but—to Vidor's eyes, anyway—extremely young sentry stationed there watched his approach with a mixture of interest and respect. Vidor didn't wear the full regalia of a priest of Morrow anymore, and not everyone was sharp-eyed enough to notice his little bronze Ascendant Rowan badge at any distance. But his years as a cleric had taught him a certain gravitas. It had preserved his life on more than one occasion when dealing with the wicked and the desperate.

"Can I help you?" the sentry asked.

"I need to speak to the Watch Commander," Vidor replied.

"Then you'll have to wait or come back. He's busy."

"Meeting with Captain Sterling and the other mercenaries?"

The young man's green eyes widened. "How did you know?"

Vidor hadn't, for certain, but when he'd found the safehouse on Cooper Street empty, it had seemed a reasonable guess that the Black River Irregulars had repaired to a Watch station to report to their employer. So he'd started with the nearest such bastion and gotten lucky.

"What matters is that they're here," he said, "and they need to hear what I have to tell them. Show me in, please."

Frowning, the sentry considered for a moment, then ushered him inside and onward. He tapped softly, somewhat hesitantly, on a door, and a masculine voice snapped, "What?"

The young officer opened the door, revealing Vidor and himself to the occupants of the conference room and vice versa. Vidor had seen Colbie Sterling, Gardek Stonebrow, Milo Boggs, and Canice Gormleigh previously. He inferred that the lanky blond man in scratched black plate was Eilish Garrity and the middle-aged fellow with the black hair was Julian Helstrom. Grim-faced, they'd all gathered around a table to ponder a map of the Undercity that was curling up at the edges. No doubt it was as incomplete, if not downright misleading, as every other such chart that Vidor had ever seen.

"Mr. Rusling," Colbie said with a rising note of hope in her voice that Vidor would hate having to crush. "Given how we met before, I assume you're here about the Black Dogs."

"Unfortunately, yes." Vidor entered the room, and Helstrom gave the sentry a brusque wave of dismissal. The young man closed the door.

"It won't be unfortunate," the Watch Commander said, "if you can tell us anything that will help us hunt the wretches down. They're committing outrages aboveground now and making us look like fools while they're about it."

"I know," Vidor said. "They kidnapped Natak Warbiter and a Dr. Regan Falk from one of your safehouses. Sadly, the reason I know is because a Black Dog told me himself. Olekse, the one in the steam-powered armor, charged me to deliver a message. To all of you." He looked at Canice Gormleigh. "But to you in particular."

The gun mage made a spitting sound. "Naturally. What's the threat? Or the ultimatum?"

"The Khadorans want you to stop meddling in their business. You presumably want Natak and Dr. Falk back. So they propose a trade. Olekse, Ivan Varnek—the boss—and three others will bring the hostages to a patch of neutral territory, an open space where wary people can take stock of one another at a distance. You five mercenaries will meet them there at midnight. They'll turn over your friends in exchange for your vows to leave them in peace thereafter. Olekse warns that if you attempt any trickery—for example, by trying to sneak in reinforcements—the Black Dogs will know, and Natak and the doctor will suffer for it. If you don't show up, the result will be the same."

"Damn them," Eilish said.

"There's more," Vidor said, "and it's just as bad or worse. Olekse suspects you're the ones who sent a gobber spy named Pog to spy on the bratya. If so, he wants you to know the Khadorans identified him, and he's dead now. A swarm of devil rats ripped him apart when he was trying to escape. So you won't be getting any help from him."

The mercenaries all registered dismay in their various fashions. Her face looking ten years older, Colbie closed her eyes. Gardek's scowl deepened. Plainly, this fellow Pog had been their confederate, and they'd all been depending on him.

After two or three seconds of silence, Milo hitched his narrows shoulders in a way that reminded Vidor of a hound shaking itself. "Let's worry about people who are still alive," the alchemist said. "What 'neutral territory' do the Khadoran bastards have in mind?"

"The cave containing the main entrances to the Anthill."

"Then you can bet they've made an alliance with the diggers. *Their* reinforcements will be hiding in the burrows waiting to pour down on our heads if we're crazy enough to turn up."

"I agree," Canice said. "It's a trap. Not one that would ordinarily work, but they're hoping concern for our friends will make us stupid."

"I think so, too," Vidor said.

Eilish frowned. "Yes. Obviously. But the truth amid the lies is that if we don't walk into the ambush, they'll follow through on their threat against Regan and Warbiter. How do we prevent that? Is there a way to slip a Watch company into the cave, or somewhere close at hand, before the rendezvous?"

"No," Gardek said, "not if the Black Dogs have the Anthill on their side."

Colbie turned to Vidor. "How are you supposed to pass word back to the bratya? If we capture Olekse, or someone else important, maybe we can arrange an actual hostage exchange."

"I'm sorry," Vidor said. "He didn't tell me to deliver a reply. It would seem he doesn't think they need one."

Helstrom turned his flinty glower on Canice. "Give us something, expert."

The gun mage glared back. "I'm thinking."

"Think harder."

"We've never determined just how many Black Dogs there actually are," Canice said, "nor do we know if Sele of the Anthill is truly happy about her new alliance. If the five us go alone but prepared for the worst, is it possible—?"

"No," Milo said, "it isn't. Not when the Black Dogs will be ready for us, too." He turned to Eilish. "I like Regan. I'd take a risk to help her, or you. But I don't want to commit suicide. I don't want you to do it, either."

The mage scowled. Then his expression softened as he seemingly thought better of what he'd been about to say. "You're talking sense. But I'm the one who dragged Regan into this. I have to try something, even if I go alone."

Gardek spat. "Do you think—"

The door banged open. Both naked from the waist up, a pair of gobbers barged through with the sentry, who evidently hadn't seen fit to admit them, in pursuit. One was Az the tunnel explorer, now battered, bruised, and welted. Vidor didn't recognize the other, but judging from their sudden animation, the mercenaries did.

"Pog!" Colbie cried. She hurried to him, put her hands on his shoulders, and beamed down at him. "You're alive!"

Seemingly embarrassed by her welcome, Pog glanced back at his fellow gobber. "Thanks to him."

Az shook his head. "We saved each other." Behind him, the sentry registered that both Helstrom and the mercenaries were glad to see the intruders and hastily backed out of the doorway, bumping his elbow on the frame in the process.

"That's all very nice," Eilish said, his voice clipped. "But do you know where the bratya's hideout is? Can you lead us there?"

"Yes," said Pog.

"And we won't even have to wade through devil rats," said Az, grinning, "not this time. I know how to go around."

Peering about, Vidor perceived that in just a few seconds, the mood in the room had changed utterly. Thought the threat to the hostages remained, any trace of despair or despondency had departed. Instead, his companions were energized. The excitement was contagious, and, fingering the button on his black coat, he thanked the Ascendant of the impoverished and oppressed that he was not sending good people to certain death after all.

"Good work," Colbie said to the gobbers.

"That it is," said Canice. "We can raid the hideout today, before midnight, and with the Black Dogs believing the gobbers here are dead, we'll catch them by surprise." She gave Colbie a crooked smile. "When I say 'we,' it's with the understanding that you're the captain of your company."

"With that understanding," Colbie said, "we can use your help." She turned to Helstrom. "Watch Commander?"

Helstrom grunted. "Despite what she promised, I don't see where Gormleigh's been all that much help so far. Maybe now she can finally earn her keep. And just so you both understand, I don't care who's the leader among half a dozen ragtag mercenaries. What's important is that everyone knows that *my* officer, leading *my* Watch company, is in command of everybody."

Colbie inclined her head. "Of course. Who are you sending?"

"The same man I was going to send before. Lieutenant Bartley."

— 15 —

UP AHEAD, THE MERCENARIES PROWLED in a conjured haze of blue-white glow. Someone needed to serve as advance guards, and they'd volunteered for the job.

Yes, Lonan Bartley thought, of course they had, arrogant murderers-for-hire that they were. They imagined themselves braver, tougher, *better* than the honest officers of the Watch who followed a number of yards behind them. It would serve them right if they came to grief because of it.

Serve them right. Serve them right. He made the thought a drumbeat inside his head. Though it kept him marching forward, it couldn't truly erase his self-disgust. Even if Gormleigh and the Black River Irregulars deserved what was about to happen, their knavishness wouldn't make Lonan any less a traitor to his oath of office and his city.

Still, with his son in the hands of the Black Dogs, what choice did he have? He was just lucky that Az had explained the route in detail before they all descended into the Undercity. The knowledge had enabled Lonan to formulate a desperate plan. It wouldn't keep Helstrom from censuring him, demoting him, or perhaps even discharging him for gross incompetence. But if everything went perfectly, it might prevent anyone from realizing that he'd deliberately sabotaged the raid.

The blue light revealed a place where most of the floor of the broad tunnel fell away; beyond that point, a gulf yawned to the right of the path. When the mercenaries and their steamjack stalked out onto the shelf, they looked like travelers working their way along a horizontal stretch of mountain trail. Holes dotted the cliff beneath them, and according to Az, rumor had it that deep drakes laired in them and sometimes emerged to pick off people who sought to pass overhead.

As Lonan waited for Gormleigh and the others to reach the midway point, he looked around at the men of his company. In most situations, they were steady, dependable officers, but most situations didn't take them underground, and he was glad to observe the tautness in them, alertness shading into jumpiness. That should help.

Eilish Garrity's magical phosphorescence washed across the opening of one of the holes. The way that the glow caught the particular contours of the wall created a vague yet suggestive flutter of deeper and lesser shadow. Lonan determined that it provided as good an excuse as he was likely to get. He tried to bestir himself but couldn't.

Because what if he was wrong? What if the raid would go perfectly if he only allowed it to, so perfectly that he and his companions would rescue Wyatt along with the other hostages?

But no, he didn't dare risk it. He pictured the boy's face, and that punched through his reluctance. He pointed and shouted, "Kill it!"

Eyes wide, his men peered about. "Kill what, sir?" Borlock asked.

"The thing in the burrow!" Lonan said. "Everyone open fire, or it's going to kill them all!" Shouldering his rifle, he shot at the hole with the deceptive mesh of grey and black.

Other watchmen discharged their own weapons. Maybe they were firing at the same hole their commander had indicated, maybe at different ones in which, thanks to distance, darkness, and anxiety, they imagined they saw a threat. It didn't really matter.

But the four watchmen armed with slug guns didn't fire. In theory, they'd brought the heavy weapons with their massive shells to take down the Black Dogs' steamjacks, and apparently they believed they were supposed to reserve them for that purpose.

As he slipped another round into the chamber, Lonan pivoted toward the slug gunners. "I said, *everyone* fire!" he screamed.

Finally, they did. Presumably they were also trying to shoot into one or another of the openings. But the shells flew wild and slammed against the scarp instead, not far below the mercenaries' feet, while Gormleigh, Sterling, and the others peered wildly about trying to discern what all the watchmen were firing at.

Dirt and rock spilled down the cliff, and when the structure underneath it gave way, a section of the path crumbled, too. Arms flailing, Milo Boggs tipped backward into space.

• • •

MILO JACKKNIFED HIS WEIGHT FORWARD, and when his center of gravity shifted, he was able to take a frantic step. For a second, he had solid earth under one of his feet again, and then that bit of path disintegrated as well.

He started to fall, and Eilish grabbed him and heaved him forward. It seemed an impossible feat until he noticed that Canice had seized hold of the arcanist's belt to anchor him.

Milo bumped into Eilish and nearly knocked both him and the gun mage off their feet. Meanwhile, the ledge was still crumbling underneath them. He grabbed hold of the arcanist and wrenched him around. "Run!" he shouted.

They didn't stop until they reached the spot where the pit ended and the tunnel became a proper tunnel again. Colbie, Gardek, Az, and Pog, who, with Doorstop, had reached safety ahead of them, clamored to know if they were all right.

As Milo nodded, he realized the shooting had stopped. He peered back at the Watch company on the other side of the gulf. The lawmen stood in a haze of gun smoke that diffused the light of their lanterns.

Colbie stepped forward. "What was that?" she called.

"Sorry!" Lonan Bartley replied. "But a beast was climbing out of one of the burrows! It would have killed you all if we hadn't shot it first!"

Some of the other watchmen nodded.

"But now you're cut off!" Colbie said.

"We'll find another way around!" Bartley said. "Wait for us!"

"There isn't another way around!" Az shouted. Grumbling to himself, he added, "Not that you'll find, anyway."

"Wait for us!" Bartley repeated. He turned away and started preparing his men to go back the way they'd come.

"Did you hear the catch in his voice?" Eilish asked, and there was no mistaking the anger in his own. "I don't believe he actually saw a threat. He meant to destroy the path."

"Really?" Milo asked. Such a possibility would never have occurred to him, but if Eilish posited it, it might well be so. "Damn all lawmen. I knew I was better off steering clear of them."

"Why would he betray us?" Gardek asked, hefting his war hammer as though Bartley were already within reach.

"Forget him for now," Colbie snapped. "We have decisions to make and no time to make them. Az, are we close enough to the Black Dogs' hideout that they will have heard the shooting?"

"Yes," the explorer said.

"Then they're going to get ready for trouble," Colbie said, "and the longer we give them, the readier they'll be. So, we advance as fast as we can."

"You mean, fight anyway?" Milo asked. "Without the Watch?"

Canice grinned. "All the more sport for us."

"That's how you see it, is it?" Milo turned to Az. "You could get us out of here? We're not boxed in?"

The gobber nodded. "I know a way."

"But then what becomes of Regan?" Eilish asked. "And Warbiter? This is still our only chance to save them."

"Colbie's right," Gardek said. "Every second that passes is a second we can't afford. We need to go *now*, and alchemist, if you don't want—"

"Oh, shut up," Milo said. "I'm coming. But if it all goes wrong, remember that I warned you it was stupid."

• • •

NO ONE WAS WAITING in the last stretch of tunnel. Colbie wondered if that was because by some extraordinary stroke of luck, the Black Dogs hadn't heard the shooting and explosions after all. But when she peered out into the vault containing the Khadorans' refuge, she abandoned that pleasant fancy.

Pog and Az said they had no idea who had built the massive old brick building or why, and she couldn't tell either. If it had started life on the surface, it could have done so as a government facility, a factory, or even, given Corvis' penchant for ugly architecture, a church. But it was plainly defensible, and if she'd been leading the outlaws in residence, she too would have waited behind the walls for her foes to come to her.

Fortunately, the situation wasn't hopeless. Although the doors looked sturdy, she was confident that her slug gun, Milo's explosives, or Doorstop's mace could take them down. The trick would be getting close enough to use them. No doubt the Black Dogs would start shooting through those narrow windows when the attackers headed across the cave.

"Eilish, Canice," she said, and the arcanist and the gun mage moved up beside her. "Get rid of the lamps outside the building. Except the ones beside the doors."

Drawing the pistols holstered on her hips, Canice glanced at Eilish. "You take the one on the left."

"My pleasure." Eilish pointed his sword, and blue symbols flickered in the air around him. A bolt of blue power leaped from the end, hurtled at the stronghold, and smashed a lamp. Meanwhile, Canice fired twice and shattered two more. Now only the two shining beside the doors remained, at least on this side of the building.

As expected, guns started flashing and banging in response. Shots thudded into the earthen arch that was the mouth of the tunnel. Milo swore.

Gardek strode past Colbie, Eilish, and Canice to the front of the passage, where he poised his spiked shield to protect everyone from the incoming fire. Colbie turned to tell Doorstop to do likewise, but in one of his occasional moments of initiative, possibly imitating the other hulking combatant equipped with an enormous shield and melee weapon, the steamjack was already in motion. Smokestack fuming, suffusing the air with the smells of burning coal, oil, and hot metal, he clanked up beside the trollkin and assumed a similar stance.

Colbie raised her voice to make herself heard over the clatter of bullets striking the shields. "We're about to move. Milo, make a smokescreen. You, Gardek, and Eilish take the door on the left. Canice, Doorstop, and I will take the one on the right. We don't stop moving until we've rescued our friends and cleared out all the Black Dogs."

Canice frowned. "Or we could all stick together."

"The way Pog and Az described the interior," Colbie said, "there are plenty of spots where the six of us wouldn't all have room to act at once. Besides, breaching in two places gives the enemy twice as much to think about and doubles our chances of finding the hostages before someone takes it into his head to go kill them or trot them out at gunpoint to make us stand down."

The gun mage nodded. "Fair enough. You're the boss."

Colbie turned to the gobbers. "Pog, Az, the two of you have done enough already. If—"

"I'm coming," said Pog.

"I'm not," said Az. "Even if I were a soldier, I'm not in any shape for a fight. But I'll wait here. If things go badly, come back and I'll do my best to get you away."

"Thank you," Colbie said. It was a sensible precaution, but she doubted it would truly help. If she and her companions lost the battle, they were unlikely to make it back to this position alive.

So, she supposed they'd better win.

"Pog," she said, "you're with my group. "Doorstop, march to the door on the right. Keep your shield up."

Unlike the steamjack, the mercenaries advanced without needing to be told. Milo threw grenades in front of them all, and the clockwork orbs burst into clouds of grey vapor. Combined with the darkness, the further concealment should make the attackers all but impossible targets, and Doorstop and Gardek's armor ought to neutralize the occasional lucky shot. Meanwhile, Colbie and her comrades had the lamps beside the doors to steer by.

She could no longer make out the entrances themselves, but as the mercenaries separated into two groups and Milo threw another smoke bomb, she heard them open and slam shut again. Moments later, three shadows as big as Doorstop appeared in the gloom. The Khadorans had sent out their steamjacks.

Colbie might have done the same. Outside the building, there were no tight spaces to hinder the steamjacks, and they could use all their weapons without endangering their human masters.

Steam lobbers boom-hissed. A projectile smashed into Doorstop's newly repaired shield, denting and twisting it all over again and knocking him off balance. He fell onto his back and then, to Colbie's relief, rolled onto his side and began the ponderous process of standing up.

Turning to Canice, Colbie said, "We can't let them keep shooting him while he's down."

The redhead returned a nod. "Distract them. Got it." She ran forward, circling toward an enemy 'jack's flank, halting for an instant to fire one of her pistols, and then sprinting onward.

Her slug gun cradled in her hands, Colbie dashed to assail the same 'jack from the other side. A bullet, likely discharged from an upper-story window, whined past her ear and made her wince. Without Doorstop for shelter, she was more vulnerable to enemy fire than she'd been before, but for the moment, she was just going to have to take her chances.

• • •

WHEN DOORSTOP TOPPLED BACKWARD, Pog scrambled to keep the 'jack from landing on top of him. He avoided getting squashed, but at the cost of putting several paces between Captain Sterling and himself. As a result, amid the sudden outbreak of noise and general confusion, he missed whatever she said to Miss Gormleigh and so was taken by surprise when the two of them went tearing off into the darkness and the smoke.

Should he follow? It was entirely possible that the captain had ordered him to. But his instincts told him to stay with Doorstop. If his skills were of any use in the present situation, surely it was to direct the 'jack whose marshal had for the moment abandoned him.

Besides, even when lying on the ground, Doorstop provided a significant amount of cover for a fellow no bigger than a gobber. He crouched behind the 'jack and waited for him to get to his feet.

When Doorstop succeeded, he shifted his now-battered shield into its original defensive attitude and once again tramped toward the blotch of lamplight on the murk. Pog's muscles tensed in anticipation of a second shot, one that might penetrate the 'jack's compromised defense, disable him, or even make his boiler explode.

Though steam lobbers were roaring and hissing and shells were exploding elsewhere, no such attack struck Doorstop. Pog decided Colbie and Canice had run forward to keep that from happening.

Soon, he came close enough to see the enemy 'jack clearly—it was turning with its steam lobber outstretched, trying to aim a shot at Canice. She was scrambling to stay ahead of it.

Somewhere ahead and off to the right, Colbie shouted, "Doorstop, kill this 'jack!"

Doorstop altered his course and hefted his mace. The Khadoran 'jack gave up trying to target Canice and readied the enormous blade it carried. It seemed it wouldn't use a steam lobber on another 'jack at close quarters lest a ricochet or explosion damage it as well.

Pog smiled in anticipation. No doubt, working together, Captain Sterling, Miss Gormleigh, and Doorstop could demolish the Black Dogs' 'jack. But his confidence wilted when the dark woman and the red-haired one ran off again. He belatedly remembered there were three enemy automatons, and presumably the humans were needed to contend with another.

Doorstop reached his target and started striking. The Khadoran 'jack did, too, producing a rhythmic, jolting crash of metal on metal.

With no one directing them, each attacked directly over and over with only minor variations. Pog wondered fleetingly why Olekse had sent his 'jacks out onto the battlefield without him. Maybe the ironhead was still engaged in the laborious process of donning his armor, or maybe he simply hadn't deemed it necessary to put himself in harm's way.

Whatever the reason, it appeared to Pog that the result was stalemate. By sheer chance, most likely, the two combatants meshed like moves in a training exercise, which was to say, each 'jack was protecting itself well enough that the other's attacks couldn't penetrate its defense.

Or so it seemed at first. Then Pog discerned that, already weakened by the steam-lobber shot, Doorstop's shield was gradually buckling before the Khadoran steamjack's onslaught. When the sword broke it away from its grips or crumpled it around his arm, then the enemy automaton would slam in a crippling blow.

Pog had watched Colbie run Doorstop through various fighting drills as a part of the repair process. He struggled to remember which was which, strained, too, to comprehend the fight unfolding before him and figure out which moves could break the impasse before the pounding sword did it first.

"Doorstop," he cried, "Pat him on the head!"

Doorstop feinted as instructed. The enemy 'jack reacted properly to the deviation and raised the sword to parry.

But it needed an instant to adjust. The parry was late, and when the mace swung down to threaten his adversary's midsection, the defense lagged a tick further behind.

Done feinting, Doorstop heaved the mace high for the true attack. Evidently recognizing that it couldn't block in time, the Black Dogs' 'jack started to step back, but it was slow attempting that as well. The mace smashed into its shoulder, crumpling the carapace and breaking open the seams. Arcane energy crawled and crackled around the breaches, and the Khadoran machine froze.

"Yes!" Pog howled. Up until this moment, he hadn't liked anything about actual fighting, but maybe he could get used to it.

• • •

CANICE FIRED THE MAGELOCK PISTOL in her right hand. The rune shot hit the steamjack in the chest, and a spiderweb of rust spread out from the point of impact.

She fired the gun in her left hand. She'd charged its round with extra force, and she hoped it would do devastating damage to the spot she'd just weakened.

The rune shot hit the center of the spiderweb. Metal cracked, and corrosion rained from the point of impact. But the 'jack stayed upright and kept moving, swinging its steam-lobber forearm to threaten her.

As she faked a dodge to the left, then lunged to the right, she wished she still had Doorstop to hide behind. But when she and Colbie had seen two Khadoran 'jacks were blasting away at Gardek, Eilish, and Milo, it had been clear that somebody had to neutralize one of those machines, and so they'd left Doorstop behind to contend with the third Black Dog steamjack on his own.

She grinned because she was circling faster than the 'jack could adjust its aim. When she maneuvered behind it, that would give her the second necessary to reload one of the magelock pistols.

Then the 'jack's arm swiveled downward. The steam lobber boomed, and a burst of vapor shrouded the limb. The 'jack had given up trying to point the weapon right at her and instead discharged it at the ground a stride or two behind her.

A blast flung her through the air. She hadn't anticipated the change of tactics because the previous projectiles hadn't been explosive. Evidently, Olekse the ironhead had loaded different kinds of rounds into the magazine.

Canice slammed down hard, and clods of earth thumped down on top of her. The 'jack pivoted, putting her directly in front of it again. The pieces of a mechanism in its steam lobber slid and hitched to reload the weapon. She tried to roll and scramble sideways, but her head was ringing, and she was clumsy and slow.

Just as the components of the reloading mechanism snapped back down, Canice dashed in front of it, interposing herself between it and Canice. Her slug gun roared, and the projectile punched into the 'jack's torso where the rune shots had already damaged it.

The steamjack tipped backward and, seemingly unable even to try to recover its balance, fell onto its engine and smokestack. It didn't move afterward. The shot from the slug gun had severed some fundamental linkage and paralyzed it as thoroughly as a human being with a broken neck.

Colbie scurried to Canice. "Are you all right?"

"I think so," Canice said. The dazed, shocked feeling was passing. She made sure she still had the magelock pistols in her hands, and then a firearm in a second-story window flashed and barked. Hit, Colbie grunted and dropped to one knee.

"Let me see," Canice said. She scurried behind the mechanik and checked the new perforation in the black armored greatcoat. "It didn't go all the way through. You'll be fine when you catch your breath."

As she finished speaking, she reloaded one of the magelock pistols with a rune shot enchanted for accuracy and waited for the Black Dog in the window to reappear. Hindered by the darkness, the smoke, and the distance, she perceived only a fluttering hint of motion when he did. Still, when she fired, he flopped forward. His upper body dangled down the wall, and the rifle slipped from his grasp and fell.

• • •

MILO, EILISH, AND GARDEK HAD FOUND A LONG, low hump in the ground to lie behind. One steam-lobber projectile screamed over the alchemist's head, and then another one hit in front of him. His particular bit of hump burst at him like a breaking wave and half-buried him. He yelped.

As he clambered out from under his covering of dirt and swiped more of it from the lenses of his gas mask, he spied the smoking projectile, half-buried also, just a few inches away. He was lucky it had run out of momentum when it had.

He couldn't expect to be lucky twice, not if he stayed framed in the newly made gap in the makeshift rampart. He scuttled right, which brought him closer to Eilish. Gardek was on the other side of the arcanist.

"We can't stay here!" Milo cried.

"With two 'jacks shooting at us," Eilish said, "we can't do anything else."

"But they're coming closer!" Milo said. "This little bit of cover won't *be* cover in a minute." He looked past the mage to Gardek in the hope that the trollkin would say he was right.

Gardek had raised his head with its crest of quills just high enough to peer over the hump. After a moment, his wide mouth stretched into a grin. "The 'jack on the right's stopped firing at us. I think Canice engaged it, maybe Colbie too. Anyway, we can handle the other one. Milo, make some more smoke."

"I'm out of smoke bombs."

"I'll distract the 'jack," Eilish said. His eyes narrowed, and a furrow appeared above the bridge of his nose. Milo knew the signs. His partner was working magic by thought alone. After a moment, a pale blue glow sprang up around the three of them.

Or rather, just around Eilish. When he crawled away from his companions, still using the long bump in the earth for cover, the light traveled with him and left Milo and Gardek in gloom.

The bounty hunter popped his head up again. "The 'jack's turning. Following the light. Come on!" He jumped up and ran, circling to remain unnoticed as long as possible.

Milo darted after him and discovered that the smoke he'd created was thinning. That was unfortunate, if "unfortunate" was an adequate word for increased risk of gunfire riddling you from head to toe or a single shot from a steam lobber tearing you apart. But maybe the darkness and general confusion would protect him. He pulled a grenade from his bandolier.

Meanwhile, steam-lobber projectiles hammered the rounded ridge in the earth, blowing it to bits. Then Eilish's light went out. Inwardly, Milo winced.

At least he was coming into throwing range. Halting, he called, "Watch out!" A couple of strides ahead of him, Gardek stopped and covered up behind his shield. Milo thumbed the clockwork timer, hurled the grenade, and ducked.

He couldn't tell if the blast did any actual damage, but at least it staggered the 'jack. Gardek charged up to it and bashed it with his war hammer.

Even the trollkin looked small assailing a steamjack. But he landed four solid blows all in the same spot, because the heavy automaton was ponderously turning to face Gardek and attack with its sword.

Gardek jumped back and so avoided the first slash. Then he circled, forcing the 'jack to turn with him. The hammer clanged against the huge blade but without breaking it or knocking it out of the steamjack's grip.

Milo hovered, waiting for the right moment, although how a person was supposed to know when a 'jack wasn't paying attention to him was anybody's guess. When instinct prompted him, he dashed in on its flank.

He grinned when he spotted the cracked place in its chassis. Colbie and Pog had explained where the steel shells of the Khadoran 'jacks were weak—relatively speaking—and Gardek had pounded at such a spot repeatedly.

Milo jammed a grenade into the jagged opening. It wouldn't slide all the way through, but he hoped it would stick. "Get back!" he yelled, scrambling away. Gardek retreated and covered up again with his shield.

When the grenade detonated, some of the acid inside sprayed out to steam and sizzle on the ground. But some of it spattered the steamjack's interior as well. The 'jack kept moving its arms, but its legs shuddered, rattled, and froze. After a moment, it turned and pointed its arm at Milo. He threw himself to the side, but the steam lobber only clacked and spurted hissing vapor.

A hand gripped Milo's shoulder, startling him. He jerked around and discovered Eilish, now as filthy as no doubt he was himself. Grinning, the blond man said, "It ran out of ammunition shooting at me."

Milo grunted. "Your light went out."

"I extinguished it when the 'jack came too near. I was done playing decoy."

"Shut up and run!" Gardek snarled. "Get to the damn door!"

They sprinted onward while guns flashed and banged from the upper reaches of the vague black mass of the building ahead. Milo felt—or imagined he felt—one round after another burning past him. But to his surprise, as he and his partners neared their destination, the shooting abated. Maybe it was awkward for the Khadorans to fire at people who were too close to the building, or maybe they were running out of ammunition.

He looked to the right and made out Doorstop poised before the other entry and other, smaller figures as well. He hoped he was seeing everybody: Colbie, Canice, and Pog. In the dark, it was hard to be sure.

No doubt on Colbie's command, Doorstop pointed at the building with his mace to give the order to breach. Milo took a deep breath and grabbed another grenade.

— 16 —

ON COLBIE'S COMMAND, Doorstop pounded the door with his mace. The third blow smashed it off its hinges. Slug gun leveled, using the steamjack for cover, Colbie peered around him. She was expecting a barrage of gunfire, but the lantern-lit space before her was empty.

"Would they run away?" she asked. "We did just neutralize three 'jacks."

"No," Canice said, meanwhile peeking around the other side of Doorstop. "Given the chance, they'll always choose to overwhelm a foe with superior numbers or stab him in the back—preferably both—but they don't run from a fight. They're lying in wait for us where they think they'll have the advantage." She cocked her head. "Should someone run over and tell the others that?"

"No," Colbie said. "They have sense enough to go warily, and we should keep moving. Doorstop, advance down the hall. Check in the doorways as you go. Any stranger you see is an enemy."

His hugeness filling the corridor, Doorstop tramped forward.

As ordered, he paused, pivoted, and peered into each doorway. Even when he moved on, though, that didn't necessarily mean the room beyond the threshold was clear. His senses were no sharper than a human being's, and it was possible that a skilled ambusher hiding in the gloom could evade his notice.

In fact, if Colbie were in the defenders' place, she might well let the 'jack pass by in tight quarters. Then she and her soldiers would attack the people following behind him.

Thus, she checked the doorways herself and frequently glanced back down the hall to make sure no enemy had slipped around behind the intruders. Canice was proceeding in the same fashion, and after a while, breathing heavily, eyes wide, and looking nervous enough to jump out of his skin at the slightest provocation, Pog started doing it as well. Colbie and the gobber peered into one opening while Canice checked its counterpart on the other side of the passage. Seeing nothing dangerous, they crept onward. Then Colbie heard the faint scuff of a stealthy footstep.

"Watch out!" she cried, spinning around. Sword raised, a Black Dog was lunging out of the room she'd just checked. She pulled the trigger and, the boom of its discharge deafening in these close quarters, the slug gun splashed his torso into mush and smashed a chunk out of the doorframe. The recoil kicked her hands up.

The Khadoran who'd been right behind that first assailant sprang from the opening painted with gore, his comrade's destruction not deterring him. Bellowing, he slashed at Colbie's head. She just managed to block with her empty weapon, then swung it in a riposte. He skipped back out of range and sneered at the awkward effort.

He was still sneering when Doorstop, wrenching himself around with an effort that scraped his shoulders, engine, and shield and tore bits of brick from the walls, thrust his mace over Colbie's head and into her adversary's face. The weapon smashed the Black Dog's skull, and he fell backward.

Glancing about, Colbie spied four more Black Dogs sprawled

dead on the floor. Canice, her hands almost preternaturally quick, simultaneously reloaded the pistols that had killed them and looked around for any remaining foes.

"Doorstop, turn back around," Colbie said. "And sorry for the dings and gouges."

• • •

GARDEK HAMMERED DOWN THE DOOR, then immediately made sure his shield covered him as completely as possible. No bullets battered it; the Khadorans weren't waiting right beyond the threshold.

Milo stepped out from behind him to survey the space. He tossed up the grenade in his black-gloved hand and caught it again. "I don't think they just ran away," he said.

"Neither do I," Gardek said. "They're as sick of us as we are of them."

"Even if they aren't," Eilish said, "they can't let us chase them out of their own secret stronghold and hope to continue intimidating the rest of the Undercity. And then there's their vendetta against Canice. No, they're waiting for us somewhere inside this pile. I just wish we knew how many are left."

Gardek grunted. "One way to find out."

Checking doorways and branching passages as he passed, he led his companions down a corridor. Then he caught a whiff of coal smoke.

"Olekse's up ahead," he whispered.

"It looks like there's a room at the end of the hallway," Eilish replied, "and he needs space to clank around in his armor and swing an ice maul." He pointed his sword, and fire flashed in the space he'd indicated. The flame couldn't reach any of the foes lurking there, nor did its light reveal them, but someone gave a startled cry.

"Good," Milo said. "Now that we're sure they're there, let's say hello." He thumbed the timer gear of the grenade in his hand and bowled it into the space ahead.

The metal egg blew apart in a dazzling flash of vitriolic fire.

Voices screamed and, squinting against the glare, Gardek smiled.

As the floating cloud of fire faded, he said, "Now we go in. Me first." He hefted his war hammer and charged. After a few strides, he could make out smoking bodies on the floor, some motionless, some writhing.

Still, he doubted Milo had accounted for all the Black Dogs, so he kept running and plunged through the doorway fast. Fast enough that he avoided a blow from the ice maul, though only barely.

He'd entered an open area with several doorways and the bottom of a staircase along the walls. It had other functional Khadorans in it, too, but he elected to leave them for Eilish and Milo as he whirled to face Olekse.

"You bastards wrecked my steamjacks," the ironhead growled. "If I could have gotten outside to command them, it would have been different."

"Your 'jacks were junk," Gardek replied. "Just like your stupid armor and your stupid ice maul." He threw his shield at Olekse's face.

Ordinarily, he wouldn't dispense with the protection. But if he held onto it, a few blows from the maul would freeze and shatter it anyway.

Olekse jerked up his arm, and the shield hit his armored limb instead of his unarmored face. That was too bad, but Gardek still didn't regret throwing it. He was quicker and more agile than the human in his ponderous steam-powered shell, and discarding the bulky shield would maximize that advantage.

Shifting from side to side, Gardek struck repeatedly. Sometimes the blows rang on the Khadoran's armor, and sometimes Olekse parried them. But even when he did, Gardek dodged or retreated out of range of the human's ripostes, though often only by a whisker.

After several seconds, Olekse retreated as well. At first Gardek thought he was pushing the ironhead back, then he realized his foe had intentionally put himself in a corner, where there was no room for his foe to sidle as he had up to now.

Gardek kept pressing anyway. He was still faster, and when the maul swept down at him, he hitched back out of range as he had before. The Khadoran's weapon slammed into the floor.

As Olekse began to lift the maul, Gardek lunged to hit him before he could come back on guard. His feet slid, and with a jolt of alarm, he realized that the floor was icy now.

The sudden loss of balance turned the trollkin's attack into a weak, clumsy stroke that Olekse easily blocked. The answering blow smashed into Gardek's breastplate. The maul knocked him on his back, hammered the breath from his lungs, and stabbed coldness into his very core.

The maul rose and swept down again. Gardek tried to roll out of the way, but he was too slow. Olekse's weapon bashed him in the ribs. Sheathed in frost, the armor there cracked, and pieces of it fell away. Another shock of cold pierced him.

Gardek sensed that a third such blow would finish him, and maybe that gave him the strength to wrench himself aside when the maul pounded down. It slammed into the floor a finger length away, and the impact sent rime flowing over his back like fast-growing fungus, but the new frigidity was insignificant compared to what he'd already endured.

As Olekse swung the maul upward, Gardek hooked the head of it with the head of his war hammer. The might of steam-powered armor had no difficulty contending with the added weight, and thus the Khadoran jerked him to his feet.

As he did, ice ran over the hammer, and the pull of the maul stressed the now-brittle weapon beyond its capacity to endure. It shattered into several pieces, and Olekse grinned. Then, an instant later, he gasped, and his bloodshot eyes opened wide.

The two weapons had remained tangled long enough that the pull not only hauled Gardek to his feet but also yanked him forward, and Olekse couldn't shift the long, cumbersome maul to make another attack or even simply to interpose it between his opponent and himself. Not in time to keep their two bodies from jamming together.

Gardek whipped his forearm at Olekse's face. The spikes on his vambrace crunched into the Black Dog's skull.

• • •

MILO AND EILISH DASHED INTO THE ROOM a second behind Gardek. The trollkin spun to the side, denying his two partners the cover his shield and massive frame had previously afforded them. Milo saw that Gardek had done it because he needed to square off with the ironhead, but that didn't make him like it any better.

Doorways opened along the walls, and Black Dogs who'd survived the first cinder bomb were waiting on the other sides. Milo picked out the space that appeared to hold the most—things were moving so fast that he could scarcely pause to make a careful count—snatched another grenade, thumbed the clockwork timer for a quick detonation, and hurled it at that opening.

It exploded into another blast of fire. This close, he flinched from the sudden heat, but it didn't harm him. The Black Dogs caught in the flame were less fortunate. Burning, they screamed, thrashed, and fell.

That improved the odds, but it didn't deter the swordsmen in the other spaces from charging. In an instant, they were close enough that any grenade Milo used against them would catch him and his partners in the blast as well.

He snatched a knife from its bandolier and threw it, then did the same again. The first knife pierced a Black Dog's chest and dropped him to the floor for the swordsman behind him to trip over. A swirling cape slapped the second blade tumbling off course.

Now the several men rushing Milo were almost near enough to use their blades. Hoping to find shelter behind Eilish with his spells and his own deft swordplay, he glanced around and found the imperatives of the fight had separated them. The lanky blond arcanist was only a few steps away, yet even so, Milo would never reach him in time.

The alchemist whirled and ran back down the corridor. His adversaries' footsteps pounded after him. Fear howled that he was about to feel a sword shear into his back.

Fortunately, fear underestimated just how fast he could move when he had to. He kept ahead of his pursuers long enough to pull out another grenade, yank the pin, and drop it at his feet.

The grenade banged, and grey vapor gusted past him. He'd known the cloud would engulf him, but this particular preparation couldn't incapacitate a man wearing a gas mask. It would, however, knock out people who weren't, and behind him, bodies thudded into one another and onto the floor.

Grinning, Milo stumbled to a halt and turned around just in time to face the sword he'd been dreading a moment before. Tottering but clinging to consciousness, one tattooed Khadoran was still on his feet and had his blade upraised.

Milo lunged and grappled, grabbing hold of the Black Dog's sword arm just in time to keep the blade from slashing down at him. The two men strained against one another, and then the Khadoran went limp, his legs giving way beneath him.

• • •

WHEN HE BURST INTO THE OPEN SPACE, Eilish pivoted, taking stock. All but one of the openings along the walls led to adjacent rooms or other hallways, and with luck, Milo would kill some of the swordsmen lurking in them. But one archway connected to an ascending staircase with a pair of riflemen kneeling at the top, and the odds of the alchemist throwing a grenade all the way up the steps and eliminating them were slim. Eilish decided to attend to them himself.

He dashed toward the foot of the staircase to give himself a better angle. The rifles flashed, banged, and puffed smoke. One round grazed his shoulder, staggering him but glancing off his armor.

The riflemen started to reload, and Eilish grinned because they weren't fast enough. They were still inserting fresh cartridges into the breeches as he concentrated, visualized the proper glyphs, and hurled a bolt of blue light up at the shooter on the left. The flare of magic struck the Black Dog in the face, and the man collapsed. Eilish followed up with a second bolt, one that knocked down the Khadoran on the right.

He whirled to see what else was going on, but there was too

much motion, too much chaos, for him to take it all in. Metal clanged as Gardek battered Olekse the ironhead's armor. Beyond one of the doorways, Milo had produced another bright, hanging cloud of flame, and men were reeling and falling down within it. More Black Dogs swarmed out of other openings with swords and capes in hand, and four of them were rushing Eilish.

Given the chance, they'd flank him and attack him from behind. He retreated and put his back against the wall. At the same time, he centered his thoughts on fire. His newly acquired command of that element was still shaky compared to his mastery of his other spells, but his intuition told him it was flame he needed.

He rattled off an incantation and pointed with his sword. Symbols of blue light danced in the air around him, and flame leaped up on the cloak in the grip of the Black Dog in the middle. The Khadoran cried out, and he and his trio of comrades all balked, perhaps because over the course of the last few moments they'd twice seen explosions of fire engulf groups of their fellow Khadorans to lethal effect.

Before they could register that the new fire was less dangerous, Eilish lunged and attacked. He sliced one Black Dog's neck, pivoted, and cut open the stomach of the next man, who wasbathed in the arterial spray. The outlaw whose cape had caught fire was still flinging it to the floor when Eilish's sword pierced his heart.

The fourth Black Dog managed to recover his wits before Eilish spun toward him. Coughing, but seemingly no less quick or steady for that, the Khadoran flicked his cape at Eilish's face.

Eilish dropped into a crouch, and both the cloak and the sword thrust it had masked passed over his head. He stabbed his own blade up into the Black Dog's abdomen, and the other swordsman doubled over and collapsed.

Panting, Eilish straightened up. An instant later, somewhere beyond one of the doorways in the opposite wall, a woman screamed.

Regan! The mercenaries had hoped to rescue the captives before anyone thought to menace them but, lacking the support of Lieutenant Bartley and the men of the Watch, they seemed to have failed.

Eilish cast about. Olekse was down. Gardek was busy slaughtering other outlaws, a big piece of his cuirass broken away but his shield once again on his arm, the hammer he'd somehow lost replaced by an axe that looked dainty in his grip. Milo had disappeared, although with luck the cloud of gas back down the corridor meant he was still alive and using his preferred weapons to good effect. If Eilish meant to answer Regan's call without delay, he'd have to do it alone.

He moved toward the doorway from which he judged the scream had come. A stray Black Dog charged him, and he flung a bolt of magic that stabbed into the Khadoran's chest and dropped him facedown on the floor.

Eilish hurried into a room lit only by a single lamp, and there he hesitated. The plump silver-blonde woman sprawled in the darkest corner wasn't Regan. But she plainly needed help, and perhaps she knew where Regan was being held.

He strode toward her. "I'm a friend," he said. "Are you hurt?"

She groaned and shifted her hand a little. He looked for blood but didn't see any. Then, behind him, cloth made a tiny flapping sound.

He whirled. A young man with a sword in one hand and a cape in the other was creeping up behind him. Perhaps he'd been hiding in the gloom.

Eilish pointed his sword, and the Black Dog whirled his cloak and dodged. The combination threw off Eilish's aim, and when the blue flare of magic blazed from the tip of his blade, it missed. At the same moment, the arcanist registered that the Black Dog was fleshy with a round face and white-blond hair too—he realized there was a familial resemblance between him and the woman Eilish had just turned his back on.

He sprang to place himself beyond her reach, but he did so too slowly. A shock jolted his thigh and made him totter.

As he stumbled back around, she rose with a bloody-tipped sword in her hand. She must have had it hidden underneath her, and her thrust had found the gap between two pieces of his leg armor, although his evasive action had kept it from stabbing deep enough to cripple him completely.

For the time being, anyway. The wound was starting to throb, and he hobbled as he put his back against the wall.

The capes in their hands swinging and snapping, the two Black Dogs maneuvered to flank him to the greatest extent possible.

"Does your leg hurt?" asked the woman. "I'm so sorry! I promise that if you surrender, no one will hurt you any further."

"Then I surrender," Eilish said. At the same instant, he hurled a bolt of power at her. Casting the spell produced an ache that told him he was close to exhausting his stamina and thus his ability to weave magic.

His target wrenched herself aside, and the shaft of blue light missed by a hair. Eilish pivoted to confront the white-blond man, who'd lunged into striking distance in the hope of cutting Eilish down while he was looking the other way. The mage parried a head cut and riposted to the torso. But the Black Dog hopped back out of range, and Eilish didn't chase him lest he lose whatever meager protection the wall afforded.

The female Black Dog sighed. "Dearie, you said you gave up. Didn't your mother teach you it's naughty to lie?"

"I think she would have made an exception in your case." Eilish visualized arcane symbols, and they glowed in the air around him. He pointed his sword at the woman but then sent the bolt of light hurtling from his off hand.

The resulting pain and jolt of weakness made him grunt. But the magic smashed the white-blond man in the throat and flipped him onto his back.

"Fodor!" the woman wailed, whirling in the fallen man's direction. Hoping to kill her while she was distracted, Eilish charged.

Or rather, he tried. The wound in his leg slowed him, and it nearly buckled beneath him. She spun back around, parrying so forcefully that she came close to knocking the blade from his grip, and riposted with a thrust to his face. He jerked his head sideways, but her sword still sliced him just above the ear.

Screaming, she attacked relentlessly, and it was all Eilish could do to parry and limp backward until a cut slipped past his guard and clashed on his breastplate. It didn't penetrate the armor, but it knocked him staggering, and his head banged into the wall with stunning force.

With a snarl, the plump woman raised her blade for another stroke. He tried to shift his sword to defend but could already tell he was going to be too late.

Then she jerked and faltered. Without hestitation, he thrust his sword into her torso, and she flopped forward, driving the blade deeper into her body. Her dead weight carried him to the floor along with her, and as it did, he saw Milo's throwing knife sticking out of her back.

The alchemist himself was a few paces away. "I'm glad she didn't hear me coming," he said. "That was my last weapon." He waved his hands to indicate his empty bandoliers.

"She was too furious over what I did to her… son, I guess he was," Eilish wheezed, pressing his hand to the gash in his temple. "How are we doing?"

Milo shrugged. "We won this part of the battle. You can still hear Colbie and the others fighting elsewhere in the building, but we need to regroup before we go running to their aid. Gardek's hurt too, though he says it's nothing."

"Well, I'm not too proud to avail myself of your elixirs and ointments. But first, check on that fellow lying over there. Make sure he's dead."

• • •

DOORSTOP TRAMPED INTO A HIGH-CEILINGED, open area with several doorways opening off it. Canice, Colbie, and Pog followed behind him.

Canice spotted several Black Dogs lurking behind the arches, but they didn't rush out instantly. If they were like their fallen comrades, they were savage fighters, but even so, the sight of a huge 'jack with gore dripping from its mace might give them pause. Or maybe it was the realization that the foes before them had fought their way through the automatons and rifle fire outside and the ambush in the hallway without taking a single loss.

Then, as she looked around, she met eyes glaring at her—*her* in particular—with maniacal intensity. They belonged to a hawk-faced man with fur-trimmed garments and gold adorning his scabbard and boots. He was surely Ivan Varnek, the leader who'd brought the bratya to Corvis in order to kill her.

He bellowed a command in Khadoran—*attack*, *kill*, or something similar—and lunged out into the open. Howling like wolves, his men swarmed after him.

Hoping to make him pay for his boldness, Canice fired at him. But he was moving fast while Doorstop was shifting sideways and inadvertently interposing himself between them, so despite the enchantment of accuracy on the rune bullet, she missed. After that, the action was too quick and its demands too incessant for her to pause and search for a particular target.

Pivoting, Doorstop swung his mace and occasionally his shield, which, with his might and weight behind it, hit hard enough to smash a man into a mass of pulped flesh and shattered bones. Some of the Black Dogs dared to meet him head-on anyway. Evidently they hoped that agility and the whirling, flapping obfuscation of their capes would keep them alive until superior numbers came into play and their swords found vulnerable spots in the metal giant's chassis.

Other Khadorans sought to circle around behind Doorstop and kill the thin, dark woman giving him orders. Colbie met one with a blast from the slug gun that left some of him in scraps on the floor and the rest oozing down the wall, but mostly she relied on Canice to pick them off before they maneuvered into striking distance. Meanwhile, Pog played spotter, pointing out threats in one direction if the gun mage was looking in the other.

One by one, the Black Dog underlings fell until only four were left. One of the survivors turned to Varnek and jabbered. The leader raised his sword as if he intended to cut his fellow outlaw down, but then he yelled something instead. He and the other Khadorans turned and bolted for one of the doorways.

Doorstop smashed two of them with a single sweep of the

mace before they could get out of range. And Canice had a perfect opportunity to shoot Varnek in the back—except that she'd just emptied all six pistols. As she reloaded one of the magelocks, the Khadoran dropped a metal egg like one of Milo's grenades on the floor. Smoke burst forth to shroud the archway through which he fled.

Canice fired anyway, then reloaded and did it again. No one cried out from beyond the cloud to indicate either round had found a target.

"Damn it!" Colbie snarled, and Canice understood the thoughts that underscored her frustration. Maybe the mercenaries could afford to let a couple of the rank-and-file Black Dogs escape. Until they disposed of the boss, however, their job wasn't finished, and knowing the mazelike building as they did not, he might well elude them.

Canice stepped out from behind Doorstop and shouted, "Where are you going, coward? You want to kill me? Then let's finish it!"

No one answered.

"I'm coming after you!" she continued, reloading her pistols. "Just me! You'd hear the 'jack if it was coming, and my comrades here don't fight without it!"

"You can't chase after him alone," Colbie said. "They'll lie in wait until they can pounce and be on top of you in an instant."

"I have to dangle bait he can't resist," Canice replied. "Otherwise, he'll disappear and come at me in a week or a month or a year when I'm not expecting it. I'm not having that. One way or another, this ends now. But thanks for trying to look out for me." A magelock pistol in each hand, she advanced into the archway and the now-thinning smoke.

A few paces down the corridor, a Black Dog was crawling on his belly and leaving a trail of blood behind. One of her blind shots had hit an enemy after all. The Khadoran just hadn't cried out to let her know. He struggled to crawl away faster as she approached, but his strength was running out.

"I found the man you abandoned!" she shouted. "He looks like he could still be saved!" She shot the crawling outlaw in the back. "Wait, not anymore!"

Varnek still didn't reply.

Canice reloaded. Then, moving onward, peering into each shadowy doorway, branching passage, or stairwell she passed, she called, "At least tell me why you hate me so much that you were willing to sacrifice all your followers just for the chance to kill me! I have no idea! Won't it be more satisfying if I die knowing what it was all about?"

Finally, he responded, his voice echoing out of the gloom ahead. "In Laedry, you tortured a Black Dog."

Unfortunately, the sound was of little help in determining how far away he was, let alone exactly where. But if she could keep him talking, maybe she could home in on him as she approached.

"I remember." She paused. "Well, vaguely."

As she answered, she glimpsed movement on the other side of an arch. She spun, searching, but there was nothing there—nothing but the glow of a guttering lantern wavering over crumbling brick. Her heart thumping, she took a long breath.

"That boy was my brother," Varnek said.

Though the Khadoran presumably couldn't see it, Canice shrugged. "Then you ought to be grateful I left him alive with most of his parts still working."

"You broke him! You turned him into a coward and a weakling, and he gave up other Black Dogs to be slaughtered. When I found him and learned what had happened, I had no choice but to kill him myself. My own little brother, with my own hands!"

She resisted any feeling of sympathy; to do so would likely get her killed. Instead, she licked her lips, thought about how to cut him the worst, and finally shouted, "Did he die begging and pissing himself? That's the way I remember him!"

Varnek didn't answer.

"It was sad!" Canice yelled, trying to imagine what he would find infuriating. "But funny, too. I couldn't help laughing!"

There was still no response to her calculated provocation, just the fading echo of her own voice.

Their exchange hadn't enabled her to pinpoint Varnek's location. But now that he'd reverted to silence despite her efforts to hurt him, he and his underlings were likely close at hand. Close enough for him to restrain himself in hopes of taking her by surprise.

She scrutinized what lay before her. Two doorways facing one another and then, just a couple paces farther on and directly ahead, another where the corridor made a right-angle turn. It was a good spot for a trio of swordsmen to pop out and attack from three directions simultaneously.

She advanced in the same wary, deliberate manner as before, as if nothing were different. Then, when she'd nearly reached the point where she expected her foes to spring their trap, she exploded into a sprint.

Her headlong charge took the Black Dogs by surprise. She heard the pair from the facing doors scramble forth to attack, but she was already farther past them than they wanted her. A sword swatted her back but, she judged, without cutting through her armored greatcoat. If the other Black Dog struck at her at all, he missed her entirely.

A black-bearded Khadoran with wavy tattooing crawling up his neck lunged into the archway in front of her. She was surprised it wasn't Varnek. He must have been one of the assailants at her back.

The man before her thrust with his sword, and she twisted lest her headlong rush fling her onto its point. At the same time, she fired the magelock pistol in her right hand.

The rune bullet, charged with magical force, caught the Black Dog in the chest and threw him backward. Still charging, Canice slammed into him, knocking him the rest of the way down, stumbled over him, and spun around. Silhouetted by the light of the nearest lantern in the hallway, the other two Khadorans were racing after her.

She fired the magelock in her left hand at the shadow in the lead. Her target's legs gave way beneath him, and as they did, he arched his back and tilted his head. The light splashed across his features to reveal that he wasn't Varnek, either.

Varnek rushed her, coming on so rapidly that she had no hope of reloading her pistols in time to stop him. Giving ground, she dropped the magelocks, drew the common pistols holstered on her hips, and pointed the one in her right. Meanwhile, he swung the cape in his hand. The weighted hem clouted the barrel of the firearm and jolted it from her grip.

Still backpedaling, she fired the pistol in her left hand. The round caught Varnek in the stomach, and he grunted and faltered. But only for an instant, and then he came on again.

His sword flashed at her. She jumped back and banged into the wall. No more retreating, then.

She snatched the little holdout guns from her greatcoat pockets and fired both at once. The shots pierced his chest. He was a dead man now, surely, but still too full of hate and rage to act like it. Screaming, he raised his blade, and Canice poised herself to dodge.

Then another shot banged. The round hit Varnek in the back of the head, punched out the front, and knocked chips out of the brickwork to Canice's left. The bratya chieftain toppled.

On the far side of him, sprawled in a pool of his own blood, the Black Dog Canice had shot first let the smoking pistol Varnek had knocked out of her hand slip from his fingers. The weapon clunked to the floor.

"You were right," the outlaw croaked in broken Cygnaran. "Ivan was bad boss." Blood trickling from his mouth, he bared red-stained teeth in a wolfish smile. "I want us three kill you, and then I kill him."

Canice nodded. "Sometimes you have to settle for what you can get."

— 17 —

REGAN SAID GARDEK HAD FROSTBITE and cracked ribs and that Natak, with his gashed, battered head and assorted other wounds, was in worse shape still. Yet each had insisted on marching to the Watch station on his own two feet alongside Doorstop, who looked thoroughly beaten up himself, along with Colbie, Milo, Canice, Pog, and Az.

As far as Eilish was concerned, this made them vainglorious idiots. With his slashed head and stabbed leg, he was happy to ride in a hired carriage holding the hand of the sweetheart he'd rescued. Granted, with a fair amount of help.

It was only when they'd found Regan unharmed in the little dungeon from which Pog had previously liberated Az that Eilish had realized just how afraid he'd been that matters would turn out otherwise. Perhaps he'd grown fonder of her than he'd intended, but the possibility didn't bother him overmuch.

As they turned into the Watch station courtyard, Doorstop's engine chugged and smoked, and the carriage horse's hooves clacked on the cobbles. Meanwhile, the sentry beside the door and the three other lawmen who were loitering outside gawked in amazement. Based on what Lonan Bartley had reported, they'd no doubt assumed the Black River Irregulars and their associates were dead.

At present, Eilish walked with the aid of a brass-knobbed beechwood cane, but the support was of limited help when he had to clamber out of the buggy. Grinning, Gardek strode over and hoisted him down like a toddler, assistance that undermined whatever figure Eilish might otherwise have cut as either a dignified scholar or an indomitable man of action. Still, he was grateful the trollkin set him on his feet gently without sending a twinge of pain through the bad leg.

Meanwhile, black coat flapping around her lean, long-limbed frame, Colbie advanced on the entrance of the bastion. "The Watch Commander," she said, her voice conveying utter certainty that Helstrom would see them all without delay. Seemingly just as certain, the sentry hastened to admit them. She gestured at her 'jack. "Doorstop, stay."

When they all crowded into Helstrom's office, the senior official gaped at them, too. Eilish stifled a grin. He doubted that many people were privileged to see the martinet looking so dumbfounded.

Colbie more or less came to attention before Helstrom's desk. "We're here to report the job's done. We wiped out the Khadorans and rescued Dr. Falk and Mr. Warbiter."

"By yourselves," Helstrom said.

"We do what's necessary," Colbie said. "Still, Watch Commander, you raise a point I intended to address. We ended up undertaking far more than we signed on for, and it was a hard-fought campaign." She waved her hand in a gesture that encompassed everyone's wounds. "We lost gear, and my steamjack needs a new round of repairs. Our contract didn't cover Az here, but he played an essential role in our success. All things considered, I believe a bonus is in order."

Helstrom scowled. "You realize, all you did was quell a spot of trouble in the part of the city nobody cares about."

"Actually, I recall the Khadorans being a matter of grave concern. It's disingenuous to pretend otherwise now that we've cleared them out."

"And it's sharp practice to try to renegotiate a deal..." Helstrom sighed. "Look, I was just saying to you what the people I answer to would say to me. They'd have my head if I simply threw open the doors to the city treasury. But I agree you deserve something extra, and I'll try to find it for you."

"Thank you, Watch Commander. Whatever you can manage."

"Speaking of what people deserve," Eilish said, "is Lieutenant Bartley here? We were hoping to see him, too."

When the grizzled little bulldog of a man came in, he had a clenched look to him. No doubt a combination of dread and hope was pulling the lawman's nerves tight as harp strings.

Beaming, Colbie walked to him and clasped his right hand in both of her own. "Thank you," she said.

He stared at her.

Helstrom's eyes narrowed. "That was scarcely the greeting I expected. I've already informed Lieutenant Bartley that I'm opening a formal inquiry into his conduct belowground."

Colbie cocked her head in seeming puzzlement. "Why?"

"Why? For destroying a section of the trail above the pit, cutting the raiding party in two, and obliging you mercenaries to continue on your own!"

"But if he and his men hadn't fired, that monstrous beast would have killed us."

"Let me make certain I understand," the old lawman said. "You actually saw a creature? Clearly?"

"Of course," Colbie said. Eilish nodded in agreement.

Helstrom looked back and forth between the captain of the Irregulars and his subordinate. Then he said, "In that case, we can dispense with the inquiry. Lieutenant, you're returned to active duty."

When the Watch Commander finished with his callers, Bartley followed them back out into the courtyard. "I have to know," the lieutenant asked, his voice low but urgent, "did you find a child in the Khadorans' hideout?"

"A little boy named Wyatt?" Canice asked.

"Yes!"

She shook her head. "Sorry, I have no idea."

He stared at her in consternation until Colbie took pity on the man.

"Your son's safe at home with your wife," she said. "We dropped him off on the way here."

"Even though," Gardek growled, "there was no beast under the trail."

"Which means," Colbie said, "that we've done you *two* kindnesses, Lieutenant. We rescued your son, and we covered for you. So from now on, you're done sneering at mercenaries or at least this particular band of mercenaries. You're going to be our faithful friend and enthusiastic advocate."

• • •

LIGHTNING FLARED IN THE EASTERN SKY. Sheets of wind-blown rain pummeled the broad expanse of water where the Black River and the Dragon's Tongue diverged. Accustomed to Corvis' foul weather, the crews aboard the ferries, barges, and fishing boats proceeded with their business anyway. Looking out one of the windows of the Headless Harper, the tavern where she and her partners sometimes celebrated the successful completion of a commission, Colbie reflected that she'd rather be a mercenary—the guns, crossbows, and blades periodically aimed in her direction notwithstanding.

Eilish raised his pewter cup of brandy. "Here's to the Undercity," he said, enunciating carefully lest drink make him stumble over the words. "It's dangerous, filthy, and generally vile, but at least we've restored it to homegrown Cygnaran vileness."

"And here's to our gobber friends," Colbie said, hoisting her beer, "who made our victory possible. Pog, you more than proved yourself. Now that you've experienced what our work entails, I hope you still want to be one of the Irregulars."

Pog made a wry face. "I didn't think I'd like fighting, and mostly I don't. It scares me and makes me sick to my stomach. But I still want to join." He hesitated. "Is that crazy?"

"Yes," Milo said. "You'll fit right in."

Colbie looked at Az. "We could use you, too. Our work often takes us into the Undercity."

"But what use would I be," Az asked, "when it didn't? Besides, when mad Khadorans aren't enslaving me, I like the life I already have. Still, if you need a guide to the deep places and the tunnels nobody else knows, come talk to me. I'll give you a rate."

"That leaves Natak and me," Canice said.

Colbie arched an eyebrow. "You two want to join?"

His head wrapped in bandages, the ogrun scowled as if it galled him to admit it. "Where my korune leads, I follow."

"The Patient Weavers are gone," Canice said. "We have to do something, and maybe a stint as 'honorable' mercenaries will make us look respectable. I can imagine that coming in handy later on."

Colbie looked to her partners.

"It's fine with me," Milo said. "It gets lonely being the only… practical one."

"It's all right with me, too," Gardek said. "Canice has done enough to lay old quarrels to rest."

"I agree," Eilish said, "and Regan told me how, injured though he was, Natak fought to give her a chance to escape." He squeezed the physician's hand.

"Am I allowed to vote?" Pog asked. "If I am, then I say yes."

With that, they all turned to Colbie. They were waiting to hear what their captain had to say, and she needed only a moment to deliberate.

Somewhere along the way, her fear of having her leadership usurped had, if not vanished utterly, at least dwindled. And it was plain that if the Irregulars were going to take on threats as formidable as the Black Dogs, they needed more fighters. Ultimately, if they were to grow into the mercenary company of her ambitions, a band of soldiers capable of fighting in Cygnar's actual wars, she was going to have to recruit and manage dozens of hard cases.

"Then it's unanimous," she said. She gave Canice and Natak a smile. "Welcome."

— ABOUT THE AUTHOR —

Richard Lee Byers is the author of almost forty fantasy and horror novels, including a number set in the Forgotten Realms universe. A resident of the Tampa Bay area, the setting for many of his horror stories, he spends much of his free time fencing and playing poker. Friend him on Facebook, follow him on Twitter, and read his blog on Livejournal.

Available Now from Skull Island eXpeditions

MURDER IN CORVIS

by Richard Lee Byers

The labyrinth of tunnels beneath Corvis is home to some of the city's worst criminals, but now even these hardened thugs have reason to watch their step in the dark, shadowy undercity. Death moves in that darkness, leaving behind a trail of horribly mangled bodies. The identity of the killer is a mystery, although his calling cards—brutally savaged corpses and a distinct, repulsive odor—are constants at each bloody murder scene.

As business falters in the wake of the murders, the shady owner of an illegal gambling hall hires a ragtag group of mercenaries and adventurers to find the killer and end his reign of terror. Among these mercenaries are the trollkin bounty hunter Gardek Stonebrow, the enterprising mechanik and soldier Colbie Sterling, the investigator and arcanist Eilish Garrity, and the skulking alchemist and thief Milo Boggs. Together, these four must work to overcome their differences, track down a killer, and end the murder in Corvis before one of their own becomes the next victim.

ACTS OF WAR I: FLASHPOINT

by Aeryn Rudel

Forged in the fires of conflict, the Iron Kingdoms is a fantastic realm where the combined power of magic and technology thunders across a landscape shaped by war. Dominating the field of battle are rare individuals who have mastered both arcane and martial combat and who boldly lead mighty armies in the ongoing struggle to claim victory over these ancient lands.

Lord General Coleman Stryker is one of the greatest heroes of the Iron Kingdoms. As a warcaster, Stryker leads the armies of Cygnar and commands the power of the mighty steam-powered automatons known as warjacks. Chosen by his king to liberate the conquered lands of Llael from Cygnar's long-standing enemy, the Empire of Khador, Stryker finds himself forced to work with one of his most bitter enemies—the exiled mercenary Asheth Magnus, a man to whom Cygnar's king owes his life. Unchecked, Magnus could easily betray Stryker, undermine the mission, or even bring Cygnar to its knees. But to claim victory for his king, Stryker will have to find a way to put his faith in a man he can't trust.

As the war against Khador and its own fierce commanders looms, Stryker's success or failure will become the flash point that determines the fate of all the Iron Kingdoms.